Here's Clare

Also by Robert L. Haught:

Now, I'm No Expert

The POTUS Chronicles

Here's Clare

a novel by

ROBERT L. HAUGHT

This is a work of fiction. With certain stated exceptions, the characters, incidents and dialogues are products of the author's imagination and are not to be construed as real and any resemblance to actual persons, living or dead, is entirely coincidental.

Design and pre-press by Lighthouse24
"Clare" cover photo by Lisa F. Young / Shutterstock

ISBN-10: 0692220755

ISBN-13: 978-0692220757

Published by Haughtline

For The Sisters

I

*I don't understand how a woman can leave the house
without fixing herself up a little … you never know,
maybe that's the day she has a date with destiny.*

Coco Chanel

1

CLARE DE LUNE braced herself for the landing. The flight had been bumpy, and she was facing one of the two most dangerous parts of flying – the other being takeoffs.

Wheels on the ground safely, she settled back in her seat and reviewed her plan of action as the giant Boeing jetliner homed in on a landing like a pigeon returning to its nest. She had only an overnight bag as a carry-on so deplaning went smoothly. Getting a cab was easy and leaving the SEA-TAC terminal, traffic was light but traffic lights were not. It seemed there was one every half a mile. She was more than ready to arrive at her downtown hotel.

Once in the room, she kicked off her shoes and quickly unpacked her bag, tossing undies and hose into a drawer and laying out her nightie. As she started to hang up her "little black dress" there was a knock on the door.

She opened it to find a uniformed housekeeper.

"May I turn down your bedcovers, ma'am?" she asked.

"No, that's all right, thank you."

"Then you won't want the chocolate?"

"I didn't say that. Come in, please. May I have one for each pillow? Thank you."

The housekeeper's work done, Clare hung up the dress and returned to the bag and started scrambling madly among the remaining contents.

"Damn!" she exclaimed, throwing up her hands. "I got away without my black slip!"

And there she stood: slipless in Seattle.

2

AFTER CHECKING FOR messages, and regaining her composure, Clare realized she hadn't eaten anything but airline pretzels and two chocolates in several hours. She went down to the lobby cafe and took a seat in a booth near the back of the room. At this hour there were only a few customers, and that suited her just fine.

The middle-aged waitress set down a glass of water, with lemon, and offered a pleasant greeting.

"Good evening. I'm Rubella."

Feeling a bit embarrassed about staring at her name badge for verification, Clare stammered:

"Rubella? That's your name?"

"Yes, it is. Rubella Sunday."

"Really?"

"Yes. I was born during a telethon."

"How interesting. But you must go by a nickname, maybe Ruby?"

"No, actually it's Bella. My father was Italian."

"I see."

"My older sister is named Citronella."

"Oh?"

"He proposed to my mother by candlelight."

"Well, well."

"What would you like?"

Clare ordered an appetizer serving of calamari and a glass of pinot grigio and mused about the strange ways of the world. Still fretting about her forgetfulness, she tried to take her mind off her undergarments and slowly surveyed the room. Her gaze caught sight of a nice-looking gentleman in his 40s, sipping a martini, dining alone. As he turned her way, she quickly resumed enjoying her meal.

For the first time since leaving LAX, Clare felt like she could relax. She would have enjoyed continuing to unwind, sipping her decaf and putting her mind on hold. But she had a very important mission to accomplish and she needed to retire early and get a good night's rest.

Leaving a generous tip for Bella, she made her way to the cashier, check and credit card in hand. In one of those moments that seldom occur in real life, the customer in front of her turned and she stood face to face with the handsome stranger from across the room.

"Oh, excuse me," he said with a polite nod.

She stood transfixed, studying the features of his friendly face. She saw eyes the color of a Belgian praline, soft brown hair without even two shades of gray, let alone 50. He started to move away but hesitated.

"Say, aren't you ...?"

"I'm J. C. de Lune, state senator from California," she said, reflexively extending her hand.

"I thought so. You're running for governor, aren't you?"

The question, here and now, took her by surprise. But she had been on television a time or two, including a C-SPAN special report.

"Let's just say I'm exploring the idea."

She knew she was allowing the handshake to linger too long. He didn't seem to mind the touch of her soft skin and her firm grip. But he sensed her discomfort and loosened his fingers.

"It's a pleasure to meet you," he said. "My name is Henry Jackson. I'm on the Republican state committee."

Stifling a snicker and resisting the urge to mutter, "What would Scoop think!" (Republicans have no sense of humor) "Well, what a coincidence – two pols who are polar opposites," she stammered, desperately wishing her mouth had a delete button.

"We could have some interesting conversations, I'll bet."

"Probably."

"Are you staying in the hotel?"

"Why, yes."

"Would you – could you – join me in a cup of coffee tomorrow morning?"

"If you think there's room," she blurted. "Sorry. Old joke."

A big smile beamed on Not-Scoop's face.

"Thank you. I would lov-- like that very much."

"Great. Nineish in the coffee shop?"

"I'm more eightish."

"You look Irish." Now it was his turn to be flustered.

"How about a compromise – eight-thirty?"

"Wonderful. Good night."

As he walked away, Clare took a deep breath, then exhaled. She stopped at the newsstand to pick up a paper, then headed toward the elevator. Once again she came face to face with the man who no longer was a stranger but someone she had agreed to meet again for a – no, not a date – just a cup of coffee.

"I had to go by the check-in desk," he explained.

He motioned her ahead and both stepped on the elevator. As the doors closed she pushed nine.

"Floor?" she asked.

"Nine."

"We're on the same floor. Another coincidence."

"How about that!"

They were the only passengers. After the longest elevator ride of her life, in complete silence, the doors opened. They said goodnight and walked in opposite directions down the hall to their rooms.

Clare got ready for bed but she was too wired to sleep. This chance meeting was not in her plan. She had to sort through her feelings.

She hadn't felt this way in a long time. To be truthful, not since her husband died had any man triggered a spark such as this. She had resigned herself to a life alone, buried in her work, focused on a career in politics. She had no time for this – not if she had any thought about trying to get elected governor of California.

Yet this very desirable man – desirable even with his inevitable faults – had shown an interest in her. And it set her to thinking. With her head resting in the pillow, staring at the ceiling while the lights of the city blinked through the drapes, she took a mental inventory of herself.

She gave herself some points for not being bad looking.

Her hair was auburn. Her football team was the Georgia Bulldogs.

Her eyes were a color of blue that defied defiling by Crayola.

Her teeth were not so white as to look artificial – just right for a beauty queen.

Henry Jackson (she couldn't resist a chuckle) was right about the Irish part. That combined with just a touch of Cherokee Indian.

She had not allowed the California sun to damage her skin.

She had a figure her late husband had described as "sculpturesque" – like a Venus de Milo with arms, maybe?

At 38, she was hot as a pistol of the same caliber – at least so she had been told by the boys in the Democratic cloakroom at the state Senate.

She was indeed a bit of a seductress. She could have her way with any TV camera, any place, any time.

Enough of these foolish fantasies, her brain commanded. You don't even know if he's available.

3

CLARE FOUND HENRY waiting in a booth, the same one he had occupied last evening. He was more casually dressed, wearing a wine-colored sports shirt and gray slacks. Henry was staring at her as if he were transfixed by her appearance. She was a model of a career woman in a black dress and black lightweight leather jacket, pearl earrings and small pearl necklace, carrying a bright red shoulder bag. He rose as she approached, smiling, said "Good morning, Henry" and slid into a seat.

"And good morning to you. I'll get the waiter's attention so you can have some coffee. Anything else?"

"Maybe a croissant."

They both ordered the pastries and he told the waiter to keep the coffee coming.

"I'm glad to have a chance to continue where we left off last evening," he said.

"We didn't really have much of a conversation."

"No, and I do want to know more about you. How did you come to run for the California state senate?"

She related the story about how she had succeeded her husband, wealthy racing enthusiast Gary de Lune, after he was killed in a car wreck 16 months ago. He was returning from a late session in Sacramento and a semi-trailer truck ran across the median and totaled his classic Corvette. He died instantly. Expressing his deep sympathy, Henry handed her a business card.

Clare took the card from his left hand. She couldn't help noticing it was as bare as a clean sink.

"Politics is a hobby. This is my job." The card read: Henry Jackson, President, Mt. Jackson Vineyards.

"You're in the wine business!" Clare exuded. "How wonderful! I mean, wine is wonderful and that makes you ... and president already at such a young age."

"Well, I'm 41. And it's a family business. My father has been urging me to settle down and get serious about my life. I kept telling him I was learning a lot about life from the time spent in England and traveling around Europe."

"How fascinating!" she said, then "Excuse me, I have to take this call."

He tried not to appear to be eavesdropping, but he did hear her say, "I'm seeing Mr. Zee at 10 a.m. after a stop at a department store near his office ... I'll explain later."

"You've aroused my curiosity. Who's the mysterious Mr. Zee?"

"Oh, just someone with more money than he needs."

Henry refrained from saying, "typical Democrat judgment."

"I'm hoping to get a big campaign contribution commitment."

"Well, your time is running short and I don't want you to miss your appointment. But I want to … I've got to see more of you. Please have lunch with me before you return to L.A.," Henry said.

"All right. Meet in the lobby around noon?"

"That's perfect. Good luck."

"Thanks."

4

CLARE GAVE THE cab driver the address of a Nordstrom department store near the building where Mr. Zee's office was located. She made a quick purchase at a lingerie counter, pulled on the black slip in the ladies room and set off to carry out her mission.

It was only a short walk from the store to the glass tower that was the home of the World Headquarters of Forever Yung cosmetics. After a long elevator ride to the top floor, she arrived at the elaborate double door entry. She entered with an air of confidence and announced herself to the receptionist, an attractive young Chinese woman. She welcomed Clare and asked her to take a seat.

Clare positioned herself on an uncomfortable thinly-padded bench and took note of the office décor: subtle tones, low lighting, commercial carpeting with a Far East design. Copies of Chinese silk prints adorned the walls, the focal point being a large oil painting of a colorful five-tiered pagoda standing against a background of snow-capped mountains.

She impatiently checked the time on her watch and cast an occasional glance at the receptionist, who eventually announced, "Senator de Lune, Mr. Zee will see you now." Clare arose and walked toward an older woman whom she guessed to be the man's secretary. Her path was suddenly and sharply blocked by a fashionably dressed figure, trailed by a snooty Pekingese, who burst into the office and went straight to the secretary, demanding in a shrill voice, "I must see him immediately!" Then followed a heated exchange, the secretary protesting the interruption and the visitor forcefully insisting that she get out of the way and let her by. There was no stopping this rude interloper.

The secretary humbly and graciously apologized. "I'm so sorry, Senator. It's Mr. Zee's sister-in-law and she drives us up the wall. But there's not much we can do about it, I regret to say. I'm afraid you'll have to wait a while longer, or we can reschedule your appointment."

Clare was severely irritated and said through clenched teeth, "No, thank you. I can't waste any more time. Please give my regrets to Mr. Zee."

She spun around and marched out.

5

CLARE STORMED INTO the hotel, went up to her room and called Henry.

"Let's get out of here."

"What's wrong?"

"I'll tell you over lunch if I've calmed down by then. I'll meet you in the lobby as soon as I freshen up a bit."

"Fine. Are you up for a little walking?"

"Sure. I didn't even bring high heels on this trip."

"Okay. See you soon."

She brushed her teeth, applied some lipstick and prepared to forget Mr. Zee and his rude in-law.

Henry's first words were: "On the phone you sounded like hell's fury unleashed, but you certainly don't look the part. Where's your red bag?"

"I left it behind," she smiled, "on purpose."

"Oh-kay," he said, with a quizzical look. "Well, let me show you Seattle."

"I can't wait."

Outside both the day and Clare's mood were sunny and the sounds of the busy city beckoned them.

"We're pretty close to the monorail," said Henry.

Clare grimaced and said, "Yes, I could see the Space Needle from my hotel window."

"A quick ride gives you a nice view of the city," he said, leading her down the sidewalk.

His plan was natural but it caught her by surprise. How was she going to explain that she had a fear of anything beginning with "mono"? She had been plagued with monophobia ever since she had mononucleosis as a teenager. Just the sound of "mono" gave her chills. She couldn't even play Monopoly without shaking all over, which was all right for rolling the dice, but a definite handicap in moving the tokens on the board.

"Would you mind terribly if we just took a cab?" she said, rubbing her stomach. "I'm a little queasy. My light breakfast, maybe."

"Oh, of course. I'm sorry you're not feeling well."

"I'll be fine, I'm sure. Where are we going?"

"Well, you've got to see the Pike Place Fish Market. And there's a restaurant not too far from there that I think you'll enjoy."

"That sounds marvelous," said Clare, trying to work up some enthusiasm about going to a fish market. As soon as they finished the cab ride, she could see why Henry recommended it.

The whole marketplace area was alive with activity. Throngs of eager customers, both local and out-of-towners, flocked to various vendors busily transacting sales of fresh flowers, crafts and all kinds of food – fruits, cheeses, produce, baked goods and seafood. The center of attention was the fish market. Before going in, Henry pointed and said, "See that?"

"You mean the coffee shop?"

"That's where the first Starbucks opened in 1971."

"And now there's one on almost every corner."

"Seattle has more than 400."

Clare's eyes opened wide as they walked into the fish place and she saw a large salmon flying through the air, tossed by a bearded guy in orange waders. Amazingly another fishmonger wearing a trademark apron caught the fish and plopped it on the chopping block.

She paused to take in the scene. There were fish of almost every variety spread out on ice in the long counter. Intermingled in the aerobatic juggling were wisecracks and insults which delighted the crowds gathered in the market, one of Seattle's leading tourist attractions.

Clare was fascinated. "It's like watching a tennis match." Henry hadn't thought of that comparison. "If you've seen enough, how about some lunch?"

"I'm ready if you are."

They strolled a couple of blocks north, enjoying the breezes from Elliott Bay, as well as various waterfront scenes. As they approached a small unpretentious place with a sign reading Etta's, Henry slowed his pace. "This is a Tom Douglas restaurant – one of his first, actually – before he built his reputation as an award-winning chef.

"We're lucky to be early enough to beat the usual lunch crowd," Henry said. They were seated at a table with a window overlooking the waterfront park. Clare was pleased by the cozy charm and playful decor.

"Don't let the casual look fool you," Henry said. "I think Etta's has the best seafood in Seattle."

"What do you recommend?"

"Oysters on the half shell are always fresh and delicious." Reading her uninterested look, he followed by describing a house specialty. "The grilled salmon, seasoned by what they call 'the rub of love' is superb."

"You've sold me," she said.

Henry gave the order to the waiter – he chose the Dungeness crab cakes – and picked a bottle of Mt. Jackson chardonnay from the wine list.

"I have to do what I can to keep Pop's winery in business," he chuckled.

"It's your winery, too."

"I know. Somehow I just can't put my heart into it. Please tell me what got you so upset this morning."

"Oh, I was just irritated. I really wanted to make a good impression on Mr. Zee because he has been known to back certain candidates rather heavily. But I didn't even get to see him. After cooling my heels in his office beyond my appointment time, a very obnoxious woman barged in and took charge. She was a relative. They offered to reschedule my appointment but I declined."

"But you left your red bag?"

"Yes. I had prepared a personalized presentation and included it with my standard information kit. So perhaps I'll get some kind of response later."

"Smart thinking!"

"So since you were staying at the hotel I take it you don't live in Seattle?"

"No, I was just here for a state committee meeting. I have a place on the vineyard grounds, about 35 miles from Seattle. And you're in the Los Angeles area, right?"

"North of LA, near Santa Barbara. After Gary and I were married, he bought what I called the 'villa of my dreams', overlooking the ocean."

"It must be a very beautiful home with spectacular views."

"Yes, but it's just not the same."

"I can well imagine."

The waiter poured the wine and Henry raised his glass and said, "Here's to happier times." She smiled and tasted the elixir of paradise – at least that's what her brain told her.

The mood was more upbeat as they dined and they engaged in mostly small talk about their likes and dislikes – including food. Clare highly approved of Henry's recommendation on the salmon. She also sampled a bite of his crabcake and pronounced it top rate.

She also ventured to explore a bit about this man she had known less than 24 hours.

"So you didn't join the family wine business right after school?"

"No. I'm afraid I didn't learn a lot in my four years at the University of Washington. I guess I was focused too much on basketball – and girls," he said with a bashful grin. "So I drew an advance on my inheritance and went abroad. Studied at Oxford …"

"You, too? I got a Rhodes scholarship after I finished at the University of Georgia. We might have been in England at the same time.."

"Could be, because Pop encouraged me to stay and go to the business school. I think he figured I wasn't ready to come home, anyway. And even after that I wanted to see more of the world so I traveled in Europe, living a rather Bohemian life for a while."

"It's amazing how our lives took the same direction. I studied and traveled in France, Spain and Italy primarily. But then I decided to return to the states and enroll in an art school in southern California. I took up sculpture and got to be pretty good at it."

"I'd like to see your work. I was more foolish. I went back to London and got into the party scene. That's where I met this woman. I'm ashamed to say so now, but I really fell for her. I should have known better."

"Were you going to get married?"

"We-ll … she had other plans. I took the rejection pretty hard. And then when my mother became ill I went back home and accepted my father's offer to succeed him as president of Mt. Jackson Vineyards."

"You've had quite a life."

"We both have."

The wine had its relaxing effect and perhaps led to Henry's impulsive suggestion.

"Clare, I am so happy to have met you. And I can't stand the thought of you going back to California before we can spend some more time together. Will you please consider delaying your return for at least one more day? I'd like to show you Mt. Jackson and let you meet my father."

Obviously somewhat startled by this provocative proposal – but at the same time feeling a strong temptation – Clare responded hesitantly, "Oh, I don't know." She reached in her pocket, which was empty. "I can't believe I left my phone in the room. There's probably something on my schedule I need to get back for. Although at the moment, I can't think of what it might be."

"Whatever it is, I'm sure your campaign staff can work it out."

"My staff!" she laughed. "In this exploratory stage, it's just Luna and me."

"Luna?"

"Gary's daughter. She's my acting campaign manager."

"You should call her. Here, use my phone."

"All right, thanks. Excuse me."

Luna answered on the second ring. "Well how did it go with Mr. Zee?"

"It didn't. I'll fill you in later. Right now I need to know what my schedule is for the next few days. I left my phone at the hotel."

"Where are you?"

"I just had lunch with the nicest guy. He wants me to delay my return for a couple of days. Am I committed to anything?"

"I don't believe this. Hold on. Let me check. No, not until the Hollywood fundraiser. But what do you know about this stranger?"

"Enough that I want to do this."

"Clare, are you crazy? He could be the Craig's list killer for all you know!"

"No, he's not. In fact, he's president of a Washington winery."

"Yeah, right. I'll bet he even had a fancy business card all printed up."

"Don't worry, Luna. I can take care of myself. Besides, I have my protective team with me."

"Smith and Wesson?"

"Yes."

"Well, be careful. And check in with me often."

"Okay, thanks."

She could see that Henry, having heard only her side of the conversation, was mystified.

"Luna was upset, I take it."

"Oh, well. She tends to be overprotective sometimes."

"What was the reference to your 'protective team'?"

"That's an inside joke – about my firearm."

"You carry a gun!"

"Yes. It's just a small revolver. It's like the one Dianne Feinstein used to carry."

"Senator Feinstein? That fierce gun control advocate?"

"It was years ago. But quite a number of elected officials have concealed weapons permits, ever since the Gabby Giffords shooting."

"Have you ever used it?"

"No, thank goodness. But the martial arts training I had in college has come in handy several times. Dealing with redneck drunks, for example. And one time at a NASCAR event one of my late husband's racing buddies had too much Jack Daniels and got a little out of hand. But a well-placed kick made him lose his carnal desires very quickly."

"I can imagine," Henry said, with a shudder. "So if you're cleared to spend some more time with me, let's go back to the hotel and check out and we'll head for the hills. I do need to make a brief stop at Chateau Ste. Michelle on the way out of town. I've gotten to be close friends with one of their management people. He and I have attended some winemaker meetings together."

Clare was flushed with excitement, but clearheaded enough to have some practical thoughts, like, "I didn't bring enough clothing for a stayover!"

"Tell you what," she said. "You go on. I have to make a stop and pick up a few things and I'll see you at the hotel as soon as I can."

Feeling elated about the turn of events, Henry profusely thanked Clare for her decision and they separated – momentarily.

Clare made her second trip of the day to the department store and took a moment to go to the ladies room where she encountered her guardian angel.

"You made a pretty hasty decision, you know," she said softly.

"Don't listen to her!" came a coarse whisper from the devil inside her.

Silently she said to herself: "I hope I'm not making a mistake going off with a total stranger. But I feel drawn to this man and I think I'll be safe."

Clare's inquisitive nature won out and she proceeded to do her shopping.

She bypassed lingerie and took the escalator to women's sports attire where she found some garments to extend her meager traveling wardrobe – a pair of denim pants and a long sleeve top (mountain country was bound to be cooler than the city).

She rushed up to her room, rapidly changed to the slacks and blouse she had worn on the plane, and tossed everything else into the suitcase – except for a yellow sweater which she carried. Then she dialed Henry's room and arranged to meet him in the lobby.

Both of them had done the "instant checkout" so they headed out the hotel entrance where they found Henry's car waiting. The bags were loaded in the trunk, he tipped the attendant and they were off on an exciting adventure.

6

HENRY'S CADILLAC HAD every comfort feature a creature could crave. The soft chocolate brown leather seats had hidden technology that detected body temperatures and maintained the appropriate level through internal heating elements of the car's climate control system. The seats also easily adjusted to a comfortable but safe position for the driver and an ultra-comfort setting for the passenger. The flexible tinted window feature ensured a "no squint" trip for all occupants. Pleasant music from a variety of Sirius XM channels floated to the ear from a quality multi-speaker sound system.

"With all the time you spent in Europe, I'm surprised you're driving an American- made car," Clare ventured.

"Pop would kick me out if I didn't," Henry said.

"Oh, a true blue American?"

"A flag waver through and through."

"Well, so is my dad."

"A generational thing, I guess."

Clare enjoyed the feeling of complete relaxation. She was comforted by the belief that nothing which had occurred during her brief acquaintanceship with Henry had given her any misgivings. She must tell herself, however, to be on guard until the relationship had progressed further, as she hoped it would.

"Henry?"

"Yes?"

"I owe you an explanation."

"For what?"

"For the way I reacted to hearing your name for the first time."

"Oh?"

"As someone who's in politics and who happens to be a Democrat, my first thought was of Henry 'Scoop' Jackson, the longtime U.S. senator from Washington. He made quite a name for himself in Democratic politics and even ran for president in 1972 and again in '76, but failed to get the party's nomination either time."

"Was 'Scoop' a newspaperman?"

"No. Some say his sister gave him the nickname because she thought he looked like a comic strip character of that name. Another story says he got it because he delivered newspapers as a boy."

"Well, as far as I know our families are not related. My full name actually is Henry Jackson III. My father is Henry Jackson, Jr., and he's chairman of the board for our wine business. My grandfather Henry Jackson, Sr., was the founder of the operation."

"Is he still living?"

"Oh, yes. He is no longer active in the business but he is very much alive. He says he owes his longevity to a glass of Mt. Jackson wine and a grilled cheese sandwich on whole wheat bread every day for lunch. And a glass of our wine and soup for dinner. Plus he does yoga."

"Any brothers or sisters?"

"One brother – he's the vineyard manager."

"I'm eager to meet them," she said. After a moment's pause, Clare felt obliged to divulge a bit of her family history.

"I'm about as far away from home as I could be. I was born in Georgia. My father owns a large pecan growing business. My mother helps out but she's primarily a homemaker. I have one sibling, a younger sister."

The rest of their respective backgrounds would have to come later because they were nearing their first stop. On the interstates, it didn't take long to reach the suburb of Woodinville where Chateau Ste. Michelle was located. Soon the historic French-style chateau and its beautiful grounds came into view. As they passed through the wide gates of the estate, Clare marveled at the vast expanse of lush green lawns accented with shrubbery, shade trees, fountains and a terraced lake, which caught her eye.

"Look – the ducks and geese are enjoying themselves," she exclaimed.

"If you're lucky you might see one of the peacocks strutting around," Henry added.

The winery loomed large in their path, making that conversation one to be continued. With a deep sigh, Clare said, "I feel as if I've been transported back to Europe." The long two-story structure with its twin towers was indeed an impressive sight.

As they entered the front door, Henry said, "I won't be long. I just need to drop off some material for a project we've been working on for the Wine Institute. You'll find the gift shop a pleasant place to wait."

As Clare made her way into the interior of the winery, she admired the light gold-painted archways that defined the various areas, including the tasting room. She knew there wouldn't be time for that pleasure on this stop but she made a mental note to add it to her "to do" list. She found a number of interesting gift items but reminded herself that she was traveling light. Another reason to make a return visit.

Henry finished his business in short order and they were on their way again.

7

TAKING A FAREWELL look in the side view mirror, Clare said to Henry, "That's quite a place. Thanks for showing it to me. I'd like to come back some time."

Henry went into his wine salesman mode. "Chateau Ste. Michelle is Washington's oldest winery. It had its beginning in 1934, a few months after the repeal of prohibition. The building we were in dates to 1976. The winery has gone through many changes and several ownerships, but it has maintained its place as the state's largest wine producer, in terms of the number of gallons sold. It is the leading producer of Riesling wine in the United States."

"I'm impressed," said Clare, sincerely.

"While I'm boring you with statistics, I know it sounds like bragging – to a Californian – but Washington ranks number two in U.S. wine production behind California," Henry said.

"I'll bet that's a pretty distant number two," Clare jibed.

"Well, you're right. And actually it's impossible to compare California with Washington – or any other state, for that matter – because California has a much different business model for wine. Washington ..." (Clare thought she detected a swelling of his chest) ... "doesn't make jug wine. And that's where a lot of California's grapes go."

"Oh, well-l-l ..."

"But what is important is to compare Washington wine, which is in the premium category, with California's premium regions. For example, Washington runs even with the Napa region in wine grape acreage – 43,000 for each area. In 2012 Washington led Napa in total tonnage, 188,000 to 181,000. For Merlot tonnage Washington outranked both the Napa and Sonoma/Marin regions. And, of course, they fall far behind us in Riesling tonnage."

"Oh, of course ..."

"Now you're mocking me," Henry said, sounding a bit hurt. "Wine makers use the number of tons of grapes crushed in a given year as a standard measurement ..."

Clare couldn't resist a musical retort: "I think I'm getting a crush on you ..."

"What!"

"I don't know. Something you said reminded me of George Gershwin."

"As I was saying ..."

"You ferment for me ..."

18

"Oh, come on!"

"Henry, I really am overwhelmed by your knowledge of the product, but the only thing that's important to me about wine is whether I like it or not. And I'm looking forward to tasting a lot more Washington wines."

She hadn't paid much attention to where they were going, except to know the roads had become a little rougher and more winding. She caught an occasional glimpse of Mt. Rainier in the far distance.

"Are we getting close to your place?" she asked.

"It's not too much farther," he said.

"How did your grandfather get started in the wine business?"

"It was a combination of his interest in growing things and changing economics. He was what they used to call a truck farmer. He had a rather sizeable acreage and he grew a wide variety of produce, which he trucked to his buyers. Somewhere along the way he decided to experiment with growing grapes. It turned out that the soil on his land and the climate were very good for that purpose. And by a fortunate circumstance around the time he started losing customers to large scale producers coincided with the beginning of the growth in the state's wine industry."

"What period was that?"

"Are you going to make fun of me again?"

"No, I promise to be good … and listen."

"All right. First, a little history. Washington's first wine grapes were planted in 1825, but the first commercial scale plantings began in the 1960s, and that's when my grandfather began to convert his cropland to vineyards. He was 33 when he began growing grapes full time.

"It was another five years before he decided to open his own winery. That was 1967. It was a significant year for Mt. Jackson Vineyards and also for the Washington wine industry. That was the year Chateau Ste. Michelle emerged to become a commercial giant by starting to produce classic European varietal wines. Another winery, Columbia, was moving in the same direction, and these two wineries were instrumental in giving the state a modern industry making some highly rated wines."

"What about the name – Mt. Jackson Vineyards?"

"That's a good story. My grandfather was a bit of a huckster. He really had a flair for promotion, and that had a lot to do with his success. Even before he thought about going into the wine business, he took a notion one day to give a name to what you might call a high hill on his property. What could be better than using the family name. So he christened it 'Mt. Jackson.' You won't find that in any atlas or any other kind of official listing. That carried over into his business enterprises."

"Is that it?" said Clare, pointing ahead.

"You guessed it. We're almost there."

As they approached their final destination of the day, Clare noted the entrance was not as grand as Chateau Ste. Michelle but every bit as welcoming. She admired the rustic charm of the building that housed offices, tasting room and gift shop with a lovely view of Mt. Jackson as the backdrop.

Inside Henry took her back, passing a portrait of his grandfather, to meet "Pop." They found him on the floor behind his desk finishing a set of pushups. He rose, caught his breath, and greeted the visitor with a broad smile that spread the whiskers of his ungainly mustache from cheek to cheek.

Henry introduced them and there was an instant connection. "So happy to meet you, my dear," he beamed. "Please have a seat."

Before sitting, Clare noticed a photo on his desk. "Is this your wife?" she asked.

"Yes, that's Clara," he replied "She died four years ago. Breast cancer."

"Oh, I'm terribly sorry," Clare said, squeezing his outstretched hand.

She became readily aware that the old man was quite a flirt. He asked if she played tennis.

"Not in quite a long while," she responded.

"It will come back to you," he said. "Meet me on the court at 7 in the morning."

"I'm not sure …" turning to Henry.

"Yes, we're spending the night," he confirmed.

With that settled, Pop laid into his son about settling down and taking over the business, "so I can retire." As they began to argue, Clare excused herself to wait elsewhere. As she showed herself out of the office, she overheard Henry saying he was not ready to settle down, but that he just might have met the woman he's been looking for. She lingered long enough to hear his father admonish him not to make the same mistake he made before with "that woman in England."

8

NOT TO HER surprise Henry's conversation with his dad was brief and he rejoined her shortly. Taking her hand he led her up a path to his home, a small log cabin. On the way she met Lucky, the chocolate (her favorite color) Lab, the official winery watchdog and greeter. Henry explained the name derived from the fact that the animal she was petting was not the same starving mongrel who showed up about two years ago desperately seeking human companionship but most of all food and shelter. He had indeed lucked out by finding the Jackson family.

"Do you have any pets?" he inquired.

"Did have a cat. Like Lucky, she was homeless, too. She showed up at our home shortly after Gary and I were married. He tried to run her off, but I wanted to keep her. He called her 'that mangy yellow cat.' But to me she was like California gold. I named her Goldie. She gradually won over Gary and they became quite close."

"You said you did have a cat. What happened to her?"

"Strangely, she disappeared on the day after Gary died."

Moving closer she got a peek at a three-car garage at the rear of the cabin, his car parked outside. He pointed to a row of cottages to the right.

"These are one-bedroom suites we make available for guests," he explained. "They come in handy when we have our quarterly winemaker's dinners. The patrons can have as much wine as they like and not have to worry about driving home."

"How nice," she said.

"I had your bag taken to number one. I'll take you over, but first would you like to see where I live?"

She was most interested. The cabin was small and rustic, especially compared to her five-bedroom villa, but also well designed and luxurious in its furnishings. Especially striking was the contrast between the traditional log cabin look of the exterior and the bright, bleached-out appearance of the interior.

Henry volunteered that he had borrowed an idea from a model in Portland, which featured openness instead of the usual walled-off divisions of space. A 17-foot tall pitched ceiling over the great room also contributed to the spacious look and feel of the cabin. The brightness was the result of large energy-efficient windows which allowed views of the fresh green surroundings and the most important decision of all: to paint the inside portion of the logs with a European super high-gloss, reflective white paint. Honey-toned fir stairs to the sleeping loft and natural cabinetry with stainless counter and shelving completed the modern masculine environment of Henry's living quarters.

He offered wine and they had a brief chat about the events of the long day, then he escorted her to her lodging.

"Dinner in the restaurant at 7?" he asked.

"That will be fine," she replied with a warm smile.

Clare still had a hard time believing she had taken this uncertain fork in the road, but "so far, so good."

9

THE HIGHLIGHT OF the day came after they dined. They enjoyed a light meal with Mt. Jackson wine and continued to get better acquainted.

Clare knew it had to be a sore subject but she felt moved to bring up the apparent thorny relationship between Henry and his father.

Sighing, he said, "Yes. It gets rough at times, like when he calls me an overeducated bum."

"Oh, my!"

"It's just his rough manner. And he is close to being right. I've never had a real job until now. I hadn't had to."

"But you don't impress me as being the irresponsible playboy type."

"Well, not anymore, anyway. Let's not talk about me. I'd like to know more about how you got interested in public service – enough so to motivate you to seek the state's highest office."

"I guess Gary's zeal for his job in the state Senate and his passion for helping people rubbed off on me. And it grew even stronger after I went to the state capitol."

"Anything you miss about your former life?"

"Yes, I was happily pursuing a career in art and I was really getting to be pretty good at sculpture. And I enjoyed my TV show. I hated to give that up." Henry raised his eyebrows.

"I had a daytime program called 'Here's Clare' on a local TV station," she explained. "I had a lot of interesting guests and as the show began to attract more and more viewers I got to be pretty well known. Of course, that turned out to be a plus factor when I decided to go into politics."

Because the hour was getting late they didn't tarry. At the door to Clare's suite, they fell into a mutual embrace which eased all tensions – and then bade each other goodnight. As she watched Henry walk to his cabin, she found herself thinking, "Well, here I go again, taking a chance on love."

10

AFTER BREAKFAST CLARE and Henry got ready to return to Seattle. A light rain was falling. The tennis match with Henry Jr. obviously had to be postponed. She asked if she could take a rain check and he disappointedly but graciously agreed.

Finishing their coffee Henry surprised Clare, telling her that he not only would take her to the airport to catch her flight but also that he had decided to go back to Los Angeles with her. "I have a business reason," he said, not too convincingly. She was thrilled but tried not to show it too much.

Because of his last minute plans, they weren't able to sit together. First class was full and there was only limited seating in business class.

That circumstance gave them both some time to think about the abrupt change in both of their lives.

11

CLARE HAD LEFT a car at LAX. She drove to Santa Barbara and on the way she told Henry how she had met Gary de Lune.

After getting a degree from the University of Georgia, another four years on a scholarship at Oxford and an extended period of living in Europe, she did a two-year study at an art institute in California. Finally she told herself it was time to get a job. She joined a Los Angeles real estate firm where she became the top seller.

One day she found herself alone in the office and thus had telephone duty. A short time after she finished her carry-out lunch the phone rang and a familiar voice said, "Hello, this is Gary de Lune."

She, along with millions of other Americans, knew all about Gary de Lune. The son of a Pittsburgh steel worker, he had become fascinated with engines at an early age. He got a bicycle as soon as his parents could afford it and as he grew older he moved on to motorcycles and later to fast cars. He invented a carburetor modification that made him a wealthy man in his 20s. He migrated to California and began to live the life of an overnight celebrity. He owned a NASCAR car and did some racing. In so doing he made quite a name for himself.

As he grew older he gradually settled down and bought a chain of California radio stations, with one TV station. He continued to date widely and ended up married to Alana, a flighty social climber. They had a daughter, Luna.

Gary turned to politics and got elected to the California state senate. He and Alana divorced. In the settlement, she got their big, expensive house. That led him to make his phone call.

Maybe it was because the date on the calendar was April 1. Whatever the reason, Clare was skeptical.

"Gary de Lune? Yeah, right."

"Hey, it's really me," he said. "Vroo-oom, vroo-oom!"

"Okay, if you say so. How can I help you?"

"You may have heard about my divorce?"

"Sure – along with five million other people."

"Then you also know I gave her the house. So I need for you to find me a place to live. I can only stand staying in the Beverly Hilton for just so long."

"That must be quite a hardship," said Clare, with no attempt to conceal the sarcasm. (Her better angel whispered, "Be nice. This might really be Gary de Lune.") "We'll be glad to put the full resources of our firm to work for you to put you in a wonderful place that will make you forget you ever lived in the other one."

"That's just what I'm hoping for."

Within a few weeks she had fulfilled her promise. During that time they had begun to date. They were each enchanted by the other's charms and with Gary's urging (after all he was a fast mover) they found themselves going to the altar.

Gary gave her not only an embarrassingly large diamond ring but an open-ended offer of "anything else you want." She had always wanted an Italian-style villa. So Gary said, "You've got it."

Clare finished her story just as they were arriving in her exclusive neighborhood. She turned onto a private drive and Henry's interest rose. Her address was marked by an elegant sign, "Villa de Lune." Henry was quite impressed by the stunning two-story dwelling on a cliff above the Pacific Ocean.

Approaching the house he took in the well-planned landscaping and well-kept gardens. As they unloaded luggage he noted the extra-wide front door and the large number of windows on the front side of the villa. He saw at least three chimneys on the tiled roof.

A brick walk with floral borders led to the entrance. Once inside he got a better idea of the design of the mansion-style residence. The first thing that got his attention was the vaulted ceiling over at least half of the ground floor. To the right was a loggia that admitted the eastern sun as it rose over the mountainside. It led to a garage.

On the left an open door revealed a gourmet kitchen with a double-size marble-topped island. It was equipped with top-of-the-line appliances.

"Welcome to Villa de Lune," Clare said.

Henry marveled at the paintings by world famous artists which lined a grand hall with a full-length runner. At the end was an arched open doorway into the living room. On the way they passed a dining room with a long antique table and chairs.

Clare motioned Henry to turn right into the great room filled with expensive furnishings. The vastness of this area accentuated the bright, airy feeling of the exquisite interior.

Another open hallway led past two flights of stairs to second floor bedrooms. In between was a stone wall and sitting in front of it was a classic mahogany bar cabinet which held a Roman-style bust. Carved in the base was "de Lunus." Clare motioned him to leave their bags at the base of the stairs.

12

MOTIONING HIM THROUGH the living area toward the outside, Clare said, "Come, I want to introduce you to my campaign manager."

She opened floor to ceiling sliding glass doors and ushered Henry onto a large terrace, encircling a pool, overlooking the ocean.

Standing in silhouette was a slender figure – bordering on anorexic – almost all legs, wearing short-shorts, pulling on a top, which had barely cleared her chin. She was braless.

"Luna!"

"What!" came a raspy voice behind the thin fabric. When Henry was able to refocus his eyes he saw a shock of blonde hair pop through the neck of a T-shirt reading "de Lune for Governor – the right woman for the job", and revealing a tanned face with button eyes and no discernible makeup.

"What's wrong? There aren't 100 guys in all the continents who haven't seen a pair of boobs," she scolded. "Not that there's much to see here."

"Well, now that you're decent … correction, now that you're covered, I want you to meet someone."

"So this is the guy? Good going, girl!"

"Henry, this is my campaign manager, L. J. de Lune. She's also my stepdaughter."

Striding toward Henry, she said: "Been looking forward to this moment ever since she told me …"

"Never mind!" Clare burst.

Sizing up "the guy" from head to toe and back again, L. J. aka Luna cracked, "I can't decide whether to call you Hank, or Hunk."

Extending his hand, he said, "Henry will do. Henry Jackson."

"Yeah, we had a good laugh about that."

Mortified, Clare was relieved to hear her cell phone ring.

"I've got to take this call."

Henry decided to take the initiative.

"I'm glad my name gave you a chuckle, Miss *Luna de Lune*."

"Okay, I asked for that.."

"How did you come to have a name like that?"

"It was my mother's idea. She told me I was conceived by the light of the moon. Luna? Moon?"

"Yes, I get it."

"It was a romantic evening on a moonlit beach in Tahiti …"

"You can skip the details. I'll bet that name was quite a burden to carry in your early years."

"Oh, yeah. Kids called me 'Looney' until I got into high school, and even then some of the boys couldn't resist. They got some black eyes to show for it."

"So where's your mother now, still in California?"

"Oh, hell, no. After the divorce she ran away to Hawaii with a mungbean magnate with a mansion on Maui."

"Mungbeans?"

"He cornered the market on bean sprouts. He's got acres and acres of them. Worldwide distribution. He made it big. And it's ironic, because he's such a little sprout. Quite a bit older than my mother. Had three wives before he married her."

"What did she see in him?" Henry asked, as if he couldn't guess.

"She fell for him when he called her 'Princess Alana' …"

"How nice."

"… and after she checked his Dun & Bradstreet."

"May I ask – did Clare and your father have any children together?"

"No, they both led such busy lives, and they weren't all that young – starting a family just wasn't a priority. And then we lost Gary …"

"That must have been a terrible heartbreaking experience."

That's for sure. I've finally moved on. But Clare's still not over it. She strokes her bust every day."

Seeing the startled expression on Henry's face, she frowned and scolded, "Not that. Get your mind out of the gutter. I'm talking about the bust of Gary that she sculpted. She'll pause and rub the top of his head, as if smoothing his hair."

"Oh, I see."

"No, she hasn't moved on yet. I'm not sure she wants to. Your coming into her life is a good thing. It's just what she needed."

Henry was visibly moved by that blunt observation. He quickly changed the subject.

"I'm sure running for governor has taken her mind off her personal feelings."

"It sure as hell demands a lot of her time and attention."

"Why is she running anyway? That was a big decision. Why did she take the leap?"

"Quite simply, she did it for Gary. After he settled down from his playboy lifestyle and got elected to the state Senate, he began to think seriously about what he wanted to do with the rest of his life. The more he saw of the problems facing the state, as well as the unexplored opportunities – he was quite an idealist, you know – that combined with a creative mind and an ego he fed with successful endeavors – well, he naturally got to thinking, 'I can do a better job than the guy that's in there, or anybody else for that matter.' So he began to formulate a plan for taking this big challenge …"

"And that's when …"

"Yeah. All that came to a sudden halt one fateful evening in 2011."

"And Clare wanted to fulfill his dream."

"Yes. Not right away, of course. She had to have time to recover from the shock of losing the love of her life. It was quite a while before she could think clearly. She didn't want to live, let alone do something dramatically different with her life."

"Did you help her make that final decision?"

"In a way, I suppose. Clare and I had not been close up to that point. I didn't dislike her or resent her taking my mother's place. I knew she was the best thing that could have happened to my dad after the split-up. But Gary's loss brought us together. My mother flew back for the funeral but didn't stick around long. She had a company luau to host. So we were two lonely women struggling to find our way."

"I'm sure she appreciated having someone to lean on."

"I think so. With her parents living clear across the country, and sad to say, few genuine friends, Clare did turn to me when she was trying to find direction."

"Did you point her toward public service?"

"That sounds so noble. If you mean politics, yes – but not directly. Things just sort of came together."

"How is that?"

"Under California law, if a vacancy occurs in the state legislature, the governor has to call for a special election within 14 days of the vacancy. That's not a whole lot of time, especially when there's a grieving family focused on funeral and burial arrangements and other matters. But politics makes certain demands that must be met regardless."

"No matter how much you and Clare were hurting."

"The governor showed respect for about 24 hours, but the day after Gary's funeral calls began coming in from his office. I took the calls. They had already selected a date and wanted the go ahead. The governor's administrative assistant also inquired whether Clare would be interested in running to serve out the remaining 16 months in Gary's term."

"They didn't waste any time."

"Neither did Gary's friends in the legislature. Some of them were wondering what kind of competition they would face if they chose to run themselves. The newspaper stories speculated the seat would be hers if she wanted to serve. I couldn't put it off any longer. I had to fill her in."

"What was her reaction?"

"Her mind was confused, as you might imagine. Her instinctive response was to say no, so she wouldn't have to think about such a major decision. It didn't help that some influential members of the Democratic state committee were putting pressure on her, saying she was by far the best candidate the party could have. Gary was a very popular state senator and they knew his widow would get a heavy sympathy vote. She begged to let her sleep on it."

"And then what?"

"The next morning at breakfast she only picked at her food. She sat in silence for the longest time. Then she wiped away her tears and looked up at me with sad eyes and asked plaintively, 'Luna, what do you think I should do?'"

"That must have shaken you up a bit."

"I'll say. It was the first time she had ever asked me for advice about anything. I had volunteered my opinion from time to time, but she usually made up her own mind."

"What did you tell her?"

"I took a long breath, looked her straight in the eye and said: 'Clare, I'm only answering your question because I know it's the last thing you want to think about right now. But we don't have the choice of putting off a decision. I want to help, and God help me say the right thing. First, there's no question in my mind that you are fully capable of taking the reins. In many ways, you're smarter than Dad. And you're as good, or better, at relating to people. You're well informed about what's going on in the state.'

"I said, 'We both know that holding public office invariably means a personal sacrifice. But you have shown through your voluntary work with charities and foundations that you have a desire to help make the world better. You have been given an opportunity to channel that desire into action and see the results. I think you would get much satisfaction from doing that, and Gary would be very proud of you. I know I would.'"

"That was quite a sales talk. I mean, you were very persuasive, but also very gentle."

"Thanks. Well, it worked. She looked at me, with tears streaming down her cheeks, and said, 'You're right. And I could live out Gary's hopes and dreams. I'll do it. And as for the special election, the sooner the better.'"

"You must have been pleased that you guided her wisely."

"I did have a wonderfully warm feeling. I hugged her close and said softly, 'I love you, Clare.' She responded with a long, tight squeeze and a whispered, 'Thank you. I love you, too.'"

After a quiet moment, Luna rose and started toward Henry, as if to give him a hug. But as he stood she stopped before him and looked up, admiring his height.

"Golly, you're a tall one, aren't you, Hank? I'll bet you played basketball at some time in your life."

"In college, yes," his gaze turning downward to rest on Clare's campaign slogan.

"I'm starving," said Luna. "I'm going to have a sandwich. Can I fix one for you?"

"No, thanks. We had some nipples – NIBBLES – on the plane. I'm okay. I'm ... okay. But thanks."

"How about a beer, then?" she said with a wink.

"I'd like that, please." he mumbled quickly.

Before Luna could reach the kitchen, her way was blocked by Clare, who demanded: "How soon are we going to get a new finance chairman!"

"We're working on it. What's the problem?"

"Things have gotten completely out of hand. That was Ned Brantley calling to ask what time he could expect me for the Santa Barbara fundraiser he's hosting."

"When is it?"

"It's tonight! Didn't you know? Why didn't you tell me?"

Checking her phone, Luna said, "Sorry. I have it on my calendar for next week."

"He said he had to switch dates."

"Well, why didn't he let us know?"

"He said he called and left word at Morgan's office."

"Well, that did a helluva lot of good. Didn't he know he resigned?"

"You thought it was best to keep it as quiet as possible, remember?"

Henry had forgotten about the beer order and what preceded it and had followed the volley of conversation with increasing interest.

"May I ask what's going on?" he inquired. Luna answered:

"Our finance chairman, Claude Morgan, had to resign two weeks ago."

"Why?"

"The dumbass is about to be indicted, that's why."

"Oh. Indicted for what?"

"Bank fraud. Sixteen charges, so the rumors say," Clare said.

Luna continued her rant. "He's one of LA's biggest bankers and he thought he could play some of the games like the big boys back East were doing. But the dumbass got caught in a federal sting."

"I see. You do have a problem."

"Thank you, Joe Friday. Now, you've got the facts. How are we going to fix it?"

"I'm new to this big state Democratic politics, you know."

"Ha! As if Republicans don't have some of the same kind of dumbasses ..."

"That's enough, Luna," interjected Clare. "We'll think of something. Meanwhile, we've got to get ready for tonight's gathering. Henry, you come along. You might learn something more about California politics."

"Well, I sure don't have any other plans."

Luna excused herself, saying, "I didn't have lunch. I've got to have something to eat. You still want that beer, Hank?"

"No, thanks. I need to make a phone call."

Clare showed him to his room, one of two large bedrooms at the top of the stairs with an all-window west wall that allowed a magnificent view of the ocean. Clare said, "See you in half an hour" and headed for the other bedroom.

13

ENTERING THE ROOM on the right, Henry plopped his bag on the bed, disregarding the imported bed linens turned back over a fluffy comforter, and surveyed his surroundings. His eye was drawn to a painting on an inside wall which he identified as a Renoir. That was before he read the brass plate which gave the artist's name and the title of the painting: "Luncheon of the Boating Party." It was a semi-outdoor scene crowded with couples sitting and standing under a pink canopy enjoying wine – and each other. There was something vaguely familiar about it.

He also noticed a copy of 'Architectural Digest' with Clare's villa on the cover. He quickly scanned the article and learned the 6,000-square-feet structure had five bedrooms and eight baths, with a three-car garage and upstairs apartment and a basement that housed a wine cellar, billiard room and laundry.

Henry didn't have time to dawdle. He needed to check in with his office at the winery. The person he was trying to reach came on the phone.

"What can you tell me? Did you close the deal?

"Great. Email the contract to them and I'll try to get it signed tomorrow.

"Good work. Thanks."

With a smile of satisfaction, he freshened up and made a quick change back to business attire for the evening. Before rejoining the two women, he paused to study a photo on a bookcase shelf. A smiling, ruggedly handsome man with tousled blond hair stood leaning on a sports car, looking every bit like a model posing for a magazine cover. In fact, it might have been just that because Gary de Lune was a pop culture personality known internationally for his daring pursuits and glamorous lifestyle.

"Henry!" Clare's voice jolted him back to reality and he went out to meet her for the ride to downtown Santa Barbara.

14

HENRY WAS SURPRISED to see a town car with the engine running waiting in the circular drive as they walked down the steps. "You have a driver?" he asked.

"This is Joe," Clare said. "He's an expert mechanic whom Gary hired to keep his cars running in top shape. He had become almost like a member of the family. So after Gary died I kept him on as the groundskeeper. He really knows a lot about landscaping - self-taught. He has a crew to keep up the place while he comes up with creative plantings and other outdoor projects. When I began looking at a governor's race, that meant a lot of travel. Joe volunteered to be my driver. He's marvelous."

As Clare slid into the back seat while Joe held the door open, she introduced her companion: "Joe, this is Henry Jackson. He's visiting from Seattle."

"Good to have you with us, sir," he said, shaking Henry's hand with a muscular grip that had secured many a wrench.

"Thank you. Good to be here," said Henry, joining Clare on the back seat. Luna, who had changed back into a skirt and blouse, chose the passenger seat in front, telling the driver, "I'll ride shotgun with you, Joe."

She wasted no time preparing Clare for the evening's activities. "You remember I told you Ned had arranged for a press conference before the reception. Have you had a chance to catch up on the day's news?"

"I scanned Drudge on my tablet and caught the lead stories on the 6 o'clock news."

"You read the Drudge Report?" Henry said, making sure he heard right.

"That's between us," she said. "But yes, I find it's the quickest way to click on the headlines, especially on national politics. Anyone I should watch out for, Luna?"

"Sam Mahoney is supposed to be there." To Henry: "He's the AP state capital correspondent. He covers the legislature and since Clare's a senator he's following her campaign ... her exploratory efforts, that is."

"I can handle Sam. And after the press conference and the reception I give them the standard pitch, right?"

"Right. With emphasis on the need for money. It takes an enormous amount just to get into a race, Hank."

"Yes, I know. I've been involved in a few campaigns in Washington, and I can imagine the costs would be multiplied in California."

Luna said, "The 2012 campaign was the most expensive governor's race in California history. Meg Whitman spent more than $160 million during her campaign, including $141.5 million of her own money. Jerry Brown raised more than $32 million for his campaign, and labor unions and other groups spent an additional $25 million on Brown's behalf."

"It's amazing that with all that money being spent, it doesn't seem to have any impact on the economy," Clare sighed.

15

ROUGHLY A DOZEN reporters were seated in a private area off the main ballroom. Three TV cameras were focused on a small table which held a tray with a water pitcher and glasses. Rather than stand behind the table Clare took a position in front – a bit of body language that's supposed to convey the thought that she had nothing to hide.

"I don't have anything to announce, so I'll take the first question," she said, nodding to a familiar female face.

"What do you think about the governor of Texas coming into California and encouraging businesses to relocate in his state? Do you share Governor Brown's opinion?"

"Offhand, I can't think of many of Jerry's opinions I share," she said with a smile. "As for Rick Perry, I'm not bothered about that. (Occasionally a Southern expression crept into her language.) Judging from his performance in the recent presidential debates, he'll probably forget why he came."

That drew a few chuckles from Sam and the others, recalling the embarrassing presidential debate when Perry couldn't remember the third federal agency he wanted to abolish.

Standing next to Luna, Henry whispered, "Off to a good start." "She's good at that," she said. "But it gets tougher."

A newsman from channel 10 cleared his throat and asked:

"If you should win a spot in the open primary in June of next year, you would have to take on Jerry Brown, an icon in California politics. Are you up for that?"

"Well, first, John, I agree with many of Jerry's friends and associates in saying that he really doesn't deserve a fourth term. And yes, I know I would face a tough battle to win the primary if I choose to run. But I am definitely 'up for it', as you put it ... if you're up for following my campaign."

That jibe drew titters from the real journalists present, who knew John Valjean never got too far away from the studio makeup room.

Sam Mahoney fired the next shot: "Senator de Lune, do you really believe you can ride your husband's coattails into the governor's office?"

Poised but defiant, Clare looked directly at Mahoney and said: "Gary de Lune not only was highly popular in California and elsewhere but he also was widely respected for his dedication to serving the people who elected him and for his devotion to responding to their needs. His time in office was cut short by his tragic death, but he accomplished a great deal in that time. During the past two years, I have sought to build on that record, certainly, but also to launch a number of my own initiatives, including improvements in education, health and social services, as well as the environment, clean energy and business and industry. In these trying times, my number one priority has been the economy, helping Californians find jobs, and secondly, getting the state budget under control. You know as well as I do, Sam, that Gary did not have to face these same problems. I am determined, if I seek the office of governor, to face the realities of the present with a strong conviction that I am the right woman for the job."

With that, Luna stepped forward and said, "Thank you," and ushered Clare out to meet the waiting crowd of potential campaign supporters.

The rest of the evening went well. Henry looked on admiringly as she somehow managed to work her way around the reception room, shaking hands with everyone present, calling many of them by name. Her brief remarks at the light supper were an extension of the answer she gave to Sam Mahoney, elaborating on the points of her platform, if she were to become a candidate for governor.

On the ride back home there was little conversation and Clare relaxed and closed her eyes. Gradually her head shifted onto Henry's shoulder and Luna, looking back, caught a glimpse of a smile on her face.

16

AFTER BATHROOM STOPS and shedding of jackets, the three reassembled in front of the huge stone fireplace in the great room. Clare excused herself and returned shortly thereafter with a silver tray bearing three crystal glasses and a bottle of red wine.

"It's a Sonoma Valley pinot noir," she said. "Luna and I like it. I hope you will, even though it's California wine."

Henry quickly replied, "Of course. I'm not a wine snob. And if you're serving it, I know it's bound to be exceptional."

"Are you Irish? You sure have the blarney down well," jibed Luna.

Henry raised his glass and toasted Clare: "Here's looking at a future governor." With a swirl and a sniff, he tasted the wine and found it to his liking.

"Let's not be too hasty," said Clare. "I do believe the evening was productive."

She and Luna exchanged views about various people who were in attendance and ways they might be helpful in a campaign.

"I must say I was quite impressed with your candor in laying out the work that must be done to conduct a campaign of this importance in this state. It is indeed quite a challenge, but you exuded the kind of confidence that leads people to get behind you and work for you," said Henry.

"That's kind of you to say, Henry." said Clare. "I hope you mean it."

"I do. Really. I must also say that I shuddered when you talked earlier about how much money it takes to run a statewide campaign these days."

"We have to face reality. More wine?" she said, eyeing the near empty glasses. "I'll be right back."

When Clare had reached the kitchen, Henry leaned toward Luna with a question:

"Tell me honestly – do you think she has a chance of winning?"

"Hell, yes, I do! That's why I'm working my butt off for her."

"How did you come to be in this position?"

"After I finished school, I just had to get away from my nutty mother and her creepy husband. So I left Hawaii and came here to study poli sci. That's political science ..."

"I know, I know," said an irritated Henry.

"There's an excellent program at Millard Fillmore University's Western Campus and I enrolled there. But I found time to work as a volunteer in some campaigns and I got hooked on politics. I also started up a public relations business."

"You took on a lot," Henry said, admiringly.

"When Clare decided to test the waters for 2014 I volunteered to help her at least get started. She hasn't kicked me out yet."

"And I'm not likely to do that," Clare said, pouring another round. "But you'd better find us a new finance chairman – quickly!"

At 10 o'clock, Clare switched on the early news, and there was John Valjean, looking very authoritative, reporting live from downtown Santa Barbara:

"Political currents were flowing here this evening as state Senator J. C. de Lune made another stop in what she calls her exploratory venture into big time politics. She has her eye on the governor's chair and she thinks it's time for Jerry Brown to vacate it."

(Video clip of Clare) "... he really doesn't deserve a fourth term."

"With his years of experience and his family background, Jerry Brown is an icon in California politics," said Valjean, quoting himself. "The senator admits that beating him might be an impossible dream."

(Video clip) " ... I know I would face a tough battle to win the primary."

"Getting one of two spots in the open primary is just the first hurdle she would have to climb. John Valjean reporting from downtown Santa Barbara."

Angrily, Clare snapped off the TV and began pacing.

"That idiotic sonofabitch! I didn't say what he said I said. He put words in my mouth!"

"You're getting your Irish up" said Luna. "The camera doesn't lie."

"No, but that SOB does. What a suckup. He's typical of the media in this state. Jerry Brown has them eating out of his hand. If I needed a stronger motivation to run, it would be to show smartasses like John Valjean that Jerry Brown didn't hang the moon. Although they do still call him 'Moonbeam' behind his back."

"Speaking of the moon," Henry interjected, to break the tension. "Look at the size of it," he said, pointing to the large picture window.

Luna rose and said, "I'd better get going."

"You're not staying here?" asked Henry.

"Oh, no. I have an apartment in town. Besides I wouldn't be spending the night anyway." Nodding to Clare, she said, "When a woman brings a handsome man home with her, she deserves some privacy."

"Luna!" scolded Clare.

Looking surprised, Luna continued, "You two *are* getting it on, aren't you? After all, it *has* been a long, dry spell."

Throwing her hands in the air, Clare sputtered, "I might just die ... right now ... right here."

"I don't think so," said Luna. "Not on that rug." Henry saw that Clare was standing in the center of a magnificent intricately woven oval rug that obviously had special meaning.

"Goodnight, Luna!" Clare said sternly, as Henry rose and thought about escorting her to the door, then thought better of it.

With the closing of the front door, Clare heaved a deep sigh and growled, "I need a brandy. Will you join me?"

"If you think there's room," said Henry.

That brought a smile to Clare's face, and Henry responded in kind.

After pouring two snifters from a bottle of extra-aged vintage cognac, she leaned against the marble top counter and lifted a glass to Henry, sipped, and said: "I hope you're not sorry you came."

"Not at all. I'm really glad to get to know you ... and Luna. She came on pretty strong, but first appearances really can be deceiving. And I might say, it's remarkable what a change of clothes and some makeup can do for a person's looks."

"Behind that brash exterior, she's a very warm and loving young woman. And for someone on the back side of 20, she's quite mature... and smart."

"She certainly seems to know California politics," Henry observed.

"That she does. She infuriates me at times. But I love her. She's like the daughter I never had."

"And I think she feels the same way."

Clare was beginning to feel the warmth of the brandy. Or was it the presence of this stranger in her home, a man to whom she had been drawn almost instantly. Before her thoughts drifted too dangerously, she inquired:

"I believe you said you had a business reason to make this trip?"

"Yes, I want to talk to you about that. What are your plans for tomorrow?"

"I haven't checked my schedule. Luna probably has set up one or more meetings."

"I hope you can postpone them."

"Why?"

"I want you to accompany me to look at an investment I've made for Mt. Jackson Vineyards. I've purchased a winery down the way."

"Really? How exciting!"

"It's among several small boutique wineries on the Central coast and from the photos it looks quite charming."

"Oh, I'd love to see it! I'm sure you must have seen some good potential. But that was rather a hasty decision, wasn't it?"

"Perhaps. But I thought I ought to own some California real estate if I'm going to be your finance chairman."

She almost spilled her brandy at this astonishing news, but recovered quickly and almost leaped into Henry's arms and kissed him, wildly, all over his face, ending on his lips. Her new money man returned the kiss with interest. And in that sublime moment, the earth moved ... for both of them ... literally.

Paintings swayed on their hangers, glasses tinkled in the wine rack and the bust made an ominous rumble rocking back and forth.

"What's happening?" Henry shouted.

"It's okay. It's just an earthquake. Or I should say an earth tremor. Happens all the time. Earthquakes, forest fires, mudslides ..."

"Not in Washington, it doesn't."

Clare couldn't conceal her excitement about Henry's announcement.

"I can't believe this. It's a dream come true!"

"Let's hope it doesn't turn out to be a nightmare."

They talked a little further about campaign plans, his role and the challenges that had to be met.

"I can't wait to tell Luna," said Clare. "But I guess I won't call her this late. Oh-h-h, tomorrow's going to be a good day." She took his hands in hers, smiled and said, "Good night, my new and very special friend."

"Goodnight, Clare."

They turned and took the separate staircases to the upstairs bedrooms. Both decided to take their brandy and finish it as a nightcap.

17

ALL THE WAY through her bath Clare thought of Henry and his generous gift – of himself – to her campaign. Visions of a knight in shining armor astride a white horse floated through her mind. "How quickly he's winning your heart," whispered her devilish baser instinct. "Don't go there, Clare!" admonished her guardian angel. "Slow down." She had to tell herself things were moving far too quickly. Yet she hadn't felt this good in a long time and she didn't want that feeling to end.

She slipped a cream-colored terry cloth robe over her silk nightgown and sat on the edge of her bed, relishing the last taste of cognac. She was wide awake and her gaze caught the bright light of the moon shining through the window. Almost as if in a hypnotic trance, she followed the beams out to the balcony. She stood at the rail and listened to the surf and the distant sound of a loon.

In the other bedroom, separated from hers by twin bathrooms, a similar scene had been played. Henry had downed his remaining brandy, showered quickly, pulled on his pj bottoms and donned a dark brown Pierre Cardin robe he found folded carefully on a teakwood bench. His mind was racing with thoughts of a new adventure, an exciting challenge that touched his competitive genes and aroused his long-stifled desires. He was thrilled with the good fortune of meeting Clare and the possibilities that might lie ahead. He couldn't completely escape the nagging realization that he had been badly burned in his last relationship with a beautiful woman, however. He had told himself he would never fall that hard again. But then he got struck by a magical moonbeam which lured him outside.

As he moved toward the ocean to get the full effect of the moonlight on the splashing waves, he caught site of a dream walking toward him. The vision was real. It spoke: "Couldn't sleep either, hmm?"

"Too much to think about."

"Me, too. Wondering whether this odd partnership between a Democrat and Republican is going to work."

"I really hope so."

"Why don't we go explore bipartisan relations together?" she said, pointing to a double wide deck lounge facing the starry sky.

They reclined comfortably and felt the enchantment of the full moon. As they lay there bathed in the moonglow, Clare thought to herself: "Should we be bathing together so early in a relationship?"

They both remained silent until Clare felt an ever-so-slight chill. A soft "br-r-r" signaled Henry to extend his arm and she moved closer, subconsciously stroking the collar of his robe. "I like that robe – maybe because it's the color of chocolate." Clare would recall sometime later that Henry was a bit slow on the uptake but did make up for it.

"I'm really interested in knowing more about you," Henry said. "How about a game of 20 questions?"

"All right, if they're not too personal."

"What did you order at the ice cream shop when you were growing up?"

"A chocolate malted."

"After coffee, what's your favorite hot drink?"

"Cocoa."

"What's your favorite cookie?"

"Chocolate chip."

"What's your favorite kind of dessert?"

"Chocolate e…Clare!" she giggled.

"What's your favorite after dinner liqueur?"

"Crème de cacao-oh-h."

"I'm not sure I'm going to make it to 20. Maybe one more. What's your favorite candy bar?"

"Oh ... oh ... oh-h-h ... Henry!"

18

CLARE WOKE WITH a jar. She didn't remember getting up and going to the kitchen to get that jar of chocolate sauce, but there it was, almost empty. Her cell phone was jangling madly. As she reached for it she suddenly realized the light that made her squint wasn't the moon's rays but the bright morning sun. She screamed, "Oh, my G... Get up, Henry (with a sharp jab of the elbow) ... Get up and ... and get some clothes on!"

Luna was calling to say she was on her way.

"On your way ... here? To pick me up for what? ... I didn't remember any meeting in Sacramento with Tim Barnham.... No, I didn't check my calendar as usual last evening. My mind was on something else. ... Now, hold on, Luna. You'll be happy to hear this. Get a firm grip on the wheel. Henry is going to be my finance chairman. ... That's right. ... Yes, we know all that. But he's taken care of it. He's a new Californian. You heard me. He's a property owner. ... Yes, he bought a winery and we're going down to see it today. ... Darned right it's important for me to go. ... Just cancel the meeting with Barnham. Tell him I'll call him on the way. And you can turn around and go back to Santa Barbara. Gotta go now. Bye."

She jumped up and ran to her bedroom, with the exhilarating feeling that a new day is dawning in the life of Clare de Lune.

19

WHEN CLARE CAME downstairs, dressed for their drive to the winery, she encountered Luna sitting on a kitchen stool drinking coffee, having a steaming duel with the mug.

"I told you to go back home," Clare scolded.

"You hung up on me while I was trying to tell you I was coming up the drive. You want to clue me in on this sudden change of plans?"

"Why don't you go out and come in again, this time smiling. You ought to be turning handsprings about the news that Henry's going to be our finance chairman."

"He seems like a nice guy, and he's drop-dead gorgeous. But what does he know about raising money for a multi-million-dollar governor's race?"

"He's had some fundraising experience in Washington state. And he's willing to take a leave of absence from the family business to help me. And I'm thrilled and delighted!"

"I don't know. It just sounds like a very hasty decision. I can't help but think he's got some ulterior motive."

Clare heard footsteps. "Shh! He's coming downstairs."

"Good morning. What are you two fighting about now? Your voices were rattling the chandelier."

"Oh, nothing much," said Clare. "Luna doesn't like it when her schedule gets changed."

"It's your schedule, dammit! And when you cancel plans I always have to make the apologies."

"Well, that won't be necessary today. I told you I'd call Tim."

Henry sensed Luna was upset about more than a schedule change. "Do I get the impression you're not all that excited about me replacing the crooked banker?"

Feeling the heat of Clare's stare, Luna said, "No, I'll be all right."

"How much cash on hand did you say we have?" (Clare liked the sound of "we.")

"It's around $50,000."

Henry pulled out his checkbook and hastily scribbled a figure, signed it and handed it to Luna.

"You can fill in the payee."

Startled but smiling, Luna said, "The 'Friends of de Lune Committee' will be most grateful for this. Now we've got $100,000. Welcome aboard, Hank."

Beaming, Clare took Henry's arm and they headed for a back door to the garage.

"I don't exactly know where we're going," Henry said. "All I have is the address."

"Well, we'll just give it to Sadie," said Clare.

"Sadie? Is she your other driver?" Henry inquired.

"Oh, no. I'm driving. Sadie is the GPS lady."

Feeling a bit embarrassed, Henry held the door for her, then took the passenger's seat. And off they went.

20

TRAFFIC WAS MOVING well as they headed south on 101 toward Ventura. The clear, sunny day offered marvelous views of the Santa Barbara Channel and Henry relaxed as Clare hit a button on her phone and a rascally voice rattled the Bluetooth speaker.

"Hello-o-o, Clare! Yer lookin' good!"

"Thanks, Tim. And how are you?"

"Terrible!" he shouted. "I'm drowning in a mudhole of misery."

"What? Why?"

"You stood me up, that's why."

"Is that what Luna told you?"

"Well, she said you had to cancel our meeting."

"That's true, Tim. But I had a very good reason. And you'll agree when I tell you."

"What could be more important than seeing me?"

Henry rolled his eyes.

"We have a new finance chairman!"

"Great. Anybody I know?"

"I don't think so. He's not from around here."

"Where's he from?"

"Washington."

"What! You got a federal bureaucrat to do your fundraising?"

"No, not Washington, D. C. He's from the state of Washington."

"Well, that's almost as bad. What's his name?"

"Henry Jackson."

"Henry Jackson. Is he any of Scoop Jackson's kin?"

"No, it's a different family. They own one of the most successful wineries in the Northwest."

"Does he know anything about fundraising?"

"He's been involved in some campaigns. There's one other thing, Tim."

"What's that?"

"He's a Republican."

The Bluetooth went silent. Then they began to hear the ravings of a madman.

"A Republican! It's not bad enough that he's a carpetbagger, but also a Republican? Clare, are you out of your cotton pickin' mind?"

"Now, don't get your boxers in a bind. Just calm down and wait until you meet him. Luna wants to have a campaign strategy meeting sometime right away and he'll be there. Of course, I want you to be there."

"Well, all right. You know I'd do anything for you, Clare."

"That's my Tim. Talk to you later."

Clare glanced over at Henry's pained expression. "Tim is a little rough around the edges …"

"That's for sure …"

"… but he's got a heart of gold. And he's a very good friend. He has been a rock for me since Gary died, and I couldn't have done without him in learning the ropes of the California legislature."

"What's his background?"

"He was a roughneck in the Oklahoma oil fields … claims he was on a crew once with Toby Keith … you know, Red solo cup, come fill me up, let's have a party…"

Henry nodded, pretending to know all about the country singer who shot to stardom while he was partying in Europe.

"But when the boom ended in the '80s he worked on offshore drilling rigs, first in the Gulf of Mexico and then when some activity was allowed again in the Santa Barbara channel after the terrible oil spill he came west. I kidded him one time about being a 'latter day Okie.' He replied, 'Well, I sure ain't a latter day saint.'"

A few miles north of Ventura Sadie's voice commanded: "Turn left at the next intersection – one-half mile."

"If there's time after we visit the winery, we might want to go on to Ventura. There are some good places to eat on the waterfront."

"Sounds good," said Henry.

21

LEAVING THE PACIFIC Coast Highway, they headed up into the hill country. The Mt. Jackson acquisitions manager had told Henry some of California's finest vineyards and a number of excellent wineries were located there. They were eager to see for themselves and especially to discover Chateau Lapierre.

"I'm looking forward to this, because I've only been to the Napa and Sonoma regions," said Clare.

"Well, that's two more than I have. Let me read something from our acquisition guy Roger's report: 'Long known for its agricultural roots and history of winemaking, Ventura County is home to many world class wineries and sits at the gateway to the scenic California Central Coast. Sourcing grapes from top growers in Napa, Sonoma, Paso Robles, Santa Barbara and Lodi, Ventura County vintners produce award-winning wines that deliver a memorable tasting experience.'"

"Interesting."

Before long they were in the Ojai Valley, situated between the towering Topatopa Mountains on the north and the southern ranges of the Sulphur Mountain. Lying about 15 miles inland from the Pacific coast, the valley was blessed with a Mediterranean climate, characterized by hot, dry summers and mild winters.

"Reminds me a bit of home," said Henry, surveying the mountain scenery and the serene environment.

"Hope you're not getting homesick already," Clare chided.

"Oh, no. Not at all."

Presently there appeared a sign reading, "Ojai 9 miles".

"How do you pronounce that?" Henry asked.

"Oh-hi." Clare answered.

"Oh. HI!" he said. Henry was beginning to get in sync with Clare's sense of humor.

Sadie interrupted their laughter with the command, "Take the next right turn."

That maneuver took them up a gravel road to Chateau Lapierre. They had been away from Clare's villa less than an hour.

"Sadie's seldom wrong, but I wonder if this is the right place."

"Roger did say not to expect anything like Chateau St. Michelle," said Henry.

He was right. The scene that opened up in the clearing ahead was a far cry from the huge European-style structure they had visited in Woodinville, Washington only a few days ago. In fact the plain brown building at the end of the drive bore no resemblance to it or any castle she had seen in France. But it was beautiful in its own right.

Set in a wooded area with an abundance of wild flowers blooming, the one-story winery had a large open deck overlooking an expertly landscaped rock garden. It was reminiscent of Henry's log cabin at Mt. Jackson.

They parked the car and climbed the steps, pausing to take in the view. A cat ran out as a youthful gray-haired lady opened the door and greeted them warmly. "Good morning. I'm Jean. Please come in."

They introduced ourselves and followed the widowed soon-to-be former owner inside. Both Clare and Henry were startled to see the contrast between the outside and the modern appearance of the interior. Henry was especially impressed with the lighting.

"I've never seen lighting like this before in any winery I have visited," he exclaimed.

"My husband designed it. He was a lighting specialist before he went into winemaking," said their greeter.

"He really knew his business," Clare added, as they proceeded to the tasting bar. A portrait of Jean's husband hung on the wall among an assortment of photographs and framed award certificates. He wore a black beret, turtleneck shirt and tweed jacket and with some imagination could pass for a lord of the manor.

"That's Jean, of course," said Jean.

"Excuse me," Clare said, with a quizzical look. "You must get this question a lot. But both you and your husband have the same name?"

"Well, he sometimes went by 'Zhawn' but, yes." She pointed up to a lacquered pine board which read: "We want our winery guests to feel comfortable. And there's nothing more comfortable than a pair of Jeans. Jean and Jean Lapierre."

"Wouldn't you agree?"

They all broke out in laughter.

"May I offer you a tasting?"

"Later, perhaps," said Henry. "First, I'd like to have a short tour."

"If you don't mind, I need to stay near the door," Jean said. "But our winemaker, George Randall, can show you around. And he can answer your questions better than I can. I've been more the business side of the partnership. Let me locate him."

She punched a number on her phone and said, "George, will you come to the office, please. The new owners are here." Clare blushed slightly.

"If you don't mind my asking," said Henry, "I'm interested in knowing more about your husband. I understand his father was a vintner in France but that Jean was in the movie business?"

"That's correct. He didn't want to follow in his father's footsteps and he became an electrician. He developed an interest in lighting and was hired by a movie studio as a lighting technician. He was so good the studio won an award one year for a film at the Cannes festival. One of the Hollywood studios brought him to California from France to do lighting for a major motion picture. He moved up to become a lighting director and established quite a reputation. But all that success came to an end one tragic day."

"What happened?" said Clare.

"He was on a very tall ladder making an adjustment to some lights and lost his balance and fell. He suffered some crippling injuries and was unable to continue working for the studio."

"How did the two of you meet?"

"It was a chance meeting. I was his physical therapist in the hospital and he had to continue with his therapy for several weeks – months, actually. We got to know each other pretty well and when the therapy sessions ended we began to date. Neither of us had been married but we decided to take the plunge."

"From your accent you're obviously not French," Henry observed.

"Oh, no. I'm a native Californian – a 'Valley Girl' – well, in my time," she giggled.

"What about the winery?"

"Although Jean declined his father's offer to join the family business all those years ago, he did maintain an interest. He had learned quite a bit about winemaking just from observing his father and brothers. It was something he thought he could do, even with his handicap. So we took our savings and bought this place after the disastrous fire."

"Fire?"

"Oh, it was terrible. It destroyed the beautiful chateau that was here. We had to start anew, constructing this building and the wine shed. And maybe it was cheating a bit, but we decided to keep the 'chateau' name and attach ours to it."

"What a lovely romantic story!" Clare exclaimed.

"Thanks for telling us, Jean," said Henry. "And by the way, I for one am feeling very comfortable."

Clare smiled at him and said, "So am I."

They turned and saw a tall, swarthy and quite muscular figure approaching. "Here's George," Jean said.

George Randall was pleasant but more businesslike as he led them through the various processing stages from crushing through fermentation, aging, fining and bottling and then storage. As they entered the storage area the lights came on automatically and went off when they exited.

"Another Jean Lapierre touch," Henry observed.

"Do wines keep better in the dark?" Clare asked.

"Light really doesn't affect wines very much unless it's direct sunlight and then it's the heat that's a concern." George explained. "But Jean's ingenuity does save on electricity."

"Well, you certainly have an impressive operation," Henry said.

"And such a lovely setting," Clare added.

"Jean told me that this valley inspired Frank Capra to select it as the site of Shangri-La, the legendary utopia of his 1936 classic film, Lost Horizon," George said proudly.

"How interesting. Jean Lapierre sounds like a very remarkable man. I can see why Jean fell in love with him."

"He was, indeed."

"It's a shame they didn't have the chance to grow old together."

"He had so much to live for," said George, looking down at the scarred wooden floor, "but the lung cancer got the best of him." He quickly recovered and sighed, "He had been a smoker all his life. And it finally caught up with him."

Everyone was quiet for a moment. Then Henry broke the silence.

"By the way, George," he said. "I think you know my father wants you to stay on as winemaker."

"I appreciate that. I enjoy what I do," said George.

Henry and Clare went back to the reception area to thank Jean for her hospitality and to bid "adieu" but she protested their leaving.

"You'll stay for lunch, won't you?" she pleaded.

"We didn't know you also had a café," Henry said.

Pointing to a doorway Jean said, "It's just a small soup and sandwich operation. Jean was a very good cook and he thought it would be a good addition to the business. He gradually turned it over to me, along with his recipes."

Clare lifted her head and sniffed. "Oh, whatever that is smells delicious!"

"It's a traditional French cassoulet."

"Oh, that's for me!" said Clare, her eyes lighting up at the thought. Jean took Henry's order and asked them to take a seat at one of the small bistro tables. She returned shortly with wine glasses and bottles of chardonnay and cabernet sauvignon.

They noted the color, the aroma and the taste and pronounced the wines very good. Clare enjoyed a steaming bowl of stew and crusty French bread and Henry a croque monsieur sandwich hot off the grill.

"We'll do the Ventura waterfront another time," said Clare, with a well-satisfied smile.

22

ON THE RETURN trip Henry showed he had been doing quite a bit of thinking about the potential campaign. The immensity of the challenge was daunting. But he was so inspired by the qualities of the woman sitting beside him he was eager to get involved in whatever it was going to take for her to achieve her goal.

"Clare, as you know I've had very little campaign experience, and certainly not anything like a large scale governor's race. Can you give me a rough outline of the plan you intend to follow?"

"I don't want to scare you off, Henry. But the plan is still evolving. The 2014 campaign will not be like any we've ever seen before."

"Why is that?"

"Political party affiliation won't be as important because of the open primary system that has gone into effect. On June 3, 2014 all candidates for governor will compete in a non-partisan primary. The two candidates who get the most votes will oppose each other in the November general election. That could be two Democrats …"

"Or two Republicans?" Henry interjected.

"Possible but not likely, considering recent electoral history. The effect of this new system is that old patterns of campaigning along party lines go out the window. That means what has worked before might not be effective this time around."

"In other words, you won't be running as a Democrat?"

"No candidate is apt to abandon long-held beliefs and positions. But voters won't be swayed by party labels as they have been in the past."

"Offhand, I'd say that gives us a perfect opportunity."

"What do you mean?"

"To come up with some brand new ideas, some fresh approaches to getting votes. And that gives *me* an idea. I know just the right person to help us with that."

"I'm interested. Tell me."

"There's a Seattle public relations and advertising firm that has done some amazing ad campaigns for Mt. Jackson Vineyards. It's headed by a dynamic guy named Gene McQueen. He and his wife Shirley run the firm and they have built an admirable record of success."

"You're moving a little fast for me, Henry. It's one thing to have a Washingtonian for finance chairman – we'll have to do a selling job on that – no offense. But to have an outsider doing p.r. and advertising … I don't know."

"I get your point, but …"

"And another thing. Luna has a small p.r. operation of her own. I'm sure she probably is counting on using her resources and reaping some rewards in the process."

"I don't want to put her down, by any means. But I doubt that she has established a record that even comes close to Gene's. He's got a whole wall full of awards, some national."

"I hear you. But it definitely will be a factor we'll have to face."

"Tell you what. Let me call Gene and invite him to come to L.A. and look over the situation and talk to us. He might not even be interested."

"I guess that's the least I could do in exchange for what you're doing – buying a winery just to be acceptable as my chief fundraiser. And speaking of that, I just remembered. I've got a fundraising event to go to tonight. It's a Hollywood reception hosted by a very successful movie producer. You can go with me, and start getting your feet wet at shaking the money tree."

23

AS HENRY AND Clare entered the villa they met Luna on her way out.

"You aren't going to the big Hollywood party?" asked Henry.

"No, no. Not when the Lakers are playing at home. Why don't you go with me? You'll have a lot more fun than being with that stuckup crowd."

"Sorry. I'm an Oklahoma City Thunder fan."

"Gee, I thought you would be cheering for a West Coast team."

"The Thunder formerly was the Seattle SuperSonics. They relocated to Oklahoma City in 2008."

"Have a good evening, Luna," said Clare, ushering Henry down the hall.

"Are you sure you want me to go with you? I didn't pack my tux."

"Hey, this is California. You'll see guys there wearing shorts and Hawaiian shirts."

"Well, okay. I'll get ready."

Henry changed into a business suit – he also hadn't packed resort attire – and went down to the living area to wait for Clare. She appeared shortly, looking like a model in a sleek black gown with a diamond necklace and earrings, carrying a red evening bag.

"My, you look nice," said Henry, rising.

"So do you," she said. "We have time for a drink if you like."

"May I mix some martinis?" he offered.

"Can't think of anything I'd like better. I like mine dry with a lemon twist. I think the bar has everything you'll need."

She was right. He found a silver cocktail shaker on a shelf with glasses, Bombay Sapphire gin and dry vermouth. He got ice and a lemon from the built-in freezer-refrigerator. Clare watched with admiration at the skill he displayed in mixing a perfect martini.

She displayed her pleasure with the first sip. "M-m-m, marvelous. I'd better have only one, though, because this is an important evening."

"What do I need to know?"

"The host is J. B. Donahoe, a wealthy movie producer. He made his millions on so-called spaghetti westerns, filmed in Italy and other countries. He liked Gary a lot and helped launch his political career. He's one of a small circle who encouraged me to carry forward Gary's plans to run for governor."

56

"He probably carries quite a bit of weight in the Hollywood community." said Henry.

"Enough to turn out a heavyweight crowd for tonight's event. And their contributions will give a tremendous boost to my campaign."

Joe had the town car waiting for them in the drive. The martinis had settled their nerves and had them feeling in good spirits. Their conversation was light, mostly small talk, exchanging stories about some of their experiences in Europe. In what seemed like no time at all Joe had them cruising the ritzy neighborhoods of Beverly Hills.

"Donahoe's mansion will be coming up soon," Clare said.

"Is there anything else I should know about Mr. Donahoe?"

"He has a supersized ego, and likes to show off the fruits of his success."

"That's understandable."

"He's also very smart and he has a knack for making good decisions … except in one area."

"What's that?"

"He's an absolute fool when it comes to women. You'll see what I mean when you meet his wife. She puts on the act of being a movie actress – I say act because she's only had a few bit parts her husband gave her for some of his movies."

"Interesting. What's her name?"

"She calls herself – are you ready? – Gigi L'Amor."

"Wow!"

"Before she came to Hollywood, she was Fifi LeFemme. That's when she was a stripper."

"Double wow! Thanks for warning me."

When the car pulled to a stop, Henry's eyes were drawn to a scene that could have been right out of the movies: a magnificent estate with a grand Spanish Colonial Revival residence.

Seeing no other houses in any direction, Henry commented, "Donahoe must own half of Beverly Hills."

"Not quite," said Clare. "But this is one of the few properties zoned for horses."

A butler in formal attire was at the front entrance to greet them and a uniformed server with sparkling eyes offered champagne from a silver tray. Their experiences in France told them it was Dom Perignon.

With glasses in left hands (freeing the right for handshaking), they made their way down a wide hall toward the grand ballroom. J. B. Donahoe's aide was on the lookout and he signaled him that the guest of honor had arrived. He strode toward

Clare with the air of a self-made mogul, grasped her hand with both of his and exclaimed with a booming voice, "Clare, my elegant, most beautiful Clare. How marvelous it is to see you. Welcome."

"Thank you, J. B.," she said, carefully extracting herself from his grip, and turning to face Henry. "I would like for you to meet a special friend. This is Henry Jackson, my new finance chairman."

"My great pleasure," he said, with an ordinary handshake. "Please come in and see everyone who is here." Translation: "Look who I've brought together for you to see."

The baldheaded, barrel-chested billionaire was in his 70s but he had the swagger of a much younger man. As he squired Clare into the ballroom's vast expanse, the glittering crowd parted as if he were Moses. He positioned the pair in the center of the room and bellowed, "Ladies and gentlemen, our special guest of the evening, the next governor of California, J. C. de Lune."

A small brass ensemble did a brief fanfare and Donahoe continued: "Clare will have some remarks later but now is the time to mingle. Enjoy yourselves, everyone!"

The room immediately became abuzz with conversation. It was steamy with air kisses and arms-length hugs: Hollywood hypocrites on parade.

Clare and Henry had become separated during the grand procession but she caught his eye and motioned him to join her. "I want to show off my new finance chairman."

She introduced him to a few friends and finance committee members in their immediate circle and planned to escort him around the room to meet others. But her good intentions were interrupted when she encountered an old acquaintance named Zacharias Bacharach, a film director who is a young genius with old school fantasies. It was said he wears a hairpiece resembling a beret and on a movie set he wears breeches and high top boots.

"Zach! I'm glad to see you back," Clare greeted him.

"I've barely had time to unpack," he responded.

"Where have you been, by the way?"

"Just returned from shooting a film in North Carolina."

"North Carolina. Really?"

"That state has a rather healthy movie industry going. Actually it began developing several years ago and it's been off and on."

"So tell me about your film."

"The title is 'Good night, Mrs. Calabash' and we shot part of it in the actual town of Calabash, North Carolina."

"How interesting."

"The story begins with the night Jimmy Durante stopped there while he was on tour and loved the food at one of the restaurants as well as the service provided by the woman owner. As he started to leave he stopped at the door, turned to her and said, 'Goodnight, Mrs. Calabash.' And that, of course became his signature signoff."

"Is that a true story?"

"Supposed to be. That's just the setting for the movie. The plot involves a young couple who were there and how the incident affects their relationship."

"Of course. Well, I hope it's a great success."

"So do I. My last film, 'Cleveland', didn't do too well. It was a biographical review of the life of former President Grover Cleveland, but too many people thought it was about Cleveland, Ohio."

"That's too bad, Zach. But better luck with this one."

"Thanks and good luck to you in your campaign."

Clare got a glimpse of Henry, who was surrounded by attractive women – not surprisingly – and she began to make her way to rescue him when she heard a familiar voice.

"Clare, DAR-ling!"

She looked back to see a snappily-attired gentleman headed her way. She immediately recognized him as Charles Lee Wiley, who was gaining notoriety as the author of a new best-seller, "I'm Not Happy Being Gay."

"Charles, how are you?"

"Absolutely fabulous," he gushed. "I'm so excited about my book. There's a good chance it's going to be made into a movie."

"Really! How wonderful."

"I tried to get Bruce Cameron to write the screenplay. He's the author, you know, of '8 Simple Rules for Dating My Teenage Daughter' which was adapted for the ABC hit series that starred the late John Ritter."

"Oh, yes."

"But Bruce is busy working on a new novel. I asked him if it was another dog story, to follow 'A Dog's Purpose' and 'A Dog's Journey.' He said no, it's about a cat who learned about Stubbs, the feline mayor of Talkeetna, Alaska and decided to go into politics. Didn't get very far, however. She couldn't even get elected dogcatcher of Pasadena."

"Sad story."

"So I may have to write the script myself."

"I'm sure you can do it, Charles."

"Carson Kressley is just *dying* to play the lead. But I'm afraid he lacks credibility. What do you think?"

"He does seem pretty happy, all right – especially after his performance on 'Dancing With the Stars.' For that matter, anyone who knows you would say you don't have much credibility to be the author of a book about not being happy. I've never seen you when you weren't very upbeat."

"Well, I just happened to think of the title one day and I just sat down and fashioned a story. So maybe I took a few liberties with the facts – doesn't everybody? Besides that's what it takes to make things sell."

"Doesn't your conscience hurt you, even just a little bit?"

"Not when I see those royalty checks. And just think of all the head shrinks who are being asked to go on TV talk shows to discuss the book. They're not sorry … and neither am I. Great to see you, Clare. I see someone I need to see. Good luck in your race."

As Charles was excusing himself, Clare was distracted by the appearance of a new member of Henry's circle of admirers and she almost groaned out loud. Gigi L'Amor was about to pounce. And she could be heard above the din.

"Well, hello there, handsome stranger. You must be one of my husband's new leading men. I'm Gigi L'Amor," she said, presenting her cheek for a continental kiss. Henry smoothly took her hand and bussed it lightly.

"I'm Henry Jackson. I am …"

"Henry! I love that name. Henry Fonda was my all-time favorite actor, as I was telling Jane just the other day."

Clare swallowed hard when she overheard Henry say: "I understand your husband has had great success making macaroni westerns."

Gigi's familiar cackle rang out and the sound waves made the crystal chandeliers tinkle. Noticing her empty champagne glass, she said, "I need a refill," and taking Henry's arm, headed for the bar.

"I want to know all about you," she said with a giggle. As those words blended into the crowd noise, Clare's anger began to rise. She wanted to follow them but it was impossible to take three steps without meeting someone who probably had made a large contribution and was likely to give more later.

It was much quieter away from the chatter of the masses. The bartender saw the lady of the mansion approaching and poured a glass of champagne to present to her. "Thank you, honey," she said. Henry ordered a spritzer.

The long dark oak bar looked out through a wall of glass windows onto a green pasture with a gray barn and a board-fenced lot where two brown horses were frisking about in the fading sunlight.

"My favorite guys," she said, pointing. "J. B. gave them to me for my last birthday."

"So you ride, then?" Henry inquired.

"Oh, yes. Do you?"

"Not in a long while."

"Well, it's just the same as riding a bicycle, or sex. It's something you don't forget how to do," she said with a wicked wink.

Gigi continued to flirt outrageously with Henry, even after he managed to let her know he was at the party with Clare. She paid a few faint compliments to the featured guest but focused mainly on herself, mentioning some of the movies in which she had played roles ranging from secretary to nurse.

"Have you seen that movie?" she asked, frequently, to which Henry replied, in one form or another, "No, not that one."

As the evening moved on, Clare grew more anxious about Henry's absence and she had an increasingly strong desire to find him and Gigi and wring both of their necks. Before she could make another attempt to break through the throng of visitors she heard J. B.'s loud bass voice:

"Friends, your attention, please. When I invited you to this reception I promised you some entertainment. So please join me downstairs," he said, pointing to a grand spiral staircase. He spotted Clare and escorted her down the steps and into a 200-seat auditorium which was used to screen his movies and others in the comfort of his home. He sat her on the front row. She looked back and saw no sign of Henry and his captor.

When everyone got settled J. B. stood and, disdaining a hand mike offered him, addressed the audience.

"We are privileged to have as our special guest this evening one of California's most outstanding women. She is an accomplished artist, an industrious and successful member of the state Senate and an individual of all-around high achievement in all of her endeavors. She is highly qualified to lead this state as its next governor. Please give a hearty welcome to J. C. de Lune."

Clare did take the mike and as the applause began to subside she smiled and began by thanking everyone for attending and for their donations to her exploratory committee. She did a rapid-fire summary of the state's problems and touched briefly on her plans for change. She was eager to have the evening over so she did not invite questions and none were offered. After another round of applause, she took her seat. To her dismay, J. B. rose and began talking again.

"As I said, I promised you entertainment and I can assure you that you will not be disappointed. I am pleased to tell you that I have persuaded one of the hottest rising stars in show business to be with us this evening. He happened to have a night off from his club act in Las Vegas and I flew him here for a special performance. Ladies and gentlemen, presenting Okie Bob."

To a musical introduction by the brass ensemble that had reassembled itself into a four-piece combo, a tall, lanky musician with shaggy blonde hair and a shy smile walked onstage, carrying a ukulele.

"Howdy, folks," he said, making instant contact with the bar-happy audience. "How's everybody doin'?"

There were scattered responses of "Fine," "Wonderful" and "Great."

"I'm Okie Bob and I'm here to play and sing for you a spell. First, I want to thank our host, Mr. J. B. Donahoe, for bringing me here tonight. It was awfully nice of him to send his executive jet to get me. One thing, I didn't have to pay an outrageous fee to bring my bag. I thought the 20-dollar charge was quite reasonable."

Donahoe's face turned two shades of red but he roared with laughter.

"Sending that fancy plane was quite a favor for a Californian to do for an Okie. You know, we got that name when some of our ancestors went West in the Dust Bowl days of the '30s to find jobs. Things have kind of turned around some since that time. Last time I checked, Oklahoma had an unemployment rate of 5 percent, and California's was 9.4 percent. (Laughter) Sorry about that, Mr. Donahoe. I'm sure Senator de Lune will be able to get that down at least to the level of Texas – 6.4. Texans like to brag, you know, and they think 6.4 is good.

"Well, y'all aren't here to listen to my corny jokes so let's get this shindig started. I'd like to do the song that put me on America's music map, so to speak. It's still holding its own on the charts after over a year. Here's 'Lonely Okie in L.A.'"

I'm just a lonely Okie, all alone here in L.A.
I came out West to find a job, pulled in late yesterday.
I found a cheap hotel room, only 90 bucks a day,
I'm just a lonely Okie, all alone here in L.A.

I left my wife and baby boy back home in Chickasha,
I told them I'd get settled and send for them right away.
But I've been here a week now, and still no job, no pay,
I'm a lonely, hungry Okie, all alone here in L.A.

I stood in the employment line for almost half a day,
Then learned there were no openings that fit my resume.
I had to sell my guitar, 60 dollars on eBay,
Enough for half a tank of gas and lunch from Chick-Fil-A.

Why did I ever leave Oklahoma?
The life I had there wasn't all that bad.
I miss my family back in Oklahoma,
I didn't appreciate all that I had.

I took my pickup truck out for a spin on the freeway,
I came across a film crew shooting scenes along the way.
The leading man had come down sick. This was my lucky day.
They said, "You're perfect for the part, this is your role to play."

I'm sitting mighty pretty now, no matter come what may,
An overnight sensation, that's what the papers say.
And more good times are still to come, that's what I hope and pray,
For this once lonely Okie, on the top here in L.A.

I need to tell my wife and son back home in Chickasha,
To share in this good fortune that has quickly come my way.
I found a house in Malibu for just 950 K,
Come join your lonely Okie, waiting for you in L.A.

Pack up your bags and leave Oklahoma,
I know you're going to miss your Mom and Dad.
You say you hate to leave Oklahoma,
But I want my family with me really bad.

On second thought, to tell the truth, I decided I would say:
This California life is great, gets better every day.
I'm dating a young starlet, you can stay in Chickasha,
No more a lonely Okie, not alone here in L.A.

That went over like a lead balloon, to use an old cliche,
She sent me a hot e-mail, here's what she had to say:
You'd better dump that starlet, boy, or there'll be hell to pay.
If I show up you'd best be all alone there in L.A.

I think I'll head on back to Oklahoma,
My wife sounds like she needs me pretty bad.
I'll leave my dreams behind in California,
And learn to appreciate all that I had.

Okie Bob's bashful charm kept the audience happy throughout the rest of his set. He performed several of his other hits including: "I've Just About Had My Fill of Jacksonville (Louisville, Nashville)", "I'd Like To Get My Boots on Your Ground", "Wine Hangover (Grapes of Wrath)", "I'm Not Woody" (a tribute to Woody Guthrie and other Oklahoma singers) and the sentimental "Cherokee Moon", which touched a nerve with Clare because of her small bit of Indian heritage.

While the entertainment downstairs was going on, Gigi kept downing champagne while Henry coasted. When he heard the music stop and the guests began moving back upstairs, he said: "Gigi, I've enjoyed the time I've spent with you but perhaps it's time to call it an evening."

"If you say so. But wait … I've got a brilliant idea. Do you like polo?"

"Polo? Why, yes."

"Have you played?"

"Just a little, a few years ago when I was at Oxford."

"Wonderful! There's a charity polo match tomorrow at the Will Rogers Ranch in Santa Monica. J. B. bought a bunch of tickets. You can go with me as my guest!"

"Well, I don't know …"

"We can outfit you with all the gear and find you a compatible horse … oh, this is going to be so much fun."

"It sounds very tempting. I really would like to see the ranch."

"All right, then. I'll pick you up at 9 in the morning. Where are you staying?"

When he told her he was Clare's overnight guest she frowned slightly, but responded, "I know where she lives. So be ready to go at 9."

Flabbergasted at what he had gotten himself into, he was hardly prepared for a face-to-face encounter with Clare.

She was in no mood for a reunion with Henry, either. Her evening had been spoiled by his disappearing act with Gigi and it was made even worse when she was stopped by a woman she utterly despised as she was leaving the auditorium.

"Clare! Oh, Clare!" She recognized the annoying voice of Evangeline "Vangy" Goddard, a snooty high society hostess known for her offbeat gatherings in her palatial residence in the Pacific Palisades area.

"Oh, hi Vangy," Clare said, and kept moving.

"I'm having a tea party tomorrow afternoon and you simply must come."

"I'm pretty busy this week ..."

"Oh, but there will be people there you simply must meet. And it's a very special occasion The tea party will follow a yoga session out by the pool. I have a wonderful yoga instructor coming and he will teach us all about this marvelous exercise. It cleanses the spirit, you know."

"Yes, I know."

"I simply won't take no for an answer. So I'll see you at two-ish. 'night now." And she was off in another direction.

When Clare and Henry finally got back together, neither had much to say. They exchanged farewells with a few close by guests, thanked J. B. for his gracious and generous hospitality (Gigi was nowhere in sight) and headed out to their waiting car.

24

IT WAS A frosty morning in Villa de Lune. Clare and Henry had retired to their respective bedrooms the night before with very few words exchanged because of the evening's unsettling events. They had barely had a sip of breakfast coffee before Gigi announced her arrival with the blaring of the horn on her yellow convertible.

Henry said a quick goodbye and went out the door to meet her. She was appropriately dressed in polo attire and she told Henry she had brought clothing and equipment for him. "You can change at the ranch," she said, "unless you'd rather do it on the way – change, that is."

Henry, just shy of blushing, said, "No, thank you. I'm not that much of an exhibitionist."

"How much of an exhibitionist are you?" she teased. He let that go by and turned on the car radio.

Meanwhile, back at the villa, Clare finished her coffee and began to attack some briefing papers. She found it hard to concentrate for thinking about Henry spending all day with that brazen hussy. She could visualize the scene, having been to the Will Rogers Ranch with Gary once – a friend of his was playing polo.

Visitors reached the 186-acre ranch, which Rogers acquired in the early 1920's and developed over a period of years, by turning off of Sunset Boulevard onto Will Rogers State Park Road. In addition to the 31-room ranch home, the property contains stables, a riding arena and a spot set aside for roping. The focal point is the regulation-size polo field, a grass-covered expanse 300 yards long and 160 yards wide. A gentle slope down from the house offers an area for viewers to watch the games.

Clare's thoughts were interrupted by the entry of Luna, carrying a bundle of mail.

"Morning. I stopped by the post office box and you have a package." Curious, Clare checked the return address and said, "It's from Seattle."

"Well, open it," said Luna.

Clare tore the wrapping paper off the box and pulled out the contents. It was her red shoulder bag that she had left in Mr. Zee's office. It appeared to be holding more than she had left in it. She reached in and pulled out a bag marked "Forever Yung" which contained an assortment of Mr. Zee's products.

With a shudder Clare said, "I can't believe that man. This is his idea of an apology for snubbing me?" And with that she ceremoniously dropped both bags into the kitchen wastebasket.

"Are you out of your mind?" screamed Luna. "That's a designer bag!"

"Don't be silly. It's just an upscale knockoff."

Luna looked at Clare in disbelief, then at the wastebasket, then back at Clare. Regaining her composure and shifting back into campaign manager mode, Luna said, "Don't forget the civic club luncheon you're attending today in Santa Barbara."

"Yes, I know. I'd better go make a few notes and figure out what I'm going to wear."

After Clare was safely on her way upstairs, Luna quickly dug the bag out of the trash, brushed it off and held it up to admire. She took out the container of cosmetics and made a mental note of the products she could use. It was then she noticed an envelope addressed to "Senator de Lune." She opened it and read the note inside:

"Please accept my sincere apology for being unavailable for our recent appointment in Seattle. I deeply regret that I had to take an overseas call that I had been expecting and it turned into a lengthy conversation. I hope my secretary explained the situation and told you how sorry I was about this unexpected development. I do so hope we can set up another meeting again soon because I am quite interested in your plans to seek the governor's office in California. I have not committed my support to any other candidate, pending a conversation with you."

The note bore his trademark signature, a giant "Z".

"Clare needs to see this," Luna thought. Then she realized she would have to tell her she dug the bag out of the trash ... "I'll think of something."

Luna took the bag and its contents and left. Around 11:30 a.m. Clare took her sedan and drove to the luncheon, where she outlined her views on the budget and other problems facing California. She stopped short of announcing as a candidate for governor but made it clear she was grateful for the support she had received from the people of Santa Barbara and that she would not forget it in whatever role she played in the future.

Returning home at mid-afternoon, Clare changed into shorts and a loose-fitting top. She poured a glass of lemonade, took the briefing papers and her cell phone and found a shady spot on the terrace where she would try again to get her thoughts on something besides Henry and Gigi.

She was about to drift off while reading an analysis of California's agricultural economy when the phone rang. To her great surprise, the call was from Henry

Jackson, Jr. He said he had flown down from Washington to check out his son's impulsive acquisition.

"How delightful to hear from you," Clare said. "Henry will be back later. But please come on to the villa and wait for him." She gave him directions and went inside to change into more suitable attire -- slacks and a striped blouse.

Presently she heard the front door chime and found Mr. Jackson standing outside holding a heavy box under one arm.

"Please come in," she said. "Let me help you with that."

"I brought you a case of 'good' Washington wine," he chuckled. "By that, I mean it's a sampling from Mt. Jackson Vineyards."

"From what I have tasted already, I know it will all be good." She showed him the kitchen and he set the box down on the counter.

"Thank you so much, Mr. Jackson. This was most generous of you."

Let's drop the formalities, Clare. Call me Henry. And I'm always happy to share my wine with friends. How about a glass right now?"

"I'd like that." She got a corkscrew out of a drawer and handed it to him. "It's nice on the terrace. I was out there getting some fresh air when you called."

"I could use some of that. We had a small problem with the air conditioning on the flight down. Leo's going to get it taken care of before we go back."

"Leo?"

"My pilot."

"Henry didn't mention you had a company jet."

"With all the talk out of Washington about raising taxes on executive jet owners I figure we'd better use it before they tax these planes out of existence."

As the Washington wine and California sunshine combined to give Clare a warm glow, she said, "This really hits the spot. I needed something to help me calm down."

"What's the problem, dear?"

"It's your son. He is one of the nicest, most charming men I've ever met. But he can be so exasperating."

"You don't have to tell me about that. I could almost strangle him sometimes. What's he done now?"

Clare took a few more sips of Mt. Jackson merlot and proceeded to pour out her heart about Henry traipsing off to a polo match with a witch named Gigi. She was on the verge of tears when Henry leaned back and roared with laughter.

"Why, I believe you're jealous!" he said. "From what you've told me about this floozy, I don't think she's anyone you should be concerned about."

"But I thought Henry cared about me."

"He does, my dear. Believe me. I can tell by the way he looks at you. And he told me at the winery that he thinks you're very special. And so do I."

That brought a smile to Clare's face along with a feeling of relief. She decided to change the subject and commented, "I hadn't noticed your hearing aids before. Have you been wearing them long?"

"Yes, my hearing has been impaired for quite some time now."

"One of my uncles lost his hearing when he was in the artillery. Is that the case with you?"

"No, nothing like that. I missed out on military service. What made me hard of hearing was the loud music of a band I played in."

This revelation piqued Clare's interest. "Really? What instrument did you play?"

"More than one, actually. Piano, a little guitar, but mainly drums."

The wine kept flowing and Clare got her current love interest off her mind as she listened, fascinated, to Henry's stories about his youth. He had formed a five-piece band in college and they played at dances and other events even after they had all graduated.

"We got to be quite popular and very much in demand," he said. "In fact, we thought we were good enough to cut a record and we went far enough to get an agent. The first thing he said we had to do was to pick a name for the band. I came up with 'The Jackson Five' but there was another group already using that name and they threatened to sue us."

"And I can imagine their lawyers were a bit more powerful than yours."

"By a long shot. We did go ahead and cut a record. I don't remember what we called ourselves. But we didn't catch on beyond our local area and we gradually quit playing so much and eventually broke up."

"Did any of the band members' children carry on the tradition?"

"No. But a few years ago three of the grandchildren who all live in the Bakersfield area started a country-rock band."

"Bakersfield ... well, Buck Owens and Merle Haggard did all right."

"Sounds like you know something about country music."

"I was part of the show on a cruise ship one summer and we had to learn all kinds of songs. Does the band have a name?"

"They all love sailboats so they call the group 'Clear Sailing.'"

"I hope I can see them play sometime. It's really too bad your musical career was cut short because you obviously enjoyed your time with the band . And all you've got to show for it is poor hearing."

"Well, I put all that behind me when I got involved with the winery. As for the hearing, you don't use your ears to taste wine, you know."

"That's a wonderful outlook. I'm afraid I would have felt a great deal of bitterness."

"Oh, no, no, no. I have many wonderful memories of those times with the band. It's the same as with Clara. Losing her left a big hole in my heart and the only way I've been able to find any peace is to remember the good times we had."

Clare took a deep breath. "You're right, Henry. That's what I've tried to do since I lost Gary. Getting over his death is one of the hardest things I've ever had to do. But I tell myself he wouldn't want me to dwell on the past but to look to the future."

"And you're doing that by building on his legacy of public service."

"Trying to make Gary's dreams come true helps a lot. But there's also a vacuum of human companionship I need to fill. I had some hope after meeting Henry, but ..."

"There you go again! Listen to me, Clare. You impress me as being a very strong woman ..."

"I am a strong woman ..."

"Then don't show any weakness when it comes to men. That turns us off. Henry does have a weak spot for women. That's why he fell so hard for that woman in England and when she rejected him he came home with his tail between his legs. I think he learned his lesson. He has applied himself to learning about the wine business. He hasn't spent any time at all with women since he's been back."

"Up to now," Clare said quietly.

"Pop" Jackson (and his wine) proved to be the perfect prescription to chase away the blues for Clare. He drew smiles which elevated to laughter telling stories about his wild youth and the adventures he had experienced while building on his father's wine empire. He was obviously delighted to have his son Henry back home and moving into position to take over. He recounted a trip they took to Washington, D.C. for a national meeting of wine company owners which drew them closer together.

Clare in turn reminisced about her life – the good times and the bad – and as the sun was getting low in the sky their spirits were high.

"So you're going to check out the new addition to your empire tomorrow?"

"I have a lot of confidence in my acquisitions guy but since I know Henry doesn't always exercise the best judgment I have some apprehension."

"I think you're going to be well pleased. And the former owner is a really delightful woman, and a marvelous cook. You must stay for lunch. But more immediately, bring in your luggage. You're staying here tonight. There's plenty of room."

After some mild protest, Jackson headed out to his car for his bag. He saw Henry getting out of a yellow convertible with a frizzy blonde at the wheel. "Bye, bye, sweetie. Had a wonderful day. See you tomorrow," he heard her say.

Clare was right. There's trouble in paradise.

25

"WHAT ARE YOU doing here, Pop," a befuddled Henry asked.

"I'll answer that if you'll tell me what you're doing running around with that cheap broad," Jackson snapped.

"C'mon, she's a high society lady from Beverly Hills. I met her at a fundraising reception for Clare given by her husband last night. She invited me to a polo match at the Will Rogers Ranch today."

"I've got a lot more questions but they can wait. I'm here to look at my new winery. Going down there tomorrow. Clare has graciously invited me to spend the night at the villa."

Clare met the two of them in the hall. "Well, look who's here," she tossed Henry's way. "Your father and I have been having a grand old time waiting for you to return." Taking Jackson's arm she said, "Come with me, Pop. I'll show you to your bedroom." They disappeared into an area of the main floor Henry had not seen.

He went up to his guest room and made a quick change into slacks and a fresh sports shirt and started downstairs, pausing momentarily at the sound of merry laughter from the vicinity of the bar. He found Pop opening a bottle of Mt. Jackson's best-selling blend, which he poured for his hostess.

"Care to join us, Henry?" Jackson said, offering a glass.

"Thanks. It appears you're way ahead of me."

"Aw-w, poor Henry's so neglected," Clare teased.

Henry felt the sting but withheld a retort. The tension was eased somewhat when Luna walked in. "Looks like somebody's having a party. And who is this handsome stranger," she said, speaking directly to Jackson.

"This is Henry's father, Henry Jr.," said Clare, and to Jackson, "my step-daughter and campaign manager, Luna."

"Delighted to meet you, Luna," said Jackson. "May I offer you a glass of Mt. Jackson's finest wine?"

"Thanks. I dropped off some things in the kitchen and opened a beer," she said, raising a bottle she had been holding at her side. Turning to Henry, she said with sarcasm dripping, "How was your day with Zhee-Zhee, Hank?"

"Okay," he said. This definitely was an occasion for "the less said the better."

While Luna engaged Pop Jackson in get-acquainted chatter, Henry approached Clare, who avoided his hangdog look.

"Clare, please don't be angry with me. It was just a polo match."

"You were with that bitch all day long," she snapped. "You've almost spent more time with her than with me."

"Now you know that's not so. And I certainly intend to spend a lot more time with you."

"Well, we can talk about that. But right now I need some more wine," she said, and turned away.

The evening didn't get any better for Henry. Luna sniped at him for being "a typical guy" and again expressed skepticism of a Republican working compatibly with Clare, a Democrat, in her high-stakes political venture.

"Oil and water don't mix and neither do Democrats and Republicans," she said.

"Luna, you're smart enough to know that Washington Republicans and California Democrats aren't all that different," Henry said. "Besides you had a good example of compatibility right here in California with Republican Arnold Schwarznegger and Kennedy Democrat Maria Shriver."

"Yeah, and we saw how that worked out," Luna said, to chuckles from the others.

Even Pop got in a dig or two, along with some flirtatious flattery.

"Henry, how in hell could you prefer the company of a painted hussy over these two beautiful, refined ladies?" he said.

"The only company I enjoyed today was Dusty – that's the horse I rode – and some very good polo players."

"Did they include Gigi?"

"No, no. She didn't want to get her costume dirty. She spent most of her time posing for cameras. And she played a little croquet with the other women present. But again, mainly to get her picture taken."

"A woman who wants to be a showoff usually doesn't have much to show," Pop growled.

"It was a real treat playing polo on the field Will Rogers built. But I'm certainly paying for the pleasure. Why don't we all go somewhere and get something to eat. I'm hungry."

That was Clare's cue to enter, wearing a bright red apron. She had an important announcement.

26

THRUSTING A LARGE wooden spoon in the air and holding it like a scepter, the queen of the villa silenced the chatter and proclaimed, "We're having dinner here. Maria had baked an extra lasagna and left it in the refrigerator. I warmed it up, threw a green salad together and put some garlic bread in the oven. Bring your glasses and let's go to the dining room."

Clare seldom used this magnificent room, with its hand woven rugs and a sparkling crystal chandelier. It held too many memories of her happy life with Gary. He loved to entertain friends and there had been many grand dinner parties in this room. This evening it only served a functional purpose.

Pop quickly opened a new bottle of wine and followed the crowd into the large paneled room with a long table and enough gold-cushioned chairs to seat a governor's cabinet. A gold-trimmed Oriental bowl held a huge arrangement of fresh flowers from the villa gardens. The table was not set.

"Pick a spot, put your wine down and follow me. We'll serve up in the kitchen," Clare said.

The steaming aroma from the lasagna which filled a baking dish in a silver holder stimulated the appetites of the guests. From a stack of china sitting on the tiled island Clare offered generous servings. "Help yourself to salad and bread, and grab some silverware," said the hostess, motioning to a crystal vase containing knives and forks.

Clare served her own plate and joined the group, which showered her with compliments on the elegant, but casual, dinner. The table conversation gravitated to the impending campaign.

"We're about to get back on track after losing our finance chairman. I'm sure Henry will want to focus on the job he is taking on," Luna said, with a glare in his direction."

"We all need to get focused," Clare said.

"Is that what they mean by focus groups?" Pop asked, with a grin.

Ignoring him, Luna continued. "We need to get all of our key people together for a planning and strategy meeting."

"Right," said Clare, "and that brings up something Henry and I discussed while traveling the past few days. He wants to bring in a Seattle advertising and P.R. guy to help with the campaign. He's got quite a record of success."

Luna's face fell and with a tone of disbelief she said, "I thought my agency was going to fill that role. What are you saying?"

"That hasn't changed. We'll just be using him as a consultant."

"Well, will someone please tell me the name of this con-sult-ant. I need to find out something about the Seattle boy wonder I'll be working with," seethed Luna.

"Gene McQueen," Henry said. "His name is Gene McQueen and he'll be here later this week."

"Boy, you really move fast! Well, I want to get my poli sci professor to check him out. I'll call him first thing tomorrow."

"I really don't think you need to do that."

"I do think I need to do that." She paused to let her assertion of authority soak in, then added some reinforcement of that declaration. "I also think an important change needs to be made." Looking straight at Clare, she said, "I think it's a bad idea for Henry to continue sleeping under the same roof as the candidate."

"What! Why, that's ..."

"Wait, Clare," Henry broke in. "She's right. I had already made the decision to leave. I just hadn't had a chance to tell you."

"I still don't think that's necessary ..."

"You know it's best."

"Well, there are plenty of good hotels in Santa Barbara."

"I know. But there's another possibility," he said, and after a deep breath added quickly, "Gigi offered me free lodging in her beach cottage."

Clare's face slowly reddened and through clenched teeth she said, "I'll just bet she did."

"I'll lease a car and move out tomorrow," Henry said, as if that settled everything. Everyone but him knew he had just made things worse.

Clare rose and slowly left the room. The group sat in silence, their gaze fixed on the condemned man.

The hostess returned carrying a tray with a carton of ice cream, three bowls and saucers, and a small plate of wafers. "Please help yourself," she said quietly. "I'm going to bed."

27

HENRY NORMALLY RELIED on his body clock to awake him at a regular time every day. But he had had an almost sleepless night. He kept thinking about Clare and how angry she was with him. He didn't understand what he had done to make her so upset. Maybe his absence will make her heart grow fonder. Maybe someday he'll understand women. Maybe there's gold at the end of a rainbow.

When his watch alarm which he used as a backup jolted him awake, it was eight o'clock. His leased car was to be delivered at nine.

He rushed through his morning routine, got dressed and began to pack when he heard sounds of activity. Downstairs he found Pop on the terrace reading the morning paper and Clare tapping away at her laptop. "Good morning," he said to her. She responded with a quick wave, not looking up or missing a beat.

"There's coffee over there," said Pop, pointing to the outdoor bar. Henry poured a cup and pulled up a chair.

"So you're going down to Chateau Lapierre today," he said. "I would go with you ..."

"That's all right. I got directions from Mrs. Lapierre. Besides you've got other plans."

"Yeah."

Clare absented herself momentarily and returned with a basket of warm breakfast pastries, which she set on the table between them. "Thanks," said Henry. She ignored him and went back to her computer.

Henry was going to stop for breakfast on the way to Gigi's beach house, but he decided to have a croissant with his coffee. "May I see the sports section, Pop?" He handed it over. Henry's perusal of the performance of his favorite teams was interrupted by a call on his cell phone.

"The leasing company," he explained. "They're on the way with the car." He excused himself to go get his bag.

On the way out he stopped to thank Clare for allowing him to stay in her lovely home. "I'll call you," he said. "OK," she said.

Pop walked out with him. Putting his hand on Henry's shoulder, he said, "I hope you work things out, son. She's a very special woman."

"I know," Henry said.

They walked outside as the cars were pulling up. One was his leased vehicle, the other the driver's ride back to the office. "Here you are, Mr. Jackson," the driver said, handing him the key.

"Is that a foreign car?" Pop asked, heatedly, pointing to the slick electric blue Camaro. "No, it's a Chevrolet."

"Well, okay. Drive carefully." They shook hands and Henry was on his way.

Pop went to brush his teeth and grab his sunglasses and a cap for his trip to the winery. When he stopped by the terrace to say goodbye to Clare, she stood and hugged him tightly. She was fighting tears.

"I'm sorry," she said. "This just isn't a good day for me."

"I know. Henry's being very stupid."

"That bothers me, all right. But I also got myself in a bind by agreeing to do something I really don't want to do."

"What's that?"

"Oh, it's a stupid yoga class at the home of a woman I really can't stand."

"You'll get through it. I know you will. Don't let it get you down."

"Thanks. I needed that," she said and gave him another short hug. "I'll see you when you get back ... and tonight we'll drink my wine."

"Well, maybe. So long, Clare."

Bucked up a bit by Pop's reassurance, she went to her room and surveyed her closet for some attire that might be appropriate for her horrible day. She settled on a pair of white slacks and a sleeveless fuchsia top.

Clare wanted to drive her silver Mazda sedan and called Joe to see if it had plenty of gas. He assured her it did and said he would bring it around. She thanked him and set out for the Pacific Palisades home of Evangeline Goddard.

She decided to chance the traffic on Route 101 – she wasn't in any great hurry to get there – and return on the Pacific Coast highway. The California sun was living up to its reputation and the breeze was warm and gentle. Vangy had chosen a perfect day for an outdoor party.

Most of the guests had already arrived and were sipping mimosas around the pool when Clare made her entrance. She gave a friendly wave to the crowd and then looked around for the hostess. She swept into view shouting across the small pool, "Clare, dah-h-h - ling! You're here at last!"

"Hello, Vangy. Sorry I'm a little late."

"Go get yourself a drink. The yoga class is beginning soon."

The House of Goddard was a marvelous place for a party, even a daytime event like a tea, and Vangy was a perfect hostess. She had arranged for an open bar, with dashing young bartenders mixing "mar-tea-nis," "tea-quila" sours or other drinks of your choice. There was no waiting for a mimosa or bloody Mary – just help yourself to a glass. Clare was selecting a sparkling water when she brushed elbows with a willowy blonde wearing black leotards and a skintight top.

"Hi, I'm Wendy Daye," she said, as if anyone wouldn't recognize the face that sold millions of tabloids. The young starlet had been the center of one scandalous incident after another and most recently had spent time in the Los Angeles County jail for punching out a papparozzi lying in wait for her as she left a well-known night club.

"Yes, I know," Clare replied. "I'm state Sen. J. C. de Lune. Call me Clare."

"Gary de Lune's widow!" Wendy said, as tactless as the gossip columnists who made their living from her exploits. "It's wonderful to meet you."

"You probably know a mutual friend, J. B. Donahoe?"

"Donzy? Of course. And his awful wife. Oh, sorry. Friend of yours?"

"Hardly," said Clare bluntly.

"I hear she was seen with a very good-looking guy at the polo match a few days ago."

Clare steeled herself and asked, "Does she run around on her husband all the time?"

"She does have a fondness for men. But don't we all?" Wendy laughed. "But she would never really cheat on her sugar daddy."

"Oh?"

"Oh, no. She knows he would toss her out of that fancy house and the life that goes with it in less time than it takes to finish a vodka shooter," she said, downing her drink with one gulp. They heard Vangy calling the guests to assemble.

"I'm absolutely thrilled to have one of the world's finest yoga instructors here today – Yogi O'hara!

"His father was Irish," she explained. "Let's make him feel welcome." She led the group in a hearty round of applause – at least those who were willing to put down their glasses.

After an unexpectedly long wait Yogi, wearing a turban and a flowing white robe, emerged carrying a drink which he set on a table and took a deep bow.

"Beautiful ladies, it is my great good fortune to be with you. Please get comfortable and step onto your mats."

With a flourish, he threw off his robe, revealing a slender, tan body clad only in a skimpy white Speedo – and the turban, of course.

"Let us assume the lotus position," he said. As he lowered himself to the floor, he teetered from one side to the other, plopping clumsily onto his mat.

Clare thought to herself: "I do believe Yogi O'Hara has been into the Jameson's."

"The first asana," Yogi said, almost in a chant. He put his hands behind him and leaned forward over his folded legs until his face was turned downward on the mat. Vangy and the others attempted to duplicate the posture. Vangy didn't quite make it all the way and her eyes focused on her high-paid yoga instructor. He was staying in the position far too long. His eyes were closed, his breathing was shallow.

"Yogi!" she shouted, rising to her knees. "Yogi!" He didn't move. He had passed out.

Muttering an epithet related to his biological ancestry, Vangy picked up a bucket of half-melted ice from the bar and angrily dumped it on his head.

"Ai-yee-e-e!" he screamed and jumped to his feet.

"Now," said Vangy, "shall we resume our lesson?"

Clare was in good physical condition because she worked out regularly. She didn't even have to leave home. Gary had arranged for a fully-equipped gym in the basement of the villa. She also had attended yoga classes for a period of time, so she was confident assuming the variety of postures Yogi demonstrated for the group. He concluded his lesson with members of the group trying to maintain their balance standing on one leg and reaching for the sky. (A bit of tai chi for a finish, Clare mused.)

At one point during the exercises, Clare noticed a helicopter circling over the area. Vangy was annoyed by the noise, but it was only momentary.

The yoga session was followed by a tea party featuring organic vegetarian Indian dishes with soy milk and yogurt. Clare took a small serving and found a table with some vaguely familiar faces.

"Did you enjoy the yoga session? Clare asked, straining to appear interested.

A bosomy brunette in a flowery mumu answered: "For the most part. But I just couldn't get that pachysandra posture." Clare stifled a giggle and made a mental note to share that remark with Maria, her gardening companion.

"Do sit down and tell us about your plans for the governor's mansion," said a plump matron daring to wear bright orange tights. "I was there for an affair several years ago and it really needed work."

"The state no longer owns it," Clare said. "It was sold in 1982. Ronald Reagan was the last governor to live there, and then only a few months."

"Then where will you live?" asked a bony septuagenerian with streaked hair.

"Probably where I'm living now. But that decision is a long way off. Right now I'm just exploring the possibility of a race for governor. If I do run, it will be a very difficult, extremely costly campaign. That's the other thing I'm concentrating on at this time – raising money. I hope I can count on your support," she said, panning the clueless faces at the table. She excused herself to find the hostess.

"Oh, there you are, Vangy. It has been a lovely party. Thank you for inviting me. But I really must go now. Another campaign commitment," she fibbed.

Clare knew what she had to do. She retrieved her car and headed west, turning south on the Pacific Coast highway. Gigi's beach house was only a few miles down the road.

Her thoughts were bouncing wildly. "Am I doing this? Am I really spying on Henry? Have I fallen that hard?" "Yes, yes, yes."

She found the turnoff and drove about a mile. As she drew near to Gigi's property, she heard sounds of splashing and giggling. Rounding a curve she reached the top of a ridge which offered a clear view of the scene below. It made her tremble with angry disbelief. She lowered the car window to get a better look. They were both in shallow water in the pool. Gigi was wearing a skimpy flesh-colored bikini. Henry had on sunglasses and who knows if anything else. Clare's blood ran cold.

The screech of tires as she whirled the car around and sped away could be heard as far away as Malibu.

28

CLARE WAS FEROCIOUSLY dead-heading spent blooms in a bed of petunias with Maria when Pop arrived back from Chateau Lapierre. He parked at the curb, got out of the car and walked around to the other side. He gallantly opened the door and out stepped Jean Lapierre.

"Good afternoon, ladies," he called out. "I would like for you to meet my new friend, Jean." She smiled and waved.

Clare stood erect and said, "We've met, Pop." Extending a hand to Jean, she smiled and said, "Hello, again. This is Maria. She and Joe are permanent houseguests."

"Well, you were good enough to put me up for the evening," said Pop, "but I'll just pick up my bag and check out."

"Nonsense," said Clare. "I've got plenty of room. Come on in. Maria, the flower bed looks a lot better. Let's call it good."

Mr. Jackson popped the trunk lid and got Jean's bag. He fell behind the two women.

Jean was as impressed with the villa as Pop had been. He had described it to her on the drive up from the winery, but he couldn't really do it justice."

"This house is so beautiful," she said.

"Wait till you see the ocean view," Pop added.

"Pop, you know the way to your room," Clare said, and to Jean, "I have a room for you upstairs."

When they reached the room, Jean put down her bag and admired the antique bed and other furnishings. "The bathroom is in there, if you want to freshen up," Clare said, pointing. "I'll go fix some refreshments."

By the time Pop joined her in the great room she had brought a tray with a bottle of wine, a pitcher of ice tea and glasses, along with some almond biscotti.

Pop was bubbling over with enthusiasm after his experience in seeing Chateau Lapierre and meeting the charming former owner. He kept talking about her, more so than the winery, but he sensed that Clare's day had not turned out as well.

"What's bothering you, Clare dear?"

She had just begun to pour out her heart about Henry frolicking with Gigi when Jean entered. She observed the two were having what appeared to be a private conversation.

"Excuse me, I'll just grab a glass of ice tea and go sit on the terrace," she said.

"Please stay," said Clare. "I don't mind." It might be well to get another woman's point of view, she thought.

She shared her frustration about Henry and "the other woman" and they expressed understanding and some sympathy. She also asked more questions about the woman in England with whom Henry was enamored. But she learned very little because his father had been unable to get his son to talk about the episode.

"All I know is that he met her while he was club-hopping and her name was ... Katie, or something like that."

"Has he dated a lot since he returned to the states?" she inquired.

"Hardly any. He's been spending most of his time learning the wine business."

"Well, he certainly doesn't have his mind on business these days," said Clare, caustically. "Monkey business, maybe."

"Now, dear, I tried to tell you that's just Henry. He's been playing the field so long it's a habit. But from what you've told me, in this case it's the woman who's making the advances and I can't believe he's really falling for all the attention she's been giving him."

Jean decided to speak up. "Henry's not that much different from my Jean. I tried to tell myself he was just a typical Frenchman, but we had to go through a difficult period before we were married when he was phasing out of his life as a single man with many female admirers. My impression of Henry is that he's somebody you don't want to give up on."

Remembering what Wendy Daye had said about Gigi not cheating on her husband, Clare calmed down somewhat. The crisp Riesling might have had something to do with her mellowing mood.

"I'd like to take everybody out to eat," said Pop. "Clare, can you suggest a good place?"

"Why, that's very kind of you. Santa Barbara has a number of good restaurants. Do you mind if we include Luna?"

"No, of course not." Turning to Jean, he said, "That's Clare's stepdaughter. She's also her campaign manager. You'll like her."

Luna answered Clare's call on the first ring. "Hi, how's it going?" Clare opted not to mention the tea party or what followed and just filled her in on Pop's return from the winery visit arm in arm with the former owner. "He'd like for you to join us for dinner. How about meeting us at Costello's at 8 o'clock?"

"The Italian restaurant?"

"Yes. On Abbott."

"At the corner of First street, right?"

"No, Chef Costello is at the corner of Third and Abbott."

"Then, who's on First?"

"I don't know."

"Never mind. I'll find it. See you at eight."

When they arrived at the restaurant they found Luna waiting for them. She was enjoying a beer at a table in a remote corner she had chosen in an effort to obtain a modicum of privacy.

With introductions out of the way they ordered and plunged into campaign talk. Pop and Jean excused themselves to go admire a huge wheel of parmigiana reggiano which had been broken for tasting.

Luna finished her beer and burrowed in. "So what's the latest with you and Henry?"

Clare glossed over the day's events and then confessed, woman to woman: "I can't decide whether I want to strangle him or smother him ... with kisses."

"Oh, boy. You've really fallen hard. Well, be careful. I don't want you to get hurt. And remember you've got a hard race to run."

"I know. Where are we?"

"Professor Perido has some more position papers for you. Also, he wants to check out Henry's PR guy. He's arranged to call him tomorrow at 10 from my office and do a telephone interview."

Hector Perido was Luna's political science professor at the Western Campus of Millard Fillmore University. The main campus is in Washington, D.C. In addition to a solid academic background, he also had spent a few years in Washington as a member of the Democratic senatorial campaign committee staff. He had worked in campaigns for some individual senators. Most importantly he had connections with some leading pollsters who owed him some favors.

"I'd like for you to be there to hear the interview," Luna said.

"I can do that. Ten o'clock, you say?"

When Jean and Pop returned with their salads they were laughing – probably about one of Pop's stories.

Pop actually kept everyone entertained through the evening as they enjoyed a fine Italian meal. The Washington (and now California) winery owner displayed an admirable knowledge of wines from various Tuscany vineyards and he made excellent choices for every course.

In the table conversation, Pop brazenly inquired about Luna's marital, or other, relationship. She gave him an appropriate answer.

"I want to see what life has to offer before I decide to share it with someone else."

She also learned that Jean had accepted Pop's invitation to return to Washington with him – to see his winery, of course.

During the dinner Clare found herself becoming more relaxed and less fretful about her roller coaster love life. The feeling remained until she had returned to the villa, Pop and Jean had retired to their rooms and she was getting ready for bed.

Then she saw the moon, which lured her out onto the balcony. She took a position by the rail and stood mesmerized by the moonlight. She knew the moon also was shining on Henry, miles away, and she wondered if he were also under its spell ... alone.

29

UPON AWAKENING CLARE became aware that she had received a message on her answering machine. She clicked on "play" and was pleasantly surprised to hear Henry's voice saying he missed her and hoped he could see her soon. She didn't quite know how to take that, after what she had seen going on in Gigi's pool. But she tried to see it as a positive sign.

Over coffee she told Pop and Jean about her appointment with Luna and that they should kick back, enjoy the villa terrace and pool and stay as long as they liked. He thanked her but said they were planning to take the plane back later that morning.

Clare apologized for not being able to offer breakfast but she welcomed Jean to explore the kitchen for whatever she could find to satisfy their hunger.

When she got dressed and returned, she discovered Jean had prepared some delicious pancakes with a side of bacon and assorted jams and jellies.

"What a delightful surprise," said Clare. "I had no idea all these good things were hiding in my kitchen cabinets. Thank you, Jean."

Halfway through their impromptu meal, Clare excused herself to answer the doorbell. It was a UPS delivery person with an interesting-looking package. She brought it into where they were sitting and opened it. To her surprise, and delight, it was a box of Oh Henry! bars with a note: "With sweet thoughts of you. Henry."

"How nice," said Jean.

Pop piped up. "Looks like he's got the good sense to admit he's making a fool out of himself."

"Now, Henry. Don't be so hard on your son."

"Well, if you say so, my dear."

Clare noticed the twinkle in his eye and felt it might be catching. She took her chocolate fix to her room and donned a light jacket. On an impulse she decided to polish off her breakfast with an Oh Henry! bar. Returning to her guests, she found Pop finishing a phone call.

"Well, I guess we won't be going to Washington as planned. The pilot says he's still waiting on a part he needs before we can take off."

"All right, then," said Clare. "My invitation still stands. Please enjoy my villa and stay as long as you like. I'll be back in a couple of hours."

"Thank you very much. I might give Jean a chance to show me some of the sights in this area of California," Pop said.

Luna's office (and ad agency) was conveniently located in a strip mall a couple of blocks from her apartment building. When Clare arrived, she and Professor Perido were already conferring about the impending campaign.

He rose and greeted her. "Good morning, senator."

"Clare, please. How are you, Dr. Perido?"

"Hector. Fine. Luna and I have been plotting your path to victory."

"Or my inglorious downfall."

"We can't let that happen. California needs you in the governor's office. I've been hearing about the p.r. whiz from Seattle and I'm eager to have this telephone conversation with him."

Luna said, "He's expecting our call. I'll get him on the line and then we'll go to speaker phone. All set?" They nodded. She dialed and had a brief exchange.

"He's coming to the phone."

"Hello, hello!" a mellow voice boomed. "Gene McQueen at your service."

Luna made a brief introduction of Hector and mentioned that the candidate was sitting in.

"I'm delighted to hear that," said McQueen.

Hector began his interview on a friendly note. "Do you by any chance have any connection with Ackerman McQueen of Oklahoma City?"

"I wish!" said the voice on the other end. "That National Rifle Association account they snared back in the early 1980s was one of the biggest coups in advertising history. Their public relations skills turned a sportsmen's group into a powerful Washington lobby, earning tens of millions of dollars. No, I'm from an eastern branch of the family."

"You did have some ad agency experience before forming your own company, right?"

"I did my apprenticeship with an agency that has some claim to fame – I worked in the New York office of the Martin Agency of Richmond, Virginia. They're probably best known for the Geico Insurance Company account."

"Oh, yes. How is the Gecko, by the way?"

"He's retired and living off his residuals."

"Well, you come highly recommended by our new finance chairman, Henry Jackson."

"Yes, Henry and I go back to Harvard Business School days. He's a good friend and comes from a fine family."

"We've heard some accounts of the work you've done for Mt. Jackson Vineyards. Could you elaborate on that?"

"I'm happy to. We've put together a number of multimedia presentations for Mt. Jackson to use at trade shows in the U.S. and abroad. We're very proud of the success we've helped them achieve. One of our most effective campaigns was a bit daring. We directly took on Mt. Jackson's strongest competitor, Washington's oldest winery, Chateau Ste. Michelle. I want you to see a video, but for the moment I'll describe the basic theme, which goes like this: The video opens with a shot of the chateau and the announcer says, "Great wine is not about great buildings. It's about the great people inside." Next shot is the Mt. Jackson winery. "Mt. Jackson wines are the product of people like ..." And then there's a series of closeups on the vineyard manager, the winemaker, the founder and a two-shot of Mr. Jackson Jr. and Henry. And the finish is: "These fine folks, with their experience, their know-how and their dedication to outstanding quality – that's what makes the wines of Mt. Jackson Vineyards truly exceptional. Taste them and you're bound to agree."

"I'm sold!" said Clare.

"Another presentation, and this one won a number of awards for pictorial design and cinematography, was what we called our 'Clear Choice' campaign. In it we featured Mt. Jackson's use of pure mountain spring water in its processing of the grapes. You'll see what I mean when you look at the video I'll get to you."

"You've probably given some thought to how you can apply your expertise to our campaign," said Hector.

"Oh, yes. I've got a brain full of ideas and I'm eager to get with you and share them. Some of them you probably won't like, but others you just won't be able to resist," Gene said, laughing.

Luna saw an opening and said, "We're putting together a meeting of key people to try to finalize a two-phase plan – the exploratory stage and if that shows what we think it will, a roughly six-month campaign. We're trying to get everybody together at the de Lune villa tomorrow. Do you think you could come down for it?"

"Let me see. Why, yes. I can do that. What time?"

"We can make it late morning, say 11 a.m. It might mean an early flight ..."

"Not a problem," said Gene. "I'll see you in the a.m. Pleasure talking with you, and I'll be happy to answer any other questions you might have."

Luna did have one big question: Would he have any problem with her agency placing the ads so she could bring in some revenue? But that could wait.

"We'll need to check with Tim Barnham," said Clare.

"And our finance chairman."

"It so happens I had some communication with him this morning." Clare decided not to mention they hadn't spoken directly. "Well, I'll be off. See you tomorrow."

As Clare pulled into the villa drive, she saw no sign of Pop's rental car. He and Jean must be enjoying their sightseeing, she thought.

The first thing she wanted to do was to get in touch with Henry. And when she did, how should she approach him. She decided to be calm but firm. He answered his cell phone on the first ring.

"I got your message and the package," she said.

"Good. Am I back in your good graces?"

"It's a start. But I'm not going to be quick to forget your carrying on with another woman."

"Clare, I'm not carrying on, as you put it, with anybody."

"Well, you could have fooled me. I saw you cavorting with Gigi in the pool yesterday."

"I thought that might have been you up there on the ridge spying on me. All that happened was that she came by to show me some things about the house, including the pool supplies. I said I was tempted to take a dip and she decided to change into a suit and do the same. She didn't stay long."

"Uh-huh. Well, the reason I called – oh, I guess I should ask, am I interfering with anything you and Gigi might be doing today?"

"Obviously you don't read the gossip columns or see the tabloid TV shows. She and her husband left this morning for a film festival in Indonesia."

"Oh ... so you've been having to endure it there all alone."

"I'm alone, yes."

"Just sitting by the pool, sipping a drink and working on your tan, eh?"

"Hardly. I've been keeping busy."

"Doing what?"

"For one thing, I got in touch with the former finance chairman – Morgan – and got him to email me his prospects list. I called every name on it and managed to reach all but two. Of the ones I talked to, I got pledges from at least 75 percent and only negative responses from a very few."

"Good work, Mr. Finance Chairman. I'm impressed."

"I figure the more money resources we can get committed the fewer our opponents can get."

"Right. I wanted to let you know we're having a meeting of key people in the campaign organization tomorrow and I hope you can be there. Or I should say here, in the villa, at 11 a.m. Gene McQueen's coming down from Seattle."

"So you got in touch with him?"

"Yes. We had a good telephone exchange."

"He's a good man."

"He thinks well of you, too."

"I want you to think well of me, Clare."

"I'm coming around. By the way, your father's still here ... with Jean. She came back from Chateau Lapierre with him, and she plans to accompany him to Washington for a visit. But their flight has been delayed because the plane needs some kind of a part."

"It will be good to see all of you tomorrow."

"You'll get to meet Tim Barnham in person, as well as Luna's poli sci professor, Hector Perido, who's our volunteer political consultant."

"Looking forward to it."

"Goodbye, Henry."

"Goodbye, Clare."

She had a spring in her step as she went to the kitchen for a glass of iced tea. "Looks like I got upset about nothing," she mused. "Guess I really didn't have anything to worry about."

There were sounds of activity at the front of the house. Pop and Jean were returning from their outing.

"Well, Pop. Did Jean do a good job of showing you some California sights?" said Clare.

"She certainly did. We toured the Ronald Reagan Presidential Library – now, he was my kind of president – and we did a couple of wine tastings and had a delicious lunch in Ventura."

"Oh, where did you eat?"

"Some place on the pier. I forgot the name. We also took a stroll around town. That's a charming area."

"I'll bet you're ready to sit a spell, as my folks used to say. I'm having some iced tea. May I get some for you?"

"Thanks," said Pop. "But I think I'll take a short nap."

"I'll have a glass, thank you," Jean said.

They decided to enjoy the breeze on the terrace and engage in some "girl talk." Clare told Jean about her phone conversation with Henry, and she was happy to know they were about to get things patched up.

"Men are hard to figure out sometimes," said Jean. "But you've got to love them anyway."

"I really do like Henry," Clare said.

"And I think his dad is a pretty nice guy."

"Lucky us," said Clare, raising her glass to toast their good fortune.

When Pop got up from his nap, he checked in with his pilot and learned they were still grounded for at least one more day. Neither Pop nor Jean seemed to mind.

Clare told them about the campaign planning session scheduled for the next day. Both were excited and Pop asked if they could sit in, "as interested citizens."

"Jean can. She's an eligible voter," Clare kidded Pop. "But I guess we can let you join us, too."

"That's very big of you," he said.

Nobody was very hungry so Clare phoned in a pizza order and they took their wine out to the terrace and dined al fresco. By mutual agreement, they all retired early.

30

AFTER ANOTHER OF Jean's marvelous "make-do-with-what-you've-got" breakfasts, the trio turned their attention to the day's activities.

With help from Jean, who volunteered her assistance, Clare got the great room ready for the group meeting. She brewed another pot of coffee, this time decaf, and found some cookies in the freezer that would be ready for snacking by the time the visitors assembled.

First to arrive was Luna, who lugged in a briefcase loaded with papers, writing pads and pens. "Did you get hold of Henry?" she asked. Clare gave her a report on the work he had done laying the groundwork for future fundraising.

Next came Hector Perido and he wasn't alone. "This is Houston Conover," he said. "He's a graduate student who has been working with me on a project. He'll be assisting me throughout the campaign." Everybody welcomed Houston as a member of the team.

Tim Barnham signaled his arrival by opening the front door and shouting, "Anybody home?" Seeing Clare, he extended his arms for a hug and said, "Yer lookin' real good!"

"And the same to you, Tim. How are things going in the legislature?"

"It's pretty slow going this time of year," he said. "We miss you."

"I guess I ought to make an appearance from time to time. But since none of my committees are meeting and there haven't been any votes, I think my time is better spent elsewhere."

"You're absolutely right, of course."

"Well, come on in. I think you know everyone, except Houston." She introduced them to one another.

"I also want all of you to meet Henry's father, Henry Jackson Jr. (who was coming down the hall with Jean) and his friend, Jean Lapierre."

With a hearty handshake, Tim said, "Yer lookin' real good." Pop's quizzical expression didn't faze the friendly Oklahoman.

After exchanging greetings with the rest, Pop – casting a critical eye at Hector's ponytail – said to Clare, "Are you sure it's all right for us to sit in on your meeting?"

"Of course. You might have some good ideas to offer."

Next to arrive was Henry. Clare answered the door and they greeted each other warmly. "Sorry I'm late," he said.

"We're still getting assembled. Your father and Jean are joining us."

"They're still here?"

"Yes. Something about a part they needed for the plane. By the way, they're really hitting it off."

"Well, I'm glad to know Pop has met someone. He's had a hard time getting over the loss of Mom."

"Yes, I know how that is."

As they headed toward the meeting they met Pop starting to go out.

"Hello, son. I'll be right back. I need to get something out of the car."

They heard the door chime and turned to observe a priceless encounter.

Pop opened the door and found himself staring at a hairless brown head which held a massive black mustache framing a set of brilliant white teeth.

"Good morning," a bass voice boomed. "I'm Gene McQueen."

"Who?" Pop asked, cupping his hand behind an ear.

"Gene McQueen, from Seattle."

"Oh, well come in, Dean."

"Thank you. And it's Gene – it's short for Genius."

"What's that?"

At this point Henry walked down the hall and welcomed his old friend to Villa de Lune. He gave a glowing introduction of Clare, stopping short of calling her California's next governor.

Gene didn't hold back. With a blinding smile he roared, "So this is the woman I'm going to help get elected governor."

"That's what we're here to talk about," Clare said. "Please follow me."

She presented Gene to the crowd and said, "All right, let's get started. Luna, you start us off."

As campaign manager, she outlined some preliminary plans which included Tim Barnham as head of the field organization and Hector Perido in charge of issue development with Houston Conover assisting on position papers and opposition research. She had drawn up a rough budget, which she handed to Henry. He looked at it and emitted a low whistle. But he said he thought it was doable.

Clare interjected and informed the group about Henry's efforts in mining the donors prospect list and thanked him publicly.

She also complimented Luna on her report and addressed Gene McQueen. "I know you're brand new to our operation, but we'd like to offer you the opportunity for any on-the-spot ideas you wish to share."

He stood, rising all the way to his 5-foot-six-inch height and said, "Thank you very much, Clare. Meaning no disrespect to your position, but my first suggestion is: No more Sen. J. C. de Lune. From now on, it's Clare."

This blustery beginning drew a fierce protest from the candidate. "If that's your idea of a good idea …" she sputtered, "having Clare de Lune on campaign materials … I don't even like Debussy!"

Gene argued, "Now, look. How many of your likely voters have ever heard of his song about moonlight? And you simply can't run as J. C. de Lune. Initials are only for business executives – no offense, Henry – and government agencies. Now, my second proposal is this: I envision a statewide get-acquainted tour traveling in a bus with 'Here's Clare!' on the sides."

With infectious enthusiasm he detailed a multi-track plan for the immediate future: Get Californians talking about Clare, build an organization using her friends in state senate districts as a nucleus, and bear down hard on raising a campaign chest.

"What can we do about critical press coverage?" Luna inquired.

"Ignore the traditional news media," Gene retorted. "Use Twitter and other social media, like the Obama campaign organization has done so successfully."

"Any other questions?" Clare said. "If not, let's break for lunch and resume our discussion at 2 p.m. There are box lunches and wine on the terrace."

Members of the group paired off, except for Tim and he sat with Pop and Jean. Clare did some table-hopping, but not until after having a one-on-one with Henry.

"It's good to be back together," she said.

"I really didn't like being away from you," Henry said. "I've got to find a place to live that's more close by."

"Luna knows the Santa Barbara area pretty well. Let me check with her and find out what might be available. In fact we can do that right now. I need to talk to her and Gene both."

"I also would like to have a chance to catch up with Gene," Henry said. "We keep in touch but we haven't seen each other in quite a long time."

Luna and Gene welcomed Clare and Henry to their table. Luna began by telling them that she and Gene had discussed his working arrangement. His agency would handle the creative side of the p.r. and ad campaign, but the advertising would be channeled through Luna's firm.

"I'm happy to work on a consultant basis," Gene said. "I should say, Shirley and I. My wife is a writer and is a valuable part of the McQueen operation. We function well as a team."

"I can certainly testify to that, from the standpoint of Mt. Jackson Vineyards," Henry said.

"And being an outside consultant will help defuse potential criticism about the campaign being run by out-of-staters," Luna said.

Clare mentioned Henry's interest in getting out of his temporary situation, staying in Gigi's beach cottage, and finding somewhere closer to campaign headquarters.

Luna's eyes brightened. "I know the perfect place!" she said. "There's a vacancy in my apartment building. The only thing is, it's the penthouse suite. That might be more than you want, but it sure would be convenient."

"It sounds fine to me. I'll take a look at it as soon as I can."

"Right after this meeting, maybe?" Clare suggested.

When the group reassembled, Gene showed a couple of his TV ads on the large TV screen. The one he was most proud of was for a national cereal company that increased their sales by 35 percent. It showed a small boy eating cereal rapidly with a small spoon. He stops and in disgust says: "I'm a big boy now. I want a big spoon." The camera shows his mother's hand giving him a large spoon. He reaches for the cereal box and pours another bowl.

"We did the same ad using a little girl. We changed America's breakfast habits," Gene said.

The rest of the meeting didn't take long. While Hector was summarizing the work he and Houston had done and roughly what they planned to do in keeping Clare and the others informed about pertinent issues and other candidates, Luna sketched out a plan for the "Here's Clare" tour covering the state from south to north, starting June 1.

Gene suggested starting in the north and going south.

"Is there a strategic political reason for doing that?" asked Luna.

"No. It's just cooler in the north in the summer."

Hector Perido asked for a moment and Pop observed him seriously fixed on a strange device.

"What's that thing you've got there, professor?" he asked.

"Why, it's a Ouija board," said Hector.

"A what?"

"Wee-gee, wee-gee!"

Pop shrugged his shoulders and looked straight at Luna with a skeptical expression.

Hector Perido shook his head, his ponytail slipping back and forth, and spoke in a commanding voice: "I'm going to have to object to Gene's North-South suggestion for the tour. It should be just the reverse. Gary, and thus Clare, is not as well known in the southernmost part of California, so that's where we should start building more name recognition."

Gene shrugged and offered another suggestion. "We need to get a campaign biography out as soon as possible. Clare, my wife Shirley is a writer and she can work with you on a book that will let all Californians know who you are and what you stand for.

"By the time you're ready to launch your campaign, they'll be calling you a wonder woman of California politics," Gene said.

Clare was somewhat taken aback but she didn't protest. She ventured a request that Henry and Luna join her on the tour. With the understanding that nobody would be sleeping on the bus the group gave approval.

"Good. Meeting adjourned. Let's go celebrate the beginning of a great adventure!"

31

BEFORE RETURNING TO Seattle, Gene urged Clare to start roughing out her book and gave her a few tips on organizing the facts of her life.

"This is rather a daunting task," she said. "I will certainly be leaning on Shirley for the actual writing."

"You'll find she is a remarkable writer and very easy to work with," he said. "She'll get in touch with you right away."

Pop got word that his plane at last was in satisfactory mechanical condition and announced that he and Jean were flying to Washington. They thanked Clare for her hospitality and at her insistence they promised to return to Villa de Lune when the time was right.

Henry found that he would have to wait a couple of weeks to occupy the penthouse apartment in Luna's building, so he decided to go back on the plane with them. He told Clare he would return soon with more clothing and some other items for a long term stay. He said he was looking forward to traveling with her on the bus tour.

Clare settled in to get her thoughts together about the tour and the book, overwhelmed by a feeling of loneliness in the now empty house.

Late in the day, Luna called Clare on her cell phone. Her message was short and shocking.

"Henry's been in an accident."

32

"SAY THAT AGAIN, Luna … you said Henry was in an accident? Please don't tell me the plane crashed!"

"No, nothing like that."

"How is he? Was he hurt? What happened?"

"He's okay. Just a broken leg. Pop called from Washington. Henry was involved in a traffic accident. His car collided with a duck."

Stifling an impulse to giggle, Clare said, "A duck? How did that happen?"

"Henry was crossing an intersection and the duck ran a red light."

"Must have been flying pretty low."

"Oh, Clare. In Seattle a duck is one of those amphibious vehicles they have to take tourists around town. It rammed the passenger side of Henry's car."

"And he suffered a broken leg. The right one, I suppose?"

"No, the left. And that wasn't from the accident. When he got out of the car to go talk to the driver of the duck, he tripped and fell over a traffic cone."

"I don't think I want to hear any more about this bizarre accident. Where is Henry now?"

"Pop said he had to go to a hospital and have the leg put in a cast. They sent him home with a pair of crutches and orders to take it easy for at least six weeks."

"That means he can't go on the tour!"

"'fraid not. It'll just be you and me."

Clare breathed a deep sigh. "Just when we were about to get back together, this had to happen. I feel like I'm living on the dark side of the moon."

II

*A strong woman is a woman determined to do something
others are determined not be done.*

Marge Piercy

33

CLARE WAS ALONE in her library. She was glad she had converted the room that had been her studio until her interests changed from sculpting to public service. It was a quiet haven where she could be alone with her thoughts.

With Henry sidelined by a broken leg, she turned her attention to the campaign biography Gene wanted her to write. She had blocked off a day to start working on an outline. She dreaded the task and had put it off by calling Henry. He was back at home at the winery and was lounging on his deck. He reassured her he was getting along all right, that his leg had begun the healing process. Being a nurse, Jean had been checking on him every day. She was enjoying her life at Mt. Jackson and had been preparing some of the meals both for Pop and Henry Sr. She had won over the senior Jackson right from the start.

Henry and Clare talked longer than she had intended but she was glad to have some togetherness, even if it had to be long distance.

What began as a casual "catch-up" conversation turned into a serious discussion of the campaign when Henry said he had done some thinking and he urged postponing the bus tour until October and November.

"It's not just because I have a broken leg and can't go now," he said. "I just believe you need to be really ready for this undertaking.

"As a businessman (he wished Pop could be hearing this) I think to launch a big project you need to make sure you have all your ducks in a row – and I'm an authority on ducks, right?

"You also need to establish some priorities. There's the bus, the book, campaign buttons, signs, a press kit, and your overall image. That's a very important element of your campaign."

Clare was most favorably impressed with Henry's advice. She had been thinking along the same lines but he had his thoughts better organized.

"Thank you, Henry. You make a number of good points. I'll talk to Luna, but I think I'll take your suggestions."

"Okay. Well, I'll let you get back to your book project. I'm thinking of you, and I'll talk to you again soon."

"Me, too. Bye now."

Relaxing with a cup of coffee, Clare began to leaf through the first of several photo albums and scrapbooks from her earlier life that she had taken off the shelves. It was fun to reminisce sometimes.

She smiled as she looked at a photo of her high school senior class. Next she came across a picture of her in a prom dress with her date, a boy who had gone on to be the president of a small college.

Other shots showed her starring in a junior-senior play, a musical – with her parents on various university campuses – as a member of the chorus – in cap and gown – at Oxford – as a member of a cruise ship staff (she and another coed signed on for a summer and got jobs as waitresses by day and stage performers in the evening) – and after graduation as a tour guide in Italy.

Another album contained mememtoes of her career: studying at art school – samples of her sculpture – clippings related to her real estate sales.

She couldn't hold back the tears as she re-read articles about Gary, thumbed through their wedding album and finally came to his obituary in the Los Angeles papers and other publications.

She was glad to be interrupted by Luna, who arrived to give her a campaign update. She had found a vacant store front to use as a temporary headquarters. It had adequate space for Luna, Houston and Melody Turner, Hector's social media intern, and was in a good location to begin publicizing Clare's interest in running for governor. While an official announcement would come later, a sign at the headquarters, "Clare 2014", left little doubt of her intentions.

Luna also wanted to tell her the tour schedule was set and the bus was ready to go. It had been decided to begin the tour with a big rally in Santa Barbara and work their way south. Melody was to travel along and do Twitter feeds and posting of photos on Facebook, as well as arrange brief Q&A sessions with local news reporters.

After hearing her out, Clare decided to be straightforward, painful though it might be.

"I can tell you've been busy and you've done a terrific job with all those arrangements …"

"Well, thanks …"

"But there's been a change of plans."

"What? What are you talking about?"

"We're going to delay the bus tour until fall – September and October."

"Fall? Whose idea was that?"

"Mine. Well, Henry suggested it. But I think it's a good idea and that's what we're going to do."

"Henry, huh!" she huffed, her dark eyes flashing.

"So he's your new campaign manager?"

"Of course not. You are and I'm glad you are. But there are some good reasons to delay it."

"Sure. I see. It's so his leg will have time to heal and the two lovebirds can be together. This juvenile crush is blinding you to reality and warping your judgment and I can't allow it to affect the campaign."

"You're wrong, Luna. Now, hear me out."

Clare leaned forward and looking directly at her fuming stepdaughter outlined the disadvantages of rushing the tour and the advantages of delaying it, "to be sure we're absolutely ready."

"Melody can use this time to build a Twitter following and establish a fan base. I'll continue to make speeches and fundraising appearances. I'll have time to do the book and we'll get it published and in circulation. In the long run I truly believe a slow buildup will be more effective than a summertime splash and lost momentum later in the year."

"I still think it's outrageous and a real slap at me," Luna said.

"Please don't feel that way. It's not personal. Tell you what – talk to Hector about it, and maybe Tim. Get the benefit of their political experience. Meanwhile, I'll get busy and finish an outline for the book. Gene's wife is coming later this week to work with me on a production schedule. Please try to see it from my perspective."

Luna rose and stormed out, muttering, "I've got to cool off." The front door slam underscored her bitter disappointment.

34

CLARE ANSWERED THE door and was a bit startled when she looked up and saw the woman who introduced herself as Shirley McQueen. A tall Swedish blond with the grace of a gazelle, she strode into the hallway and cast admiring glances at the splendor of the villa.

"Welcome. I'm so happy to meet you," Clare said. "I have to say you're not quite what I was expecting."

"Gene and I do make a couple that draw stares," Shirley replied, with a worldly accent.

"Please come in. There's a powder room on the left. I'll take your bag. You are welcome to stay at the villa."

"Why, that's very generous of you. Thank you. Leave the other, please."

Clare, a bit puzzled about the boxy case, said, "All right. Would you care for some coffee?"

"That would be nice, thank you."

Clare emerged from the kitchen carrying a tray with a carafe and two cups and invited Shirley to join her in the library.

"I've been trying to organize my thoughts about the book, but I'm going to need a lot of help from you."

"That's why I'm here. From the preliminary research I've done, I know you have a fascinating story to tell."

"I suppose a person's life is always more interesting to someone who hasn't lived it."

They took chairs at a round cherry table and Shirley set the case on a table mat and removed a strange device that prompted Clare to ask: "What in the world is that?"

"It's a stenotype – a machine stenographers use for shorthand."

"Really!"

"One of a series of unusual jobs I've had was being a court reporter. In fact I had my own business for a while."

"That's very interesting," Clare said. "We could work on the terrace, but I find the outdoors can be somewhat distracting."

"This will be fine," Shirley said. "You just tell me your story and I'll take notes."

"All right. But I'd like to have an understanding that I'll probably tell you things about myself, my family, my husband and maybe others that will help you know who I am, but I trust you'll have the good judgment not to include everything I say in producing this biography."

"I know this book is primarily a political vehicle and not a commercial venture, so naturally there has to be a degree of discretion. And, of course, you'll have final approval on the manuscript," Shirley said.

"Good," Clare said. "Shall we begin at the beginning?"

"I can't think of a better place."

Clare essentially repeated what she had told Henry about her early years in Georgia growing up in the mid-80s and early 90s on a pecan tree farm as the daughter of Pat and Betty Sullivan. Her mother always called her Judy Clare; she preferred simply Judy and went by that through high school, then changed to Clare because she thought it was more grownup. She had little to say about her younger sister, who remained in Georgia, got married and raised a family.

Referring to her scrapbooks and photo albums, she related a few anecdotes about her years at the University of Georgia. Making notes on the photos, Shirley's eyes fell on one showing Clare and other female students in Kung Fu costumes. "What's the story on this one?" she asked.

"That's a martial arts class. My last semester I had a light class load so I decided to enroll. I thought the training might come in handy, and it did – several times. Dealing with unruly drunks in European taverns and on cruise ships, for example. And one time at a NASCAR event one of my late husband's racing buddies had too much Jack Daniels and got a little out of hand. But a well-placed kick made him lose his carnal desires very quickly."

"Yes, indeed."

"I might add, just so you know, I got a concealed weapons permit after I went to the state senate."

"So you carry a gun?"

Clare found herself having the same conversation she had had with Henry in Seattle.

"Yes, a small revolver – like the one Dianne Feinstein had years ago when she was a member of the San Francisco board of supervisors. A number of elected officials have decided to arm themselves after the shooting of the Arizona congresswoman."

She added that there hadn't been an occasion where she had had to use the firearm.

They resumed talking about Clare's academic experience. She graduated Phi Beta Kappa and got a Rhodes Scholarship. That marked the beginning of a new phase in her life.

The initial session went well, with Shirley asking a minimum of questions to fill in some gaps, but it was tedious. Clare sat back and stretched and said, "Shall we take a short break? We can walk out on the terrace and stretch our legs."

"I'd like that," Shirley said.

Breathing in the cool, fresh air, Clare relaxed a bit and asked an impulsive question.

"I know this is rude, but how did you come to be named Shirley and not something like Ingrid or Elsa?"

"My mother was a fan of Shirley MacLaine."

"Oh, well that explains it," Clare said, laughing.

"When you were at Oxford, did you expect your life ever to turn out the way it did?" Shirley asked.

"No, not at all. I guess at that age we really don't know what the future holds. I felt as if it was a good move for me and I was so grateful for the scholarship. My folks couldn't have afforded to send me to graduate school."

"We can get some more details on your London experience later. What was the next turning point in your life?"

"Being over there made me want to travel more, to see more of Europe especially. During my summer experiences working on cruise ships – I'll fill you in on that – I got to go to a number of ports. But there wasn't much opportunity for staff to really see much of the countries we visited.

"So after graduation I used a connection I had made on one of the ships and applied for a job as a tour guide in Italy. I was surprised and delighted when they hired me."

"That was definitely a big break. I'm sure you must have enjoyed that time in your life very much."

"Yes, indeed. I received a thorough education on the various regions of Italy. I learned all about Rome, Florence, Naples, Venice and other large cities. But I also discovered the beauties of the Amalfi coast, Messina and Sorrento."

"Did you have a favorite region?"

"I loved Tuscany with its wonderful food. And so many great wineries."

"I know I'm getting ahead of myself. But it appears wine is something you and Henry have in common."

"Yes, one of many things. Not the least of which is that we both spent a good bit of time traveling in Europe – not at the same time. But we find ourselves making comparisons about what we saw and enjoyed."

"Perhaps we should get back to the library and my machine."

Clare resumed her story with her decision to return to the states and undertake a serious study of art. She located an art school in California she found desirable and it also satisfied a long-held desire to go West.

Perhaps inspired by the works of Michelangelo and da Vinci, she chose sculpture as the medium she wanted to pursue. "It's more hands on than sketching or painting," she said. "The three-D aspect also makes sculpture more of an in-depth art."

"Sculptors get to do the hair at the base of the neck," Shirley said.

"I never thought of it that way. But I prefer to work with the front of a subject, if you know what I mean."

Laughs lifted the monotony of plodding through the various phases of Clare's life. The remainder of the morning brought them to her decision to get serious about finding a job and how she got into selling real estate.

Clare had prepared a light lunch of albacore tuna salad with tomato wedges and avocado slices, fresh tropical fruit and whole grain rolls. She offered beverages, including wine.

"I'm accustomed to a shot of vodka, if it's not too much to ask," Shirley said.

"Of course not. And you probably prefer Absolut," Clare said.

"Sweden makes the best."

"You'll find a bottle chilled in the fridge." She led her to the bar.

"And this is one of your sculptures?" Shirley said.

"Yes. It's the only bust I kept. It's a comforting connection with Gary."

Clare opened a bottle of New Zealand sauvignon blanc and they took seats on the terrace.

"Thank you very much for the vodka," Shirley said. "It helps the digestion, you know."

"No, I didn't. I do know a vodka gimlet certainly improves my mood."

"The next phase brings us to your meeting and marrying Gary. Are you sure you're up for reliving those memories?"

"I never tire of remembering this remarkable man and all the wonderful times we had together."

Clare skimmed over the successes she had that earned her the top salesperson award at her agency and eagerly recalled her first meeting with Gary.

"When he called that day I couldn't believe I was talking to this famous celebrity. Just from the sound of his voice I took an instant liking to him."

"And when you met him in person?"

"I swooned like a teenager seeing Frank Sinatra for the first time."

"He must have been quite a charmer."

"That he was. I don't know what he saw in me or whether it was one of those rebound things but we seemed to connect from the very beginning."

"Was he all that you expected him to be?"

"Oh, yes, all that and more. I didn't mind that he was a bit shorter than me. His blond hair and gorgeous green eyes, along with a stunning smile, stirred a primal instinct inside of me that wouldn't subside."

"I read that Gary's father worked in a steel factory in Pittsburgh and that he became fascinated by engines at an early age. I found it very interesting that when he was 10 and his parents took a family vacation to Corning, New York, that they went to see the glass museum but he wanted to go to the Glenn Curtiss museum."

"That's where he got hooked on bicycles, then motorcycles, and later fast cars."

"And he invented a carburetor modification that made him a wealthy man in his 20s?"

"That's right. He became the owner of a NASCAR car and did some racing. He made quite a name for himself. A Hollywood studio contracted with him to be a technical advisor on some racing films and he moved to California. As he grew older he sort of settled down and bought a chain of radio stations and one TV station."

"I suppose he was a popular man about town in L.A."

"Yes. He dated widely and ended up married up to Alana, a flighty social climber. Maybe you shouldn't put that description in the book."

"All right."

"They had a daughter, Luna. She is now my campaign manager."

"Now, that's an interesting story in itself."

"Gary turned to politics and got elected to the California state senate in 2010. He and Alana divorced. She got their big, expensive house. That's why he came to our agency."

"What a fortunate chance meeting."

"It certainly was. But I never thought it would lead to anything."

"Even so it brought you together and maybe that was meant to be."

"My Presbyterian upbringing tells me that. At any rate, we did spend quite a bit of time together with me showing him houses. At some time in that process we were running late and he asked me to have dinner with him. I was thrilled and the evening went well."

"Meant to be, as you said."

"By the time I found him a place that he really liked, we realized we were falling in love. We continued seeing each other and before too long he asked me to marry him. I knew it was an impulsive thing to do, but I also knew in my heart it was the right thing."

"So you were married. And did you move into the house you had found for him?"

"No. Gary was a very generous man. He offered to build me the villa of my dreams."

"Wow! That's some wedding gift."

"He ran into problems with a suitable building site, but he happened to find a property that came very close to what we were planning."

"And that's where we are right now."

"Yes. And I couldn't have been more pleased."

"It sounds like a fairy tale romance."

"We had a fabulously good life until one night in 2011 … driving home from Sacramento after a late session in the senate … a semi-trailer ran across the median … and killed him instantly."

Clare couldn't hold back the tears. Shirley understood. She decided it was time to call it a day.

Shirley took Clare's suggestion for a swim, which was good for both of them. After cocktails at poolside, they had dinner in Santa Barbara with Luna and Houston and retired rather early. Clare couldn't have bags under her eyes for her important morning appointment.

35

RETURNING FROM THE hairdresser, Clare combed out her auburn locks and adjusted some curls at the back of her neck. She had worn her hair fairly short since she entered public service.

This was the day she was to have an official campaign portrait taken. Gene had lined up a photographer he knew – Lynn Dykstra, who lived in the San Francisco area but had the use of a studio in Los Angeles for special assignments. A first class photographer with more than 25 years experience, Lynn had founded her company, Focused Images, in San Francisco but moved to Washington, D.C. where she established a reputation for photographing prominent public figures (including seven presidents) and significant events (such as the Ford's Theatre annual fundraising gala which attracted stars of the entertainment world). A few years ago she had decided to return to her roots.

For her public appearances Gene had said Clare had to have a distinctive look. She had asked Henry what struck him about her appearance. He said it was the way she was dressed to see Mr. Zee: black dress, black lightweight leather jacket, pearls, red shoulder bag. She told Gene she would go along with everything but the jacket. She wouldn't wear that on every occasion.

Clare thought she would need to replace the bag she threw away in anger, but Luna had said not to worry.

Right on time, Luna and Houston arrived to take her to the photo studio. Luna was carrying a large paper sack from which she produced a red bag (the same one she had rescued). Clare was delighted and decided not to ask any questions. In view of their argument about changing the schedule for launching the bus tour, she opted to thank her profusely.

"We've got time for a cup of coffee, I believe," Clare said. They joined Shirley on the terrace where she was organizing her notes from the first day's session.

"It's coming together very well," Shirley said. "Tomorrow we can get going on your views about what California needs and your positions on various issues."

"I'm glad you think we're making progress," Clare said.

With Houston driving, they were at the studio in about half an hour. As they walked in the door, Clare's eyes immediately focused on a bear standing in the reception room. It was a life-sized stuffed bear, about five feet tall, wearing a blue T-shirt with USA in large letters and an American flag, and a Los Angeles Dodgers baseball cap.

Still staring at the friendly-looking creature, Clare walked toward the receptionist and said, "I just have to ask …"

"Oh, that's Charlie Bear, 'America's Official Adventure Bear'," she responded.

Clare felt a bit awkward about asking her next question, but did so anyway. "Is this his office, too?"

"No, he travels with Lynn."

"Really! I don't want to get personal, but exactly how long have they had this relationship?"

The receptionist laughed and said, "I don't blame you for being curious. Actually, Lynn has loved bears since she was very young. She even has a special license plate, BEARVAN. Once when she was on an assignment in Chicago she saw this bear in a store and had to have it. She immediately came up with a name: Charlie Bear. She had him delivered to her home in the Virginia suburbs of Washington."

"But the story didn't end there."

"Oh, no. It really began when Lynn decided to make a cross-country trip to California. She wanted to take Charlie but he wouldn't fit into the van with all the other things she had packed in it. So she set out without him. She was about three hours away on the Pennsylvania Turnpike when she changed her mind and turned around."

"She went back for Charlie?" Clare found herself getting into the story.

"She took out a seat in the van so Charlie could lie down flat. He doesn't bend, you see."

"I see."

"That was an 8,000 mile journey. They took the Northern route with stops at several places in the West. Along the way Lynn got the idea of getting Charlie out and posing him for pictures with people they met. She had great shots of Charlie at Yellowstone, the Grand Canyon, Lake Tahoe and other interesting places. It was the beginning of what she calls 'Charlie Bear's Grrreat Adventure.' He now has friends throughout the United States and some foreign countries. And of course he has his own website."

"Of course."

At that point Lynn emerged and with a smile and warm greeting introduced herself as Charlie's "Adventure Pal."

The portrait shoot went very well. Clare saw right away that a major key to Lynn's success was her ability to make her subjects feel at ease. She also observed the high degree of professionalism gained from her rare experiences. So what if she enjoyed creating "grrreat adventures" with a large stuffed bear?

36

LUNA AND HOUSTON returned to the villa the following day (Clare had noticed they seemed to be spending a large amount of time together. She also had observed that Luna was paying more attention to her hair – the boyish bob had given way to a softer, more feminine style). They brought along Hector's intern Melody to discuss social media plans.

Hector had impressed on Clare the growing importance of the Internet in campaigns, especially in going after the youth vote. He said 50 percent of the public says the Internet is their main source of national and international news. The figure for adults under age 30 is 65 percent. Campaigns use the Internet to provide information about candidates, get people to sign up for a campaign and for fundraising. Social media has been found to be a highly effective way to get information quickly to journalists.

Melody didn't look the part of a key campaign aide. A junior in high school, she was still at an awkward stage of the tweens but Clare soon became aware she was very keen on knowledge about how to use the Internet for building and maintaining a public image.

"Research shows that social media can provide a basic measurement of public opinion, y'know," Melody said. "And it can serve as an 'early warning system' for a campaign, y'know, especially in a crisis. And it can measure basic reactions to a major event more quickly than polling.

"Professor Perido said one study of the 2010 race between Jerry Brown and Meg Whitman showed a spike in social media volume – the highest of the campaign – when Whitman's housekeeper held a press conference and said all that stuff about her treatment and firing. That was one of the main reasons she lost the race, y'know."

Melody said she had established a Twitter account, @Clare2014, and it was beginning to get some followers, one reason being Facebook accounts for Clare and Friends of Clare. She showed on her iPad a proposed design for a website clare2014.com with a blog, "I Can See Clearly."

"As soon as we get an official photo, y'know, we can go live with it."

Clare liked everything she saw and told her so. Melody said, "There's more."

"We need to start posting videos on Youtube and photos on Instagram and Pinterest. Pinterest has a heavy female demographic, y'know, and women are a potent source of candidate backers."

Luna interjected: "Email is really the first social network. We should take our list of email addresses and build on it at every opportunity. The list can be used to send campaign updates, scheduled events and even fundraising pitches. Can we have a spot on the website where people can sign up for emails?"

"No problem," Melody said. "I mentioned photos. Maybe I can get a few candid shots with my iPhone of you and Luna working on campaign ideas. We can get some more when you visit the campaign headquarters. And, y'know, anything you have in your files that might be good to use."

"I'll take a look to see what I have stored on the computer," Clare said.

While Melody was taking pictures, Clare and Luna huddled to talk about scheduling appearances, press notices, procedures for voluntary contributions and use of volunteers, among other things.

When everyone was ready to leave, Clare approached Houston, having noted that he hadn't said a word all the time he was there. He had just sat or stood looking sexy with his beach-blown hair and blue eyes. While Melody was getting some single shots of Clare, he and Luna had gone out to the terrace to speak to Shirley. They returned shortly.

"Houston, you haven't had much to say," Clare said. "Any thoughts on how the campaign is developing?"

"I guess I'm more of a listener than a talker," he said. "I've been working with the professor on position papers and I've done a bit of exploring on researching the potential opposition. That's rather limited since we don't know for sure who's running."

"I think it might be well to start building a file on Congressman Bull," Clare said. "If he's not an actual candidate, I know he'll be doing everything he can to defeat me."

"Okay, I will."

By the time the group went on their way, it was time for happy hour. Clare opened a bottle of wine and took it and two glasses out to the terrace to ask about Shirley's day.

37

A GLANCE AT her schedule told Clare this would be a busy day. She and Shirley had arrived at the point in the biography where she gave her thoughts about topics that might be issues in a campaign. She had asked Hector to join them. But that was in the afternoon. Before that session she was meeting with Tim Barnham to get his viewpoint on potential opposition and general campaign advice from an old pro. The door chime signaled that he was on time.

"Good morning, Tim."

"Hello, there, Clare. Yer lookin' real good. Got any coffee?"

She carried a tray with a pot and cups into the library and they took seats on a long sofa.

"Well, Tim, what's latest from Sacramento?"

"Nothing that hasn't been in the news. Several of your friends send their good wishes."

"That's nice. I guess you know we postponed the bus tour. Luna wasn't very happy about that. But I think she's over it."

"I know. She called me. I told her it was a good decision. It wouldn't look too good for you to be out traveling while the legislature is still in session."

"That's another good reason to wait till fall. Well, what's the race looking like from your perspective?"

"As I said at the meeting, Jerry Brown appears to have a pretty strong hold on his seat if he wants to go for another term. His re-election campaign organization has raised over $2.8 million this year. Nobody is even close to that."

"I know we certainly don't have that kind of money yet."

"His biggest donor is the Democratic State Central Committee, so he's got the backing of the state party organization. Other big givers are the nurses association, the school employees association and several Indian tribes," Tim said.

"That sounds pretty discouraging," Clare said.

"Now, just remember what I've told you. First, Brown hasn't declared his candidacy. He will be 76 by November 2014 and would be 80 after serving another term. But if he does run, and that's generally expected, he more than likely would finish first in the June 3 open primary. But he would still have to face the second-place finisher in the November general election. If we run an effective enough campaign, that could be you, Clare."

"What kind of opposition would I be facing from other candidates?"

"Well, the scuttlebutt around the Capitol is that John Bull definitely plans to run. He thinks it's a good time to get out of Congress – and he's right about that – and he's looking at a grudge match."

"Oh, really?"

"Yes. He has bragged to his former colleagues in the state senate that he's going to beat – quote – 'that rich bitch whose husband stole my seat.'"

"He's saying that about me? Why, that son-of-a ..."

"Well, you know what they say: forewarned is forearmed. And Bull has a reputation for playing dirty. So it's bound to be an ugly campaign."

"I don't believe in dirty politics," Clare said. "But you'd better believe I can be tough."

"Oh, I have no doubt about that."

"Let's look at the odds. As you've pointed out, California has never elected a woman governor. Meg Whitman spent more than $170 million and got only 41 percent of the vote to Brown's 54 percent."

"But Clare ... she's a Republican," said Tim. "California is a Democratic state. Just look at the electorate. Roughly 18 million of the state's 24 million eligible voters are registered to vote. Of the 75 percent who can vote, 44 percent are Democrats. Republicans have 29 percent."

"Okay ..."

"Larry Sabato, a respected political science professor at the University of Virginia, in his list of predictions for 2014 governor's races calls California 'safe Democratic.' So you've got an edge just being a Democrat."

"Although with an open primary it will be a different kind of race than the usual Democrat versus Republican. What about independents?"

"That's a good question. Those who register to vote and list no party preference increased 11 percentage points from 1992 to 2012 as numbers declined for the major parties. So-called independents now total around 21 percent of the electorate. And that's a good group to target."

"I've made it clear I will not abandon the principles of the party my husband I both supported," Clare said, "but I also am inclined to believe that in these times voters look at what kind of a person is the candidate rather than a label. This view has guided me in reconciling my association with Henry, a Republican, both personally and as a valued member of my campaign organization."

"I think I've heard him say that California Democrats and Washington Republicans aren't that far apart," Tim said.

"Any other observations?"

"Just one. Another advantage you have is living in the Los Angeles area. This is the area with the largest concentration of the state's population and it has 24 percent of the state's likely voters, followed by the San Francisco Bay area at 22 percent and Orange and San Diego counties at 19 percent."

"So in spite of the odds, you're not here to tell me to forget about running for governor?"

"Oh, no! Not at all. You have the opportunity to offer Californians a new kind of candidate and a new kind of campaign. From what I've seen of the team you've assembled, I think you have the makings of a successful run."

"I hope you're not just saying that, Tim."

"No, I mean it."

Clare glanced up to see Shirley with her coffee cup headed toward the kitchen.

"Shirley," she called. "I want you to meet someone. This is state Sen. Tim Barnham. He's an old friend and trusted adviser."

"Hello," Shirley said with a downward nod and an outstretched palm. Tim returned the handshake with a broad smile and his usual greeting. "I'm pleased to meet you, Shirley. Yer lookin' real good."

Shirley winked and said, "I'll bet you say that to all the women you meet."

"As a matter of fact, he does," Clare said.

"No, just the good looking ones," Tim said.

"I was just going for a coffee refill," Shirley said.

"It's getting close to lunchtime. Maybe you'd rather have your usual," Clare said. "Tim, will you stay for lunch? I can offer a ham and cheese sandwich."

"Why, thank you. Next to Oklahoma chicken fried steak, that's my favorite meal," he said.

That was a familiar response. She had heard him say the same thing about everything from pizza to turkey enchiladas.

Shirley stopped by the bar and poured her shot of vodka and they all went to the terrace. On the way out, Clare overheard Shirley saying to Tim, "Tell me about this chicken-fried steak of yours." It was going to be an interesting lunch.

38

TIM WAS LEAVING as Hector Perido arrived for his afternoon session with Clare. Houston also came along, this time without Luna. They said she was busy with another project.

"Did you and Sen. Barnham have a good meeting?" Hector asked.

"Yes. It was quite enlightening." Clare decided not to elaborate. It would be better to focus on preparing for the challenge against Bull rather than talk about him.

"I know you've studied the position papers Houston and I have done for you and we'll continue to provide these," Hector said. "A candidate needs to be knowledgeable on a wide range of matters, but perhaps we should begin to concentrate on developing a short list of issues that will constitute your campaign platform."

"That sounds like a good approach."

"Let's begin by looking at a recent survey by the Public Policy Institute of California. I'll hit the highlights. The findings show that crime and public safety issues are surfacing. In the survey 52 percent of the respondents support the plan approved by the governor and the legislature to reduce prison overcrowding. But strong majorities are concerned about the possible early release of thousands of prisoners. As you know, this was something the plan was designed to prevent. Half of those polled are concerned about violence and street crime in their communities.

"Education continues to be a major topic. School districts are now getting more control over how state education dollars are spent, and the survey showed 60 percent are confident districts will use the money wisely. Almost half favor more strategies to manage water more efficiently and 55 percent okayed a proposed $6.5 billion bond measure to fund water projects.

"Majorities support legalizing marijuana, same-sex marriage, preserving access to abortion and, by a slim margin, the Affordable Care Act.

"Governor Brown's job performance approval was 48 percent and the legislature's 38 percent."

"Those findings certainly give us a lot to think about," Clare said.

Hector added, "a survey four months earlier indicated support for Brown's revised budget plan, increased spending for public schools, health and human services and corrections, but also listed problems that included the state budget, a distrust for state government and too many propositions on the state ballot. The respondents felt the government does not do enough to regulate access to guns and 78 percent said illegal immigrants who meet certain requirements should be allowed to stay."

"I think state finances will continue to be a topic of high interest," Clare said, "and with the economy still anemic I would like to see more being done to strengthen the small business sector. During our upcoming statewide tour I plan to visit some successful local businesses along the way.

"I have a strong interest in education and I want to hit that hard. I'm genuinely concerned about the natural disasters that are a recurring threat to the state. Forest fires especially have caused a great deal of damage this year to our woodlands and private property, along with loss of life in many instances. Using more state resources to help contain the fires might fit into the crime and public safety category as an issue I could adopt."

"That's certainly worth exploring. Houston, will you put together a background paper on that right away?" Hector said.

Houston nodded and made a note to himself.

"You mentioned Governor Brown's approval rating is under 50 per cent. Tim had some reports that as things stand now he would be unbeatable if he runs for another term," Clare said.

"That's probably right. And he has a hefty campaign chest," said Hector. "So for that reason my advice would be not to waste your resources running against Brown. Let the other candidates do that. There are some well-financed Republicans getting set to make the race. They can make themselves useful by spending their time and money running down Brown, and you can put yourself in a good position to challenge him if the two of you emerge from the open primary as the two contenders next June."

"That makes a lot of sense."

"I've seen it happen before."

"Shirley and I are at the point in the book outline to cover my positions on matters of interest to California voters. This discussion we've had will be very helpful, and I thank you for all the information and guidance."

"Let us know if you think of anything else in particular that you need," Hector said.

Clare walked out with them and then decided to give Henry a call. He answered after several rings.

"Were you away from the phone?" she asked.

"Yes, I was getting a little exercise," he said. "I'm still getting used to the crutches and I can't move very fast."

"I could use a walk myself. I've been holed up here having meetings. Besides working with Shirley on the book, I met with Tim this morning. He tells me that the word around the state capitol is that John Bull definitely is going to run and says he's going to – and these are his words – 'beat that rich bitch whose husband stole my seat.'"

"He called you that?" Henry exclaimed. "Wait a minute. He's a congressman, isn't he?"

"Now he is. But he was in the state senate and Gary ran against him and won."

"Well, I don't care who he is. I don't like anyone calling you names."

"Get used to it, Henry. Politics can get down and ugly. There is one thing that bothers me."

"What's that?"

"Referring to me as 'rich.' If he's spreading that around it could hurt our fundraising."

"Let's face it, Clare. You don't exactly live in a shack."

"Gary did leave the villa to me, and the will had adequate provisions for both me and Luna. But his investments and real estate holdings had taken a heavy hit during the recession. He had to sell his radio and TV stations and some other businesses. And then taxes and attorney fees took a big chunk of the estate."

"I see. Well, I'll let you know if I get any feedback about Bull's insinuation. The other thing is that you've made it clear that you won't finance a campaign from personal funds as Meg Whitman and others have done."

"I just thought you should be aware of this development. I also had a session on issues with Hector Perido. He had some good research information and we had a pretty productive meeting."

"Good. I don't think I told you that Pop doesn't have a very good impression of Hector."

"Why is that?"

"His long hair for one thing. Pop's kind of old fashioned. And he also was turned off when he saw Hector using a Ouija board at the meeting we had at the villa."

"Oh, for heaven's sake! That has nothing to do with the expert advice he's giving me. He's just testing a theory to see how close some election predictions come to the answers you get from a Ouija board."

"I figured there was a good explanation. So you're getting along all right, not getting stressed out or anything?"

"Yes, other than missing you terribly. When can I see you again?"

"Believe me, I hope that's very soon. I miss you, too. I'm so glad you called."

The conversation gave Clare a bit of a lift. But she decided that after a brief session with Shirley about her meeting with Hector she would take that walk she had mentioned. Strolling through the gardens on the villa grounds and taking in the ocean view always did wonders for her mood.

39

THE NEXT FEW weeks were busy but productive ones for Clare. Shirley finished her interviewing work on the book project and returned to Seattle to convert her notes to a draft for Clare's review. The schedule was filling up with speaking engagements and other public events, the most immediate of which was a charity walk to support cancer research and dog adoptions.

"Paws for a Cause" was different from the "Relay for Life" and similar walkathons. It was a one-mile walk through the beautiful grounds of the Koehler Winery at Los Olivos in the Santa Ynez Valley. Located on the Foxen Canyon Wine Trail in Santa Barbara County, the Koehler vineyards had tall oaks nestling among the vines. The walk was truly a delightful outdoor experience.

This was one public appearance Clare wanted to keep private if at all possible. She was sincerely devoted to the cause and participated with no intent of gaining publicity for political purposes. As it turned out, no photographers were on hand but she was recognized by one of the other walkers.

"Clare?" a voice called. She turned to see a mid-fiftyish woman with beads of sweat on her face approaching. "I'm Sarah Metz. I'm on the county 'Friends of Clare' committee."

"Oh, yes. I believe we met at the meeting we had a while back."

"That's right. How's the campaign going?"

"Well, we're still in the preliminary stages, raising money and preparing for a statewide tour in October."

"How exciting! I'll look forward to that."

"We want to have a bus christening or some kind of event locally before beginning the tour up north. Please pass the word."

"Oh, I will, and let us know how our group can help."

"I'll definitely do that. Good to see you."

That conversation would be worth more than a photo in a local newspaper.

Also coming up on the schedule was an important speech. The Southern California Art Teachers Association had invited Clare to attend a quarterly meeting and share some of her ideas about improving the quality of education. She was eager to accept.

On the day of her appearance she was pleased to see an encouraging turnout. The association president, in introducing her, underscored Clare's career as an artist as well as her role in California government as a member of the Senate Standing Committee on Education.

Clare's remarks focused on the broad topic of education in the state, primarily on grades K-12, but she preceded her main talk with some comments on art education in particular.

"We are all aware of the 2012 report from the U.S. Department of Education on the availability and characteristics of arts education programs in the nation's schools. A disturbing finding of the report was that despite being designated a 'core academic subject' in the No Child Left Behind Act and being included in the mandated elementary school curriculum in 44 states, access to arts education remains elusive to a tremendous number of students across the nation.

"This is of special concern in light of new evidence that is continuously emerging about the essential skills, character traits and success factors students gain through learning in the arts. I commend the Arts Education Partnership, a division of the Council of Chief State School Officers, for its recent work in publishing an excellent report: 'Preparing Students for the Next America: The Benefits of an Arts Education.'

"The findings show that arts education helps students become better readers and writers while also advancing math achievement. Students involved in the arts are more motivated to learn, they are more creative and better able to solve complex problems.

"There is ample proof that all of you are doing very important work in preparing today's students for living productive and successful lives."

Clare reviewed her involvement with legislation considered by the Senate Education Committee, including the Common Core State Standards. She said she had been skeptical of a bill establishing a new statewide student assessment system because it had been opposed by U.S. Education Secretary Arne Duncan as well as some education groups in California.

Among bills she said she favored was one to allow aspiring teachers to pursue an additional year of training and another to increase access to digital textbooks and educational materials.

"Education is a key issue in all future political campaigns in California and it will certainly continue to be a major interest of mine in whatever public role I choose to take," Clare said in closing. She left the audience wondering whether she would seek the governor's office, but she got a valuable group of voters talking about that possibility.

After her speech she was approached by a woman who identified herself as a reporter for the state edition of the Los Angeles News. She queried her about her political plans and Clare gave her the same answer: that at this point she was exploring the possibility. The reporter, Laurie Miller, said she would like to accompany Clare on some of her travels in the state and write some articles. Clare said she would think about it.

Laurie reminded Clare of some of the women reporters in the state capitol press gallery: bad complexion, "muffin top" figure, a hairdo that could only be described as "hasty". But she knew that more than one of them had won top honors in the annual state press association awards.

After reading what Laurie wrote about her speech to the art teachers the following day, Clare and Luna discussed her request and concluded that she might be a helpful ally for the campaign.

A short time later Clare followed through on a scheduled luncheon with a local firefighters union group. Luna had alerted Laurie Miller, who already was at the meeting place when Clare arrived. She was talking to Ed Winn, a Texaco station owner who was fire chief for the volunteer fire department. Clare greeted him immediately.

"We're glad you can be with us, senator," he said. "I think the food is ready so we might as well proceed."

The chief had invited some other firehouses to send representatives so the meeting hall was pretty well filled. They were mostly men, with a few women among the attendees.

"I'm delighted to be with you today," Clare began. "I appreciate your taking time away from your duties to come and I hope you don't have to respond to any calls.

"I know how important you are to the communities you serve. As most of you know, my late husband was a volunteer fireman. He considered it a valuable service and he missed going on those engine runs after he went to the state senate."

With her preliminary remarks establishing rapport with the audience, Clare got down to her main message, in which she made these points, among others:

"The safety of firefighters is a major concern. Americans were horrified at the deaths of 19 brave men who died in a raging wildfire in Arizona. It was the worst tragedy of this kind since the Griffith Park fire in southern California in 1933 which claimed the lives of 29 firefighters. We'll never forget 9/11, the deadliest day for firemen, when 340 perished.

"It is imperative that we have the resources to provide firefighters with the best protective clothing and other equipment to reduce the risks they take to the fullest extent possible.

"With firemen now being exposed to danger as first responders to domestic terrorist incidents, necessary safety equipment should also include body armor.

"Wildfires have plagued California for many years and each new season brings more disastrous outbreaks. The number of acres destroyed in these fires has grown with each successive year. Our state has had some of the worst fires, like the 2007 season when fires covered more than 500,000 acres and displaced nearly 1 million people. It is especially tragic when the cause can be traced to humans, accidentally or intentionally starting the blaze. If more stringent law enforcement is needed to fight arson, I will certainly support it.

"And if more funds are needed, either from state or federal sources, I will do my utmost to see that local firefighting units get their fair share.

"As long as I am in public service I will fight for those who risk their personal safety to protect the lives and property of our citizens. I will champion your causes and my door will always be open to you."

At the conclusion of her remarks and after answering a smattering of questions, Chief Ed Winn thanked her for her support and presented her with a fireman's hat as a token of appreciation.

"This would have come in handy in some of my battles in the legislature," she joked.

40

LAURIE MILLER'S STORIES in the Los Angeles News were beginning to draw attention to Clare as a potential candidate for governor. Her article about Clare's appearance at the firefighters' meeting prompted some offers of support from fire-and-police union groups. But her earlier report on the speech to the art teachers association had more far-reaching impact. It was picked up by the Associated Press and that resulted in commentary from some columnists who wrote about the political scene.

A surprising development was an invitation for Clare to speak to the Women's Correspondents Club in Washington, D.C. in September. At first she was undecided about whether to accept an out-of-state engagement, but when she learned that the date coincided with a meeting of winegrowers that Henry was interested in attending, that settled it. She would make the trip, even though the journalists' group could pay only minimal expenses.

Henry's plans were dependent on his broken leg recovery, of course, but he was coming along pretty well. He had gone from using crutches to dependence only on a cane.

Meanwhile, rumors of other potential candidates had begun to get media attention. The name mentioned most often was Rep. John Bull. During the August congressional recess he held town hall meetings in his district in which he gave the impression he might run, asking constituents more about what they wanted from state government than federal. He had quietly hired John Valjean as an aide in his district office, conning taxpayers into covering some of his pre-campaign expenses. In interviews he played down Clare's expected candidacy, saying some very mean things. "She has such a shamefully light record of public service, I can't imagine anyone taking her candidacy seriously," he told reporters.

During one of her frequent telephone check-ins with Tim Barnham, Clare told him she thought it would be a good idea for her to make an appearance in the Senate before the end of the legislative session. He agreed and she decided to go the first week in September.

Clare often recalled sadly that Gary almost always made the trip by automobile, even though the normal driving time was about six hours. But Gary loved cars and he enjoyed driving. He also liked to drive fast. That fetish resulted in a lot of speeding tickets, but he gladly paid them and managed to stay out of jail.

He was a very good driver and speed was not what caused his death. The crash was clearly the fault of the semi-trailer driver, who apparently fell asleep at the wheel. But Clare couldn't help but wonder if he had returned home by air instead of the highway if her husband would still be alive.

Flying time was only a little over an hour and there were plenty of flights from either LAX or the Santa Barbara airport. She booked a morning departure on Tuesday, September 3.

Arriving in Sacramento on time, Clare picked up a rental car, checked into her hotel and drove to the State Capitol. The neoclassical structure, modeled after the U.S. Capitol in Washington, houses the bicameral state legislature and the office of the governor.

On the way to her office she exchanged greetings with a number of state employees she had gotten to know. In her absence her secretary had informed her of mail and messages that needed her attention so the stacks of paper on her desk were not matters of great importance. She didn't remain long because a vote was in progress on the Senate floor.

Clare saw more acquaintances as she walked through the second floor corridor toward the Senate chamber. It is an eye-catching sight for tourists with its coffered ceiling and Corinthian columns. The large room is decorated in red, as is the British House of Lords.

As she entered the chamber, she spotted Tim Barnham right away and got him to fill her in on the vote in progress. It was on a bill previously passed by the state assembly which would make it state policy to reject "indefinite detention" powers from the federal government under the National Defense Authorization Act. Clare voted affirmatively and the bill passed by a unanimous vote. The governor later signed it into law.

As members returned to their offices several of Clare's friends paused to tell her they had missed her presence. A few inquired about her political plans and more than one encouraged her to make the governor's race. She and Tim went to his office and closed the door for a private chat.

"Clare, I think you should know that I've had some inquiries about whether you intend to run for a full term in the Senate. What's your thinking?"

"Before I began to look at a run for governor I was undecided. In a way I felt I shouldn't quit after serving only 16 months. But after forming this exploratory committee my situation has changed. And I've come to realize that I really can't devote the time necessary to do a good job for my constituents if my focus is on another office.

"I'm glad you brought it up because I had been wanting to talk to you about what would be best. I've pretty well decided I should not seek a full term. The question is whether to resign now so that my successor could begin to establish incumbency."

"Your decision to concentrate on running for governor is the right thing to do. As for giving up your Senate seat, that's a matter of personal choice, but I don't think it would be too damaging to you politically if you didn't. John Bull will pounce on it, but he's going to do that at every opportunity. After the legislature goes into recess, there won't be anything happening for the rest of the year. And there's never too much done during the early part of a new session.

"I've got a couple of folks in mind who would make good candidates for your seat. And knowing they wouldn't have to run against you they could go ahead and start planning to file for the office in January."

"Tim, as always your advice is sound and based on reason. I can't thank you enough for being such a good friend and counsel," Clare said.

"I value your friendship, too."

As Clare was on her way out of the Capitol, she saw Sam Mahoney of the AP approaching. They greeted each other cordially and he asked, "Are you ready to announce you're running for governor?"

"You know I'm still exploring the possibility, Sam. I'll be closer to making a decision after the statewide tour I'm beginning in October. But I will give you a little scoop."

"Oh, what's that?"

"Don't quote me directly on this, but I plan to release a statement tomorrow that I will not seek a full term in the Senate."

"A lot of people have been wondering about that. What led to your decision?"

"I'll cover that in my statement. But it really comes down to feeling that a career in the Senate is not the direction I want to take my life. It's only fair to make my intentions known this far ahead so others who might be interested in my seat can have plenty of time to make plans."

Within hours Sam's story would be in the newsrooms of AP clients all over the state.

41

A FEW WEEKS later Clare and Henry followed through on their plans to go to Washington, DC. Henry had made all the arrangements. It was an early flight for Clare – even earlier for Henry, who caught a redeye from Seattle and got a few hours of sleep at an airport hotel.

Clare was to meet him at the security checkpoint at LAX. As she approached the area she saw a familiar figure come out of the men's room and walk ahead of her. He had Henry's build and a slight limp and was using a cane. But when she called him and he turned around, it was not Henry's face she saw. The man had a full beard and mustache.

"Clare!" he said.

"Henry, is that you?"

"Surprise!"

"I'll say."

They exchanged a brief hug and she stepped back and demanded an explanation for his appearance.

"When I was bedfast for a while with my leg I let it grow out," he said.

"Well, it's going to take some getting used to," she replied.

They had seats together in business class so they were able to catch up after their absence from one another. There also was time during the five-hour flight to discuss the campaign quite a bit.

Their plane landed on time at Dulles International Airport and they took a taxi downtown. Clare's speech to the Women's Correspondents Club was scheduled to be in the J. W. Marriott hotel, but Henry had suggested they stay at the Hotel W on 15th street, about two blocks away. He had booked a suite with an adjoining extra bedroom. It was a special package that included a complimentary bottle of champagne.

While Henry picked up the room keys, Clare marveled at the spacious lobby with long red couches accenting the ample seating beneath a high wall of archways. Henry had arranged to have the luggage deposited in the suite's living room. The bellman had left the door to Henry's room ajar. After he helped take Clare's bags into her bedroom, he took care of his and they settled into the comfort of a long curved sectional couch to collect their thoughts.

Clare briefly scanned a coffee table book that highlighted W's opening in 2009 after a massive reconversion of the historic Hotel Washington's 1917

Beaux Arts building. Henry thumbed through the pages of a daily newspaper. Glancing at the "cocktail caddy" he asked, "Would you like something to drink?"

"No, thanks." After the long flight, Clare wanted to stretch her legs. The only time she had been to the nation's capital was a very quick visit years ago when Gary received an award. She looked forward to doing a little sightseeing They decided to walk over to the J. W. Marriott to take a look at the room where she would be speaking the next morning.

"Are you sure your leg is up for this?" Clare asked.

"I think so, as long as we don't walk too fast," he said. "It's not that far."

It was a nice day for a stroll. Leaving the hotel they headed on F Street toward 14th. Before they got to the corner, Henry said, "Let's cut through the Willard. You need to see the hotel that has been patronized by presidents and other celebrities for more than 150 years."

The wide hall leading from the F Street entrance to the lobby is known as Peacock Alley. They passed displays about the hotel's history, upscale shops and the famed Round Robin bar where the first mint julep was made (by Henry Clay) and the National Press Club was founded in 1908.

As they entered the lobby, Henry told Clare to look up at the elaborate carved ceiling with its hand-painted state seals. "There's a story that the term 'lobbyist' originated here," Henry said. "President Ulysses S. Grant used to come to relax with a cigar and brandy and was hounded by favor-seekers. He called them 'those damned lobbyists.' But when I was in England I learned that the term was first used to refer to wheeling and dealing that went on in the lobbies outside the chambers of Parliament."

"You seem to know quite a bit about Washington," Clare said.

"I've been here a few times for meetings of winemakers. But the fact is, I lived here for a short time a while back. The summer before I went to Oxford I got an internship with a travel magazine with an office in Washington. I wrote and edited stories about the capital city. But I enjoyed travel more than writing about it, so that career was not for me."

They exited the Willard through the main entrance and paused to take in the bustling scene on Pennsylvania Avenue and the Washington Monument standing tall in the background.

Henry said, with a gesture to the left, "The J. W. Marriott is just over on that corner." They caught a green light and walked across 14th Street. Before entering the hotel, Henry said, "Turn around and you can get a view of what the Willard looks like from the outside."

"It's really very impressive," Clare said.

Their next mission was to find which of the Marriott's 29 meeting rooms was the place for Clare's speech. Fortunately it was posted in the lobby. Henry was disappointed at the size of the room, which was set up for the next day's meeting. "It's so small," he said. "I'll bet it wouldn't hold a hundred people."

"Well, that's about right," Clare said. "The Women's Correspondents Club is a fairly small group, but as you can imagine quite influential. And that's more important than a large audience."

"If you say so. I just hope they know what kind of speaker they're getting."

"Don't worry, Henry. It will be just fine."

As they left the Marriott, Henry said, "I want to stop by the Press Club, which is just up the block. I joined the club when I was here and I think I've kept the membership renewed, but want to make sure. They have reciprocal arrangements with other clubs throughout the U.S. and several foreign countries. That has come in very handy."

A short walk past a liquor store took them to the National Press Building, which housed the club. Henry noticed a worried look on Clare's face when he pushed the elevator button for the 13th floor. "Journalists aren't superstitious," he said.

Henry stopped at the reception desk and told Clare he would "just be a minute." Knowing better she headed for an exhibit of prizewinning photographs which absorbed her interest until she heard him calling her. "Here's a schedule of events and I see that tomorrow there's a luncheon with Gov. Mary Fallin of Oklahoma as the speaker. She's going to talk about education and jobs. Interested?"

"Yes, definitely," she said. "And my meeting with the women correspondents starts at 10 a.m. so I should be through in plenty of time."

The luncheon was almost sold out but Henry managed to get two tickets. Clare read the announcement further and learned the governor was appearing as the new chairman of the National Governors Association.

"I'd very much like to meet her. This will be a good contact," Clare said.

Having satisfied themselves about plans for the next day, they walked back past the Willard and on to 15th Street on their return to the W. When they got back to the room, Henry said he had made a reservation for dinner, but there would be some time to rest up. "I think I'll take advantage of that and take a quick nap," Clare said.

"I've got some phone calls to make," he said. "So I'll see you in about an hour."

Clare reappeared dressed for the evening in a navy blue skirt and beige top with a beaded design, carrying a light multi-colored jacket. She noticed Henry looking out the window. "You can see the White House from here," he said. "or at least the roof." They could have easily walked from the hotel past the Treasury Department to see the executive mansion. But not now. Henry had crossed the room and was opening the champagne.

"I love the sound of a champagne cork popping," Clare said. Henry poured the glasses and lifted his. "Here's to our long-awaited reunion."

"A perfect toast," she said. "I trust your phone calls didn't turn up any crises. I called the president of the women's correspondents group to let her know I'm here. In the conversation I told her I was curious why the meeting wasn't in the National Press Club. What she said was unbelievable."

"What was that?"

"Women journalists have had a long battle of discrimination in Washington and there are still some remnants of it. Women were excluded from membership in the Press Club until 1971 and it was another eleven years before the club had its first woman president."

"Just another reminder that California hasn't had a woman governor," Henry said. "but I'm confident you can break the gender barrier." He raised his glass in tribute.

"Where are we having dinner?" Clare asked.

"It's the CityZen restaurant in the Mandarin Oriental Hotel."

"Chinese?"

"No, the cuisine is called 'modern American.' The Washington Post food critic, Tom Sietsema, gives it four stars, his highest rating."

"It sounds wonderful."

"Our reservation is for 7, so we can go any time."

They caught a cab in front of the hotel on F Street. Clare was startled when the driver made a U-turn in the middle of the street to turn left on 15th. She grabbed Henry's arm. "It's allowed in D.C.," he said.

"The place we're going is in Southwest – the smallest of Washington's four quadrants that extend from the Capitol. It's where I lived. In fact, my apartment was in that building," Henry said, pointing as the cab turned from Independence Ave. onto 12th Street.

Clare was suitably impressed with the 347-room Mandarin Oriental Hotel, with its marvelous views of the capital skyline and the waterfront. Their table at the CityZen was waiting and they saw a number of tempting selections on the menu. They opted for the chef's tasting menu, which featured Maine lobster poached in olive oil on a parsley coulis and Virginia beef rib-eye rubbed with Old Bay seasoning on a bed of corn pudding. Preceding the entrees was a presentation of Northern Neck tomatoes followed by seared duck foie gras and risotto. Clare loved the dessert, of course, because of the warm chocolate sauce poured over apricots with toasted sesame seeds. Henry ordered excellent wines from the restaurant's extensive selection.

Going back to their hotel, Henry told the cab driver to take a longer route to show Clare the beauty of the Capitol after dark, sitting on a hill bathed in light, overlooking the National Mall which stretches to the Lincoln Memorial. They returned down Pennsylvania Avenue, where incoming presidents ride in an inaugural parade that leads to the White House.

The magnificence of the capital city was not lost on the California visitor. "No Hollywood movie could ever do justice to this scene," Clare said.

It had been a long day and both Clare and Henry were about ready to retire for the evening. Clare kicked off her shoes and said she might go over the notes for her speech so Henry said, "The couch is all yours."

As he turned to go to his room, Clare said, "Wait just a minute." She padded over to him and put her hands on either side of his hairy face. "You are a devil," she said. "But I love you. Thank you for a wonderful evening." They kissed. "It scratches," she said. Henry said, "I'll shave it off when I get back home. I didn't bring any shaving materials with me."

"At least the beard – maybe keep the mustache for the time being. Goodnight, my dear."

Henry closed his door and got ready for bed. After about half an hour there was a soft knock and he opened it to find Clare standing there in her nightclothes.

"It's cold in my room. Can you see if you can do something with my thermostat?"

42

HENRY WAS HAVING his wakeup potion from the in-room coffeemaker when Clare made her appearance.

"Good morning. Sleep well?" he asked.

"Yes, after I got warm. Anything of importance in the newspaper?"

"As a matter of fact, there is – in the gossip column. I'll read it to you. The heading is 'Seen on the scene' and it says: 'California state Sen. J. C. de Lune dining at the CityZen with a handsome bearded companion. She's reported to be considering a campaign to become the state's first woman governor.' How about that?"

"Yeah, how about that," Clare said. " – 'handsome bearded companion.'"

"They could have left that out. But it will get the attention of some pundits and other opinion makers in this town."

"We'll see. Are you hungry?"

"Yes. I was waiting for you before ordering room service. What would you like?"

"Just some fruit and yogurt … and real coffee. I'm going to go shower."

By the time she returned her meal and Henry's ham and eggs had arrived. They eagerly poured cups of fresh coffee.

"I really would like to hear your speech," Henry said, "but after that gossip item in the newspaper, perhaps it's best that I not be there. No point in causing any kind of distraction."

"I suppose you're right. I really want this appearance to go well."

"I'll plan to be at the press club by 11:30 and you can meet me there."

"Sounds good."

Later, when Clare was ready to head to the J. W. Marriott, Henry admired her appearance. She was wearing an aqua suit that complemented her auburn hair, with a small Italian scarf and understated jewelry.

"You really look great!" he said. "I hope there are lots of pictures. We can use some on our Facebook page."

"Sounds like Melody has been talking to you."

"Luna actually. But I'm looking forward to meeting Melody. Luna says she has this social media stuff down pat."

"I guess I'd best be off. I'll take a cab this morning. I don't want to walk in these heels."

"I'll go down with you," Henry said. "But let me give you a good luck hug."

The club president met Clare in the hotel lobby and escorted her to the meeting room.

"We're going to have close to a hundred members," she said. "A number of them have told me this is a meeting they wouldn't want to miss."

"I hope they're not disappointed," Clare said.

She received a generous introduction ending with, "Please welcome Sen. J. C. de Lune."

"Thank you. Please call me Clare. I know what you're thinking. I get a chuckle, too, at Clare de Lune. I'll tell you how that came about."

She proceeded to explain that she was Clare Sullivan when she met Gary de Lune and she was so excited to be marrying him she never thought about what her married name would be.

"I'm a bit older and wiser," she said, "although you might question the wisdom of considering a run for governor of California when all the odds are against me."

She recited the historical facts about women running for elective office, citing the fact that women hold 98, or 18.3 percent, of the 535 seats in Congress – the breakdown being 20 of the 100 seats in the Senate and 78, or 17.9 percent of the 435 seats in the House of Representatives.

"In 2013," Clare said, "73 women hold state elective executive offices, or 23 percent of the available positions. Only 24.2 percent of the members of state legislatures are women. Think about that. Women encompass more than 50 percent of the U.S. population, yet we continue to represent less than a quarter of state legislative seats. As a state senator I am in the 20.8 percent of seats held by women.

"When it comes to governors, the picture is worse. At present the United States has only five women governors. By the way, one of those, Gov. Mary Fallin of Oklahoma, is speaking at a luncheon today at the National Press Club. I look forward to meeting her.

"Five women governors – that's a low for this century. We've never had more than eight. That was the record high number, which prevailed from 2001 to 2009.

"Since 1909, when Carolyn Shelton served as acting governor of Oregon for one weekend, there have been only 36 women to occupy the governor's office. A total of 24 states have never had a female governor. That list includes California, the most populous state.

134

"So you see, I'm faced with a formidable challenge. That's why I'm testing the waters before making a decision. In early October I will begin a statewide tour – I hesitate to use the shopworn phrase 'listening tour' but that's really what it is. I want to get a feel for what Californians want in a governor ... if they're happy with the status quo, or whether they are ready for a change.

"I will share some of my ideas along the way. But my campaign platform is a work in progress. It will be shaped in large part by what I learn from this tour. Whether I run also will be determined by the ability to raise enough money for the race.

"I'm sure you all know, and probably have written about it, that Meg Whitman spent something like $170 million in 2010, much of it her own money, and lost the California governor's race by a 13-point margin. It's like Will Rogers said back in the '30s: 'Politics has got to be so expensive it takes a lot of money to even get beat with.'

"Despite one of my prospective opponents already trashing me as a 'rich bitch' – yes, he said that – I don't have that kind of money and I wouldn't try to buy the office with it if I did. My campaign contributions are coming from a wide variety of sources – people who are interested in good government and qualified leaders.

"Depending on the results of my statewide tour and the outlook for financing a campaign, I plan to make a decision by the end of the year on whether to be a candidate to become the first woman governor of the state of California.

"As women, we share a common cause. Women have had to fight for recognition and advancement in every career field. I know that is certainly true for women in journalism. Women certainly have come a long way since Nellie Bly became known for her investigative reporting at the New York World. But gender inequality still prevails in America's newsrooms as in offices, factories and, yes, legislative chambers.

"In this century Sally Ride and other women have broken the barrier in space exploration and they have shattered the glass ceiling in many corporate boardrooms, but baby, we've still got a long way to go.

"I am energized by a challenge and I suspect all of you are, too. I am confident that we all are committed to continue the good fight. Thank you again for inviting me to meet with you. Now, I'll take a few questions."

There weren't too many, because she had pretty well laid out her timetable regarding a governor's race. She skirted questions on controversial social topics like abortion and gay rights, referring to stands she had taken on legislation in the California state senate, and gave general answers about so-called women's issues. One correspondent, from a New York tabloid, did indeed ask the question she fully expected:

"I'm curious to know about the 'handsome bearded companion' you had dinner with last evening. Could he be a future 'first gentleman' in the California governor's mansion?"

Clare laughed, along with the crowd. "I hate to disappoint you," she said. "He's the president of a winery on the West Coast who is in the city for a meeting of winemakers. He very kindly arranged a fundraiser for my exploratory committee here with some members of that group."

She took one more question, related to her appearance with the California educators, before doing the ritual handshaking.

Henry was waiting in the Press Club as planned. "How did it go with the women correspondents?" he asked. Clare told him she was quite pleased.

Moving into the room where Governor Fallin was to speak they found many of the tables were reserved. But they found two seats at one of the tables in the rear. As luck would have it, her seatmate was a columnist for a Washington-based political journal which had a daily online report. He pumped her for juicy news about her prospective campaign for governor. She tried to give unrevealing but provocative answers designed to start a buzz.

The governor, a youthful blonde whose looks belie her age, 58, devoted her remarks largely to the program of work she would be involved in as leader of the National Governors Association through the coming year. Attendees had received copies of "America Works: Education and Training for Tomorrow's Jobs," an initiative to close the gap between education attainment and skills needed in the marketplace.

"Governors are in a unique position to foster an alignment between workforce training and job growth because they are the primary individuals responsible for education and the economy," Fallin said. She said the United States needs higher educational standards and should demand more of its students.

"The bottom line is that we're just falling behind and many people won't reach the middle class, so it's up to the governors to build new pathways to the middle class, which must be flexible, efficient and meet both students' and employers' needs," Fallin said.

Clare was most interested in what the governor had to say. She found herself, a California Democrat, agreeing with the conservative Oklahoma

Republican on many points. She was especially taken with her response to one of the questions from the audience concerning women's participation in politics.

She commented that she encountered naysayers who minimized her chances to hold elective office, "but I've been able to hold four different offices in our state." Fallin served as a member of the Oklahoma Legislature, as Lieutenant Governor, and was finishing two terms in the U.S. House of Representatives when she was elected governor in 2010.

"We do need to encourage more women to get involved in politics in our nation," she said. "Certainly they can make a difference, whether it's running on the local level or running for Congress or the U.S. Senate or running for governor."

When Fallin concluded her remarks, Clare left Henry talking to the Washington journalist and made her way through the throng to the head table where she introduced herself and had a brief exchange with the Oklahoma governor.

Henry was eager to hear about their conversation. "She was very nice and even knowing we're from different political parties she strongly encouraged me to follow my instincts regarding a try for the California governor's office. I wished her good luck on the education and jobs initiative."

They got a cab back to the hotel where Henry had a meeting of the winemakers association board of directors to attend. Clare changed and went for a walk.

From the hotel she went past the Treasury Department, paused to take in the view of the White House and grounds, then continued on Pennsylvania Avenue to the Renwick Gallery, the home of the Smithsonian American Art Museum's craft and decorative art program. She limited herself to one exhibition, "Our America: The Latino Presence in American Art", because she wanted to allow time to see as much as possible at the Corcoran Gallery of Art.

The Corcoran was about three blocks south on 17th Street. It is a major center of American art, both historic and contemporary, and also has an admirable collection of European art. As a sculptor, Clare was particularly interested in an exhibition in the Atrium of six "ideal" busts, four of which belonged to William Wilson Corcoran, a banker and philanthropist who founded the gallery in 1874 to house his private art collection.

Clare was drawn to a bust of Proserpine, the maiden of spring in ancient mythology, carved in the 1840s by Hiram Powers. She admired the clean lines of the sculpture and the detail of a wreath of wheat adorning the hair and acanthus leaves encircling the chest.

She found she had time to at least sample a new permanent collection installation of "Modern and Contemporary Art Since 1945" before heading back to the hotel to get ready for the fundraising reception.

Henry was out of his board meeting and was waiting in the suite. Clare filled him in on her outing and excused herself to get dressed for the evening. She reappeared shortly clad in a dazzling red cocktail dress and satin slippers.

"You're stunning!" Henry said.

"You're not half bad yourself," she said, admiring her "handsome bearded companion" in his dark suit.

"There's some champagne left," he said.

"Not for me, thanks. I have to keep my wits about me."

The association president was near the entrance and greeted them, adding another compliment on Clare's appearance. She asked about his winery, which was in the Finger Lakes region of New York.

"Please pay us a visit sometime," he said. "Meanwhile, we happen to be serving some of our wine this evening."

"I'll have a glass later," she said. "Thank you ever so much for hosting this reception."

Henry squired her around the room, introducing those he knew personally, which was most of them. It was a predominantly male group, although there were a few women winery owners who were eager to meet Clare.

"I'm from California," said one, "and I'm so excited about the prospects for having a woman governor."

"It will be a hard uphill race, and very expensive," Clare said. "That's why events such as this are so important. I really appreciate the generosity of this group."

After about half an hour of working the crowd, Clare asked Henry to please get her a glass of chardonnay. They worked their way to the bounteous "light buffet" and surveyed the selection. They began with the mound of shrimp on crushed ice and moved along the table to the miniature Maryland crab cakes, stopping to talk to other diners along the way.

This didn't seem to be an occasion that called for remarks, since Clare had done such a thorough job of communicating one-on-one with everyone there. So after about two hours, as a few began to slip out, Henry and Clare thanked the host again and made their own exit.

"It's a little too soon to retire, don't you think?" Henry said. "Since we don't have an early plane to catch, what say we check out the rooftop lounge that this hotel is known for? I took the liberty of making a reservation just in case."

Clare was agreeable so they took the elevator to the 11th floor and the "P.O.V. Roof Terrace."

"I believe P.O.V. stands for point of view, and this really is a great place to get good views of Washington."

They counted themselves lucky to be there at midweek and well past the happy hour. The lounge was not too crowded or noisy. It was the perfect place to relax after a rather busy two days.

They stepped onto the terrace and settled into one of the velveteen banquettes that overlooked the brightly lit White House. A waitress came and Clare ordered a cosmopolitan and Henry a dry martini. The food at the reception had been abundant but they were tempted with the tapas the waitress recommended. They found them to be quite tasty.

When music from an unseen DJ wafted through the air some couples took to the dance floor. It was only natural that Henry asked Clare to dance.

They found a relatively unoccupied area with a different view – the Washington Monument – and Clare discovered that Henry was an excellent dancer, even with one bad leg. He moved across the floor with the skill of a professional (no doubt learned from his playboy years in Europe, she thought).

Between the musical numbers they moved away from the other dancers and paused to look at the sky. It was a night of a full moon. Memories of a moonlit night at the villa drew them closer in a magical moment.

After finishing their drinks Clare signaled that she was ready to go to the suite. Inside the door Henry took her by both hands and stood back to get another good look at the beautiful woman before him.

"I can't tell you how much I've enjoyed our evening," he said.

"Let's get out of these clothes – get comfortable, that is – and maybe we can talk awhile," she said.

When she returned wearing her robe, she saw two glasses of champagne on the table. Henry, also in his robe, handed one to her and said, "Cheers!"

"Cheers!" she responded.

They sat on the couch with their feet on the table and reminisced about the time they met in Seattle, the spur-of-the-moment trip to the Mt. Jackson winery, Henry staying at the villa, Clare being angry about the brief time he had spent with Gigi … they could laugh about that now.

"I guess you could say we have some kind of relationship," Clare said.

"I would like to think so – a good relationship," Henry said.

"A close relationship," she said, moving closer.

"A very close relationship," he said, closing the gap.

He put his arm around her shoulders and drew her even closer and kissed her passionately. She returned the kiss, ignoring the underbrush.

"We can't let our relationship interfere with the campaign, you know," she said.

"Yes, I know. But I think we have the willpower to do that."

"Please keep reminding me," she said, and kissed him again.

"The campaign seems very far away tonight," he said.

"That's very true," she said.

He took the last sip of his champagne and said, "Shall we go see if your thermostat is okay?"

43

CLARE WAS RELAXED (as much as she ever was) on the return flight. She had good thoughts about her speech and other events of the Washington trip and she could feel the excitement building about her forthcoming state tour. Luna had told her in their last phone conversation that arrangements had been completed for a red bus, appropriately decorated inside and out for a "meet the people" trip up and down the state. Members of the "Clear Sailing" band had mostly used up their vacation time for the year so while they would play for the kickoff rally they couldn't do the full tour. But the keyboardist, Ronnie Stone, and his wife, Rosa Montez, the band vocalist, would be able to go. They, along with Luna and Melody, would travel on the bus. Luna had arranged for a white SUV with "Here's Clare" painted on both sides which would carry Clare, Henry and a driver, following the bus at a distance that would allow them to arrive after the musicians had warmed up the crowd.

On arrival at LAX, Clare and Henry parted company, but only for a short time. He returned to Mt. Jackson to take care of any loose ends at the winery before relocating in California for the duration of the campaign while he took a leave of absence. The apartment Luna had found for him in Santa Barbara would be ready and waiting.

Another meeting of staff and advisors at the villa was scheduled for early October. Henry arrived ahead of the others, looking more like the man Clare met by chance in Seattle. He had shaved off the beard but kept a neatly trimmed mustache which Clare had to admit made him more handsome than ever.

For this meeting both Gene and Shirley McQueen were present. They brought a draft of the text for the book that would make Clare known to all Californians, not just those in her legislative district. Also attending, besides Luna, Melody and Henry, was Tim Barnham, Hector Perido and Houston Conover.

Luna went over the details of the tour, which would kick off with a gala launch in the Santa Barbara area and begin officially on Saturday, October 19 with Clare riding in the annual Pumpkin Festival parade at Half Moon Bay, about 50 miles south of San Francisco.

Tim gave a report on the field organization he had established with the help of his and Clare's friends in the state legislature. He also gave an update on political developments, including the emergence of Rep. John Bull as a prospective opponent with a grudge. He warned everyone to be prepared for some dirty tricks by Bull and cautioned about maintaining tight security about Clare's exploratory moves.

Hector reported on recent surveys which measured opinions on various issues, but he emphasized that it was too early for voters to be thinking about the governor's race and that they could easily change their minds as campaigns got going strong.

Gene was encouraged by growing interest in Clare as a potential candidate, fueled in part by articles that Laurie Miller had written for the Los Angeles News. Clare had rated a few mentions in the national press from her Washington speech. Gene enthusiastically congratulated Melody on the work she had done on the Internet establishing a website, building a base of followers on Twitter and expanding a presence on Facebook through frequent postings about Clare's activities with accompanying photos. Ads had been placed in local newspapers where Clare would make stops on the bus tour, and her Facebook friends would be alerted to her schedule and encouraged to meet her bus.

After the meeting, Clare and Gene huddled about doing some radio and TV ads they had discussed. He had made some preliminary arrangements with a local studio that had some time open on the following day. Clare reluctantly agreed, and invited Gene and Shirley to spend the night.

She had hoped Henry also would stay over, but he had agreed with Luna to go check into his new lodgings.

At cocktail time, she joined Shirley in a shot of vodka.

"Gene told me he really had to persuade you to give up using initials for your name and just be 'Clare'," Shirley said.

"It's just that I hate the sound of Clare de Lune. It sounds like something a humor writer would do for a cheap laugh."

"I can understand that."

"But most occasions demand the use of a full name. I'm a public official, not an entertainer like Madonna or Beyonce."

"Well, here's an idea you might want to consider."

"Tell me quick!"

"Use your maiden name."

"You mean change my name to Clare Sullivan and drop de Lune? I don't think I want to do that."

"You don't have to. Just be 'Clare Sullivan de Lune.' The 'Sullivan' breaks up the ghastly combination of 'Clare' and 'de Lune.'"

"Hey, I like that!"

"I don't know whether you would need to change it legally – I don't think so. But your lawyer could tell you that."

Lifting her shot glass, Clare said, "Shirley, you have made my day." Pensively she thought, "This might make my parents proud."

44

ON THE EVE of the bus tour kickoff rally, Clare received a surprise phone call from Pop. After the usual pleasantries he demanded to know, "Where the hell is Henry? I tried to call him."

"He's here with me. Do you want to talk to him?"

"No, you can give him a message. I flew down with Jean. We wanted to be here for your big sendoff."

"That's wonderful!" she said. "How sweet of you."

"We also wanted to see how things were going at Chateau Lapierre."

"OK. Come to the villa when you're ready. Your sleeping accommodations are available."

"That's very kind of you. We'll see you later today."

Henry said he had no idea about his father's plans but he was delighted he came.

Luna had made arrangements to hold the rally in a public park near the Santa Barbara waterfront. It was an ideal outdoor setting, with a softball field not used in the fall and nearby parking. It was not possible to predict accurately the size of a crowd but an impressive turnout was expected.

After Pop and Jean arrived and they had a round of drinks, the group decided to join Luna and Houston for dinner at a waterfront restaurant. This gave everyone a chance to get an advance look at the rally site and there was general approval.

The event was scheduled for 10 a.m. the following day. Everyone got around fairly early. Clare was dressed in her "campaign attire" – black dress, red bag. She and Henry were to travel in the SUV that would follow the bus on the tour. Clare's regular driver, Joe, had offered to go on the tour but she didn't want him to be away from Maria for such long periods of time so another driver had been hired. He showed up right on schedule to take them and their luggage to the rally. Pop and Jean followed in their rented vehicle.

Nearing the park they heard the sound of the "Clear Sailing" band playing. Pop had said he was looking forward to seeing the young men who were part of his musical family carrying on a tradition. They were set up on a temporary stage erected with the "Clare for Governor" bus in the background.

The white SUV pulled up and parked behind the bright red bus and Clare took a position at the door of the bus so she could shake hands with the visitors standing in line to tour the mobile campaign office. At the front were two rows of passenger seats divided by fold-down tables for eating. Next was a small galley with a microwave and mini-fridge and across the aisle a toilet. A roomy conference room occupied the rear space. In addition to individual chairs there were bench seats on the sides with pads wide enough for napping. What was out of sight for visitors was a computer system and audio and photo equipment in a locked cabinet.

Clare turned to see Laurie Miller, who had done the tour and exited by a rear door. She asked a few questions and passed on a bit of information. "I saw John Valjean here earlier. I'm pretty sure he went through the bus."

"I guess I shouldn't be surprised to see John Bull's aide checking out the potential opposition," Clare said.

"I can't go to San Francisco for the first stop of the tour," Laurie said, "but I've lined up one of our stringers to file a report for the News."

"That's good," Clare said, and resumed her handshaking. She passed on what she had just learned to Luna, who came to tell her it was almost time for her to make some remarks.

"Thank you, thank you," she shouted above the outpouring of cheers and applause. "I want to thank everyone for turning out to see me off on a tour that will help me decide whether to embark on a greater journey next year to try to put a new face in the governor's office ..." The rest of that sentence was drowned out by well-orchestrated chants of "Run, Clare, Run."

"I believe Californians can benefit from new ideas on education, state finances, transportation, health and safety, better support for our agricultural industry, including our vineyards, and an improved climate for small business. By going out to the people up and down the state, I'll find out what our citizens are thinking and whether they agree with me on the need for a change at the top of our government.

"I hope all Californians will get to know me and, of course, I hope they like what they see." This was followed by a repeated chorus of "We love you, Clare."

She continued along the same lines for another 10 minutes and the crowd enthusiasm kept building. She moved toward a close with a pitch for financial support.

"Political campaigns have grown to be outrageously expensive. I wish there were a better way. Too many good people are discouraged from running for office because of the enormous financial demands.

"I am very grateful for the thousands of contributors who have given to 'Friends of Clare' to enable me to explore a race for governor. We will continue

145

to raise money for my exploratory committee and we welcome support from everyone who believes in good government. Please contact one of our local offices, which are located throughout the state. Or go to our Internet website, Clare2014.com, to make a contribution online. You can also sign up to be a volunteer. Watch our Facebook page to keep up with my public appearances and other developments.

"Thank you again for coming. Now, I'm going to open our statewide tour officially by christening our bandwagon bus with a bottle of California sparkling wine," Clare said. The band played a fanfare as she walked to the front of the bus and climbed a stepladder. Luna handed her a bottle which she raised and brought it down on the front bumper of the bus. The bottle didn't break but the wine spewed beautifully into the air.

The band struck up an original tune they had been working on that might become an official campaign song. As Clare shook more hands, Ronnie and Rosa boarded the bus, followed by Luna and Melody. To the sound of roaring cheers the bus slowly rolled away on the road to San Francisco.

Pop and Jean congratulated Clare on her pep rally-type remarks, gave her hugs and said they wished her well on the tour.

"Good luck," said Pop. "We'll be in touch," Jean added.

Clare gradually made her way through the crowd back to the SUV and with a final wave, answered by a thunderous reception, she joined Henry in the back seat and the driver fell in behind the bus.

She was off and running in the first important phase of her developing campaign.

45

SALINAS, ABOUT FIVE hours north on U.S. 101, was the first day's stopping point en route to Half Moon Bay. Lodging there would be scarce because of the Pumpkin Festival and reservations would have had to have been made well ahead of time. Two hours of driving time in the morning would get the group to the World Pumpkin Capital in plenty of time for Clare to ride in the parade beginning at noon.

Luna had arranged for rooms at a Holiday Inn in Salinas. Clare cautioned everyone not to mention to Tim Barnham that they spent the night in Salinas because it was the birthplace of John Steinbeck. As an Oklahoman, Tim had a natural hatred for Steinbeck for writing about the Okies in "The Grapes of Wrath."

After checking in Clare and Henry took the SUV to drive the 18 miles to Monterey. Henry wanted to visit a winery or two – as many as time permitted – Monterey being one of the largest wine growing and producing regions in California. They made it to only one before closing time: Ventana, which boasts of being "the most award-winning vineyard in America."

They tasted a Syrah-Grenache blend that is unique to Ventana, as well as the pinot noir and some of the white varietals. With an eye on the sun they sped to the Scheid Vineyards tasting room on Cannery Row, the neighborhood Steinbeck made famous in one of his most widely read novels.

Although sunset was nearing they were too close to Carmel-by-the-Sea not to top off the evening at this European-style beach town.

Their choice for dinner was Casanova, one of several Zagat-rated restaurants. As the name suggests it is a very romantic place, reminding Clare and Henry of the small country inns they had visited in Europe. A point of interest is a table used by the Dutch painter Vincent Van Gogh when he dined at the Auberge Ravoux in France. They enjoyed the restaurant's regional cuisine of France and Italy, rustic but elegant.

Their visit to Carmel wouldn't have been complete without a walk along the pristine sand of Carmel Beach, holding hands and watching the last rays of the glorious California sunset.

46

CLARE HAD FOND memories of Half Moon Bay and that was one of the reasons she wanted to begin her statewide tour there. Years ago sponsors of the world famous "Celebration of the Great Gourd" invited her husband Gary to be the Grand Marshal of the Great Pumpkin Parade and she had displayed some of her sculpture in the Art and Pumpkin Festival. She had maintained contact with a woman on the festival committee who invited Clare to ride in the 2013 parade. Her return to Half Moon Bay was not just for sentimental reasons; it also was an excellent opportunity to be seen by thousands of visitors.

As Clare's campaign caravan approached the Half Moon Bay area, scores of pick-your-own pumpkin patches were seen along the road, offering a wide variety of shapes, sizes and colors. By the time they reached the parking area in town, Henry was overwhelmed.

"I've never seen so many pumpkins before in my life," he said.

A carnival atmosphere definitely prevailed with the streets of the coastal town filled with mobs of happy revelers enjoying the sights and sounds of an early autumn day. Music filled the air and both festival participants and visitors were decked out in colorful attire. Delightful aromas floated through the air from the food tents that featured a wide variety of mouth-watering dishes, naturally including dozens of pumpkin confections. A high school basketball team sold a breakfast with pumpkin pancakes. The 4-H club offered pumpkin rolls. There were pumpkin cookies, pumpkin cheesecake, pumpkin ice cream, and of course, pumpkin pie. Henry succumbed to an order of warm pretzels with pumpkin dipping sauce.

The weeklong celebration had begun with the judging for the 40th annual World Championship Pumpkin Weigh-off which offered $25,000 in prizes. It was really a sight to see competitors bringing pumpkins in the trunks of cars, in pickup truck beds and the largest ones hauled in on flatbed trucks. The 2013 winner was a Napa man who grew a pumpkin weighing 1,985 pounds. It set a new record, topping the previous year's 1,775-pound winner, but did not break the world record of 2,009 pounds set at a 2012 festival in Massachusetts.

The festival did have an international champion, however: the biggest, heaviest pumpkin sculpture the world has ever seen. Lake Tahoe artist Peter Hazel created a monstrous mosaic sculpture 11 feet high, 12 feet long and weighing five tons. It was made of steel, cement and ceramic tile.

Before finding the float she was to ride on, Clare made a point of shaking hands with the 2013 parade's grand marshal, San Francisco Giants fan favorite J. T Snow, who was surrounded by a bevy of photographers.

The local organization of "Friends of Clare" had done an extraordinary job of designing a colorful float for "State Sen. J. C. de Lune", which was not overtly political but also called attention to the smiling lady waving to the crowds who lined the streets. When she alighted at the end of the parade she was surprised to be greeted by people asking for autographs. She signed her name simply "Clare."

Henry met her and they saw a few art exhibits and tasted some pumpkin cookies. Luna and the others had gone on to the bus and they soon followed. Although it was only about a 45-minute drive to San Francisco everybody wanted to get there and get settled before a big day tomorrow.

47

FEELING GOOD ABOUT the first stop on the tour, Clare got on the Internet and reviewed her social media pages. Melody had done an outstanding job of posts and pictures from both Santa Barbara and Half Moon Bay and she had done it in record time. Clare's number of Facebook page friends and Twitter followers was growing rapidly. The same was true with responses to her website.

When Henry finished making some phone calls she shared the news with him. He was equally pleased.

In San Francisco Luna and the others were staying at a motel away from downtown where bus parking was allowed. But Henry had booked two rooms at the Mark Hilton because he had arranged a fundraiser to be held in that landmark luxury hotel situated at the top of Nob Hill.

Some extra time had been included in the weekend schedule to allow for some sightseeing. The rally at Golden Gate Park was scheduled for 1 p.m. Sunday and the fundraiser Sunday night.

"Have you been to San Francisco before?" Clare asked.

"Only once, and it was a brief business trip. So I didn't get to see much of the city."

"Good. You showed me around Seattle and Washington, D.C. I'll be your tour guide for San Francisco."

After Henry and Clare got checked into their rooms, he suggested cocktails at the hotel's world-famous rooftop lounge, "Top of the Mark." When the elevator doors opened on the 19th floor Clare could see why Henry was enthused. From this highest point downtown visitors have breathtaking views of the San Francisco skyline, the Bay and the Golden Gate Bridge. It is an ideal setting for enjoying a sunset over a cool drink.

The waitress came to take their order and Henry said, "Well, I'm just going to have to have a martini," pointing out the bar's signature 100-martini menu. Clare was overwhelmed by the variety of choices so she decided on a vodka gimlet. They shared some Moroccan nuts and Yukon gold chips from the "bar bites" list.

"If you're up for a bit of walking, I thought we might take a brief stroll through Chinatown and have dinner at a small place very near the hotel," Clare said.

"I would like that very much," he said.

" I notice you haven't been using your cane, so I guess your leg is getting well. "It certainly didn't hinder your dancing in Washington."

"Yes, it's fine. We might have to try out this dance floor – maybe tomorrow evening after the fundraising event."

As they left the hotel they were met with the sights and sounds of San Francisco. The rays of the setting sun painted the sky with a mosaic of red, orange and yellow. A gentle autumn breeze made Clare glad she had worn a light jacket. A rumble of wheels on rails and clanging of bells signaled the approach of a cable car.

Only a few blocks away crowds were packing the streets of North America's oldest and largest Chinese community. Sidewalks strung with lanterns and shops with pagoda roofs presented a scene to bedazzle the eyes. Street noise pounded the ears. And the distinct smells of this iconic neighborhood flooded the nostrils with scents seldom found outside of Asia.

Locals were busy shopping at the many produce markets and others where butchers and other vendors had their goods displayed. Although this wasn't her first experience, Clare still was taken aback by the sight of live turtles, chickens and other animals.

After absorbing the exotic environment they made their way back to the edge of Chinatown and found Kam Po Kitchen, a spanking-clean restaurant known for its crisp-skinned pork and duck. Clare said she could vouch for the beef chow fun and the pork-stuffed tofu over Chinese greens and both found them to be to their liking. Henry envied Clare for showing off her chopstick skills.

Clare's fortune cookie message made her blush slightly: "Your true love will show himself to you under the moonlight." Henry tried not to show his pleasure at reading his: "The object of your desire comes closer."

They returned to the hotel and after a brief kiss at the door advisedly said their goodnights.

48

FULLY RESTED, CLARE called Henry's room to make sure he was up and around and they met outside the elevators.

"We've got the whole morning, so I've got a few things planned," Clare said.

"I'm looking forward to it," said Henry.

The Mark Hopkins is located at the crossing of three cable car lines. They took the Powell-Hyde Street car to its last stop at Fisherman's Wharf and headed for the nearby Buena Vista Café. A small friendly place, it is renowned for introducing Irish Coffee to the United States. It dates to 1916 when the first floor of a boardinghouse was converted into a saloon.

The café is generally crowded but Clare explained that it was an established custom for customers to share tables. They found seats with a couple of "regulars" who were colorful both in their attire and their conversation.

After surveying the extensive menu, Clare settled on a Jack Koeppler omelet and Henry chose the Crab Benedict, each with San Francisco's famous sourdough bread, toasted. And, of course, two Irish Coffees. Clare's omelet was named for a former owner who had challenged international travel writer Stanton Delaplane in 1952 to help recreate an "Irish Coffee" served at Shannon Airport in Ireland. The two pursued their goal until the taste was just right and the cream floated delicately on top.

Their companions had finished their breakfast but had lingered to enjoy another round of Irish Coffees. Clare and Henry found their drinks were strong enough without a refill so after enjoying their meal they said farewell and went walking – past the cable car turnaround and through Aquatic Park, where couples and families were gathering for a morning outing.

"We'll come back this way and see the beach, with actual sand," Clare said.

It was a perfect day for a stroll and they enjoyed seeing the marvelous views from the waterfront. They also did some people-watching on Jefferson Street and admired the results of a recent makeover to make the main drag at Fisherman's Wharf a much improved stretch of road for walkers and bikers.

Shoppers also were milling around The Cannery, a former fruit factory converted into a mall. They peeked into a few boutiques and art galleries, then circled back to the park and found an unoccupied bench. They watched people, young and old, enjoying various forms of recreation: bikers and skateboarders, children running while their parents relaxed on beach towels or a grassy spot, a few hardy souls taking a swim. They were amused at the sea lions at play.

Clare arose, took Henry's hand and as he got to his feet she said, "There's one other 'must-do' place."

A short distance away was Ghirardelli Square, a mecca for chocaholics like Clare. A landmark San Francisco attraction with its distinctive clock tower, it was the home of the original Ghirardelli Chocolate Factory. The renovated factory buildings now are filled with restaurants, galleries and shops including, naturally, some selling the famous chocolate in many forms.

"I think I'd like some ice cream," Clare said.

"I'll treat," said Henry.

Clare also got a small box of chocolate to take with her. They headed back to the cable car stop licking their cones and basking in the sunshine and breezes from the bay.

Since they had had a hearty breakfast at the Buena Vista Café, Clare and Henry decided they could skip lunch, with the expectation they might find something in the bus galley if necessary to stave off their hunger.

The driver arrived at the appointed time to take them to the rally at the Golden Gate Park, a San Francisco treasure frequented by more than 13 million visitors a year. Less than two weeks ago, the park had been the site of a noisy rally protesting alleged park ranger abuse of homeless people. But today conditions were peaceful.

They could hear the musicians playing and sounds of a gathering crowd as the van approached and Clare was feeling the excitement of the first rally in a major California city. The van pulled into position behind the bus and Clare alighted to the cheers of the assembled supporters. With a smile and a wave she stepped into the park and looked for Luna. They spotted each other right away.

"Anything I need to know?" Clare asked.

Luna told her she would be introduced by a woman who owned a successful Japanese bakery chain. She also gave her a list of questions that had been submitted as a result of a website request in advance of the rally.

There weren't any tough questions and she worked her responses into her remarks. But when she opened up for questions from the crowd a man up front shouted:

"Congressman Bull said on the radio that you ought to resign from the legislature if you're running for governor. Will you?"

Clare smiled and said, "Well, in the first place I'm not a candidate for governor yet. I'm holding meetings such as this one to help me decide. The filing period for state offices doesn't open until after the first of the year. Secondly, an elected official has a responsibility to continue to serve the people until a successor is chosen. And third, why is Congressman Bull so interested? Is he thinking about running for governor, too? And if so, will he give up his job and his salary of $174,000 a year? Maybe you should ask him."

Her answer was greeted with cheers and applause and the questioner slinked away. "He was probably a paid shill," Luna said later.

As the crowd began to disperse, Clare heard a voice calling, "Senator de Lune." She turned to see a young woman with a reporter's notebook. She introduced herself as the person Laurie Miller had lined up to cover her appearance for the Los Angeles News.

"That was a good answer you gave to the question about Congressman Bull," she said. "He had a press conference yesterday and that's when he made that statement."

"Oh, really? Well, I guess I'll have to expect more attacks from him in the coming weeks."

After the driver dropped her and Henry off at the hotel she told him, "I'm going to go soak in the tub for a while. Call me when it's time to get ready for the reception."

Later when he came to pick her up she was refreshed and dressed to enchant the grumpiest corporate executive.

"You are absolutely gorgeous," Henry said, admiring her stylish tailored fall suit.

"Why, thank you, sir," she said.

As always, Clare charmed the contributors as she went from one to another at the reception. Since she had skipped lunch except for grabbing a light snack on the bus, she sipped a club soda as she and Henry moved around the room.

In exchanges with the attendees, roughly a third of them women, she received many words of encouragement. She got a definite impression the business community was in a mood for a different style of leadership.

When the event had almost run its course the host got the crowd's attention and Clare thanked everyone for their attendance and their support. She emphasized the tremendous cost of campaigns and closed by saying, "Just look on your contribution as an investment in good government."

She and Henry slipped out and moved toward the elevators. "Do you need to go to the room?" he asked. She declined and they rode arm and arm to the

"Top of the Mark."

"I know I shouldn't do this on an empty stomach, but I think I'll have a martini," said Clare. "All I have to do is decide what kind."

Pointing to the 100-martini list, Henry said teasingly, "How about number 93?"

Clare exclaimed, "'The Double Dirty'? Oh, well, why not?"

Later, on the dance floor, she murmured, "Henry Jackson, you have a 'double dirty' mind."

"Moi?"

The moon was bright but diffused by some light cloud cover, adding to the romantic glow of the evening. Henry and Clare glided effortlessly around the floor. On the last dance, she sang softly in his ear the Tony Bennett hit song.

"The city by the bay was good to us," Henry said, and whispered the amount of contributions produced by the reception. Clare hugged him tightly and sighed, "You are my superhero ... at fundraising ... and other things."

49

THE BIG RED bus was still parked when the SUV driver picked up Clare and Henry at the hotel to take them to Berkeley where a rally on the University of California campus was scheduled for 10 a.m. It had been organized by the UC-Berkeley Friends of Clare at the request of Luna. It was difficult to anticipate how many students would turn out for this Monday morning event.

There would be no music to warm up the crowd. Clare knew she was taking a chance on what kind of reception she would receive – some past speakers had been targets of hostile demonstrations – but she felt it was important to get an idea of current attitudes toward state government at this very liberal institution.

She was introduced by a young woman, a member of the student senate, who drew a comparison between their respective roles with emphasis on Clare's membership on the state Senate Education Committee. Facing a small, predominantly female audience, Clare began by recognizing the influential position of the Associated Students of the University of California (ASUC) as the largest and most autonomous student government in the nation.

"I am aware that your leaders envision an ASUC committed to the values of transparency, empowerment, social justice, innovation and collaboration. I want you to know that I share those same values and I have strived to apply them during my service in state government," Clare said. "Another value I feel that public officials should hold is being responsive to their constituents – all of them, young and old, men and women, regardless of color or political philosophies.

"In an effort to be as responsive as I can I have embarked on a tour up and down California, a listening tour to find out what is on the minds of the people who live in our state. I know full well we have problems, and they include achieving and maintaining a level of support for education that will enable our universities to provide the kind of learning experience that will help today's students become tomorrow's leaders in health, science, business and industry, government and other walks of life.

"As I consider facing the challenge of becoming California's first woman governor, I want your ideas on what we can do to find solutions to our problems and make this a better state for everyone who lives here, or who desire to come here."

As she got farther along in her remarks, Clare observed her audience was growing as students began to show up and join the group. "Some texting has been going on," she thought. "They're telling their friends there's a politician here who is worth listening to."

By the time she finished, with plugs for her social media accounts, she had a good-sized, appreciative crowd. Several of the students gathered around her and offered compliments, many of them including the word "refreshing." She tucked that away in her brain as a good thought for campaign advertising.

Henry, who had been watching and listening from the perimeter, also was complimentary. "Well, at least I didn't prompt a demonstration," Clare said.

They rejoined the bus and the others at Jack London Square on the waterfront. Everyone had time to grab something to eat before the 1 p.m. rally. There was a wide choice of restaurants. Henry and Clare opted to have a beer at Heinold's First and Last Chance Saloon, the historic watering hole of the colorful adventurer and writer Jack London. He studied at the saloon's tables as a schoolboy and later made notes there for "The Sea Wolf" and "Call of the Wild." Clare warned Henry about the bar's slanted floor, resulting from uneven ground formed during the great San Francisco earthquake in 1906.

They got a takeout lunch at a place specializing in wood-fired pizza and ate it on the bus before the rally. In contrast to the Berkeley campus gathering, this was a more relaxed setting and Clare gave her brief, peppy appeal for support of her preliminary efforts at building a campaign for governor. While she was speaking she noticed a TV cameraman moving into position. After her remarks he approached and she learned he was with a local TV station with studios at the Square. He did a brief interview, which delighted Luna and Melody.

Clare and Henry spent the remainder of the day and the following morning making calls on executives of major corporations with headquarters in Oakland. They were pleased to receive pledges of support from a number of them.

Next stop on the tour was Fremont, named for an American explorer. It is characterized by its highly-educated population with high-paying clean technology jobs and is one of the most ethnically and culturally diverse cities in the Bay area. Around half of the residents are Asian.

The local Friends of Clare group had no difficulty finding an appropriate location for a rally in one of the city's many parks. Sensing the entrepreneurial character of the business community, Clare bore down hard on the need for government to work hand in hand with private enterprise for the overall good of the economy. She purposefully did not mention the disappointing failure of Solyndra, the solar panel company that was forced to close its doors despite a heavy infusion of federal funds and a strong endorsement by President Obama.

She delivered a similar, but more emphatic, message later in the tour in San Jose, the third largest city in California. Known as the "Capital of Silicon Valley", it is the home of several prominent high-technology companies. Henry and Clare devoted almost a full day visiting plants and offices in the affluent urban area, mindful of its importance not only to the California economy but its position in global commerce.

Before moving on, the group had a prearranged meeting on board the bus. Gathered around the conference table, they assessed the success of the first week of the tour. Henry said he felt the tour had been worthwhile from the financial standpoint. Melody had some highly encouraging reports on rising numbers on the social media sites, including visits to the website and inquiries from users interested in becoming involved in a possible future campaign. Luna had made a point of listening for comments by rally attendees and for the most part what she had overheard was favorable.

They concluded that Clare had put herself ahead of the field in sounding out Californians on whether they were satisfied with the direction state government was moving or if they felt a need for change.

Before breaking up, Melody spoke up. "I wanted to mention a Twitter message that came in. It was an invitation from the owner of a small business named 3-P for Clare to stop in."

"That sounds interesting," Clare said. "I'd like to do that if we can work it out."

"It so happens that it's on our route back home," Luna said.

Heading south from San Jose the travelers began to follow the business owner's directions after about 1 ½ hours. Before too long they saw a sign on the highway reading "3-P next exit." Presently the bus and the SUV pulled up alongside a plain factory building and the passengers (minus the musicians – they were napping) found the front entrance.

A smiling middle-aged woman greeted them. "Welcome to 3-P – Peppers' Packaging Products. I'm Olive Pepper. My husband's in the back."

Clare presented herself and introduced the others. "Thanks for inviting us to stop by."

"We don't get too many visitors, but this has been a special day," Olive said. "You're the second VIP we've had today."

"Really?" said Clare. "Who else?"

"Congressman Bull paid us a surprise visit this morning."

The startled looks on the faces of the new visitors prompted Olive to continue. "Mr. Bull said he knew we weren't in his district but that he had heard about our business and was interested in seeing it."

"Oh, he did, huh. Well, that's why we're here. So can your husband show us around?"

"Sure. Please follow me."

Peter Pepper was in his office at the computer with a chart on the screen. He stood to shake hands with Clare and told her he was glad she accepted his invitation. He also referred to John Bull.

"Yes, your wife told us. So tell me about your business," Clare said.

"We make packaging products – bags, boxes, tape and other materials for worldwide distribution from this little plant in California," he said.

"I'm impressed. And it must be profitable – otherwise you might have gone under like so many other businesses in these rough times for the economy."

"I'm pleased to say we're doing quite well. And it's largely because of a big government contract."

"And what's that for?"

"We supply the federal government with red tape."

"Is that a fact!"

"Let me show you," he said, leading the group out to a stock room. "Look up there." They did and saw rolls and rolls of red tape.

"Do you know how the government uses all this red tape?"

"No. They said they couldn't tell me because of national security reasons."

"But that doesn't matter, right?"

"Not at all. Supply and demand. That's what it's all about."

"And something tells me there's always going to be a demand for government red tape."

As she ended her visit, the owner casually mentioned that the congressman had told him he had connections in Washington in case he ever needed any help getting a government contract.

On the way to their vehicles, Clare opened a discussion about John Bull's odd visit. "We didn't announce anything about the invitation or our plans to stop here did we, Melody?"

"No, we didn't."

"Bull must have known we were coming and beat us to the punch," Luna said. "Wonder how he found out?"

"Maybe he has a friend at the National Security Agency," said Henry.

"I'm sure his people monitor our Twitter account. That's easy enough to do," Melody said. "So he could have known about the invitation. And the tour itinerary for each day is posted on Facebook. But, y'know, this visit wasn't listed."

"Well, no harm done. Let's just be alert for any further instances of spying."

159

50

THE LONG WEEK on the road, though productive, had been tiring and Clare was glad to have the weekend to renew her energy. She arose early Saturday and went for a brisk morning walk around the villa grounds. Living in sunny southern California she missed the turning of the leaves in the fall that she remembered so well from her years in Georgia. But the tradeoff of the blue sky view from her cliff-top home was worth it.

When she returned to the villa she found Henry having coffee on the terrace. A tray with a carafe was on a nearby table.

"May I join you?" she said, pouring a cup.

"Please do," he said. "Thanks again for allowing me to be an overnight guest."

"Well, it was so late when we got back it just seemed the right thing to do. Sorry I faded so quickly last evening."

"I understand. How are you this morning?"

"Better after stretching my legs. Sitting in a car for lengths of time is not my favorite thing to do. But I know it's a necessary part of mounting a campaign."

"How do you feel about the first week of the tour?"

"Very good. I enjoyed getting out with the people. It's invigorating. And Melody told me we got very good news coverage. She gets news summaries off the Internet on a regular basis. And some kind of automatic notification by email of a mention of me in the news media.

"That's good."

"And I'm amazed at all the photos and publicity she can spread through social media. It's helping a lot to build our base of support and the next few weeks should yield more of the same kind of results."

Henry left shortly to go to his apartment and finish settling in and Clare turned her attention to catching up on mail and phone messages.

51

WEEK TWO OF the tour opened at the historic Santa Monica pier, a 100-year-old landmark that is a popular location for public rallies. Beachgoers were few in number, although the mild temperature was suitable for some frolicking both on the sand and in the water. There were plenty of strollers on the pier itself.

Again, local Friends of Clare volunteers had done a creditable job of turning out a good-sized Monday morning crowd that enjoyed the music of the Clear Sailing band. When Clare emerged from the SUV she received a thunderous ovation.

She kept her remarks fairly brief and encouraged questions from the listeners. In addition to the usual queries and comments about environmental matters and taxes, one young mother expressed some concern about the delay in signing up for the Affordable Health Care program.

"I know that members of the congressional delegation are also concerned and I share their frustrations," Clare said. "This is a federal law and the core of the problem lies with the president and Congress."

She spent some time shaking hands and talking with individuals before rejoining her fellow travelers. "Let's get some lunch before we go on," she said. "One of my favorite places is Rusty's Surf Ranch."

Since it wasn't too crowded outdoors they chose a table with a view of the beach and enjoyed some fresh seafood, burgers and Mexican specialties.

Moving south, they headed for an afternoon stop at Buena Park, the home of a well-known California attraction, Knott's Berry Farm. The rally was held in a park where a number of historic buildings have been preserved.

Over the next few days Clare fired up prospective supporters at rallies in Anaheim, Santa Ana and Irvine. As might be expected in Orange County, questions reflected conservative leanings. In Newport Beach, she spoke at a meeting of People for Pro-Business California Politics, a group promoting business friendly policies. She repeated her theme of helping small business.

In Huntington Beach she touched on the controversial subject of fracking, which is being done offshore in those areas and through traditional drilling in counties from Los Angeles to Sacramento. She mentioned voting for the new fracking law signed by Governor Brown with its strict disclosure requirements on water usage and other aspects of the oil shale development boom spreading in the state.

"The new technologies for oil and gas extraction can have a tremendous economic impact on our state, creating millions of jobs and adding billions of state and local government revenues," she said, "but it's important for state officials to be able to track and monitor this activity and measure its effects on California's air and water as well as wildlife and human health."

Later when Clare appeared at a rally in Long Beach, she was met by a group of environmental protesters. She and the others speculated that John Bull's spies had tipped them off.

En route to Pasadena for the final rally of the week, the group made an unscheduled stop at Downey, birthplace of the systems for the Apollo space program and the Space Shuttle developed by Rockwell International. The Rockwell plant closed in 1999 and had been converted to a shopping and hospital complex. But the oldest surviving McDonald's restaurant was open for business and they stopped for a snack.

On the way home from Pasadena Clare also deviated from the schedule to respond to another invitation from a small business owner. It had come in an email sent to the address published on the website. Melody had shown it to her earlier in the week during a brief session on the bus and she was intrigued enough to want to see the operation.

Like 3P this business was housed in an inconspicuous building off the major highway. The sign read "Gowns to Go" and after meeting the owner, Risa Yamada, Clare learned she specialized in providing stylish wedding gowns within 24 hours at a set price of $89.

"How in the world can you do that?" she asked.

"The secret is in the low cost material," she said. "The gowns are made of paper." She led the group into a fitting room where several tailors were busy with scissors and tape putting the final touches on some stunning gowns.

"We also can supply inexpensive wedding cakes," she said. "The top layer is real cake but the base and the other tiers are cardboard."

"Business must be good," Clare observed.

"That's what Congressman Bull said when he was here earlier today."

"Well, I'll be ..." Luna exploded.

Clare and the others thanked her for the enlightening visit and went on their way shaking their heads.

"It looks as if Bull's people are monitoring everything we're doing," Henry said.

Clare was getting her Irish up. "We need to get to the bottom of this," she said.

"I have a plan," said Henry.

162

52

THE THIRD WEEK of the tour began with a breakfast sponsored by the Greater Santa Clarita Chamber of Commerce. As the third largest metropolitan area in Los Angeles, Santa Clarita was an important stop.

Clare began her remarks by immediately establishing a connection with her audience. "I'm delighted to be here," she said. "In a way this is kind of a homecoming for me. Valencia, which was one of the four communities that united to form this city in 1987, was my first home in California. I was drawn to the area by the California Institute of the Arts.

"After Oxford and a period of time in Europe, I decided I needed to settle down and get serious about a career of some kind. I had an interest in art, and at CalArts I had some excellent instructors who helped me to focus on developing the skills that eventually led me into sculpture. But for some unexpected life changes I might be showing my work or perhaps teaching instead of being here as an elected official considering a bold decision to seek a higher office.

"But this isn't a campaign appearance. That would be premature. As you may know I'm on a statewide tour to find out what's on the minds of Californians as our state faces the challenges of this fast-moving age.

"I have indeed given thought to some areas of particular interest as a state senator and potential candidate for governor. One of those, and perhaps foremost, is education."

She referred to her service as a member of the Senate Education Committee, mentioned a few new laws she had helped write and referred to her recent meeting with Oklahoma Gov. Mary Fallin and her jobs and education initiative as chairman of the National Governors Association.

"Another matter of great concern to me is the vast amount of suffering Californians have endured through natural disasters. Citizens of Santa Clarita have had more than their share. I don't have to remind you of the calamity that occurred in March of 1928 when the St. Francis Dam broke releasing flood waters that spread quickly all the way to the Pacific Ocean, killing nearly 600 people.

"Twice now, in 1971 and in 1994, the area has been affected by earthquakes. In more recent memory are the destructive and deadly wildfires which have occurred virtually every year since 2001, making Santa Clarita one of the nation's leading areas for wildfire activity. The Powerhouse fire in the Angeles National Forest in late May and early June burned nearly 50 square miles and destroyed a number of homes and outbuildings. It cost more than $11 million to fight this one fire.

"Disasters such as these are a terrible waste of our state's resources in addition to being a threat to the lives of police, firefighters and rescue workers, and above all a menace to the safety of residents of the areas affected."

Clare touched on some other concerns and then opened a discussion of matters that were troubling to her listeners. As in all of her meetings, Luna and Melody took extensive notes.

After she concluded her remarks a number of people came up to shake hands and offer support. Among those was one of Clare's former teachers at CalArts. She had read the newspaper article about her meeting with the art teachers group and complimented her on the efforts she had made in improving education.

It was a long drive to Modesto, the only other stop of the day. On the route was a small town named Chowchilla and as they approached Clare saw a sign reading, "Chowchilla Chow-Chow." We've got to stop there," she said.

"That would put us behind schedule," Henry said.

"We're coming back this way later in the week, aren't we?"

"Yes, we are."

"Let's stop then."

"Sounds like a good idea. But let's not let them know we're coming nor discuss it with Luna and Melody until later."

"Okay, if you say so."

Modesto was included in the tour to provide a contrast to the urban character of most of the other cities. Located in the Central Valley of northern California, it is surrounded by fertile farmland and ranks among the state's leading areas in farm production.

The city is known to movie fans as the setting for the 1973 film "American Graffiti" directed by George Lucas, a native of Modesto. It is also the home of the headquarters of E. & J. Gallo Winery, the largest in the world. Gallo is the city's largest employer.

Naturally Henry wanted to pay a visit to the winery. He had a contact there through someone he knew at Columbia Winery in Washington, which Gallo purchased in 2012. He and Clare took time for a tasting of reds, including the award-winning pinot noir.

Luna had found a nearby park for the rally with views of the beautiful winery grounds. There was a good turnout and the crowd was most receptive, especially when Clare spoke of the importance of California's agriculture industry. She made specific reference to the state's winegrowing operations and decided to take this opportunity to introduce Henry and his association with Mt. Jackson Vineyards, owner of the Chateau Lapierre winery. She called him "a key member of my exploratory committee." As they were to learn later, John Bull's forces picked up on this announcement.

Clare was pleased with the Modesto experience and she received an equally warm reception in Stockton, a city with history dating to the Gold Rush days when it was one of the largest cities in the state. It was a good spot for Clare to talk about public safety and to brag on the city for taking action to fight a wave of violent crime. She also took note of Stockton's self-reliant stand after it was forced to file for bankruptcy protection after the crash of the real estate market.

Following the rally Henry got the travelers together for a brief park bench summit to discuss his plan to trap the Bull forces in their espionage efforts. He told them about Clare's desire to stop in Chowchilla and gave Luna a disposable phone he had acquired to use in alerting the owner of Chowchilla Chow- Chow.

"What the hell is chow-chow?" Luna asked.

Clare responded. "The rest of you aren't from the south so you wouldn't know. It's a pickled relish made from green tomatoes, cabbage, onions and other vegetables. I'm surprised at seeing it made and sold this far West."

"I'm surprised to see it made and sold anywhere," Luna said.

"Just wait till you taste it," Clare said. Luna grimaced.

"Tomorrow morning before we head back south," Clare said, "we'll have coffee on the bus and I'll open a conversation about making another of our small business visits, but it won't be Chowchilla. It will be some place farther down the road like Fowler or Selma. Just play along and we'll see what happens."

Continuing Clare's appearances in the San Joaquin Valley, the first stop on the third day of this week's tour was Merced, known as the "Gateway to Yosemite" because it is less than two hours driving time to Yosemite National Park. It was a perfect location for Clare to repeat her concerns about the destructive force of wildfires, tying into the 2013 Rim Fire in the Sierra Nevada region which was the third-largest in California history.

"This disaster began when a hunter's illegal fire got out of control. The flames spread rapidly and eventually consumed over a half-million acres. It took more than two months and the efforts of more than 5,000 firefighters to bring this fire under control. The cost of fighting the fire was estimated at $127 million," Clare said. "We can be thankful that Yosemite never was in danger, although at times there was heavy smoke.

"Hot, dry conditions contributed to the severity of this year's fires, causing them to spread and be harder to fight. We can't do much about the weather, but we can make sure local firefighting units have the necessary equipment and that communities receive assistance they need from public funds."

As planned Luna, before leaving her hotel room, had called the owner of Chowchilla Chow-Chow on the disposable phone to let her know about Clare's drop-in visit and the group had a chat on the bus about stopping farther down the road at a factory that produced ant-resistant picnicking quilts.

When they reached Chowchilla, Mary Anne Parker was waiting at the door to her small canning company. "Y'all come right in," she said. "We're mighty glad you folks came by."

They accepted her offer to "sit and have a cup of coffee" in her kitchen, where a large canner was heating up on the stove.

"This reminds me of my mother's kitchen in Georgia," Clare said. "That's where I grew up."

"Well, I'm from Alabama," Mary Anne said. They talked about their mothers for a while and how they both made chow-chow when the girls were little.

Mary Anne had started her small business after her truck driver husband had died in a highway accident a few years back. She had built the business into a money-making enterprise with distribution in several states.

"Congratulations. Your success is quite inspiring," Clare said. "By the way, do you have many drop-by visitors?"

"No, you're the first one in quite a spell. And I really appreciate your interest," Mary Anne said.

When the visitors insisted they had to leave she sent them on their way with jars of Chowchilla Chow-Chow.

Later in the day when they pulled into Auntie Jane's Anti-ant Quilt factory, it was a different story. Clare apologized for showing up without advance notice, Auntie Jane said, "Oh, that's all right. We had another surprise visitor earlier. Congressman John Bull said he was passing through and wanted to see our operation."

"Well, well," Clare said. "You probably got behind in your work, so we won't take long."

On the way out the group exchanged knowing glances and Henry said he'd like to make a quick check of the bus. Inside he looked around the conference room and got down under the table. He motioned to the others to be quiet as they peeked and saw the hidden microphone.

Outside the bus, Luna exploded. "That bastard Bull bugged our bus!"

"Looks that way," Henry said.

"I'll bet I know when it happened," Clare said. "Didn't someone say John Valjean was among those who walked through the bus when we opened it to the public on kickoff day?"

"That's right," Luna said. "I'm sure he did it. Now what do we do?"

Henry said, "Let's not do anything until the end of the day. We could leave it and give them some more false information. But we need to be able to use that area for meetings. So I'll remove it and disable it."

Continuing south, the group passed through Madera, site of eight wineries on the Madera Wine Trail. Clare had to restrain Henry from stopping. "We don't have time to do them all," Clare said, and we can't afford to show favorites."

Fresno was an important stop. At the heart of the San Joaquin Valley, a leading agricultural area of the United States, it is the largest inland city in California with close to half a million people. As the closest major city to Yosemite National Park, it was an ideal place for Clare to repeat her message about the destructive force of forest fires. She spoke at a well-attended rally at the Fresno Convention Center.

On down the road to Visalia, one of the state's fastest growing cities, Clare was pleasantly surprised to find the local volunteer organization had chosen the Fox Theater as the venue for her appearance. The 70-year-old theater, with its distinctive clock tower, had been restored by a community group which raised more than $1 million.

Closing out the week at Bakersfield, Clare took the opportunity to brag on the members of the "Clear Sailing" band, who were from the area. In her remarks she included recognition of the city's musical contributions, but she concentrated on her thoughts about energy production. She took note of the fact that 10 percent of the nation's domestic oil production comes from Kern County. The county also ranks in the top five of the most productive agricultural counties in the nation. And on a lighter note, she said she had learned that Bakersfield is the home of the world's largest ice cream plant. "I might just have to make a stop there before leaving town," she joked.

With one more week to go on her listening tour, Clare relaxed and looked forward to a weekend of downtime at the villa.

53

CLARE DECIDED NOT to go public with the discovery of the bug on the bus until after the tour was completed. She was planning a news conference then anyway and a little juicy morsel about political espionage would be enough to guarantee some play in the news media. John Valjean would guess that the bug had been found and it would be deliciously delightful to let him stew for a few days. Bull probably was itching to beat her to the punch again on a small company and wondering why Valjean was objecting. Revenge is sweet.

The weekend sped by and early Monday morning the "Here's Clare" caravan was headed south to San Diego for a previously scheduled Veterans Day speech and rally. She was speaking to a group of women veterans at a luncheon that was suggested by Tim Barnham. It was arranged by the sister of a state senator they both knew well. She had served in the Air Force with the rank of captain.

The luncheon was at the Hotel del Coronado, a landmark beachfront resort, where Clare and Henry had room reservations because he had scheduled a fundraising reception that evening. As California's second largest city, San Diego was fertile ground both for contributions and votes. In lining up the reception Henry had detected a strong attachment to Clare, which he later discovered was due to Gary de Lune's generous support of the San Diego Automotive Museum. She had donated one of Gary's classic cars to the museum after he was killed.

With its distinctive red turrets, "The Del", as it is known locally, is most impressive both to first-time visitors and returning guests. The sprawling Victorian complex is one of the largest wooden structures in the United States. At the time of its opening in 1888, it was the world's largest resort hotel. Presidents, royalty and many celebrities have stayed there through the years. Henry and Clare were made to feel they received the same hospitable welcome as all the famous names.

For her speech Houston Conover had supplied her with some helpful background material. With more than 185,000 women veterans, California leads the nation for women in military service. Clare opened her remarks with a tribute, noting that women had served in every major conflict in U.S. history. "For years of dedicated service, we owe you and all the other women a great debt of gratitude," she said. "After serving in the military in support and combat missions, women are returning to their roles as wives, mothers, caregivers and workers in unprecedented numbers. Those of us holding public office need to uphold our responsibility to women veterans to make sure they are receiving all of the benefits to which they are entitled."

Clare referred to biennial surveys taken by the California Department of Veterans Affairs to let the group know she was tuned in on their issues. She touched on transition challenges confronting veterans returning home from the wars in Afghanistan and other areas. "We need to be more attentive to the unique challenges encountered by women," she said. She acknowledged their need for gender-specific health care, help finding employment and assistance with housing. She expressed alarm at the high rate of sexual assaults among women veterans as well as sexual harassment.

She closed by stressing the importance of knowing what help is available from both state and federal government offices and how to get it. In a Q&A session, she told a questioner who asked about her plans to run for governor to watch for an announcement after she completed her grassroots tour of the state.

In the afternoon Clare did some handshaking at a Salute to Service Festival at the USS Midway Museum where a panorama of the San Diego Bay offered some excellent photo opportunities. A rally arranged by local volunteers at the regional campaign headquarters concluded a successful day of revving up the "Clare for Governor" troops.

There was an encouraging turnout for the evening fundraising reception, which was heavy on executives from defense and military-related industries. Clare took the opportunity to meet all attendees individually and thank them for their support. She and Henry followed up the following day with calls on selected businesses, including research and manufacturing companies.

Then it was on to Fontana, home of the California Speedway – another area where Gary de Lune was well known – and to Riverside, the most populous city of Southern California's Inland Empire region for a midweek rally.

In San Bernardino, Clare made an appearance at the National Orange Show and spoke to a modest crowd at a volunteer rally. As the gateway to the ski resorts and lakes of the San Bernardino Mountains, it was an appropriate spot to restate her interest in preserving California's outdoor resources. Since it had been the largest city to file for bankruptcy protection prior to Detroit, no fundraising activities were scheduled.

In contrast, Palmdale offered numerous opportunities for soliciting financial support. Commonly referred to as the Aerospace Capital of America, Palmdale is the birthplace of the X-15 and many other aircraft used by the Air Force, NASA and airlines around the world, as well as the Space Shuttle.

All in all, Clare considered the final week of the tour to be most productive for developing resources for the campaign. Melody had dutifully maintained a steady flow of information about the week's activities on the various social media outlets. The tour windup also allowed Clare and Henry to spend more quality time together.

54

CLARE SPENT A large part of the weekend catching up on mail and phone calls. One of the calls was from Gene. Excited as always, he said that when he was in Los Angeles recently he happened to catch part of a TV show called "In the Kitchen with Ida Clare." He said she should try to line up a spot on the show to promote her book once it was published.

She also devoted an ample amount of time reflecting on the past month's activities on the road talking and listening to Californians from various parts of the state. The interaction had strengthened her desire to pursue an effort to become the state's first woman governor.

A news conference had been scheduled for Monday morning at her state headquarters to report on the tour and also to inform the public about the evidence of campaign skullduggery.

TV crews from a number of area stations showed up ahead of time to set up their equipment. Another early arrival was Laurie Miller, whose articles in the Los Angeles News had been quite effective in getting Clare's name widely mentioned as a strong possibility for the 2014 governor's race. She grabbed a few private moments with Clare before the full contingent of news reporters had descended.

"Are you getting closer to a decision about becoming a candidate?" she asked.

"The calendar has a lot to do with the timing of that decision," Clare said. "But getting out over the state and finding out what people are thinking was an essential part of the process. From that standpoint I believe the tour was invaluable."

"Any surprises along the way?"

"I had a pretty good idea of what some of the issues might be, but my visits in different areas definitely show how strong feelings are running about things like the large number of people leaving the state, protection of our natural resources and implementation of the new health care law," Clare said. "And there was one particular surprise I want to talk about."

"What was that?"

"I'm afraid you'll have to wait with the others on that, Laurie," Clare smiled.

Because of the widespread interest in the news conference, some radio stations were carrying it live. Clare had to remind herself that she was communicating with a general audience, not just those who report the news.

She began with an opening statement summing up the valuable lessons learned from the tour:

"As all of you know, I have just completed a month-long tour of California which took me to many areas of the state. Our bandwagon bus traveled up and down the state, stopping at 32 cities and towns, representing a cross-section of our population.

"This was essentially a listening tour. I shared some of my views on issues that have confronted the state legislature and which continue to be areas of concern to me, and I answered questions at rallies and town hall meetings. I went out to the people to find out what's on their minds: what are they happy and unhappy about, how do they think state government is working, how satisfied or unsatisfied they are about the current leadership.

"It is no secret that I am exploring the possibility of running for governor next year. I have recently formed an exploratory committee, which allowed me to start raising funds to help me undertake the enormous task of assessing the mood of the electorate and to decide whether I should take on the awesome challenge of winning enough votes to put me in the governor's chair.

"I have not made that decision. But it's not one that I can postpone for too long. I will give it a lot of thought over the holidays coming up. And I hope to have my mind made up early next year.

"I have to say that I have received a great amount of encouragement as I connected with people in large and small communities over the state. In most places, good-sized crowds turned out to meet me. They showed an interest in what I had to say and I certainly learned a lot from them.

"I had conversations with students and other young people, working men and women, and older, retired persons. I exchanged ideas with rural and city dwellers, people of wealth and those on public assistance, citizens of various races and ethnic backgrounds. One of the activities I enjoyed most was visiting with a number of small business owners in their work places. In an economy that is still struggling, I saw many examples of successful entrepreneurship – the kinds of successes our state needs to grow and be strong.

"To sum up, as a result of this tour, I think I have a pretty good picture of what will be uppermost in the minds of voters when they go to the polls next year.

"This will be a different kind of election, the kind that has not been seen in past elections for governor. On June 3, Californians will vote in a statewide non-partisan primary election. The two candidates receiving the most votes, regardless of party affiliation, will be on the general election ballot in November.

It could be a Democrat and a Republican – that's what we're accustomed to. Or it could be two Democrats or two Republicans. There also could be an Independent in the mix.

"It certainly will be an interesting campaign. And the easiest thing to do would be to just sit on the sidelines and watch. But that is a difficult thing to imagine for someone who has been part of the inner workings of state government, as I have, and who has a deep desire to do what is necessary to make lives better for all of our people.

"For anyone trying to win the governorship in a state like California it is a monumental task. For a woman, it is almost an unthinkable challenge. The tremendous amount of money that it takes to run a statewide campaign these days, the immense pressure on the candidate, day after day, the physical and mental energy required to remain committed to the goal – these are demands that a weaker, less determined individual could meet. But I am not that kind of individual. I aspire to higher goals. If I didn't I wouldn't even consider trying to become the first woman ever elected governor of California.

"Now, I'll take a few questions and then I'll have some closing remarks. Let's start with Sam Mahoney of the AP, the dean of the state capitol press corps."

"Senator, as things now stand it appears most likely that Gov. Jerry Brown is considered a shoo-in for reelection. I'm not alone in that opinion. He's popular, and he has a much larger campaign chest than any potential candidate. Why even consider a losing battle?"

"Well, Sam, I guess I'm not as cynical as you. But in the first place, the governor has not said whether he will run for a fourth term. I have no idea what his intentions are. But speaking for myself, if I do choose to become a candidate I will not be running against Jerry Brown – I'll be running *for* the office. I would conduct a campaign of issues, not personalities, and put forth positive proposals. I think that's the kind of politics the voters would like to see in every state and at the national level as well. Laurie Miller ..."

"Clare ... I hope you don't mind ..."

"Not at all. That's the name I've been using in presenting myself to the people – Clare Sullivan de Lune ..."

"Your bus has the words, 'Here's Clare' painted on the side. That sort of implies you're ready to go. But do you have the resources it will take to mount a campaign as challenging as this one will be?"

"Good question, Laurie. The simple answer is no, as of right now. But we are a lot better prepared than I thought we would be a few months ago. Thanks to volunteers who have stepped up to help all over the state, we have the framework for an effective statewide organization. We have groups of hardworking women, largely, and supportive men in almost every county in the state. Many of them have become interested by following the tour from reports on our website, as well as on Facebook and Twitter. And we have a good fundraising effort in progress. I don't want to tip off my potential opponents by saying how much we've raised. There'll be time for official reports later. But I am quite pleased. And in addition to the cash in the bank, I've received pledges of many more contributions if I do decide to get into the race. Let's take a question from an L.A. TV reporter."

"Our station has information that you have on your team a person who not only is from out of state but also is a Republican. Is that true?"

"That is the first of what will likely be many innuendos and half-truths spread by some news media if I become a candidate. I am an out-of-stater myself, if you count the fact that I was born in Georgia. California is a state that attracts people from all over the country, all over the world. My finance chairman is a native of the state of Washington. But he is as much a Californian as I am. He arranged the purchase of an excellent winery, Chateau Lapierre, in Ventura County for Mt. Jackson Vineyards, his family's business. Allow me to introduce him to you – Henry Jackson. He has done an outstanding job of building a campaign treasury. I believe he is a registered Republican. I think you'll agree that Republicans are pretty good at raising money. But he has nothing to do with the political side of our operation. Even so, remember the major step in the campaign is the non-partisan primary next June 3. If I do decide to make the race, I will be running on what *I* believe in, not somebody else."

Clare took a few more questions on such things as state finances, education, health care and environmental concerns, on which she was well prepared to give answers. As the TV crews were just about to pack up their equipment, she said:

"I would like to close with a statement I think all Californians will be interested in. The statewide tour I have just completed was a valuable learning experience, in many ways. One thing became very clear. There are distinct signs that if I run for governor it most likely will be a dirty campaign. During our travels we discovered evidence of spying – secretive, deliberate eavesdropping on our plans, followed by actions to sabotage them."

After a dramatic pause, she reached into her red shoulder bag and held up a closed fist, which she slowly opened to show a small object wrapped in a handkerchief. By this time the TV cameras were running and some photographers moved into closer range.

"We found this microphone had been planted on our bus." Flashes from the still cameras illuminated the room, which was abuzz with whispers.

"You mean your bus was bugged?" came a shout, quickly repeated.

"No doubt about it," said Clare. "After this news conference we will turn this item over to the State Bureau of Investigation for fingerprinting and other analyses which will identify the perpetrator."

An excited TV reporter asked, "Do you have any idea who did this?"

"I have some suspicions," Clare said. "But I prefer to let the authorities do their job. Unless, of course, the guilty party decides to come forward and confess before being arrested."

"What do you make of this stunt?" someone yelled.

"I'd hardly characterize this invasion of privacy as a stunt. It's a serious crime and needs to be thoroughly investigated, not only for my sake but for the protection of other candidates. My personal reaction is disgust that someone would stoop so low. But it's also a strong indication that there are forces at work trying to keep me from being a candidate. Maybe they're scared that a woman, and one who is not part of the 'old guard' might actually become governor and shake things up a bit."

She met the barrage of questions with a silencing hand gesture and said, "That's all I have to say for now. We'll report any developments as they occur."

Clare had invited her core team to the villa for a combination celebration of the tour and news conference and a free-wheeling discussion of future plans. On the way Henry expressed his admiration.

"Clare, your remarks were splendid. You hit all the right notes. And with the dramatic ending, you really knocked it out of the park."

"Thank you, my fellow Californian. That's very sweet."

"You also handled that very well. It's a matter that needed to be addressed and it was good to get that response out early."

"Well, I thought so."

"By the way, I had a call from Pop."

"Really? What did he have to say? Is everything all right?"

"Oh, yes. He sounded very good. He wanted to wish you well on meeting what he called 'the Fourth Estate bastards.' But he also wanted to invite us up to Mt. Jackson for Thanksgiving."

"How nice! I'd love to see him and Jean again, and maybe meet the rest of your family."

"Pop also said he had an important announcement to make."

55

CLARE'S SENSATIONAL REVELATION was the lead story on newspaper websites and evening newscasts. Whoever planted that bug on her bus to derail her effort to become better known throughout the state unwittingly had thrust her into the news spotlight and aroused interest in her possible campaign for governor. Her announcement about bringing the State Bureau of Investigation into the case was bound to be causing the culprit to have some cold sweat.

She smiled as she scanned the news reports on her tablet and imagined the chaos in the Bull camp. She had some wicked thoughts about John Valjean resigning from the congressman's staff with a public apology for his actions. At the same time she hoped he would keep the truth bottled up. A guilty conscience could lead to more mistakes in judgment that could do serious damage to Bull's future plans.

Although she was off the road for a spell, the newly-crowned "potential candidate" – Sam's AP story referred to her as "a darkhorse with long odds" – had a mountain of work to get done before taking a Thanksgiving break. Topmost on her "to do" list was reading the manuscript for her book and giving the final signoff so the Canadian publishing company Gene had lined up could get it printed and in distribution.

She disciplined herself to set aside a certain number of hours a day for the somewhat monotonous job, allowing time for walks and other kinds of exercise to keep her body and her mind alert.

Clare liked the title Gene and Shirley had suggested – "Clearly I See" – and was pleased with the portrait photo by Lynn Dykstra that would appear on the front cover. Shirley had woven the story of her life around the theme of reaching a decision point and after careful thought "seeing clearly" the right course to take. The steps in her career included the choice to leave the comfortable surroundings of home in Georgia to go out into the world; deciding to return to the states and become a sculptor; her chance meeting with Gary de Lune which developed into a romance that led to a marriage proposal; and following his death carrying on his work in the California legislature. All of that brought Clare to the point of boldly embarking on the search for what some might call the Holy Grail of American politics: becoming governor of the state with the most people, and being the first woman to do it.

The latter part of the book pertained to her views on leading issues:

"Clearly I see that California needs to do a better job of educating its young people …

"Clearly I see that not enough is being done to protect California's natural resources from the ravages of wildfires and other natural disasters …

"Clearly I see that California is losing too many of its people moving to other states …"

Clare had very few corrections or suggestions to make. It was obvious – clear, even – that Shirley was a highly skilled professional writer. She had transformed her interviews and their conversations into a smoothly flowing story told in Clare's words, incorporating her sense of humor along with her sincerity about public service. It had been their understanding that Clare would be candid about many things, which would win favor with readers. But the person with her name below the title reserved the right to edit out references that might be politically damaging. One such instance was her ownership of a gun. While she was prepared to admit it and justify the possession, she could "see clearly" there was nothing to be gained by tossing raw meat to the hungry dogs of the press and her opposition.

By the end of the week she had finished the review to her satisfaction and sent an email to Shirley with a three-page attachment which included, along with requested omissions the addition of a short paragraph about her hair: "It is naturally auburn, but I do enhance the color a bit." That was in anticipation of inquiries that were fully expected to arise. The press has a curious fascination about women politicians' hair, as Hillary Clinton and Michelle Obama would testify.

Henry had given her the privacy necessary to concentrate on the book project, remaining in his apartment and keeping busy with followups on contacts made during the tour with potential donors. When Clare called him on Friday afternoon to report she was free for the evening, he eagerly drove to the villa, stopping only long enough to purchase a large bouquet of red roses.

The flowers were a delightful surprise. They earned Henry a missed-you-so-much kiss and a thank you hug. She put the roses in a vase and took them to the terrace, where they sat and sipped wine and enjoyed each other's company until after sunset. He remembered he had left a change of clothes in "his" guest bedroom so he accepted her invitation to spend the night. It would have been a shame to waste the magical spell of a moonlit sky apart from one another.

56

AFTER A CHECKLIST session with Luna in Santa Barbara, Clare joined Henry to drive to the airport. Pop had sent the company jet for their Thanksgiving trip, saying, "you'd have a hell of a time getting reservations" on the most heavily traveled holiday on the calendar. After the hectic schedule of the past month, it was a pleasure to be relieved of the hassle of a commercial flight.

Henry's brother, Andrew, had volunteered to meet the plane and drive them to the winery and it gave Clare a chance to learn a little more about the Jackson family.

Henry Jackson, Jr. and his wife Clara had raised two sons, neither of whom aspired to be on the executive ladder. As Clare had learned, Henry Jackson III, the eldest, had a chronic case of wanderlust that led him to leave home and see the world rather than settle into a desk job at the winery. Andrew, on the other hand, wanted to remain with his parents and the family business, but his interest was outdoors, not in an office. His love was in growing grapes, developing new varieties and overseeing that important function of winemaking and was perfectly content being the vineyard manager.

Clare's first impression of Andrew was that he was a gentleman, like his older brother. As he took her bag to load into the car, she observed a bit of shyness in his smile but deep sincerity in his brown eyes. His hair was a lighter shade of brown than Henry's, blending well with his naturally-tanned skin. His build also was different. Henry had the body of an athlete, muscular and well-proportioned. Andrew was sinewy, his muscles more subdued – the look of an outdoorsman.

As they settled in for the ride, Clare surprised Andrew by asking if he had any ambition to be president of the United States. "No, why?" he responded. "Well, you have the name for it – Andy Jackson," Clare replied. Henry interjected, "He usually goes by Drew."

Arriving at Mt. Jackson Vineyards in the daytime was quite different from Clare's first trip. She could see more of the beautiful woodland scenery, for one thing. But there was more of an "at home" feeling about the place.

Andrew parked at the winery and left the car with them. After an initial greeting from Lucky, the official winery dog, she received a warm welcome from Pop and Jean, who told her to get settled and meet them at the main house.

Henry drove up to his place, all the while Clare wondering about what he had planned.

"Am I staying in one of the guest cabins as before?" she asked.

"If you wish. There's also an extra bedroom in my house."

"That arrangement worked out wonderfully at the villa," she said.

"Then let's get our bags and go inside and get unpacked," he said.

Neither thought it necessary to change for the casual dinner that was expected.

Pop's home was at least three times as large as Henry's, as would befit the head of the company. The exterior of the two-story rambling brick structure was not imposing – they did notice an attractive carriage house at one end where Pop had said Jean was living – but once inside it was quite luxurious, in a low key sort of way. It had a good-sized living room and dining room for formal occasions, but Jean suggested they gather in a more informal sitting area. The muted tones of the walls and built-in bookcases blended with the glow from a huge fireplace to give the spacious area a warm, friendly feeling.

On the way to their destination they passed a roomy kitchen designed for a host or hostess who enjoyed cooking. Clare had to stop and admire the butcher block-top island, plentiful cabinets and top-of-the-line appliances. She peppered Jean with questions while Pop and Henry continued on their way. Jean picked up a tray of appetizers and they soon joined the men for a glass of wine and a toast to the success of the tour.

After some approving comments from Clare, he said, "It's a vintage released just recently and it is selling well. Andrew is largely responsible."

They spent the early part of the evening nibbling on Jean's delicious stuffed mushrooms, brie and other finger foods and chatting about a variety of things other than politics. Although her mind was never too far from her political plans she welcomed the break.

She couldn't help but notice Pop's relaxed manner and lack of his typical gruffness. He and Jean seemed very comfortable with one another, as if they had been together much longer than about five months.

Eventually Pop announced he was ready for some "real food" and the group moved to a table near a large window which in daylight offered a splendid view of Mt. Jackson. A starlit sky was visible this evening.

Jean had prepared steak au poivre with herbed frites and dijon leeks with a pear tart for dessert. Pop served a fine selection of dinner and dessert wines.

"What a wonderful meal!" Clare said to Jean.

"If this is a preview of what to expect for Thanksgiving dinner, I can hardly wait," Henry said.

"Jean is a marvelous cook," Pop said, and turning to her: "This was one of your finest performances, my dear."

"Thank you all. I do enjoy cooking."

"Tomorrow will be a little different," Pop said, with a wink to Jean. "Our Thanksgiving feast will be catered."

Detecting a look of disappointment on his son's face, he quickly added: "Jean and the chef at our dining room have formed their own catering company – Mt. Jackson Caterers. It's our newest business sideline."

"Oh, I see," Henry said. "Was this the big announcement you told me about?"

Pop laughed. "No, that's something else. But it will have to wait until our family circle is all here."

Henry and Clare later learned that the circle would include the senior Henry Jackson, Andrew, the winemaker and other key staff members.

"Anyone care for an after dinner drink?" Jean asked, easily slipping into the role of hostess of the main house.

"No, thank you," Clare said. "But this has been a very special evening. I'm so glad you included me in your family Thanksgiving plans."

"Certainly, dear. Sleep well," Pop said. "You, too, son."

57

THE AROMA OF coffee drifting up from the kitchen gently aroused Clare from her slumber. She was momentarily alarmed by seeing how late she had slept, but she was grateful to have had that opportunity.

After getting dressed she walked downstairs and joined Henry, who was warming some cinnamon rolls in the oven.

"Jean had sent these over with a welcome home note," he said.

"How nice," Clare said. "She is really a sweet lady. And I think your dad is quite fond of her."

"That appears to be the case, all right. I believe the rolls are ready."

Henry's only dining area was the lip of his kitchen island and two stools so they moved to the sitting area and actually used the coffee table for having coffee. He shoved aside two stacks of large flat illustrated books to make room for their cups and the basket of warm rolls.

"It's too bad we can't sit on the deck but I think it might be too nippy this morning," Henry said.

"But we can still look out the windows and see the beautiful mountain scenery."

"Quite a bit different from your view of the ocean."

"These are some of the best cinnamon rolls I've ever tasted," Clare said.

"Right. Jean's a real winner."

"She seems to be adjusting quite well to the loss of her husband."

"I guess it makes a difference knowing it was just a matter of time before the cancer would finally take its toll on him."

"Not the same as when death is unexpected and sudden. Like Gary's."

"That must have been very painful for you."

"Yes. But time is a great healer."

Feeling a need to change the subject, Henry said, "We have some free time before gathering at the main house for the Thanksgiving feast. Would you like to take a walk around the grounds?"

"That sounds like a marvelous idea. Maybe I'd better get a light jacket."

"Okay. I'll put away the cinnamon rolls."

"Not so fast. I believe I'll have one more."

"More coffee?"

"No, thanks. I'll just finish this."

Henry took Clare by the hand as they strolled along the paths strewn with pine straw that led to a number of scenic spots on the property. There were benches carved from timber along the way for occasional pauses. As they sat Henry told her more about his early years when he used to run and play with his younger brother, Andrew. He mentioned that one of the things they liked to do most was to go fishing in the pond.

"Would you like to see it?" he asked.

"Yes, of course," she said.

They playfully kicked aside pine cones that had fallen on the path to the pond, which was visible through the trees as they approached. The water glistened in the morning sunlight and Clare could imagine the two Jackson boys spending hours in this lovely setting matching their wits against the fish. The pond had been stocked with trout for as long as Henry could remember. A reward for a good catch was a tasty meal, sometimes prepared on an open wood fire.

After an hour or so of enjoying the beauties of nature, Henry said he was beginning to work up an appetite so they headed back to his house. Casual dress was the rule at the vineyards, but both decided to change to something a little classier than jeans for Thanksgiving Day.

Henry gave a call to Pop to see if it was too early to make an appearance.

"Nah, come on up," he said. "Your grandpa is here and he's eager to see you and meet Clare."

She was equally excited about meeting him, and a bit nervous. Henry assured her there was no reason for that. "I have a feeling the two of you will hit it off the way you and Pop have."

"I hope so," she said.

The elder Jackson was sitting in a wheelchair near the fireplace. Henry guided Clare over to the white-haired gentleman who gave her a big smile and with a twinkle in his eye said, "Come sit here by me, my dear."

"Thank you, sir."

With a hearty laugh, he said, "None of that. Just call me Gramps."

"All right, Gramps. I'm so happy to finally meet you."

"That goes for me, too. We don't get too many visitors up here so I'm glad to have some company. Since I don't get around as well as I used to, I spend a lot of time by myself."

"You must be very lonely at times," she said.

"Hell, he spends all his time watching old movies," Pop said. "He loves those musicals with stars like Ginger Rogers. The reason he's in a wheelchair is he had to have a hip replacement after he fell one day acting like he was Fred Astaire."

"You want to hear a chorus of 'Puttin' on the Ritz'? "

"I'd love to," Clare said.

"Some other time," said Jean, who approached with another woman whom she introduced as Louise, her catering partner. She sat on the other side of Clare and enthusiastically told her about her experiences running the winery restaurant and recently working with Jean on catered events.

"We get along so well together," she said.

"I understand today's meal was prepared by Mt. Jackson Caterers," Clare said.

"Yes, but it's being served by my restaurant staff. Mr. Jackson wanted Jean and me to be among the guests."

"Isn't this a busy day for the restaurant?"

"Actually, it's closed. On Thanksgiving most people had rather be with their families. Or if they're dining out it's in the city and not out here in the woods," Louise said.

"Well, Henry and I are really looking forward to this dinner."

As the time to dine grew near, other guests began to arrive. First was Andrew, who politely inquired of Clare if she was enjoying herself. "I'd like to give you a tour of the vineyards if you have time," he said. "I'd like that, Drew," she said. "We'll see."

Henry introduced her to the acquisitions manager and the winemaster, whom she had heard of but had not met, and the manager of the gift shop, who also was in charge of online orders.

Uniformed waitresses from the restaurant passed sparkling wine and light hors d'oeuvres from silver trays and at precisely 2 p.m. Jean announced, "Dinner is served. Please be seated."

Gramps took his place at the head of the long dining table and said the blessing. Others found their place cards and pulled up chairs.

The table, laden with a display of appetizing food, accented by colorful small gourds and other autumn touches, was like a page out of Sunset magazine. At each setting was a salad and a small printed menu:

> Mussels with Sausage and Thyme
> Spinach and Persimmon Salad
> Ojai Roast Turkey with Rosemary, Lemon and Garlic
> Giblet Gravy
> Apricot and Wild Rice Dressing

Gorgonzola Broccoli Casserole
Sweet Potato Gratin
Cranberry Pomegranate Sauce
Louise's Special Rolls
Chocolate-Pumpkin Marble Cake

Clare thought to herself, "I could just skip the preliminaries and go right to dessert." She could hardly contain her excitement anticipating this gourmet meal.

She was seated to the right of Pop, who occupied the chair at the end of the table opposite his father. Jean was across from Clare. Henry and Andrew were sitting with Gramps.

The magnificent bronzed turkey was on a platter right in front of Pop (and her) and the scent of rosemary drifting into her nostrils heightened her expectation of a glorious meal. He skillfully carved the big bird and served portions as guests passed their plates.

Clare soon had a full plate because she wanted a taste of everything. She complimented Jean and Louise on all the dishes – she knew they had either prepared them or supervised the cooking. She gave special praise to Louise for her yeast rolls.

She had some conversation with the winemaster, who was seated to her right. But primarily she was engaged in talking with Pop and Jean. She became aware that Jean, in addition to providing companionship for Pop, had become an integral part of the winery operation. She drew on her own experience to offer ideas for the restaurant and gift shop. She was a natural greeter for visitors, who told her she made them feel so welcome they would plan to come back.

All the while Pop was beaming. After dessert was served (and Clare scraped the last crumbs of cake off her plate) he tapped the water glass with his fork and said:

"Folks, I want to tell you how happy I am that we could all be together this day. I hope you have enjoyed the meal as much as I have. (Murmurs of assent were heard.) Before we adjourn for football or naps, I have an important announcement to make.

"Over the past several months I believe all of you, at one time or another, have commented that you've noticed a change in me. And not that I've gotten grumpier or ornerier, but rather the opposite. You've told me I've become less uptight, more relaxed, an all around happier person.

"Well, I agree. And I have one person to thank for that. My life hasn't been the same since Jean Lapierre came back from California with me after my visit to our new winery addition. Her warm and gentle personality, her sense of humor, her calming influence – not to mention her wonderful cooking – have really made a difference in the way I feel about living.

"So much so that I can't even think about her ever leaving Mt. Jackson. And so …"

Pop reached into a pocket and produced a stunning diamond ring.

"… I have asked her to be my wife." As he slipped the ring onto her finger, Clare burst out:

"You and Jean are getting married? How wonderful!" From the other end of the table, Henry shouted, "Congratulations – to both of you." Others joined in the showering of good wishes on the smiling couple.

"This is exciting," Clare said. "Have you set a date for the wedding?"

Jean replied, "Not exactly. But both of us feel there's really no need for a long engagement. We've gotten to know each other pretty well."

"It will be sometime before the end of the year – just a small private ceremony – maybe in Europe," said Pop. "At any rate, we're going to have a honeymoon in Paris, starting on New Year's Eve."

"Wow! You really do have exciting plans," Clare said. "I would love to dance at your wedding, but you know what's best for you. And I know you'll have a great time."

By this time Henry and Andrew and the other guests had brought their dessert wine around the table to where Pop and Jean were sitting. Henry raised his glass and offered a toast:

"Here's to a remarkable couple. Like a properly aged wine, you are ready to open and enjoy a new experience. May it be the beginning of a long and happy new life together."

With that he gave Jean a tight hug, his father a firm handshake and Clare a surprise kiss, which drew a joyous murmur from the group.

An unidentified female voice (maybe Louise?) was heard saying, "Maybe there's a double wedding in the offing."

Both Henry and Clare responded quickly, saying, "No, no, don't get any ideas." Clare said, "If we're still friends after this political venture I'm engaged in …" Henry finished her sentence, "Well, we'll see how things go."

The guests whiled away the rest of the afternoon chatting among themselves – those who weren't gathered in front of the large TV screen, that is.

Before the gathering started to break up, Pop sought out Clare, who was huddled with Jean and Louise talking about recipes.

"Are you looking for me, Pop?"

"Yes, Clare. I want to remind you about the tennis game we had to postpone the first time you were here. How about tomorrow morning?"

"Well, I don't think there's any rain in the forecast."

"We don't have to play tennis, of course. Maybe you'd prefer pickleball."

"I've heard of that, but never saw a game. I don't know too much about it."

"Well, it originated here in Washington state, as you may know, back in the summer of 1965, on Bainbridge Island in Puget Sound. A state legislator and a couple of his friends made up the game, combining the elements of tennis, badminton and ping pong," Pop explained.

"But why is it called pickleball? Don't tell me you bat a pickle back and forth."

"No," said Henry. "The game uses a small whiffleball."

"Then why not just call it whiffleball?"

"Because of Pickle."

"Was that the state legislator's name?"

"No, it was the dog's name."

"What dog?"

"The one who used to catch the ball in his mouth and run into the bushes with it."

"I'm surprised they ever finished a game."

"The game ends when a team runs up a score of 11 points and is leading by at least two points."

"These guys who thought up this silly game – did they use tennis or badminton rackets to hit the pickleball?"

"Neither one," Pop said. "But they used a badminton net, except they lowered it two inches."

"And they hit it with ping pong paddles?"

"No. The guys got some scraps of plywood from a shed and made paddles that were almost straight across the end."

"Well, I hope the rules aren't as complicated as the invention of the game."

"Not really," Henry said. "The main thing you have to remember is when you get into the 'kitchen.'"

"Wait. The game's not played inside the house, is it?"

"No. "It's played on a shortened tennis or badminton court. The 'kitchen' is a zone seven feet from the net on either side."

"What happens when you get into the 'kitchen'? Do you switch your square paddle for a round frying pan?"

"Inside this zone, you can't play a volley."

186

"Or volleyball either, I suppose."

Pop got a stern look on his face. "You can make fun of pickleball if you like, Clare, but it is a serious sport played in all 50 states. It even has a governing body called the U.S.A. Pickleball Association."

"I almost hesitate to ask," she said, "but is pickleball an Olympic sport?"

"Not yet. But as fast as it's growing across the U.S. and in some foreign countries, who knows?"

"Well, I guess I'll just have to try it, if the invitation still stands. What time?"

"I'm up and around pretty early," Pop said. "Just call me when you're ready and I'll meet you at the court. I'll have all the equipment ready."

"Good. I'll try to remember everything you've taught me."

58

BACK AT THE villa after a four-day break, Clare delighted in filling in Luna on details of the trip – getting acquainted with Henry's grandpa and younger brother, the scrumptious meals topped by the elegant Thanksgiving feast, Pop's surprise announcement about his and Jean's engagement, and almost as exciting, Clare's surprise win in her first pickleball game. She had beaten Pop two out of three and then when Henry and Andrew showed up for a doubles match, she and Pop showed them who was best.

For the remaining days of the year, Clare and Luna laid out a schedule of book signings and other public appearances. Clare also was looking ahead to January and her big decision.

"You still have some doubts about running, don't you?" Luna said.

"Let's say I don't have my mind completely made up," Clare sighed. "It's really a giant undertaking. The odds are so much against me. The fight would be very ugly. Do I actually want the job that bad?"

"But as you've said, it's not just about you."

"That's true. As a result of what we've done so far, I probably have a lot of Californians counting on me. It would be a shame to let them down. I do think I could be a good governor – that I have the ability and determination to get things done. But getting elected is such a big challenge. How do you feel about our resources, our organizational strength, Luna? And be honest with me."

"I have a good feeling – about everything. You've had some very good advice from Hector, Tim and Gene and we've followed through on it with our publicity, our use of the Internet, plus your personal appeal, which counts for a lot."

"Melody has been very helpful, as has Houston."

Luna continued. "The themes that Gene suggested have caught on with the people, I believe. They see you as a different kind of politician – one who will listen, who will understand – and when you talk to them they believe you're telling the truth. That's a rarity in today's politics.

"I have been pleasantly surprised at how far we've come in developing a statewide organization. The responses to your appearances on the tour and our postings in social media have been amazing. There appears to be genuine enthusiasm out there for your candidacy.

"And, as you know, I had some skepticism about Henry being our finance chairman. But I'm happy to say I misjudged the man. He has done a terrific job of raising money for us. He has the right kind of personality, persuasive ability and boundless energy. As a person of wealth himself, he relates well to those who have it to give. It helps that he's loaded with charm, of course. But I don't have to tell you that. And Clare, you know, any negative things I had to say about him earlier were just because I didn't want you to get hurt."

"I know, Luna, and I appreciate that. I do like him very much and I'm pretty sure he feels the same way about me. Both of us have had experiences that make us very reluctant to have a close relationship. And we've been so busy with this political journey I'm on there hasn't been time for that anyway. I guess we'll just have to see what the future will bring. By the way, how's your love life?"

Luna replied sharply. "I'm too busy to have a love life."

"You and Houston spend a lot of time together."

"That's work. You know that."

"He's very good looking."

"Yeah. He has a nice body, too."

"Oh?"

"We went to the beach on Labor Day weekend. He wanted to go surfing."

"He's also pretty smart."

"Very smart. But we're getting off the subject."

Clare paused for a sip of coffee. "Before you go, I want to ask you about something else I've been thinking about. What would you say to the idea of me filing my candidacy by petition?"

"You mean instead of just paying a filing fee?"

"Yes. Not to avoid the fee, of course. But I think it might be a good way to get people involved in the campaign from the very beginning. And it only takes 10,000 signatures. With the kind of organization we have, that shouldn't be too much of a challenge."

"Not if we capitalize on the momentum we've got going after the tour."

"We would have until February 20 – that's the deadline. If we kicked off a drive early in January that would give us at least six weeks."

"It would generate some excitement among our volunteers and surely result in some good publicity. I like the idea. But there is a downside to think about. If we didn't reach our goal of getting enough signatures by the deadline, it would look very bad."

"You're right. I could still run by paying a filing fee by March 7. But I'm really leaning toward going the petition route. I do want to talk to Tim and

Hector before going any further. But I'm glad to know you see all the possibilities."

"Well, you understand that whether you make a race for governor or sit it out is strictly up to you. I will tell you this: if you decide to run I will do everything in my power to make that dream come true. And I believe sincerely that everyone on our team is 100 percent loyal and will give all of their efforts to run a successful campaign."

"I believe you," Clare said. "If I didn't I wouldn't even consider running."

59

WHEN CLARE SPRANG the petition idea on Henry, he had a lot of "devil's advocate" questions, one of them being "what if there's a challenge to signatures or some other roadblock?"

"I'm sure our friend Jack Bull would try something like that. We would just have to be very careful in the collection process to make sure everything is done right," Clare said. "We would need to get more than the number required to allow for the possibility of some of the signatures being thrown out. And if Bull raises a stink, he would just call attention to the 'dark horse' candidate."

"I guess your December calendar is filling up pretty quickly."

"Luna has lined up a number of events connected with the book release, which is scheduled for December 5. Gene says Thursday is the best day of the week for a book launch and he's had plenty of experience. He and Shirley will have books in the stores and available for purchase online early that day. Gene said he will get review copies in the hands of key people at newspapers in time for the weekend editions. He's also making wide distribution of news releases to the papers as well as radio and TV outlets. The primary announcement will be made with my appearance on my former TV program, "Here's Clare", on a local TV station.

"I'll be doing book signings at stores in the greater L.A. area in the days following the launch, and possibly a few in other major markets. It's a blitz campaign to saturate news media for a splash effect, to quote Gene, and to get people talking about me."

"It sounds like you're going to be pretty well occupied for most of the month," Henry said. "I was just wondering if we should plan to do something special over the holidays?"

"There's also my annual Christmas party for children. Gary and I began this event for less fortunate children to make sure they have some happy holiday memories. This year I've invited children from a school for the deaf to come to the villa on the afternoon of Christmas Eve to enjoy refreshments and fun activities, with a visit from Santa Claus, of course."

"That's a big undertaking. You surely don't do all of this yourself!"

"No. I found this small business – 'Elves on Call' – they do everything: decorating inside and outside the house, all the food and drink, games, gifts for everyone. They're wonderful."

"I should say so," said Henry.

"And while the villa is looking so festive, I want to have all of our staff in for an evening of adult partying – something stronger than punch. I'd like to make it an occasion to close out the year on a high note and look ahead to an exciting year of working together."

"With all that going on, it's obvious we won't be able to have any private time," Henry said.

Seeing his downcast look, Clare pulled him close and said, "Maybe we could go dancing on New Year's Eve."

60

WEARING HER CAMPAIGN "costume", Clare set off with Henry for the TV station on the morning of December 9. Luna and Melody were meeting them there, where they were to have a meeting with the producer and the show's host to go over the details of her appearance. They were both complimentary of the book.

The host, Rodney Fairfield, gave a general outline of the interview and they discussed some of the topics it would cover. Clare tried to be calm while sitting for makeup but she was glad when the time came for her to be miked and she was told to wait just off the set while the first segment was completed. Then she heard the host give her introduction.

"My special guest today is Clare Sullivan de Lune. If her face is familiar it might be that you remember her being on this station a few years back with her own show, 'Here's Clare.' She has had a most interesting life and is considering adding an exciting new phase, running for governor. The story of her life up to now is told in a biography being released today, titled 'Clearly I See.' She's here to talk about her new book and possible future plans. And now, 'Here's Clare.'"

With a wave to the studio audience, Clare strode confidently to meet the host, giving him a handshake, and sat down in the guest spot on the couch.

Almost before she knew it, the interview was nearing an end and the host was asking her a final question:

"Before we finish, I want to thank you again for coming," Fairfield said. Holding up the book, he said: "Your book goes on sale today and I believe it will be well received. I know you've said you haven't made a final decision about running for governor, but can you give viewers a hint about what the next chapter in your life might be?"

"Thank you for having me on your show, Rodney. As I've tried to say in my book, life is a series of decisions. At each phase of my life I've tried to see clearly the right decision to make. So far, I feel that my choices have been the best ones. In these times, so many of our decisions are influenced by our governmental leaders. Government affects almost everything we do. For that reason we should strive to have the best government and the best leaders possible.

"Clearly I see, from my recent tour, that Californians are not entirely happy with the present state of affairs. They've told me they see a need for a change in this election year. Having a woman in the governor's chair for the first time would be a historic change. I plan to decide which course I will take early in the new year. I hope I can see clearly whether I am the right woman for the job."

"Thank you again."

As the show went to commercial, Clare shook hands with Rodney Fairfield again and left the set, pausing to have a brief exchange with the producer and the station manager who had come from his office to watch the show.

Henry, Luna and Melody met her with hugs and congratulations on her performance. She noted that Melody had used her phone to take several photos of her on the set, which would go on Facebook and Twitter right away.

"Someone told me that calls from viewers were coming in right after the show was over," Melody said.

"Really?" Clare said. "I hope they were good calls."

"I'm sure they were," said Henry.

61

OVER THE COURSE of the next few days, Clare did a number of book signings in the Los Angeles area. Most of them were in book stores, but she also went to the Santa Barbara public library where she donated a copy of the book and made a few remarks in connection with it.

More signings were scheduled for the following week, along with calls on some newspaper and magazine book editors. She also did a remote interview for a radio talk show and at Gene's suggestion Luna had arranged for an appearance on "In the Kitchen with Ida Clare," a popular cooking show which originated in Los Angeles. When she told Gene about it, he was thrilled. "That's terrific!" he said. "Please have the studio send me a tape."

She wanted to be well prepared for the show so she set aside some time over the weekend to collect her thoughts and look over her recipe collection.

When Monday came around, Clare arrived on the set early to have plenty of time to get acquainted with the hostess and feel comfortable about her appearance.

She was met by the show's personality herself, Ida Clare, a more "down home" Oprah Winfrey, who obviously enjoyed eating as much as cooking.

"Miz de Lune, I'm Ida Clare."

"It's a pleasure to meet you. Please call me Clare."

"That might be a little confusing, but we'll give it a try. I want you to meet the sous chef at my restaurant who is with us today. Clare, this is Sue."

Clare shook hands with the slender brown-skinned woman and said, "Sue – and you're the sous chef?"

"Oui."

"Oh, are you French?"

Ida stepped in to say, "No, she's a Sioux Indian. She learned French when she studied at the Sorbonne and likes to speak it."

"So Sue the sous chef is a Sioux? "

"Si," said Sue. "I also speak Spanish."

"I see."

"Well, Clare, I understand you're going to demonstrate a bit of cooking with wine," Ida said.

"That's what your producer and I talked about, yes. I love California wines and I enjoy using them in my kitchen for certain kinds of foods."

"I do, too. And I look forward very much to your demonstration following our chat. I want to ask you about your campaign for governor."

"I'm still in the exploratory stage but the time's getting close when I'll need to make my intentions known. I've taken certain steps to be in a position to hit the ground running if I take on that challenge. The statewide listening tour I took this fall gave me a sense of what Californians are thinking about the current state of affairs. As you know, I have a book out that lets the people know more about me and some of the concerns I have."

"Yes. 'Clearly I See.' I have a copy right here," Ida said. "We'll be sure to talk about that."

The first segment of the program belonged to Ida. She took the viewers through the steps of making a "Triple Chocolate Layer Cake with Raspberry Filling." When she finished she cut a slice, took a bite, and uttered her trademark comment: "I do declare this is one of the best chocolate cakes I've ever tasted."

Following the commercial break, Ida introduced Clare and joined her on a couch just off the kitchen set. They chatted informally about Clare's life, leading up to the big question:

"Clare, you've aroused quite a bit of interest with your statewide tour and the new book that just came out. I'm sure my viewers want to know: are you going to try to become the first woman governor of California?"

"That's a very big challenge, so I don't take that decision lightly," Clare said. "I have received a great deal of encouragement from my 'Friends of Clare' supporters over the state. And I would like to hear from your viewers. I can say this: If I'm going to do it, I need to get going right away. I will make an announcement early in the new year."

"Well, since I can't get you to declare your intentions here today, let's get into the kitchen," Ida said.

After the break, during which time Clare donned an apron embroidered with "Here's Clare," the cameras were back on and Ida asked what she was going to prepare.

"This is one of my favorite recipes for cooking with wine. It originally was called the 'Lazy Oven Dinner' – but I don't think the word 'lazy' belongs in a busy woman's kitchen, so I renamed it 'Easy Oven Dinner'—'easy' being a relative term.

"We begin with a three-to-four-pound chuck roast," she said, as the recipe appeared on screen. "Turn on the oven broiler. Place the roast on a large piece of foil in a shallow baking pan and brown it on both sides under the broiler. Turn off the broiler and set the oven to 325 degrees.

"Then you take it out of the oven and top the meat with the celery, carrots and garlic, all finely chopped. Season with salt and pepper. Now, bring up the sides of the foil to form a kind of a bowl. Pour in one cup of California red wine and fold the foil tightly around the meat."

As Clare placed the pan in the oven, she said, "Set the timer for one-and-a-half hours. At that point, partially unwrap the foil and add half a cup of wine, rewrap and bake for another 30 minutes. Check for doneness and allow the meat to set while you use the wine and meat juices to make a very tasty gravy.

"Add a side dish of potatoes or corn and a green salad and you've got a hearty meal."

"That sounds absolutely wonderful," Ida said. "And, as you said, so easy. And what kind of wine would you serve with it?"

"A cabernet sauvignon or pinot noir would be fine – from California, of course."

"Of course! Thank you for being a guest in my kitchen today, Clare." And to the camera, holding her book, "And don't forget to pick up a copy of 'Clearly I See.'

"Until our next show, this is Ida Clare saying, I do declare I love good food. Bye, now."

Clare thanked her big friendly hostess and the show's producer and left the studio with Luna.

"What do you think, Luna?"

"I think you scored some points with a very important audience."

62

ONLY A FEW events were on Clare's calendar for the rest of December, so she did have some time to concentrate on her big annual party.

Villa de Lune had undergone a magical transformation by Christmas Eve. "Elves on Call" had turned the grounds and the rooms inside into a glittering holiday fairyland. The shrubbery on the lawn was festooned with colorful lights along with tasteful displays of snowmen and reindeer. A giant lighted wreath on the front door beamed a welcome to all comers.

"Kissing balls" of boxwood and mistletoe hung from chandeliers and doorway arches. Fireplace mantels were adorned with elaborate arrangements of holiday greenery. Large potted poinsettias sat in key locations throughout the house.

The elves, with Clare's permission, had moved the de Lunus bust to her bedroom and a colorful runner stretched the length of the bar. A 10-foot tall Christmas tree, decorated from top to bottom with ornaments, lights and tinsel, stood in the middle of the great room. The twinkling lights were reflected in the large gold-rimmed mirror over the fireplace at one side of the room.

A large punchbowl and cups, surrounded with heaping plates of cookies and other delicious goodies, occupied the center of the dining room table. At each end were trays of mini-sandwiches with snack plates and napkins.

Clare surveyed the work of the elves and pronounced it "superb." "The children will love it," she told the chief elf. "Santa will make an appearance at 4 p.m.," he said.

"A fine job all around," Clare said. "Thank you."

The bus from the school for the deaf arrived shortly before 2 p.m. and off-loaded its 30 passengers at the front door. Clare, looking very festive in a red velvet dress, welcomed each child with a signed greeting and a hug. Boy and girl elves, wearing their green elf caps, showed the children the way into the villa and they looked in awe at the beautiful sights they beheld.

Some of the children wandered back and forth between the dining room and the great room while others sat on the floor on front of the large screen and watched cartoons and other holiday movies.

Clare and Maria, who had come to help out if needed, were talking in the kitchen when the school director came up and thanked the hostess profusely for the party. "You are so kind and generous to do this," she said. "It means so much to the children."

Santa Claus made his entrance not by way of a chimney but bounding down the stairs with hearty "ho, ho, ho's" and a happy smile for the excited children. They gathered around him as he set his huge bag on the floor and began reaching inside and pulling out gifts. When every child had received a small package, he signed "Merry Christmas" and left by way of the front door.

A few of the children opened their gifts but most of them clutched them tightly and awaited their return home to enjoy their surprises. Clare signed "I love you" and "goodbye" to each child as they departed and she stood outside waving as the bus pulled away.

"You need to sit down," Maria said. "May I bring you some punch?"

"I think I'd rather have a cup of tea," she replied.

Relaxing in front of the fireplace as a small crew of elves picked up after the children and cleared the table, Clare felt a deep sense of satisfaction and well-being, as she had done each year she had hosted the event. She considered taking a nap before the campaign team arrived, but the tea revived her and instead she changed into sweats and took a walk around the grounds.

When she came inside she observed the elves had reset the dining room table with a bright tablecloth, two large candelabra and place settings. A special bar had been set up in the great room, large enough to accommodate the crowd. An elf who would serve as bartender for the evening was busy checking on supplies of wine and spirits.

Clare donned a pair of tan slacks and a blouse with a holly and ivy print and poured herself a glass of sparkling wine from the bottle she had brought from the downstairs wine cellar. She reclined on her chaise lounge and idly thumbed through a popular news magazine. Her eye caught a headline reading "Bull Run Expected." She put down her wine and scanned the story.

> U.S. Rep. John K. Bull is expected to announce his candidacy for governor shortly after the first of the year. In response to widely-circulated reports that he will make the race, he said: "I have been giving considerable thought to running. I plan to make an official announcement early in January."
>
> Bull aroused speculation this fall when he began making public appearances in parts of the state outside his district. He conceded he was "testing the water" to determine whether to give up his congressional seat and seek the office currently held by Gov. Jerry Brown.
>
> The 58-year-old Democrat was elected to Congress after being defeated for reelection to the California state senate by well-known racing enthusiast Gary de Lune, who was killed in a highway accident ...

Clare put down the magazine, had a sip of wine and said to herself: "And so it begins."

At the sound of the door chimes, she went downstairs to meet the first of her guests to arrive. She was delighted to see Gene and Shirley McQueen, who had flown down from Seattle for the party and campaign update.

"I'm so glad you could come," Clare said.

"The villa is shining in all its glory!" exclaimed Shirley.

"How's the new author?" asked Gene. "I thought the book received some good reviews."

"I haven't quite gotten used to it yet," Clare said. "Sitting in a book store and signing books is a new experience for me."

"It's kind of exciting, though, isn't it?" said Shirley.

"Oh, yes. And the turnout has been very rewarding. Thank you both again for all your help in producing the book."

"Is all of the team gathering here this evening?" Gene asked.

"I believe everyone is coming but Tim Barnham. He is visiting relatives back in Oklahoma."

"What about Henry's father and his friend Jean? I enjoyed meeting them at our last group meeting."

Clare told them the news about their engagement and plans to go to Paris for New Year's Eve, and they were happy to hear it.

The others had all arrived by cocktail time and the rooms were abuzz with conversations as they admired the decorations and expressed their excitement about a forthcoming campaign.

When it was time for dinner everyone took places at the dining room table with Clare sitting at one end and Luna at the other. The casual talk continued as the various courses were served and as the happy diners were finishing dessert, Clare said:

"I know this evening is a time to be lighthearted as we celebrate the joy of the holiday season. But as we look ahead to the new year, I would like to take a few moments to share some of my thoughts with you and, as always, get your responses.

"First, I don't imagine there's any doubt in your minds that I'm on a course to run for governor. A rather large field of candidates is developing so I believe it's important that our campaign be distinctively different. One way I see to do that from the start is to pass up the standard procedure of becoming a candidate by filling out some papers and paying a fee. Instead I want to know what you think about filing by petition." (This idea prompted some visible reaction.)

"We would need to gather 10,000 signatures by February 20 – more than that to be on the safe side. I believe our statewide organization of volunteers is up to the task. It would be a means of activating them right away and it would certainly draw attention."

Gene quickly spoke up. "I think it's an excellent idea. A petition drive would provide the right kind of dynamism to propel the campaign into motion. It should build momentum for the long haul that can carry you to victory."

"I appreciate your enthusiasm, Gene," Clare said, "but I want to caution everyone that we can't afford to get overconfident. We'll have to work hard every day to overcome the heavy odds.

"Get back to me on this right away, if you will, because I'd like to make an announcement early in the year.

"Now, another thing I want your guidance on is this: When I officially become a candidate, should I opt not to do it by party affiliation? (A murmur around the table greeted this surprising statement.)

"The June 3 primary is non-partisan. As an underdog candidate I would need to appeal to as many voters as I can. It's a given certainty that I am not going to have the backing of the state Democratic party. I don't want to abandon my principles, but I see nothing to gain by putting that 'D' beside my name on the ballot.

"I don't expect any reaction to this today. But please give it some thought and help me see the pro's and con's.

"Along this same line, how do you feel about labor unions? I know they are a potent political force in California. But here again, I would not expect the unions to be aligned with a longshot candidate like me. And it would free me up to be critical of, say, the teachers union if I so choose."

Clare could detect some looks of disbelief on some of the faces, not to her surprise.

"Moving ahead to a matter that is likely to come up once the campaign gets going. I would like to set a policy ahead of time on whether to participate in debates. I'm inclined not to do so unless all serious candidates agreed to it. I don't think that's likely to happen. I'm sure Congressman Bull probably will challenge me to a debate, but I just think it would be a waste of valuable time to get into a public slug match with him. By the way, I just read that he plans to announce early in the new year."

"Yeah, I saw him on ABN," Luna said.

"ABN?"

"The All Blonde Network."

"Oh, Fox News," Clare said.

Various members of the team gave indications they agreed with Clare it would be best not to engage in debates unless they were structured to give voters an opportunity to know the views of all those seeking the office of governor.

"Finally – and I think we can all agree on this – I want to run a clean campaign. From the dirty tricks we've already seen – most likely from Jack Bull's camp – there are bound to be more once the campaign gets under way. In my announcement I would like to put him and any other opponent on notice that I and my team will not involve ourselves in that kind of activity."

The response was unanimous. "Hear, hear." "Right." "You bet." Gene could hardly contain himself.

"It would be part of a great campaign slogan," he said. "Clear Vision, Clean Campaign, Clare."

"That has real possibilities, Gene. Thanks," Clare said.

From his position at the opposite end of the table, Hector said, "You've given us all a lot to think about, Clare. Thank you for a wonderful meal, a beautiful evening and most importantly, for giving us your thoughts about this exciting venture that lies ahead."

The others took Hector's cue and had their last sips of wine and said their goodnights. Henry lingered behind, as Clare hoped he would.

"I'm glad you stayed," she said. "I have a little something for you."

"May I go first?" he said. Reaching into his pocket he produced a small gift-wrapped package.

"Oh, what is this?"

"Open it and see."

Clare removed the wrapping and found a box from one of L.A.'s finest jewelers. She raised the lid and her eyes lit up at the sight of a stunning necklace – a large blue star sapphire encircled with diamonds on a gold chain.

"Oh, my darling!" she said.

"Do you like it?"

"I love it!" She drew him close with her free arm and kissed him, whispering, "And I love you."

"Merry Christmas, sweetheart."

"Have some cognac. I'll be right back," she said.

He poured two glasses and took them to a love seat by the fire.

She returned with a package bearing a small card which read, "For Henry, with love. Clare."

He unwrapped it and smiled broadly, holding up a lifelike portrait in a gold frame.

"This is so you will remember what I look like when we're apart," she said.

"I don't need a reminder – I see you in my dreams every night," he said. "But this will have a special place in my bedroom." He kissed her warmly. "You will always have a special place in my heart."

They drank a toast to "things to come" and stared into the dying embers, arm in arm.

"You don't really need to go back into town tonight, do you?" Clare said, softly.

"Not if you want me to stay."

63

THE FOLLOWING WEEK passed by rather quickly. Clare had emails and phone calls from various members of her team with comments about her list of Christmas Eve topics. Gene had no objection to any of her ideas. He could envision some fantastic promotional opportunities.

Hector thought she shouldn't take a hard line with the unions. "If you feel strongly about some of the positions taken by leaders of certain organizations, you can disagree without being disagreeable, as the old saying goes. But picking a fight unnecessarily would distract too much from your mission. And besides, you might get some support from some of the unions, like the fire and police, for example."

"I do value your advice," Clare said. "And as you probably know, Luna agrees with you."

Henry arrived to pick up Clare for their New Year's Eve date in time to have a drink before heading to the Beverly Hills Country Club. The private club tucked away in Cheviot Hills on the west side of Los Angeles was Clare's suggestion. She told Henry that Gary had been a member and she kept the membership because it was a good place to play tennis, and she also used the fitness center occasionally.

The club had scheduled a New Year's Eve party with a lavish buffet, dancing and a midnight champagne toast. Henry was thrilled, naturally. He was virtually overcome with pleasure at seeing his companion for the special evening wearing a perfectly fitted crimson evening gown, set off by the star sapphire necklace he had given her.

"I took the liberty of mixing a pitcher of martinis," she said. "I hope they are to your liking."

"Anything you do is to my liking," he said.

"Careful, you may regret those words some day."

"I can't imagine that day will ever come."

She poured their martinis and they drank to the exciting evening that awaited them.

It turned out to be a perfect date – from the food to the music and dancing to the midnight kiss.

Clare was reluctant to return to the world of reality but she had a campaign to launch. Tim Barnham, the seasoned pol, had taught her there were three steps in announcing your candidacy:

1. Announce that you are going to announce.
2. Announce.
3. Announce that you have announced.

She had scheduled a news conference for the following Friday and members of the local "Friends of Clare" group had been invited to the event at the committee headquarters. A large sign reading, "Clear Vision, Clean Campaign, Clare for Governor" formed a backdrop for the big announcement.

As expected, there was a large turnout of newspaper, TV and radio news correspondents. They busily got cameras and microphones set up and took their places as the audience of volunteers buzzed excitedly. Melody gave the press a two-minute warning and at precisely nine a.m. the woman of the hour walked to the podium and said:

"I am Clare Sullivan de Lune and I intend to be a candidate for governor in this year's election."

A loud cheer went up from the crowd followed by prolonged applause and shouts of "Clare! Clare! Clare! ..."

"In my recent travels to cities and towns, large and small, listening to Californians from one end of the state to the other, one message has come through loud and clear: the people want new leadership. They're not happy with the way the state is being run. They feel that elected officials are more interested in keeping their jobs than doing their job. The poor economy has taken its toll on virtually every household. Too many people are out of work. Those who are working are insecure about their future. Business owners feel threatened by government encroachment on their operations. City officials see thousands of residents moving to other parts of the country, weakening the revenue base and in far too many instances causing bankruptcy. Parents are concerned about the kind of education their children are receiving. Families face each day with anxiety about getting necessary health care and being able to pay for it. Everybody who drives a car or uses power to heat and light their homes, cook their meals, run their appliances, or provide them with information and entertainment in their non-working hours can't help but worry about sources of energy and its rising costs. Those of us who marvel at the beauty of our state are pained at the loss of our natural resources through nature's fury and thoughtless neglect.

"Is it any wonder that the thought that goes through people's minds is: Does anybody in the state capitol care?

"During my time in the state senate I have seen many of these problems. And I have tried, in my small way, to take corrective action through remedial legislation. But a legislative body is like a bunch of cats and dogs tied up in a bag – fighting amongst themselves, making a lot of noise, but accomplishing little. That is one reason I have decided not to seek reelection to the state senate when my current term is finished. That does not mean that my career of public service is ended, however.

"I believe I still have something to contribute. And I believe my place is in the executive branch. I know there are those who will say, 'a woman's place is in the home.' I disagree. I believe this woman's place is in the governor's office."

The largely-female audience erupted in a roar of cheers and applause, followed again by the chant of: "Clare! Clare! Clare! …"

"I intend to be a candidate in the June 3 primary for the office of governor. But I am not going to follow the standard procedure of filling out some papers and paying a filing fee. I want to involve the people in the process. So I am going to take the option of filing by petition.

"That means those of you here, and others who may be listening on the radio or otherwise learn of my decision, may participate in a petition drive that is being launched today. Any registered voter may sign the petition. Local volunteer groups that have been established in counties over the state will have circulators collecting signatures.

"We will have complete information on our website as well as in our state and county headquarters. We'll also have a helpline to provide answers to questions voters might have.

"Beginning today I will be actively seeking the support of all Californians in this difficult race. The June 3 primary was established by law as a nonpartisan election and I am not running as a partisan. A governor is elected to serve all of the people and therefore I will not base my campaign on appealing to members of any specific political party or any special interest.

"I believe strongly in the principle of fairness. As a candidate I will follow the rules of fair play, and I will take those practices into the governor's office.

"I know that some other candidates might engage in dirty tricks during the course of the campaign. We've already seen evidence of that in the discovery that the bus we used in my statewide tour had been bugged. Forces obviously hoping to sabotage my campaign before it got off the ground secretly planted a hidden microphone in an area of the bus where they could listen in on discussions that I had with members of my team about our plans and strategies. The crime is under investigation.

"I pledge today that I will conduct a clean campaign. Insofar as it is possible, it will be an open campaign. But reporters covering our campaign should know that a winning team doesn't give away its plays ahead of the game. We will be alert for any shenanigans by other opponents, and at the same time police our own troops. If anyone working on my behalf is caught doing something underhanded, that person will be out the door immediately.

"I enter this race with confidence that I can win, tempered by the reality that it will be an uphill battle. I cannot fight this fight alone. I must have help from voters who believe as I do – that California is a great state, but it can be better. Just give me a chance to prove it."

Again the room shook with the crowd's reaction – a combination of cheers, applause, the stomping of feet and the persistent chant: "We want Clare! We want Clare! We want Clare! …"

She allowed the demonstration to continue for a minute or two, then silenced the hubbub and recognized one of the many reporters shouting questions.

"You are a registered Democrat. Are you turning your back on your party?"

"I'm not turning my back on anyone," Clare answered. "I was raised a Democrat and I am not abandoning those principles. But this is a different kind of election, and I think a candidate has to acknowledge that fact and adapt to the change. Laurie?"

"Are you saying that you promise to fire anyone, even a top member of your staff, if they violate your standards for a clean campaign?"

Looking toward her campaign manager, Clare said, "I think Luna knows better than to do anything like that." That answer drew laughter. "Seriously, I can make tough decisions if necessary. My colleagues in the state senate would tell you that when I get my Irish up, I can lower the boom. You, in the shadows …"

"Congressman Bull already has taken some potshots at you. Do you view him as your worst enemy?"

"Ha, ha, ha … Jack has had me in the crosshairs for quite some time. But instead of tossing spitballs from the sideline I think it's time he suited up and got into the game. He has let it be known that he would do anything he can to keep me from being elected governor. Well, I dare him to come out in the open and declare himself to be a candidate – then let the people be the judge."

With another burst of applause, Clare waved to the audience and walked offstage leaving reporters still trying to get her attention.

"Nice lick at Bull," Luna said. Clare responded, "Well, we know he's on the verge of announcing, so why not get the jump on him?"

They found a corner where they could talk briefly about the petition drive. "Houston has gathered some information," Luna said. "We have to be sure and strictly follow the rules. Anyone signing a petition has to print and sign their name and give the address where they are registered to vote. That has to be verified by an election official. They also have to give the name of the county where they are registered and state that they are not a signer of a petition for any other candidate.

"Petition circulators have to give their residence address, the period during which they obtained signatures, and sign an affidavit swearing they are 18 years of age or older, and that they witnessed the signing of the petition."

"I couldn't agree more about adhering to the law. There will be challenges anyway, but we need to keep the petitions as clean as possible," Clare said. "I have faith that our volunteers will do the best they can, but we have to make sure they know exactly what has to be done."

"I can hardly wait to see and hear the news reports on your announcement!" said Luna, giving Clare a hug.

64

CLARE AROSE EARLY and took a jog around the neighborhood. Through her ear buds she listened to a smattering of radio newscasts – generally only one or two sentences about overnight happenings. Her heart jumped a beat when she heard this sensational report:

"On the political front, Gov. Jerry Brown has drawn a dynamic new challenger for this year's election. A fiery redhead from Santa Barbara County named Clare Sullivan de Lune has launched a petition drive to get her name on the ballot for the June 3 primary. In other news ..."

Other clips were similar. A morning drive show featuring two wisecracking hosts, Mick and Mack, devoted a little more time to Clare's announcement.

Mick: "Here's something hot off the wire. A woman is running for governor."

Mack: "The same one who ran last time?"

Mick: "No. I think she decided she didn't want the job bad enough to spend another 150 million bucks."

Mack: (low whistle). "Well, I might be able to give her a small loan."

Mick: "Not interested. But this candidate – her name is Clare something – she's not living in the poorhouse."

Mack: "Is that right?"

Mick: "This story describes her as the wealthy widow of racing enthusiast Gary de Lune."

Mack: "Hey, I remember him. I think he was on our show one time."

Mick: "Yeah, well, maybe we can get Clare to come on sometime during the campaign."

"Fat chance," she muttered, turning the dial. She slowed her pace as she heard an all-too-familiar voice saying:

"So Miz de Lune is crying about someone taking potshots at her. Maybe she's too thin-skinned to compete in the big leagues."

"So, Congressman Bull, are you saying that a woman has no business running for a major office?"

"Certainly not. California has two outstanding women serving in the U.S. Senate: Dianne Feinstein and Barbara Boxer – both Democrats, by the way. Miz de Lune doesn't seem to know what she is."

"Are you going to take her dare and get into the governor's race?"

"Let me just say that Miz de Lune will be strongly opposed if she insists on this foolish pursuit of an office for which she is totally unqualified and has no chance of winning."

Having jogged back into the vicinity of the villa, Clare switched to music to bring her blood pressure down. After a quick shower she threw on some jeans and a light sweater and began to scan the news stories on her tablet while she had her coffee. She was interrupted by a call on her cell phone from Henry. He was on his way to see her.

"I picked up some of the papers and thought you might like to see the coverage you got from your announcement."

"Fine. I'll be anxious to see them – and you," she said.

They sat in the great room with the newspapers spread on the coffee table. The AP story by Sam Mahoney was pretty straightforward:

> State Sen. Clare Sullivan de Lune ended speculation about a run for governor by announcing Friday that she intends to be a candidate in this year's elections.
>
> In a news conference at the state headquarters of "Friends of Clare", the exploratory committee she formed last year, Sen. de Lune said she decided to enter the race based on what she learned from a statewide tour last fall.
>
> "In my recent travels to cities and towns large and small listening to Californians from one end of the state to the other, one message has come through loud and clear: the people want new leadership," she said. "They're not happy with the way the state is being run."
>
> The Santa Barbara County legislator's remarks focused on problems affecting voters. She neglected to state her positions on various issues. She said afterward she will set forth several proposals as the campaign moves forward.
>
> A sampling of her views are outlined in a biographical book just released titled, "Clearly I See."
>
> She said she had seen many of the state's problems since being elected to the state senate in a special election to succeed her late husband, Gary de Lune, who was killed in a highway accident in 2011.
>
> "I have tried, in my small way, to take corrective action through remedial legislation," she said. "But a legislative body is like a bunch of cats and dogs tied up in a bag – fighting amongst themselves, making a lot of noise, but accomplishing little."
>
> She gave that frustration as one reason for deciding not to seek reelection to the senate when her current term is over. She added:
>
> "I believe I still have something to contribute. And I believe my place is in the executive branch. I know there are those who will say, 'a

woman's place is in the home.' I disagree. I believe this woman's place is in the governor's office."

If she were to be one of the two candidates with the most votes in the June 3 primary and go on to win the general election in November, de Lune would become California's first woman governor.

Her announcement contained one surprise. She said she would not follow the standard procedure of becoming a candidate but would take the option of filing by petition. Her organization has launched a drive to collect at least 10,000 signatures by February 20 as state election laws require. Candidates may also enter the race by paying a filing fee by a March 7 deadline.

While de Lune delayed stating her positions on issues, she made her views clear about the conduct of her campaign.

"As a candidate I will follow the rules of fair play, and I will take those practices into the governor's office," she said. She pledged to conduct a "clean campaign", repeating charges of "dirty tricks" she made last fall when she said a hidden microphone had been planted on her tour bus.

She said that in the nonpartisan open primary she would not be running as a partisan, which prompted a reporter to ask if she was turning her back on her party. Her answer:

"I was raised a Democrat and I am not abandoning those principles. But this is a different kind of election, and I think a candidate has to acknowledge that fact and adapt to the change."

Another question referred to criticism by U.S. Rep. John K. Bull. She laughed and said, 'instead of tossing spitballs from the sideline I think it's time he suited up and got into the game." She dared him "to come out in the open and declare himself to be a candidate – then let the people be the judge." Bull had no immediate response.

Henry said, "That one's not half bad."

"Sam knows me better than any other reporter. He's always been very fair in his articles."

"Let's see how the tabloids handled it. Here's one:"

There's a new face in the governor's race. Clare Sullivan de Lune, a fiery redhead from Santa Barbara County, has declared war on the state of state government and goes marching off to battle Gov. Jerry Brown and anyone else who might seek his job.

Exploding on the political scene like a firebomb, the combative state senator appeared ready to put on the gloves with any opponent and threatened to fire anyone caught playing dirty tricks in her campaign. 'Whenever I get my Irish up, I can lower the boom,' she said.

The would-be first woman governor dared congressman Jack Bull, a chronic critic, to get into the ring as a candidate ...

"A bit sensational, I'd say," said Henry.

"Ugh!"

"What about that woman reporter who's been following you around?"

"Laurie Miller. I think I saw ... yes, here it is:"

"Call me Clare," the youthful, bright-eyed woman says with a smile and an outstretched hand, as she asks Californians to tell her what's right and what's wrong with state government.

She got an ear full as she traveled the state from north to south last fall on a listening tour to help her decide whether to take on the biggest challenge of her life: running for governor of California.

What she heard was enough to persuade Clare Sullivan de Lune to announce Friday that she intends to be a candidate in this year's election.

She said that during her travels, "one message has come through loud and clear: the people want new leadership. They're not happy with the way the state is being run."

To get her campaign off to a lively start, Clare launched a statewide drive to collect enough signatures to file by petition as a candidate for governor. She could have just paid a filing fee, but she felt going after this prize deserved a more exciting beginning.

Clare has been setting the stage for this announcement for several months – ever since she formed an exploratory committee and began raising money for this enormously expensive race.

In one of several appearances with various groups last year, she told members of the Southern California Art Teachers Association that education "will certainly continue to be a major interest of mine in whatever public role I choose to take." She had been invited to speak not only because of her work as a state senator on legislation considered by the Senate Education Committee but also for her accomplishments as a sculptor before she met and married the well-known racing enthusiast Gary de Lune. She succeeded him in the Senate after he was killed when his car collided with a semi-trailer truck on the way home from a late session in Sacramento.

At a luncheon for a firefighters union group, Clare said: "As long as I am in public service I will fight for those who risk their personal safety to protect the lives and property of our citizens. I will champion your causes and my door will always be open to you."

To find out what is on the minds of Californians, Clare made visits to localities from San Francisco to San Diego and many places in between. During her tour it was discovered that her bus had been bugged. The hidden microphone was turned over to authorities.

She pledged to conduct a clean campaign and would not tolerate any "dirty tricks" by anyone working in her behalf. Asked if she would fire even a top member of her staff if they violated her standards, the auburn-haired candidate replied: "My colleagues in the state senate would tell you that when I get my Irish up, I can lower the boom."

For those who may not be aware of the change, Clare pointed out that the June 3 primary is nonpartisan and that although she is not abandoning her principles as a registered Democrat she will not run a partisan campaign. "A governor is elected to serve all of the people and therefore I will not base my campaign on appealing to members of any specific political party or any special interest," she said.

Anyone wishing to volunteer to help in her campaign may do so at any of her county headquarters or on her website.

Henry shook his head. "From reading that article, I would say you have really won her over."

"It is a very favorable piece. I want to make sure Gene sees it."

"All in all, I think you should be quite pleased with the coverage."

"It's the best a public official could expect, I suppose."

"I have some other news that should make you happy," Henry said.

"What's that?"

"Since you made it official that you're running, we've received an outpouring of financial support – from those following through on pledges and many making new pledges."

"That's terrific! I can't thank you enough for being my chief fundraiser."

"I'm happy to do what I can to help you reach your goal."

"How about I take you to lunch?"

"Well, that would be nice."

"I'm speaking at a luncheon of small business owners in Ventura and I'd like to bring you along."

"Oh. I was thinking of some dimly lit café. But I would be delighted to accompany you, if I've got time to go change."

"Sure it's only about a half-hour drive."

"I won't be long. Bye."

Finishing her coffee Clare decided she should give some thought to what she would wear. On the way to her bedroom, Luna called.

"I think we got generally good coverage from your announcement. And I thought you might like to know that the petition drive seems to be pretty well received by our troops. The county leaders I've talked to are all very enthusiastic."

"That's good to hear."

"I did learn something we need to be aware of, and that is there are a couple of other petition drives under way that will compete for voters' attention. The Green Party is circulating a petition for a slate of candidates, and Cindy Sheehan also is gathering signatures for a run for governor."

"Then we'll have to impress on our circulators to make sure our signers haven't already put their names on another petition."

"Right."

"By the way, Henry was here and told me more money is coming in since I made my candidacy official."

"That's very good news. Thanks."

"Well, I'm getting ready to go to my Ventura luncheon. Talk to you later."

"Okay."

Clare and Henry arrived shortly before noon at the Crowne Plaza Ventura Beach hotel where the luncheon was being held. It is the only hotel in Ventura located directly on the beach and has marvelous views, especially the panorama from the Top of the Harbor Ballroom on the top floor. This also serves as a meeting room for groups like the small business owners.

Following a buffet lunch, John Crofton, who was presiding, gave Clare a brief introduction.

"When we invited today's speaker to meet with us, she was exploring the possibility of running for governor this year. As of yesterday her exploration is over and she now is a declared candidate. Most of us are familiar with her record as a state senator. She will continue to hold that title until her term expires, but Clare Sullivan de Lune has decided to drop that formality and says, 'Call me Clare.' So now, ladies and gentlemen, here's Clare."

"Thank you, John, and (turning to audience) thank you for that warm welcome. I'm always happy to come to Ventura and I'm glad to have this opportunity to be with you today.

"From some of my past experiences and from more recent visits with entrepreneurs in various parts of the state, I believe I have a pretty fair understanding of some of the conditions you face in your businesses these days.

"Before I got married – to that exceptional man and hard-working legislator, Gary de Lune – I had a small business of sorts. I had launched a career as a sculptor and I engaged in selling my works at art shows and other places. I know my sole proprietorship doesn't compare with your businesses in size and scope, but like you I had to follow certain standards and wrestle with taxes and home business requirements. So I know a little about some of the frustrations you feel.

"One thing I do know for sure. I firmly believe that government exists to help people, not make their lives more difficult. And I will carry that belief to the governor's office if the people choose to elect me."

That statement triggered the first of many rounds of applause. Clare ticked off things she had learned on the state tour, mentioning conversations she had with the owners of the packaging plant, the bridal gown business and the chow-chow distributor. She also touched on some bills she had sponsored in the state senate and criticized some regulations she thought were unfair.

Before summing up and inviting questions, she said: "Before I close I want to introduce a California business owner who came with me today. He is Henry Jackson of the Mt. Jackson Vineyards in the state of Washington, which also owns the Chateau Lapierre winery not far from here."

Henry stood and acknowledged the applause.

"He's also the finance chairman for my campaign, so if you feel inclined to make a contribution before you leave, he'll be glad to accommodate you. Now, what's on your minds. Ask away."

On the drive back to the villa, Clare said, "Some of those questions indicated some genuine concern about the impact of the Affordable Care Act on their businesses."

"And with good reason," Henry said.

"It's a very volatile issue and I want to be careful about what I say about it."

"Even partisan Democrats are critical about the implementation of the law."

"That's true. I need to have a session with Hector on this."

65

THE PHONE RANG early at the villa. It was Luna calling to say she had received a tip from Laurie Miller that Jack Bull was going to announce today.

"I thought he was in Washington. He's surely not going to do it there," Clare said.

"No. He just went up for the opening session of Congress, then turned around and flew right back."

"All at taxpayers' expense, of course"

"Of course."

"What time is this big hot air blast happening?"

"He's having a news conference at 9 o'clock. Do you want to come to the headquarters and watch it here?"

"I'd rather not have to bare my emotions in front of our volunteers. I'll go to Henry's place and see it there. You can tell the press that I'll be available at the headquarters for a statement after Bull's announcement."

"That soon? Hadn't you rather wait till tomorrow?"

"No, I want my comments to be in the same news story with his."

She quickly called Henry and alerted him. Then, in between gulps of coffee, she got dressed and headed for Santa Barbara.

It was the first time she had seen Henry's penthouse apartment that Luna had located for him. Like a typical male, he had little furniture, which made the 2,000 square feet of space look even emptier. He had a big screen TV, naturally, and that was all that mattered this day.

The opening scenes for Bull's big splash were of the Honorable John K. Bull cutting a ribbon to open his new campaign headquarters.

"I understand ribbon-cutting is one of the first things they teach in the orientation for new members of Congress," Clare said.

"He learned well, it appears," Henry observed.

"Okay, let's listen." Bull, his paunch preceding him, marched to the platform and to the cheers of his paid campaign workers began his remarks:

"My fellow Californians. I have had the high privilege and the distinct honor …"

Clare interjected: "Come on, Bull, you're not introducing the president at the joint session."

216

"… of representing you in the Congress of the United States for the past five years."

"Gary replaced him in the state senate in 2004 and then he feathered his nest as a lobbyist before the state legislature a few years before getting elected to Congress," Clare said.

Bull took the next several minutes boasting about all the bills he introduced – not a single one of them becoming law – and all the great constituent service his office had provided to Californians. Then he said dramatically:

"But the time has come for me to return to the state I love and continue my public service on the state level.

"My friends, far and wide, I am pleased to announce that I will be a candidate for governor of California."

The crowd responded as they had been instructed to do. Then he launched into a longwinded speech in which he praised his fellow Democrat, Jerry Brown, for "his outstanding record" but adding that it might be time for him to take a rest. And therefore he was offering himself as a qualified successor.

"Do you have a barf bag handy?" Clare asked, jokingly.

Next, rather than list his purported qualifications, he tore into Clare.

"On the assumption that my friend Jerry might not run, some Republicans have the audacity to believe that this year is an opportunity for them to retake the office of governor. (Loud chorus of no's from the audience.) They're wrong, of course. But the most dangerous thing is the threat of a split in the Democratic party ranks. An upstart freshman state senator, J. C. de Lune, is foolishly seeking to fill the seat of our distinguished governor and she's running with no party label. But regardless of that curious decision, the best choice for voters is: Anyone but de Lune!" (Cheers on cue.)

"Thanks for mentioning my name, Jack. But it's Clare, get it?"

"Sen. de Lune is running strictly on the name of her late husband, Gary de Lune, who was well known to Californians. He was a distinguished citizen of our state until he decided to dabble in politics and capitalized on his fame to get elected to the state senate. His wife, who succeeded him, is no more qualified than he was to represent the people of California. They need someone with experience, like me, to fight their battles. (The audience obediently responded to the unseen applause sign.) Congressman Bull removed his jacket, loosened his tie and took a long drink of water from the bottle left for his convenience.

"For one thing, Sen. de Lune is not a native Californian, as I am. She can't possibly know the state as well as I do or hold the same principles as other Californians. (Applause.)

"Miz de Lune lives a ritzy life in her oceanside villa where she has servants waiting on her night and day. I'm surprised she would want to give that up for the hard job of being governor. The office of governor does carry with it a lot of power. It makes you wonder if she has some kind of hidden motive.

"Servants? Is he kidding?" Clare exclaimed.

"When she announced, Sen. de Lune reeled off a whole long list of things that she says people have complained to her about. She made the great state of California sound like a Third World country. And she didn't say what she would do about any of these so-called terrible conditions. (Applause.)

"She didn't give her positions on any issues. That's incredible. The people have a right to know what she stands for – if she stands for anything. (Applause.)

"One more thing. Miz de Lune threw out some wild charges about some kind of cloak-and-dagger plot to eavesdrop on conversations she had with her stepdaughter, who is on the payroll as her campaign manager. I'm sure their chatter must be fascinating, if you're interested in listening to two women exchanging recipes or talking about the best places to shop for shoes. (Some audible moans from women reporters.)

"Ha, ha. Just kidding, girls. In conclusion I just want to tell my fellow Californians that I will run an aggressive but fair campaign and if the voters choose to send me to the governor's office I will perform the job to the best of my ability, in the same manner that has characterized my life's career in public service."

Clare couldn't contain herself. "I think I'm going to throw up," she said. "That fool! After all those outrageous things he said about me to run me down, then he got carried away and insulted women in general! What an idiot!"

"But he's been able to fool the people into voting for him year after year," Henry said. "I don't think we can rest easy."

"I guess you're right. I can't afford to turn my back on a snake like Jack Bull."

"Now cool off and decide what you're going to say to the press."

"I pretty well know, but I'll make a few notes. By the way, where's your bathroom?"

"There's one down the hall, between the two bedrooms."

"You have two bedrooms?"

"Yes."

"Not that it matters," she said over her shoulder, with a wink.

When they arrived at the headquarters, reporters were already beginning to gather. Laurie came up to meet her.

"Did you hear Congressman Bull's announcement?"

"Saw it on television."

"That was quite an indictment of you."

"I expected it. But I didn't think he would shoot himself in the foot the way he did."

"You mean his joke about what women talk about?"

"I don't think too many of our sisters will find his cracks very funny."

Luna came up and steered her away until the full press contingent was on the scene.

"Are you ready to return his fire?" she asked.

"I've got both barrels loaded," Clare said, with a glint her eye.

When everyone got settled, Clare went to the front of the room and said: "I know you've come to hear my reaction to Congressman Bull's announcement. But first I want to say that I'm very pleased about the response I've had to my declaration of intentions. The reporting, for the most part, was fair and objective. Comments we've received on Twitter and Facebook have been quite positive, as well as the calls coming in to this office and to county offices over the state. And also, of no little importance, we have had a number of generous offers of financial support from various sources. I appreciate this show of confidence in me as a candidate very much.

"Now, as to Jack Bull's diatribe: I haven't witnessed that much trash since the garbage truck turned over on the freeway a while back. (A few chuckles.)

"For starters, he bragged about being a native of California and tried to brand me as an outsider. That's one big difference between Bull and me. He was born here and left to go to Washington. I came here and stayed. (Applause from volunteers.)

"I hope he's been happy living in Washington all these years but it certainly hasn't made him any smarter. He might be interested in knowing that California ranks last of all the states in the percentage of native born population. California traditionally has been a melting pot. People have been attracted to our state – at least until the past few years until they began leaving for states that have better governments and lower taxes.

"I got a big laugh out of what he said about me living a 'ritzy life' with servants waiting on me all the time. Members of Congress are the ones who live the high life, with large staffs at their beck and call, fancy receptions and dinners all the time, a free gym, free transportation back and forth to their home states – and by free, I mean it doesn't cost Congressman Bull ... it's all paid for by the taxpayers. And that doesn't count all the junkets they take to exotic places all over the world. Last year members of Congress and their aides took 1,887 free trips – that's more than any year since 2007. And while every year there's a crisis about scraping up enough money to keep the government open and running, they had no trouble finding almost $6 million to pay for these trips.

"One of the last things the congressman said this morning was that he would run a fair campaign. That came after he opened his remarks by smearing my late husband. Those kind of tactics didn't work for him in 2004 when he called Gary every name in the book. But voters turned Bull out of the state senate and elected Gary. It sounds like he's still sore about that and might be out for revenge by stopping me in this race.

"Well, I say bring it on, Jack. And he can make all the insulting cracks he wants to about me and other women, because that will just mean more women will be on my side in this race."

"Clare?"

"Yes, Laurie."

"Congressman Bull pointed out that you hadn't spoken about your positions on issues in your announcement. Why was that?"

"It's certainly not because I don't stand for anything, as he implied. I guess he hasn't read my book, 'Clearly I See'. But as we know, members of Congress pass bills without reading them. Anyone who does read my book will learn how I feel about a number of topics affecting California citizens. As I go about the state campaigning in the coming months I will have a lot more to say. Next?"

"How many servants do you have?"

"None. Sam?"

"Were you surprised about Congressman Bull's entry into the governor's race?"

"There has been speculation for some time. And as I've said before, I can't blame him for wanting to get out of Washington, with the mess that it's in. Congress has one of the worst favorability ratings of any profession – hitting a new low of 9 percent, the last I heard. But of course, Congressman Bull was one of those who helped create the mess, so I can't imagine the people of California wanting him to come back here and do the same thing. Thanks for coming, everybody."

With a cheerful wave, Clare left the glare of photographers' lights and went around the room shaking hands with the volunteers still at work. Luna and Melody helped keep the news hounds from pelting her with more questions. But there was one she sought out: Sam Mahoney.

"Sam, I'm surprised to see you here. Did you come all the way from Sacramento just for Bull's announcement?"

"No, and I was at yours, too. I got a transfer to the L. A. bureau."

"I thought you loved being at the state capitol."

"I did. But I wanted to cover your campaign."

"Really? Why?"

"I made some calls and found there's some interest developing around the state," he said. "And I know a newsmaker when I see one."

66

WHEN CLARE TURNED her phone back on after meeting with the reporters she discovered a message to call Tim Barnham. She hadn't talked to him since before Christmas so she found a quiet corner and returned the call.

He answered with his usual greeting. "Clare, yer lookin' real good. I just wanted to congratulate you on your announcement and your gigs at Congressman B.S."

"I can't let him get the best of me – especially this early in the game."

"Yer doin' the right thing. I've heard some good comments from a number of my buddies in the senate. They wouldn't want to go public quite yet but I'll bet they might endorse you later on."

"I'm happy to hear that. And I know if you learn anything that will be helpful you'll pass it along. I appreciate your call."

Tim's mention of endorsements reminded her that Gene had sent word that he had talked Ida Clare into appearing in an ad that was scheduled to air on TV and radio on the upcoming weekend. She had some bookstore events but when she was at the villa she kept an eye on TV. And just before the Saturday noon newscast she heard her own voice saying:

"I'm Clare Sullivan de Lune and I'm running for governor. As I've traveled around the state listening to Californians, one message has come through loud and clear: the people want new leadership. They're not happy with the way the state is being run.

"California is a great state, but it can be better. Just give me a chance to prove it. Please sign the petition to get my name on the ballot for the June 3 primary election. Thank you."

(chants of "We want Clare!" followed by a shot of Ida Clare, hands on hips, saying:)

"I do declare this woman has the best kind of recipe for better government. Tell your friends Ida Clare says: Sign up for Clare."

Clare wasted no time in dialing Gene. He answered right away.

"Gene, you are indeed a genius!" she said.

"Like I say."

"I love the Ida Clare ad. How in the world did you get her to do it?"

"First of all, she was really impressed with you. And then I offered her a few incentives – like getting her program on a Seattle station. And the ad does plug her show."

"Whatever you did, it certainly worked and it gets the petition drive off to a good start."

"I hope we'll see some results. I'm working on another ad to run on Super Bowl weekend."

"I can hardly wait to see it. Thanks again, Gene."

She had barely hung up the phone when another call came in. It was Henry saying he had seen the ad and "you looked really great."

"I taped that right after the announcement and did it in one take, so I wasn't sure how it would turn out. Gene edited it down considerably, of course. But Ida Clare is wonderful – I do declare!"

"Well, I just wanted to let you know I'm thinking about you. I'm going to be traveling most of next week, but I'll check in."

"I'm going to be on the road myself – a combination of book promotion and petition rallies. Generally short trips in the greater L.A. area. I'll miss seeing you."

"Same here."

On Monday morning Clare was about to begin a book signing session in The Grove at Farmers Market, where Henry tracked her down.

"Where are you?" she asked.

"At the airport getting ready to catch a plane to Las Vegas."

"What's up?"

"If you haven't made plans I'd like to ask you to save next Sunday, the 19th."

"I try not to schedule much on Sunday. What's the occasion?"

"You don't know? It's the NFC playoff game."

"Who's playing?"

"The San Francisco 49ers and the Seattle Seahawks."

"Oh. Well, I'm a 49ers fan …"

"That ought to make it interesting. I'm for Seattle, of course. I want you to come to my place and watch it with me."

"OK. I can do that. Have a safe trip."

The week went by quickly. Clare took time out from traveling for a midweek meeting with Hector and Houston to go over issues and settle on some general positions that could be published in a brochure. The campaign had drawn some editorial criticism, partially fueled by Jack Bull's attack, about Clare holding back.

"Her kickoff event was somewhat paradoxical," read one editorial. "Behind the candidate was a large sign reading 'Clear Vision, Clean Campaign, Clare' but while she had quite a bit to say about 'no dirty tricks' she didn't give a clue as to her 'clear vision.' For someone who shows promise as a fresh face in this year's election for governor, this kind of vacuum detracts from her enthusiasm for change."

It was a tactical error, but one easily corrected. In less than a month's time voters won't remember.

After a couple of hours of discussion, Clare said she would like to come up with a five-point issues agenda: Education, Budget and Spending Priorities, Natural Resources Conservation and Development, Economic Growth, and Human Resources. She asked Houston to pull together a report on public statements Clare had made on all of these topics and requested some up-to-date information from Hector on prevailing public opinion in California on current issues. They agreed to get together again in a week or 10 days.

She also said she would get her thoughts together and make notes for further discussion at that meeting.

"One other thing, Houston," she said. "We need to be building a comprehensive file on Jack Bull, including his votes on bills, missed votes, attendance record, overseas junkets and anything else you can think of that can be used as ammunition against him."

"I've already made a pretty good start and I'll keep after it," Houston said.

"Thanks to both of you for all your help."

With Henry away, Clare buried herself with research material, reviewing issue papers that Houston had provided over the past several weeks and jotting down talking points she could use in future speeches. She had anticipated that running for governor would not be child's play and her expectations were being realized.

67

CLARE WORKED LONG hours at her desk every day including Sunday and as the hours went by she kept looking for a stopping point so she could get ready to go watch the NFC football playoff with Henry. She wasn't that enthusiastic about going but she knew it was important to Henry.

She kept on going without stopping for lunch and as the hour got closer to the 3:30 p.m. PST broadcast time, she decided she had to freshen up, change clothes and be on her way. As she got her purse and started to go downstairs, Tim Barnham called.

"What is it, Tim? I'm on my way out the door."

"I think you need to know that Jack Bull is going to try to sabotage your petition drive."

"What?"

"I've got a source in his camp that told me Bull's people sent orders to county workers to take whatever steps necessary to disrupt the petition process. It's hard to believe they would break into our local offices and destroy or steal the signed petitions, but it can't hurt to put out a warning."

"That dirty SOB! Well, I guess we can't be surprised at anything he might do. I'm so glad you caught me, Tim. Thanks a lot."

She hung up and called Luna. She had to leave a message on the answering machine. She decided to try again on the way to Henry's apartment.

It was after 3:00 p.m. when Clare knocked on Henry's door. She hadn't been able to reach Luna.

"Here you are," Henry said, as she swept in the door.

"I'm sorry I'm running late. We've got a bit of a crisis developing. I'll fill you in later. Here's some cookies. I didn't have time to bring anything else."

"I'm glad you're here. But we'd better go on down if we expect to get a spot to see the game."

"Where are we going?" Clare asked, with a look of consternation.

"Oh, didn't I tell you? Everybody is gathering in the building's party room on the first floor."

"Everybody? Who's going to be there?"

"Everyone who lives in this apartment building was invited."

"Including Luna?"

"Sure."

"So that's where she is. I've been trying to get hold of her."

"Well, I'm sorry you had the wrong idea. But it won't matter whether we watch the game here or with the crowd."

Clare shot him a frown. "If I had known I could have dressed a little differently." She had worn powder blue slacks and a white sweater with a 49ers pin.

"Oh, you look fine. You always do."

Noting his cap with the Seahawks emblem, she said, "Well, you're certainly prepared for the game."

"I found this at a sports store last week. OK, are we ready to go?"

"I suppose."

He picked up a paper bag from the hall table and closed the door.

"What's that?" Clare said.

"Wine. They've got wine and beer downstairs but I prefer to bring my own."

"I could have guessed."

"And there's some food, too."

"Good! I'm starving."

They walked quickly toward the crowd noise and entered a room almost full of excited fans. They appeared to be pretty well divided between Seattle and San Francisco. There were small bistro tables with stools and most of them were taken. "Let's grab that one," Henry said, pointing to a table toward the back with a sideways view of the large television screen. On the way, a pair of busty blondes smiled and said, "Hel-lo-o, Henry," and "Hi, there, handsome."

"Who are they," Clare asked icily.

"Just a couple of residents I see on the elevator now and then."

"They are certainly friendly."

"Aw, c'mon Clare." He pulled out a stool for her and hopped up on the other one just as the game was about to begin.

Clare was busy scanning the crowd to find Luna and did spot her across the room with Houston. She started to go over to see her but it was time for the kickoff.

"Game time," Henry shouted excitedly.

There was a basket of chips on each of the tiny tables and Clare reached to get one just as Seattle kicked off to San Francisco and with the jostling of the elbow-to-elbow fans the basket went flying.

"Damn!" said Clare.

"Why aren't you cheering?" Henry said. "Your team forced a fumble and got the ball on the 15-yard line." She pointed to the chip basket on the floor, almost emptied by the fall. Henry picked it up and set it back on the table. She wondered how long he was going to wait before opening the wine. He was too intent on watching the next play to notice her frustration.

The Seahawk defense prevented the 49ers from scoring and they had to settle for a 25-yard field goal. At the end of the first quarter with San Francisco leading 3-0 Clare's mood was a little better, but she was still concerned about Tim's call and needed to see Luna. She got up to leave but was stopped by Henry, who said: "Stay here and guard our place. I'll go get something to eat."

Disgusted, Clare sat, scowling as a 30-ish couple approached. "You're Clare, aren't you?" the woman said. "Why, yes," she responded, extending her hand. The woman introduced herself and her husband.

Curious, Clare asked: "How do you like apartment living?"

"We only have a short-term lease," she said "We're staying here while our house is being replaced. We lost it in one of the fires last summer."

"Oh, I'm so sorry to hear that."

"The firefighters felt bad about it, too. They told us there were so many homes in the path of the fires and they saved as many as they could. But they just didn't have enough trucks."

"That's terrible."

The man spoke up. "We just wanted to tell you we like what you're saying about doing more to prevent the tremendous losses caused by fires and other natural disasters."

"We hope you get elected so you can try to do something about it," his wife said. "I've signed up as one of your volunteers."

"Thank you so much," Clare said. "I really do appreciate your support."

About that time Henry came back carrying two chili dogs, a plate of nachos and two plastic tumblers. Clare watched as he found room on the table for this football watch feast. She stared at the hot dog on a soaked napkin and said: "Are there any utensils?"

"Utensils? You mean like knife and fork? No," he said with a blank look.

"Not even plastic?"

"Sorry."

"Well, next time you're up, would you get some more napkins?"

"OK," he said, as he opened a bottle of wine and poured it.

Clare counted to 10 and reached for the wine and took a sip. Noting the expression on her face, Henry said, "This is one of my favorite Napa Valley wines. Don't you like it?"

"It's just that ... well, fine wine just doesn't taste the same in a plastic cup."

The teams were back on the field. Clare had a nacho, taking care not to drip the melted cheese. She was so hungry it tasted so good she had another, along with another sip of wine and joined in the spirit of the game.

"Go, 49ers!" she shouted, drawing a frown from Henry and a "Go, Hawks!"

Clare actually jumped down from her stool and clapped and cheered when San Francisco got a touchdown five minutes into the quarter. During a timeout while an injured player was taken off the field, she got Luna's attention and with a hand gesture motioned for her to call. When she did, Clare filled her in on Bull's sabotage plans and told her to get the word out to the volunteers in the field.

With the Seahawks trailing 10-0 Henry wasn't taking the game too well. He excused himself to go to the food bar and returned with a plate of California-style Buffalo wings and the napkins Clare had requested.

Clare sampled a wing and found it to be too spicy so she decided to tackle the hot dog. The greasy chili had congealed somewhat but was still messy. Carefully placing it on a double napkins layer, she screwed up her courage and lifted it to her mouth. When she bit down the chili squirted out of the bun and onto her face and down to her white sweater. At that very moment a flash went off from a young woman's phone, amidst an outburst of giggles. Henry's eyes were so focused on his team moving toward the goal line he hadn't noticed until he heard Clare shout in anger.

"Ahh-rr-ghh!"

Dropping the hot dog she grabbed up the rest of the napkins and began dabbing at her face, only succeeding in smearing the globs of chili. She had no better luck with the spots on her sweater.

Meanwhile, Henry was yelling, "Yea, Seattle" after his team kicked a 32-yard field goal.

Clare downed the rest of her wine in one gulp, stood up and said, "Henry, give me your apartment key. I've got to go get cleaned up."

Meekly he reached in his pocket and handed her the key. "I'm sorry, honey," he said, as she stormed off.

In the apartment, Clare took off her sweater and worked with the stains at a lavatory. She also restored her face with a washcloth.

Then she sat down and wrote a note, pulled the sweater back on – shivering at the damp places on her chest – left the door unlocked and headed for her car. The note said: "Henry, I'm going home. It's not just because I wasn't having a good time, but I do have a lot of work to do for the campaign. Maybe our next sports date will be better. Love, Clare."

68

AS EXPECTED, WHEN Clare did her morning scan of the news there was her photo, top and center, in a gossip column. It was awful. The camera caught her with a panicked look on her chili-mottled face, dripping down on the pristine whiteness of her sweater. The caption read: "Candidate Smeared – by Herself."

The first thought that came to her mind was, "I'll bet Jack Bull is laughing his head off."

She was guzzling, not sipping, her black coffee, trying to tell herself, "What's done is done. It's exposure, after all, and I'll just have to make light of it and go on." She felt reassured after Gene called.

"That photo of you with the hot dog is great," he said. "It's a PR guy's dream!"

"What are you talking about?" Clare said, exasperated. "It makes me look like the biggest klutz in California. And if you saw it, in the whole country, maybe."

"No, no, no. People love this sort of thing. It's humanizing. It makes them see you as one of them."

"Women, maybe. But men voters …"

"Listen. Women are your most important constituency. They wield the most influence in the family. As for men – they tend to feel threatened by an all-powerful woman. This will help make you more appealing to the male voter."

"If you say so, Gene."

As she headed back to the coffee pot for a refill, Henry called.

"How are you this morning?" he said.

"How do you think? I suppose you've seen my picture in the paper."

"No, but they showed it on the late newscast last night. I thought it was kind of cute."

"A guy might think that, all right. Oh, well. Sorry I ran out on you. I just couldn't go back looking the way I did."

"I'm sorry, too, but I understand."

"It's probably just as well. I saw that Seattle got going in the second half and won the game."

"Yeah, they're going to the Super Bowl. Well, I just wanted to check on you. By the way, thanks for the cookies. They're really good."

"I'm glad you enjoyed them, and thanks for the call. I've got a pretty busy day, so I'll talk to you later. Bye."

She called Luna to inquire about getting the word out about the Bull petition threat.

"I texted Melody last night and she did an email blast to our local offices warning there might be attempts to disrupt the petition drive and to take necessary precautions," Luna said. "I didn't mention Bull's name, but they can probably guess who's behind it. We've had some responses saying the signed petitions are being locked up every night and the workers are keeping an eye on suspicious-looking people."

"That's good. Thanks, and let me know if there are any incidents. I might need to make a statement."

"Will do."

In the coming weeks a number of reports came into the state headquarters that small groups of pickets were showing up at local offices carrying signs like, "Beware of Clare" and "Don't Sign Your Freedom Away." But they hadn't had any noticeable effect on the collection of petition signatures.

Meanwhile, Clare continued to work with Hector and Houston on drafting a presentation of positions on the issues they had discussed. Their goal was to have something ready for Clare to use in an upcoming speech to an important audience.

By late January the group had organized their ideas and distilled them into the five-point "Clear Vision" that Clare could use in her campaign. They were set forth in an illustrated brochure to be made available at all local offices and which also could be downloaded from her website. It covered these points:

"I believe I have a clear vision of what it will take to carry California forward and give its citizens a secure, productive and happy future living in this beautiful land of ours.

"I can see clearly that California needs some improvement in the *education* of our young people, from the early grades through high school and beyond, if they so desire.

"I can see clearly that the best possible use should be made of the *financial resources* which our taxpayers provide to run all of the programs and deliver all of the services for which our state government is responsible.

"I can see clearly that we need to do a better job of conserving and protecting our *natural resources* and where development is judged to be beneficial that it be done properly and result in no harm to the environment.

"I can see clearly that steps must be taken to encourage *economic growth* while preserving the quality of life that makes California attractive to both current and future residents.

"I can see clearly that our state's leaders must place strong emphasis on *human resources* and always be mindful of the health and welfare needs of all Californians, regardless of race, color, gender, religious preference or country of origin."

From this general outline Clare could present her message to any group, expanding on any or all points as she saw fit.

That important work done, Clare agreed to take a breather for the Super Bowl, but only if she hosted the party at the villa for a small group that included Henry, Luna, Houston, Melody and her friend, a freshman college athlete named Dustu.

She had prepared a buffet with a variety of selections – which did not include hot dogs.

In addition to wine, she had beer and soft drinks for the younger guests.

Henry was the first to arrive. He presented Clare with a bag containing plastic cups. "Very funny," she said sarcastically, leaving the bag on the kitchen counter.

Next came Luna and Houston, then Melody and her date. He was a tall, muscular youth with bronzed skin and other characteristics of an American Indian. Clare welcomed him to her home and he politely said, "Thanks for having me."

"Your name is Dustu, is that right?" she said.

"Yes, ma'am. It's Cherokee." Looking down shyly, he said, "In our language, it means Spring Frog."

"How interesting. I have some Cherokee blood, but I'm afraid I don't know that much about the language, or anything else for that matter. The only Cherokee word I know is Osiyo (Oh-see-yo)."

"And hello to you," the young man said with a broad smile.

"Well, come on in, Dustu."

"You can call me Dusty, if you like. Almost everyone else does."

"Thanks, but I think Dustu is a beautiful name and that's what I prefer."

He smiled again and fell in behind Melody, who headed to the great room where they joined the others in front of the television set. Since she didn't have a favorite team Clare was much more interested in the ads than the game. Gene had alerted her to watch for a spot he had produced to run on local stations during the pre-game period, which consumed a major part of the afternoon. She was waiting anxiously to see it.

Finally, just before kickoff the screen went black. That got everybody's attention. Then there was a dramatic drumbeat followed by a fanfare and the screen was filled with the bright colors of a sunrise over the mountains. The music came up and an announcer's voice said: "A new day is dawning in California." With the sound of a cheering crowd in the background, quotes from newspaper stories flashed on the screen:

"From out of nowhere an exciting new candidate for governor has emerged ..."

"Exploding on the political scene ..." (cheers build)

"She's the one to watch ..."

With the sound of a crowd shouting, "Clare! Clare! Clare!" the image of her face zoomed forward to fill the full screen and she smiled and said, "It's a whole new ball game!"

A "Clare for Governor" banner across the bottom closed the ad.

Wild applause from her guests greeted Clare, who sat on the couch, stunned at the ad's impact.

"That's terrific," Luna said, giving her a hug.

"I'll say," said Houston.

Henry chimed in with, "Great. This ad really is an attention-getter. Congratulations."

"All the credit goes to Gene," Clare said, "and to Luna, who placed the ad. All I did was tape that one short line. I'm a little embarrassed by some of the hyperbole in the newspaper quotes. But that's what it takes, I guess. Well, anyone interested in the Super Bowl? I'll bring a tray of snacks."

The ad only ran once. The campaign couldn't begin to pay the exorbitant cost of time during the game. But it did get attention, as Henry said. Clare got calls from Hector and Tim and some of her friends from the state senate and elsewhere. This football party was going to be a lot different from the last one.

An ideal opportunity to publicize her campaign platform came with an invitation to address the Southern California News Editors Association meeting in Marina del Ray in early February.

The speech went over well and the news coverage extended far beyond the greater Los Angeles area and produced a number of positive editorials containing such phrases as "woman with a well thought-out plan", "keen knowledge of the state's needs", "not just another stale and stilted campaign speech", "intense loyalty to her adopted state", "strong dedication to public service" and "shows signs of ability to get action." The campaign staff moved quickly to make wide distribution of reprints of these news stories and editorial comments.

The campaign began to gather speed and Clare and Henry were spending little time together. He called one evening to see if they might go out on Valentine's Day evening.

"Not alone, I'm afraid. There's an annual heart association dinner that I always attend. I'm on the board. But I would be happy for you to be my escort."

"Well, it's not exactly what I had in mind, but I can't turn down a chance to be with you for an evening."

The dinner was a gala affair. Along with most of the other women attending Clare wore red, and looked quite elegant. She was not expected to make any remarks, but the president of the group introduced her from the audience.

"We are honored to have with us again Clare Sullivan de Lune." She stood to hearty applause. "She is a longtime and generous supporter of our efforts to raise public awareness of heart disease. We appreciate your contribution to our work and we will follow your exciting new venture with great interest."

"That wasn't exactly an endorsement of your candidacy," Henry whispered.

"She has to remain neutral, publicly. Many of the members helped get Jerry Brown elected. I hope they'll decide he's had the office long enough and vote for me. And others are diehard Republicans who will be loyal to their party. But we'll have to turn a lot of people around all over the state if I'm to be successful."

On the way back to the villa, Henry apologized for not buying anything for Clare for this special day. "That's okay. I don't have anything for you either."

"But I do have a Valentine's Day gift of sorts. When I was in Las Vegas I got a sizeable contribution from a casino where I have a contact."

"Oh, my! That's much better than a bouquet of red roses," Clare said.

"Or a box of chocolates?"

"Now I wouldn't go that far." They both had a big laugh.

69

IT WAS LATE when Clare got back from the heart association dinner and she hadn't checked her email until this morning. One message got her attention right away. It was from Luna, who said one of the local offices, which had collected over 300 signatures, reported signs of an attempted break-in.

Rather than call a news conference on a Saturday, they decided to use social media knowing that most of the media monitored both Twitter and Facebook for news tips.

The Twitter bite from @Clare2014 read: "Petition drive going well. Over 9K sigs collected w/5 days to go. Report of attempted break-in at 1 local office. Authorities alerted."

The posting on Facebook was much longer than the 140-character Twitter limit. It gave more details and a quote from Clare: "Our volunteer petition collectors throughout the state have done an outstanding job, in spite of harassment from hecklers and picketers carrying personally insulting signs. The required number of signatures is easily within reach, but we will exceed that number in anticipation of challenges. Our local offices have been warned to be alert for dirty tricks and there has been at least one attempted break-in. It's shocking to know that someone opposed to my candidacy would break the law like a Watergate burglar. Anyone caught stealing or destroying signed petitions will be subject to severe penalties."

The press did follow through and the story got wide play during the weekend. When asked for comment, Jack Bull had sneered: "There she goes whining again. Politics is a competitive exercise. It is not a game for the weak and whiny."

A concerted effort was made on Monday, when many workers had the day off for Presidents Day. Petition tables were set up in shopping malls and other public places. Clare made personal visits to a number of these in the L.A. area, posing for photographs with volunteers and signers and giving TV crews footage for the evening newscasts.

By Tuesday the total had topped 12,000 signatures and she and Luna flew to Sacramento on Wednesday to file the petitions one day before the deadline. On her official filing papers she listed her party preference as Democrat, at Hector Perido's advice. He told her that wouldn't be noticed, but if she took the option of "no party preference" that would get a lot of attention. "You can still do what you said and run a nonpartisan campaign," he said.

She held a brief news conference with the idea of getting news coverage not only in the state capitol but in San Francisco and areas throughout the northern part of the state.

Congressman Bull's office released a statement in which he demanded that a thorough examination of Clare's petition be made, "that an absolutely accurate count be made and each signature be subjected to rigorous checking to be certain it is valid" – thus casting suspicion and distrust on state employees responsible for verifying the information from signers and final certification of the petition.

Before leaving the Capitol, while Clare went by her Senate office Luna decided to go back to the Secretary of State's office to check the list of candidates for governor who had already filed. She was glad she did.

She quickly called the state headquarters. Her co-worker and current steady answered. She said:

"Houston, we have a problem."

70

"DON'T TELL ME you're pregnant?" Houston responded nervously.

"Oh, hell, no! Get your mind out of your pants and into the campaign. Another woman with the first name of Clare has filed as a candidate for governor. Get busy and track down Tim Barnham. He'll know what to do about it."

"I'll get right on it. And Luna …"

"Goodbye, Houston."

She filled in Clare on the way to the airport. "It could be confusing to voters to have two Clares on the ballot. I smell a rat and I think the rat's name is Jack Bull."

"You did the right thing, Luna. Tim will take care of the problem."

Early in the following week, Melody – who had a system to track pertinent news stories – sent Clare a link to a two-paragraph item in the Sacramento Bee saying the mysterious Clare had withdrawn her candidacy.

"Tim's persuasive powers worked again," she thought. "He probably reimbursed her for her filing fee, with a little extra."

Hector was sending her frequent updates on what the polls were showing. He was pleased to tell her that her name recognition numbers were steadily increasing in parts of the state outside of greater L.A.

Sales of her biography also were doing well and that meant more voters were getting to know more about her.

As more and more newspapers began treating her as a serious candidate, Clare began to get more requests to meet with various special interest groups. She couldn't accept all the offers, but fortunately Luna – with advice from Tim – had formed a corps of surrogates who could stand in for her. This had a double advantage: a substitute speaker could get her message out without committing her to any promises to a particular group.

Clare was careful not to overschedule herself. She also resolved to maintain her routine of regular walks around her neighborhood and on the villa grounds. Nothing was more satisfying and stress-relieving than to take a brisk walk and then pause to stand on the overlook below the villa terrace and watch the waves rolling in from the ocean onto the rocky shore.

Not only did she discipline herself to keep physically fit but also mentally alert.

As she took her morning walk, through her earbuds she heard the grating voice of Congressman John K. Bull. He was making his post-announcement speech.

"I invite Californians to look at my record of public service. In the state senate I served on some important committees, including those dealing with legislation affecting our vital agricultural industry. I carried that valuable experience to the Congress when voters elected me to the U.S. House of Representatives.

"I am currently serving as vice chairman of the Hairy Vetch Subcommittee, and in that capacity I have worked hard to protect the interest of this important cover crop. I am also proud to have the privilege of being a member of the Tropical Fruits Subcommittee, although it has required me to take long arduous trips to far distant areas of the Pacific for extended periods of time. It is a sacrifice that a congressman must make if he is to serve his constituents effectively.

"As a result of this service, I have acquired a vast amount of experience that I can bring to the governor's office and makes me uniquely equipped to lead this great state ... unlike a certain candidate who has filed recently. She is totally unqualified to serve in the state senate, let alone hold the office of governor. She would be an embarrassment to the state and would make California the laughing stock of the country. Blah, blah, blah ..."

It was at this point that Clare wished she hadn't sold the punching bag Gary used to work out in the villa basement. She would love to paint Bull's face on it and let him have it with both fists.

But she willed herself to turn her thoughts to her positive campaign and to remind voters that she had announced why they should support her.

The incumbent governor, Jerry Brown, removed any doubts about his future plans when in late February he posted an open letter on his campaign's website saying he would run for reelection to a fourth term. By any measure Brown would have to be considered the strongest candidate in the race. With $18 million in the bank, he had by far the largest campaign chest. Brown was generally credited for bringing the state from $20 billion in the red a few years ago to the enviable position of having a budget surplus. A January poll showed 60 percent of likely voters approved of the way he was doing his job.

With Brown looking like a sure winner, political reporters weren't paying much attention to potential challengers, but that would change somewhat after the filing period closed on Friday, March 7.

Clare anxiously awaited the news from the Capitol. Tim Barnham was there and he promised to call and let her know if there were any surprise candidates.

Shortly after 5 p.m. the phone jangled. She snatched it and heard Tim's voice saying: "Yer lookin' good, Clare ... I think."

"What's the news?"

"You'll never guess who just walked in and filed for governor."

"No. Tell me quick."

"Pat Brown."

71

"PAT BROWN?" CLARE repeated. "Not the governor's father. He died years ago."

"In February, 1996."

"Then you must mean ..."

"Pat Brown, California's most popular actor at the present time. He's known in every household as the star of the most-watched show on television."

"The Chief Exec". I watch it myself when I get a chance. But he lives in New York, doesn't he?"

"He has been. But the series has finished shooting and is going off the air at the end of this season. Brown says it has been his lifelong dream to be governor of California."

"Who would have known?"

"Folks at the Capitol couldn't believe it – first that they were seeing a famous star, and second that he might be in the same building with them as governor."

"This certainly livens things up. How do you think it will affect my race?"

"Well, there are several ways of looking at it," Tim said. "For one thing, with Pat Brown running it's for sure going to be an open primary. That will be good for you."

"I suppose so. This is such an unexpected development, I'm going to have to adjust to it. But thanks so much for alerting me, Tim."

Right away Clare called Luna, who said she was in the process of reading the wire story online. "What does this mean?" she said. Clare replied, "Tim thinks it's in our favor, but I'm not sure about that. We need to have a conference call to get opinions from others on our team."

"Better still, we can use the Internet chatroom that Melody set up for us," Luna said. She gave Clare the website address and told her what to do. Then she sent an email giving recipients an hour's notice.

The first to sign in, naturally, was Luna, followed by Melody, Houston, Hector, Clare and Henry. The transcript:

Hector: This certainly changes the way everyone expected the campaign would develop, but I don't think we need to change our strategy; that is, not to run against the top contender but to run a positive campaign to come in second in the June 3 primary and carry that momentum into the general election in November.

Clare: That sounds like good advice, Hector. Anyone disagree?

Luna: No, but I can't help wonder how Pat Brown thinks he can use his popularity as a TV star to capture the top prize in California politics?

Henry: Let's not forget about Arnold Schwarzenegger. And he was a Republican.

Luna: He never would have won in this Democratic state if he hadn't been married to a Kennedy.

Hector: Never underestimate the ignorance and the apathy of the voters. The character Brown plays in "The Chief Exec" is a power figure, which voters like to see. Many voters will pick him because they think from what they've seen on TV that he is the best qualified. Some will choose him simply because he's good looking. And others – God help us – will vote for him thinking he's the current Governor Brown or his father.

Clare: It's a sad fact, but I believe Hector is right.

Luna: I have to assume he's a registered voter and he's certainly old enough to qualify. I'm a bit fuzzy on the residency requirement. Hector?

Hector: Article V, section 2 of the California Constitution requires a candidate for governor to have been a resident for five years. But it is the legal opinion of the Secretary of State's office that this provision violates the U.S. Constitution and is unenforceable. But I daresay Brown has maintained a residence in the state anyway.

Houston: It's possible his character might come into play. Based on my hasty research, I've learned that he's had two failed marriages, he has spent time at the Betty Ford Center and he was jailed for drunk driving when he was in his teens.

Hector: Houston, you need to learn that voters have very short memories and unlike us they spend very little time thinking about politics and who's running for anything. Quite often they pick a familiar name, someone they think they know.

Clare: Then I guess we need to step up our efforts to get people to know me – or think they do.

Melody: We've about five times as many Twitter followers as the leading Republican candidate and substantial numbers of "likes" on our Facebook page. Our YouTube videos also are attracting lots of viewers.

Clare: Thanks, Melody. Can you be more specific?

Melody: I'll work up a report and get it to you ASAP.

Houston: I would add one more thing about Pat Brown. He has had absolutely no experience in politics.

Hector: Sadly, that could be to his advantage. And of course, he can buy as many consultants as he wants to.

Luna: It will be interesting to see how the press treats this surprise entry into the race. Sam Mahoney told me nobody saw this coming. BTW, he wants to get your reaction, Clare.

Clare: I'll call him. Any other comments?

Clare: OK. I want everyone to know that I'm certainly not dismayed about this development. I'm fired up and ready to go, knowing I've got the best team behind me of any candidate. I'm eager to crank up the bus and hit the road.

After signing out of the chatroom, Clare called Sam Mahoney. She said: "Pat Brown's announcing for governor doesn't change anything, as far as I'm concerned. I was an underdog before he got into the race and I'm still an underdog. I am just going to continue to run a campaign to win."

72

THE RETURN OF popular TV actor Pat Brown to California to run for governor dominated the news for several days after his dramatic appearance at the State Capitol on the last day of filing. Stories about his career, his personality, his family and friends and commentary about his potential for victory in his first venture into politics filled columns of newspapers throughout the state. In many media markets, Brown rated more attention than the 6.8 mag. earthquake in northern California.

While he didn't grant any interviews for radio and TV, enterprising stations featured guests who raved on and on about his abilities and qualifications for high office, based on little more than his success in the field of entertainment.

Polls taken in the wake of his splash in the spotlight gave him exceedingly high rankings, which were highly undeserved but easily believed by the gullible public. While some publicity-seeking minor candidates sought to ridicule his candidacy, Clare stuck closely to her plan of moving ahead with her campaign without any mention of the new sensation. If asked for comment she would generalize about the election being an open primary and he has as much right to run as anybody.

With the field of candidates established, pending a March 27 certification, it was time to shift into campaign mode. The "Friends of Clare" organization remained in place, but the exploratory committee was succeeded by a "Clare for Governor Committee." The website and Facebook page were updated accordingly.

Gene's TV ads had done a lot to "market the brand" but nothing can take the place of meeting and hearing the candidate herself, so Luna and Clare were laying out a schedule of public appearances. Some of them would take her back to places she had been on the fall listening tour but there also were cities and towns she had not visited.

Members of the "Clear Sailing" band had arranged to play for the crowds on Friday and Saturday and Ronnie, the keyboardist, and his vocalist wife, Rosa, would travel with the bus the rest of the week.

In speeches to groups and at rallies, Clare planned to hit the five points of her platform, one each week, following an annual St. Patrick's Day parade in Ventura and a campaign kickoff at a St. Patrick's Day rally in Santa Barbara.

The Saturday parade began in front of the San Buenaventura Mission and the parade entrants followed a route that stretched eight blocks on Ventura's East Main Street. Clare rode in a bright red convertible bearing "Clare for Governor" banners on both sides and a "Clare 2014" sign on the trunk. She stood for the entire distance, waving at spectators lining both sides of the street. Advance publicity had stressed her Irish heritage.

On Monday, as part of St. Patrick's Day festivities throughout the Los Angeles area, "Friends of Clare" sponsored a rally in a Santa Barbara park. Since it was a holiday the full "Clear Sailing" crew could participate in the event.

Ronnie had a surprise for Clare. He had composed a campaign theme song, which the band played and he and Rosa sang to a peppy tune:

California is the nation's greatest state,
But today it's in a state of disrepair.
If you think that government can't get any worse,
Just you wait, don't despair,
Here's Clare!

With a pained expression, Clare turned to Luna and said, "Did they say what I think they said?"

"These people are so excited they probably didn't notice. But we do need to talk to Ronnie," Luna replied.

Clare took the platform. Looking out at a sea of green, she shouted a hearty welcome to the large number of loyal supporters and plainly curious people who turned out to see the woman who had been in the news so much since she announced her candidacy.

This was not the time for a long or heavy speech. She began by talking about her Irish ancestry.

"St. Patrick's Day has been a special day for me my entire life. No matter what part of the world I've been on this day, I have tried to join Irelanders and Irish-Americans in celebrating March 17th.

"In case anyone here might not be aware of it, I am running for governor of this great state," Clare said and was answered by loud cheers, "and this rally marks the kickoff of my campaign" (more cheers). "For the next several weeks, I will be going to cities and towns all over the state. I visited some of these places last fall on a listening tour, in which I heard from Californians who told me they were not satisfied with things the way they are. They're looking for a different kind of leadership. I hope I'm the one the voters choose to provide it.

"One of my opponents is peddling the silly notion that a woman would be too weak to be governor, that I could not stand up to the forces in the legislature and elsewhere who would try to get control. I say to you people and to all Californians, that's not going to happen with me in the governor's office. Whenever this woman gets her Irish up, Clare will lower the boom."

With the crowd cheering wildly, the band played a chorus of "Clancy Lowered the Boom."

She thanked everyone who had signed the petition to get her on the ballot, made a pitch for continuing support as volunteer workers and contributors, and said: "And just remember: if you want a governor who'll care, if you want a governor who's fair, 'Here's Clare.'" With that she stepped down from the platform and worked her way through the throng shaking hands.

Before beginning a campaign swing, Clare filled a previously scheduled engagement to address a key organization, Women United for Sensible State Solutions (WUSSS). She had become acquainted with some of its leaders when they had come to the State Capitol to lobby legislators.

It so happened the group was holding a quarterly meeting in the area so it was convenient for Luna, Melody and Henry to accompany her. The theme of her remarks, naturally, was getting more women into government.

"I want all of you to know that I am really pleased to have the opportunity to meet with you today. You and I have an awful lot in common. I am a woman who is strongly dedicated to finding sensible solutions to our state's needs.

"We also share a common interest, I'm sure, in seeing more women holding positions in government. Here are some cold, hard facts:

"Women make up more than half of the population of the United States – 50.8 percent, to be precise.

"Women are more than 50 percent of the population of all but 10 of the 50 states. In California, the percentage is 50.3 percent.

"Now, listen to this. At this time, in the year 2014, only 99 women sit in the 535 seats in the U.S. Congress. They occupy only 20 percent of the 100 positions in the U.S. Senate and only 18.2 percent of the House of Representatives.

"Only 24.2 percent of the 7,383 state legislators in the United States are women. And the figures are even more dismal for governors. At present there are only five women governors. FIVE out of FIFTY!

"As you already know, but I want to repeat it for you, California has never had a woman governor. It's time to bring that statistic into line with the demographic reality." Applause echoed through the room along with some cheers.

"What are the prospects for changing that inexcusable outmoded imbalance of representation in America's state capitals? Let's look at the picture of forthcoming elections.

"This year 36 states are holding gubernatorial elections. While only seven states will have open seats due to term limits or retirements, at least six other races are regarded as 'tossups.' There are 10 women running for the seven open seats and three in the so-called 'tossup' states.

"The Rutgers Center for American Women and Politics reports 14 women are running as challengers in nine states … but the Center doesn't have me in the list because I just announced.

"All that by way of saying that women are making an effort to increase their numbers in the top elective offices and break the stranglehold and end the antiquated male domination of governorships. I believe that can happen – and will happen – right here in the state of California come November." That line also drew extended applause.

"The first hurdle is the election on June 3. It is an open primary and that means for the first time in a gubernatorial election candidates do not compete in Democratic or Republican primaries. Candidates of the two major parties and others, and those who are running as independents all will be running in a nonpartisan primary. The two candidates who get the most votes will be pitted against each other in the November general election.

"Because of my background and my experience as a state senator, I believe I can offer good reasons for Californians to vote for me. But it is not a race that one person can win. And I am not too proud to say I need your help.

"I believe members of this organization and I share common goals. Let me tell you why: I have presented what I call a 'Clear Vision' for California's future, consisting of five major points …"

As Clare outlined the basics of her platform, the crowd remained attentive. But when she concluded by saying, "I believe I am the right woman for the job. And if you're looking for a governor who'll care, if you want a governor who'll be fair, here's Clare!" the attendees rose from their seats and the room reverberated with cheers and applause, so much the presiding officer had to use the gavel to be heard thanking Clare for coming and referring members of the audience to her website and Facebook page.

A number of women came up to meet Clare and give their appreciation for advancing the cause of women – some even pledging their support for her campaign – and when she began to work her way toward the exit she saw coming to meet her was reporter Laurie Miller.

"That was a good rousing speech," she said. "And now you're going out into the field, right?"

"That's right. Starting tomorrow."

"I wanted to let you know I got my editor to approve an assignment to travel with you the next few weeks and write articles on the road. I got a schedule from Luna and she said it would be all right if I rode along on the bus."

"Why, yes," Clare said, a bit uncertainly. If Luna okayed it she must think it's a good thing to do. "We'll be glad to have you along."

73

March 19, 2014
By Laurie Miller
Los Angeles News Correspondent
On the Road With Clare

PALM SPRINGS – A spirited woman seeking to become the first of her gender to attain the state's highest office has begun her quest with a battle cry of "Here's Clare!"

The self-proclaimed underdog candidate is Clare Sullivan de Lune, the 38-year-old widow of famed racing enthusiast and classic automobile collector Gary de Lune. She succeeded him in the state senate after he was killed in a fiery auto crash in 2011.

Clare's big red bus rolled out of Santa Barbara County, where she has a home, early today following a rousing campaign kickoff rally on St. Patrick's Day in which she responded to an opponent's insinuations that a woman would be too weak to be governor. She quoted the unidentified accuser as saying "that I could not stand up to the forces in the legislature and elsewhere who would try to get control."

"That's not going to happen with me in the governor's office," she said. "Whenever this woman gets her Irish up, Clare will lower the boom."

The bus, which she used in a five-week "listening tour" last fall, is taking the "Clare for Governor" campaign on a swing through lower southern California, where Republicans have been making strong showings in elections the past few years. A significant victory was scored in San Diego when GOP city councilman Kevin Faulconer was elected mayor in a special election last month.

In her speeches Clare stresses the fact that the June 3 primary is a nonpartisan contest, unlike the separate Democratic and Republican primaries of the past.

In this phase of her campaign Clare is focusing on the five planks in her "Clear Vision" platform. This week it's education.

"Today's children are the leaders of tomorrow," she tells crowds. "The most important thing we can do for them is to make sure they get the quality of education that will help them fulfill the goals they set for themselves."

She points out that it is a governor, Mary Fallin of Oklahoma, who is leading a major national effort to improve education. As head of the National Governors Association, Gov. Fallin launched an initiative on "Education and Training for Tomorrow's Jobs."

In stops at San Fernando, Altadena, Azuza and Redlands, she touched on a number of education topics including new regulations under the Local

Control Funding Formula, implementation of Common Core standards, teacher salaries and pensions, and teacher preparation programs at colleges and universities.

Drawing on her experience on the Senate Education Committee and consultation with those in the field, Clare singled out some long term issues that continue to need attention.

"Teacher tenure has been a problem since the state passed tenure laws back in the 1930's," she said. "The advent of collective bargaining has aggravated the situation greatly. It is not limited to wages and hours as is common in private industry. Rather, teacher bargaining issues can reach far into the operational policies of a district involving such things as the curriculum, teacher assignments, class size and selection of administrators."

Clare said that Proposition 13, passed in 1978, drastically changed the operation of schools in California.

"This law had the worthy purpose of preventing property taxpayers from being 'taxed out of their homes.,'" she said. "On the other hand, it destroyed any semblance of local control of schools. The state took over the financing of public schools, cities and counties. Power shifted to Sacramento. Now schools rely almost solely on state legislators and the governor to determine how much revenue schools will receive."

Clare was met by enthusiastic crowds, and a few demonstrators, all along the route to Palm Springs, where she had an evening fundraiser scheduled.

Traveling on the bus gives this reporter an inside look at the workings of a statewide campaign. The bus is virtually a campaign headquarters on wheels. It has comfortable seats for the musicians who entertain the people gathering for the candidate's appearance, as well as her campaign manager, Luna de Lune, and communications coordinator Melody Turner. A space at the rear of the vehicle contains a table and chairs for use of the staff as a conference room. There is a small bathroom and a sleeping area where the bus driver, or anyone else, can catch a nap. Computers and smart phones are available for messaging.

The bus heads westward tomorrow for a return trip to the San Diego area, where she made some appearances last fall.

March 20, 2014

SAN DIEGO – Clare Sullivan de Lune brought her campaign for governor to California's second largest city today, carrying a message of hope and optimism for the state's economic future through excellence in education.

Addressing the Southern California Council on Higher Education, she said: "We have been losing people to other states, for a number of reasons. We need to turn that exodus around. We need to bring Californians back to where they belong. And the key is education – excellence in education at all levels.

"A good education leads to better jobs. And better jobs mean stability. If we can offer that to our citizens, they will have no reason to be lured to other states that are lacking well trained, skilled workers."

Clare said she was pleased that Gov. Jerry Brown increased funding for education in his new budget. "We cannot afford to deny our schools, our colleges and universities, the money they need to provide quality education."

The candidate seeking to become the state's first woman governor also was optimistic about her chances for victory in the June 3 open primary. In remarks to a fundraising dinner audience, she said: "This election will be quite different from those in the past. There could be some surprises. I'm counting on one of them to be me."

"Please understand, I don't have anything against men in general. Some of my best friends are men. More important, many of my most generous contributors are men," she said, to laughter from the predominantly male crowd. "But this is an age of equal opportunity. And I think it's time to give a woman a chance to govern this state."

Clare continued: "I sense a feeling of change in the air. San Diego voters have certainly shown they want a change by electing a Republican mayor. I believe this indicates that at least in this area of the state people will cross party lines if necessary to choose the best person for the job.

"The June 3 open primary is a nonpartisan election, and therefore I am determined not to run a partisan, divisive race but to offer myself as someone who can best serve all of the people."

Sign-carrying protesters greeted Clare at her rallies in Moreno Valley, Tenecula and Escondido where she talked about her "Clear Vision" platform in general terms.

March 21, 2014

TORRANCE – "Community colleges are a vital part of California's education system," Clare Sullivan de Lune told a gathering of students on the campus of El Camino College. "As governor, I will continue to support and strengthen this vast network of schools where students are pursuing their educational and career goals."

In Torrance, she completed a swing through southern counties in the initial stage of her campaign to win election as governor later this year.

In scheduling the college stop, Clare knew that California has 112 community colleges in 72 districts in the state, making it the largest system of higher education in the world, serving more than 2.4 million students.

El Camino College, established in 1947, has nearly 23,000 students, of whom 32 percent are Hispanic. It offers nearly 2,500 classes in 85 different programs.

While in Torrance Clare also went to a rally in one of the city's 30 parks, where she focused on environmental concerns and expressed her desire to work harder to protect California's natural resources.

She also made a stop at the overseas office of Toyota, one of Japan's three largest automakers, which has headquarters in this coastal community of 145,000. Toyota Motor Sales U.S.A. is Torrance's largest employer.

Before coming to Torrance, Clare emphasized her nonpartisan theme to a rally crowd in the affluent resort city of Carlsbad, which has all-Republican representation in the state legislature.

She made repeat visits to Newport Beach, Irvine and Santa Ana in Orange County, the state's third most populous county and a Republican stronghold. She spoke at a fundraising luncheon with executives of Fortune 500 companies located in the area. It was closed to the press by request of the attendees.

Sunday, March 23, 2014

The candidate of the "Clare for Governor" campaign was quite pleased with her first foray into the field in her campaign for governor, having received friendly receptions in some strong Republican areas of southern California and despite unfriendly demonstrators picketing her candidacy she was met with supportive crowds in a dozen stops from San Fernando to Torrance.

On her campaign bus I had an opportunity to gain some better insights into the candidate Clare Sullivan de Lune (more popularly known as Clare) through an exclusive interview. Following are my questions and her answers:

Q: You appear to have the means for living a comfortable life. Why have you chosen to give that up for public service?

A: I gave up my private life when I was elected to fill a vacancy in the state senate after my husband Gary was killed. I wanted to continue the work that he had begun. After I had adjusted to the responsibilities of that office I gained a great deal of satisfaction from serving the people. What I'm doing now is an extension of that decision.

Q: You have freely admitted you are facing heavy odds in seeking to become California's first woman governor. What is your basic motivation for running for governor?

A: I thought long and hard about entering this race because I knew the odds were against me. I also faced the reality of knowing that a campaign of this nature these days would require a large amount of money. And I realized it would place heavy demands on me physically and mentally and would occupy virtually all of my time for a couple of years. But the staff I had assembled was very competent and willing to give their all to achieving the goal; plus, I was encouraged greatly by people I met on my listening tour last fall.

Q: Not simply personal ambition?

A: No. It's much more than that. Running for office calls for a certain amount of conceit, I suppose. And if I had thought I wasn't capable of doing a good job I never would have put myself forward.

Q: You're not trying to succeed where Meg Whitman failed last time around?

A: Oh, heavens no. From what I know of her, we are totally different. I certainly don't have nor would I be able to raise the amount of money she spent. And the other thing is, I believe I have a better chance in this year's election because of the open primary. I doubt that I could win a party nomination, for example.

Q: That brings up another question. Could you elaborate on what you said in your announcement about not wearing a party label?

A: What I said was that I would not run a partisan campaign because this is a nonpartisan election – at least the primary. I do remain loyal to my lifelong status as a Democrat. That was my upbringing in Georgia, where I was born and raised. My father and mother were both Democrats, as most people in our town were at that time. My father and I talked about politics sometimes. He told me he didn't vote for Jimmy Carter for president, but there were other reasons. And he didn't leave the party.

Q: Regarding your staff: it seems most campaigns have employed experienced campaign management people and highly trained consultants. Your campaign is different, isn't it?

A: I don't have an excessive number of people helping me. Nor have I brought in teams of high paid consultants as some candidates have. None of my staff are making much money out of this venture. In fact, they are making financial sacrifices. We are focusing our resources on the essentials, like advertising, transportation, printed materials and the like. And one of the greatest strengths of our campaign is the large number of enthusiastic volunteers all over the state. They are giving countless hours of their time and energy to this cause. Their desire for change is the driving force behind this endeavor.

Q: Your finance chairman is from another state, I believe. You don't have any problem with that?

A: None whatsoever. He is not someone we imported, like some campaigns – as I said – hire East Coast consulting firms. Henry Jackson is president of a family-owned winery in the state of Washington but he does have a California connection. Mt. Jackson Vineyards also owns the Chateau Lapierre winery in Ventura County. I became acquainted with Mr. Jackson through a chance meeting. It happened to be at a time when we desperately needed to replace my first finance chairman. He volunteered to take a leave of absence from his company and assume the monumental task of raising money for my campaign. He is an extraordinary person and I am grateful to him for his support.

Q: And Luna de Lune, your stepdaughter, is your campaign manager and also is handling campaign advertising?

A: Luna is Gary's daughter. She is working very hard. I think, in a way, she is dedicated to having a successful campaign in memory of her father. But she is very talented. I couldn't do without her. Before we formed an exploratory committee for a potential campaign for governor, she was running her own advertising agency. The creative portion of our campaign advertising is the work of an absolute genius of the industry who is based in Seattle. He has a number of clients in other states, including California. Luna places our ads through her agency.

Q: Clare, you've been very forthcoming with your answers. I believe our readers will be glad to have this information.

A: I want to be as open as I can. People now will know more about me.

74

LUNA WAS THE first to call. As Clare was prone to do, she was sleeping late on Sunday morning. She answered the phone with a barely audible, "Hello?"

"I've just read Laurie Miller's interview with you in the Sunday paper. What were you thinking?"

"Why? What's the matter?"

"What's the matter! Some of those things she quoted you as saying?"

"Like what? I haven't read it."

"Well, did you really have to say, quote, 'I doubt that I could win a party nomination'?"

"It's the truth."

"Maybe so. But it's one thing to be candid. It's another to give the impression of being a loser."

"Oh, Luna. I think you're upset about nothing."

"Nothing? Nothing? What about your description of our bare bones campaign staff operation? That doesn't do much to inspire confidence."

"Now wait a minute. I didn't make any disparaging remarks about you all. I thought I was very complimentary. And I think voters are fed up with reading about high-cost sophisticated campaigns. I am an underdog, after all. There's no getting around that. So it's natural that we'd have a lean but scrappy team. It's sort of like the David and Goliath story."

"Who are they?"

"They're a couple of characters in the Bible. What other complaints do you have?"

"All those details about Henry, Gene and me. That will give the 'Raging Bull' plenty to bellow about."

"Don't you think his opposition research people have that information already, just holding it for the right time to hit us with it? This robs them of the opportunity."

"Well, it really shook me up to see this. But I guess you knew what you were doing."

"Thanks a lot. And by the way, I'd like to remind you that you were the one to allow Laurie to tag along on the bus, not me."

"I didn't think I had to clear every decision I make with you. And the other stories she's written are giving us some good publicity."

"That's right. And so will this one. Just wait and see."

And so it went. Laurie Miller continued to write her "On the Road With Clare" series as Clare took her tour to industrial areas and newer communities talking about growth and development; to northern California to appeal to liberal voters with her stand on preserving and protecting natural resources; and to points in Central Valley focusing on human resources.

At each stop she asked for a moment of silence for the victims of the terrible mudslide that destroyed a rural community in Washington state. "It pains me to think of the families who lost loved ones along with their homes and possessions," she said.

Meanwhile, John Bull was still up to no good. As expected he let loose a blast about Clare's campaign team: "She doesn't think Californians are good enough to work for her so she went out of state to hire two of her top people," he said. "And she's getting some of her biggest campaign contributions from Las Vegas and other places like that." Bull left himself wide open on those charges. Clare could retort by pointing out Henry and Gene's California connections, and by gouging Bull about getting some of his buddies in the House to come and campaign with him. He also had received a large amount of campaign money from Washington lobbyists.

One of Bull's most clumsy attempts to turn voters away from Clare was to attack her legislative record. She made him a laughing stock by reciting all the silly, meaningless resolutions he had sponsored in Congress.

Another step to counter Bull's assaults was to equip "Clare for Governor" volunteers with signs to use as they stationed themselves at Clare's rallies in opposition to the demonstrators that most likely were being paid by Bull's campaign.

Gene's excellent TV and radio ads were having the desired effect. Those messages, in combination with Laurie's articles, were drawing more and more voters to her side. Hector was thrilled to report that she was rising steadily in public opinion polls.

On one of the bus trips, Clare took some time to have a conversation with Laurie.

"I know reporters don't want to be thanked for their coverage – they're supposed to be objective and not show favoritism – but I've been meaning to ask you something: does your newspaper have writers assigned to cover the other candidates?"

Laurie replied: "The best way to answer that is to explain that I am not an employee of the paper. I'm what's known as a freelance correspondent. What I do for the paper depends on what kind of arrangement we can work out. I wanted to cover you and I talked the editor into a deal that's really more to their advantage than mine. That's the way it has to be with newspapers these days – with all the competition they face from television and the Internet."

"Well, I didn't know that," Clare said. "Thanks for telling me."

Henry steadfastly stuck to fundraising and stayed out of the campaign operation – usually.

But he took a chance and mentioned a scheduling idea to Luna, which she liked. He learned that April 13 would be "Tax Freedom Day", a date when theoretically American taxpayers had earned enough income to pay taxes owed to federal, state and local governments. With federal tax returns due two days later, he thought it would be an appropriate time for a speech about taxes. The California Taxpayers Alliance was holding a conference that day and Luna arranged for Clare to be one of the speakers.

The alliance was relatively broad-based, including Republicans, Democrats and independents, libertarians and conservatives, large and small business owners and a few officeholders. They held a wide range of views on taxes and tax reform.

"Taxation is a double-edged sword," Clare told the group. "We have seen that quite plainly here in California. The capital gains tax and the personal income tax increases imposed by Proposition 30 have generated billions of dollars in revenues, and as a result we now have a budget surplus. One of the downsides is that higher taxes encourage migration and that causes loss of revenue.

"In my visits to corporate offices, such as the Toyota headquarters in Torrance last month, I have become keenly aware of Texas Gov. Rick Perry's aggressive efforts to use California's high taxes as a weapon to lure industry to his state.

"We realize that taxes are necessary to support government. But taxes are the natural enemy of working men and women. And one of the things they complain about the most is unfair taxation. Being fair in all aspects of governing is part of my five-point "Clear Vision."

"Another thing that gets under the skin of taxpayers is the way the government spends their money. Governor Brown's proposal to put his high rail project ahead of more urgent needs rankles even top Democrats like Lieutenant Governor Gavin Newsom."

In a Q&A period following her speech, Clare made a statement that was bound to make headlines. She was asked: "What is your general position on raising taxes?"

"Some people think that someone who has an open mind on taxes is empty-headed," she answered. "I assure you that is not the case with me. My experience in the state senate has convinced me that it is foolish to take a firm position on a matter without having all the facts at hand. Nobody can know what conditions will prevail at some future date. Former President George H. W. Bush learned that the hard way."

"So are you saying you would not sign a pledge to oppose higher taxes?"

"I believe it would not be fair to my constituents to do so. They have elected me to use my best judgment on any issue at the time it is put to a vote. That has been my practice as a state senator and it will continue to be a guiding principle in the governor's office."

Surprisingly enough, editorial comment on her politically hazardous stand was just about evenly divided. She was criticized, without basis, for seeming to favor tax increases by not being dead set against them. She was complimented for being candid and not hypocritical. It was more fodder for Jack Bull, of course. She chose not to respond to his claptrap.

Another of Clare's issues was less controversial. After the cycle of severe drought followed by heavy rains earlier in the year, another dry spell had set in, heightening the danger of wildfires.

Late one day, after a round of grueling campaign appearances, Clare and Henry were traveling homeward in the SUV. The bus had gone on ahead of them as usual. Shortly after sunset, as they drew nearer to Santa Barbara, they noticed a bright orange glow in the sky in the distance – the sure sign of a fire. Clare told the driver to head in that direction.

"Are you sure you want to do this, Clare? You're tired. You need to go home and rest."

"I have to find out what's going on," she said. She told the driver to speed up as much as he could.

The closer they got the more they could see of the wide devastation. Before long they could make out the silhouettes of fire engines and the figures of firefighters manning hoses. Clare directed the driver to get as close as possible. They got to a point where police were on duty. An officer ordered them to stop and advised them to turn around and leave the area.

Clare reached back into the cargo area behind her seat and retrieved the fire helmet she had been given after she spoke at the local firehouse some months back. She put it on and went to talk to the officer. Identifying herself as a state senator she persuaded him to allow her to find out if Chief Ed Winn was on the scene. Henry followed behind.

Without warning, the wind began gusting, feeding the flames and threatening a line of trees. Small limbs were catching fire and bouncing on the ground. Henry tried to hold her back, but she kept advancing toward the blaze as she saw a firefighter alone close to the inferno. He turned to retreat and gasping for breath collapsed. The flames eating through the dry grass were speeding toward the prone figure.

Clare broke away from Henry and ran toward the body. Chief Winn came running and shouted, "Come back. Don't go any farther!". He rushed toward her just as a huge limb high on a tree cracked and bent precipitously over the fireman on the ground.

"I'm coming," Clare shouted. "I'm coming to help you!" Henry panicked as he saw what she was doing. Running almost into the fire, she tripped over a log and sprawled forward. Henry heard the limb snap above and he plunged ahead as it hurtled toward the spot where Clare was lying. She struggled to get to her feet and felt herself being scooped up by two strong arms and carried to safety. Meanwhile, Chief Winn dragged the firefighter, overcome by smoke and unconscious, out of the way of the burning limb, which crashed down where he had been lying.

An emergency squad team bearing a stretcher carried the stricken man to a waiting ambulance. Clare, coughing helplessly, leaned on Henry as Chief Winn approached. "Are you all right, ma'am?" She was unable to speak but nodded her head. Henry thanked him and said he would get her some medical attention.

He lay her down in the back seat of the SUV and got in front with the driver. They sped to a hospital in Santa Barbara. A passerby recognized her as she was getting out of the vehicle and snapped a couple of pictures with his phone. He sent them immediately to the local TV station which put them on the air as the lead story in the 10 o'clock news slot.

She was treated for smoke inhalation and minor scratches and bruises and released.

After a fitful night, Clare was pleased to see Henry's smiling face. "Here's your coffee," he said, "and the morning paper. The firefighter you tried to rescue is going to be all right."

"Thank God," she said. "And thank you for rescuing me."

Her photo was on the front page. Her hair was blown, her face speckled with blood and blackened by smoke, her dress torn.

"I look worse than when I tried to eat that hot dog at the football party," she said to Henry. She didn't bother to read the newspaper story because she looked down and saw a disturbing result of the nightmarish episode.

"Darn!" she said.

"What's wrong?"

"Oh, nothing. Could you please hand me that nail file?"

75

A NUMBER OF NEWS commentators applauded Clare's daring and bravery at the scene of the fire, but Jack Bull blustered, accusing her of "grandstanding." "While I and the other candidates for governor are talking seriously about the issues, Senator de Lune has resorted to a cheap publicity stunt to try to save her puny campaign. What a shameful display of audacity," he said.

After several weeks of Bull's bombast, political reporters were giving him little attention. They were focusing primarily on Pat Brown, who had begun a rapid rise in the polls and his high-powered campaign was pumping up the numbers with a blanket bombing of TV ads. The commercials emphasized his TV star good looks and contained scenes of him in a "chief exec's" office at a desk, phone to ear, fully in command. For all many voters knew, he could easily pass for the sitting governor.

Clare picked up her active schedule right away and Laurie Miller kept turning out almost daily articles about her activities. The first time she and the reporter met after the fire episode, Laurie greeted her with a mixture of concern for her well-being and disappointment at not being present to witness her heroics. "This was definitely something that was unplanned," Clare told her.

As May approached and she prepared to begin the final push, Clare's ranking in surveys of likely voters also was quite favorable. So much so that she began getting calls from political consultant firms on both coasts seeking to induce her into bringing some "experts" on board to run her campaign. Her attitude was, "Thanks, but I like the 'experts' I have."

Her advertising "expert", Gene McQueen, had adapted an ad he had designed for Mt. Jackson Vineyards to underscore the "clear" theme of Clare's campaign. It began with a close-up of a middle-aged couple sitting on a couch. The man is reading a newspaper, the woman is holding Clare's biography. The man, exasperated, slams the newspaper down in disgust. "What's the matter?" asks the woman. "It's these guys running for governor. They're all alike. They promise you the moon but they never carry out their promises." The woman replies, "Well, there's one candidate that's different." She holds up the book so the cover shows and says: "Clare!" With that, the camera gives the appearance of zooming through the picture window behind them and up into a clear blue sky. An announcer's voice says: "It's clear to see we need someone with a clear vision to guide our state." With the slogan spelled out at the bottom of the ad and as

Clare's face fills the screen, the music builds to a dramatic climax and the announcer says: "Clare – the clear choice for governor."

All across the state "Clare for Governor" volunteers were hard at work developing plans for "Get Out the Vote Drives" and the effort was being promoted on both Twitter and Facebook. Luna was in touch with county headquarters in high-vote areas almost daily and she reported enthusiasm was building.

Clare's travels for the remaining weeks of the campaign were primarily to areas of the state that had been determined to be the best sources of support for her candidacy. They included the San Joaquin Valley agricultural region – making a point of going to Fresno, where President Obama had appeared in mid-February to witness damage caused by California's drought – the "inland empire", the San Diego vicinity and Orange County in southern California, and greater Los Angeles, where the largest number of voters were concentrated. At various points in her travels Clare encountered unseasonal showers but they didn't dampen her spirits.

It became obvious that the Bull campaign was stepping up efforts to crush Clare's candidacy. As she set out for a northern swing the first full week of May, Bull's PAC released a TV ad painting Clare as an elitist trying to buy the governor's seat. As viewers are shown an aerial view of the villa a narrator says patronizingly: "Why would this woman want to be governor anyway? She's living in luxury at this oceanside estate … (switch to shot of her and Henry on New Year's Eve) she hobnobs with the country club set … (another aerial view of her by the pool at Vangy's yoga tea) and parties with other rich celebrities. She's just using her millions to buy her way into the governor's office. That didn't work in the last governor's race and it won't work for this woman either."

Clare brushed that off as Bull "trying to incite class warfare without any ammunition." "It's obvious Bull's hit squad has been spying on me again. But he's wrong about my so-called ritzy lifestyle. Besides, he has no room to talk," she said, citing his salary and congressional pension. "His attempt to ridicule me just brings up another big difference between him and me. I pay taxes on my home to Santa Barbara County. He pays taxes on his home to Arlington County, Virginia."

The following week Bull's campaign leaked a report of possible employment by Clare of undocumented workers, implying that Joe and Maria had come to California from Mexico illegally. The few newspapers and radio stations that ran the story without checking its authenticity resurrected a charge that did considerable damage to Meg Whitman in 2010, when her former Latina housekeeper alleged her employer was aware of her immigration status when she hired her.

Clare called a special news conference to refute the false claims. "Of all the ridiculous charges to come forth from Jack Bull's camp, this has to be the most outrageous. They are totally without foundation, absolutely false, the product of someone's wild imagination – any way you look at it. First of all, Joe and Maria are American citizens, of Italian descent. Joe was employed by my late husband to look after the automobiles he owned. Gary provided them with a small home on our property so Joe could be close at hand if work needed to be done. He left them a modest endowment in his will. Joe and Maria are not servants of mine in any sense of the word. Maria works in the gardens at my place sometimes because she enjoys it. Joe is my paid groundskeeper and has voluntarily driven me to some of my campaign events on occasion. He likes to say he was my 'Number One volunteer.' So you can just put away any notion you might have that there is a word of truth in these allegations, because they are all lies. Just another one of those dirty tricks I warned about when I began my campaign.

"And I might add that these efforts to derail my campaign have had no adverse effect on my candidacy. I am pleased to report that my favorability ratings in the polls are very good and getting better. I believe we have the best statewide organization of any candidate in the state, with the possible exception of the incumbent. And we have enough money in the bank to finish the primary campaign in good shape.

"Now, it's on to victory on June 3rd."

On the road Clare continued the practice of riding with Henry in the SUV, but on one of the stops, while the musicians were warming up the rally crowd, she went on the bus to check something with Luna. She found her working on schedules for the last two weeks of May.

"You've got a devilish grin on your face, Luna," Clare said. "What's up?"

"Oh, it's just an idea that came in from one of our most loyal supporters. She suggested we bring our campaign to Bull's hometown by scheduling a visit to Bullport. I'm thinking about doing it on Tuesday, May 20."

"You'd have to keep it a secret so it would be an embarrassing surprise to Bull."

"Yes, of course. It won't be listed on the schedule we give out to the news media."

"Including Laurie?"

"Right."

"I'm game."

Luna prepared two schedules to add to the loose-leaf notebook which she kept as a record of the campaign. One showed daily stops for the upcoming week, minus Bullport. The other one read for Tuesday morning: "Unannounced visit to Bullport."

When that date came around Clare began to feel a bit mischievous herself. After all the grief Bull had given her it would be only fair to one-up him on his home turf.

Bullport, named for the congressman's great-grandfather, once had been a thriving seaport. But over the years, with the decline of shipping and the exodus of residents going elsewhere to find work, it had pretty well dried up. Jack Bull certainly hadn't done anything to save his birthplace. He was far more interested in raiding the federal treasury for areas where there were more votes.

As the big red bus rolled into the tiny village on the shore of a leeward cove south of Los Angeles and the musicians set up in a small park and began playing, local townspeople began to gather. Soon there was a sizeable crowd and Clare decided it was time to make her entrance. As she and Henry got out of the SUV they noticed a large black sedan bearing small flags moving down the main street.

"Maybe it's the mayor coming to give you the key to the city," Henry said.

As the car drew nearer, Clare was trying to read the writing on the flags. "I don't think so," she said grimly.

All the attention of the crowd turned to the street scene. When the car stopped, the driver – John Valjean – stepped out and went around to open the door for Congressman John K. Bull. He emerged, waved at the crowd – which responded with cheers and applause – and walked up to Clare.

"Welcome to Bullport, Senator," he boomed. "What brings you to my hometown?" He snickered and many of his friends in the park joined in the derisive laughter.

Clare knew she couldn't give Bull the satisfaction of knowing that he got to her. She smiled and coolly responded, "Why, I'm here just to show the fine citizens of Bullport that I'll be just as glad to have their votes on June 3rd as any of the other communities I've visited all over the state."

"Well, Miz de Lune, I'm sorry to have to tell you that you've made a wasted trip. Bullport is solidly behind me in this race, as are cities and towns, large and small, from the northern reaches to the southern border. So you might just as well get back on your bus, or that expensive SUV, and go on up the road."

"No, thank you, Congressman. I came here to meet and visit with the people of Bullport, and that's what I'm going to do," Clare said, with a nod to Ronnie, the keyboardist, who joined Rosa in belting out the (revised) lyrics of the campaign song:

California is the nation's greatest state,
But today it's in a state of disrepair,
Here comes a woman who is going to set things straight,
Just wait, don't despair, Here's Clare!

About half the crowd applauded, perhaps out of politeness, but it was enough to cause Bull and Valjean to get back in their car and leave.

After giving her standard talk and answering a few questions, Clare and Henry headed back toward the bus where they saw that Luna had cornered Laurie Miller and was giving her a tongue-lashing of the first order. "You tipped them off. I know you did," she said to the protesting reporter.

"Did you do this, Laurie?" Clare said. "Look me in the eye and tell me the truth."

"I, I didn't … mean to … do any harm."

"I'm very disappointed, Laurie. Come inside the bus and let's talk about this."

The group filed back to the conference table and Clare ordered Laurie to sit. "I want a full explanation. It appears you sneaked a look inside Luna's notebook."

Laurie nervously explained: "Sometime late last week I saw the book was lying open. A reporter's curiosity got the best of me and I saw the schedule that listed an unannounced stop in Bullport."

"So you couldn't wait to call Bull's headquarters?" Luna said.

"No, it wasn't that way. Over the weekend I happened to run into John Valjean. I've known him since he was a TV newsman. In fact, I dated him for a while. But it didn't last. I knew I could never be in love with him."

"Why is that?" Clare asked.

"He was too much in love with himself."

Clare suppressed a grin. Luna scolded angrily, "Get back to the subject."

"We had a couple of beers and exchanged a little campaign talk and John turned on his charm and before I knew it he was asking me to let him in on any juicy information I had learned from following you on the tour. 'I'll make it worth your while,' he said, and whispered in my ear a sum of money that made me think."

Luna threw up her hands. "I can't believe I trusted you and allowed you to travel with us. And now I learn we had a paid spy right under our noses."

"No, no, Luna. It was just this once. I slipped up, and I'm sorry."

Clare said, "Go ahead, Laurie, tell us the rest of it."

"I told John I couldn't accept his money, and besides I didn't have any big secret information to give him. But he kept pressuring, and I finally I said there was one little thing that was interesting. And I told him that you were going to Bull's hometown on Tuesday."

"And then what?"

"We finished our beers. He gave me a hug and said it was nice to see me again and he went his way and I went mine."

"And that's all?" Luna said.

"Almost. When I got home and took off my jacket, I found a wad of cash that John had stuck in my pocket."

"And you kept the money?"

"I haven't had a chance to give it back. But I was tempted to keep it. In the first place, I didn't feel like I had betrayed any confidence. In fact, looking at the situation as a reporter, I thought it would make a much better story if Bull decided to show up. I know now that was a mistake. But the other thought I had was that I really could use the money.

"I'm a single mother. Newspaper work doesn't pay very well. And as I told you earlier, I'm not on salary. I just get paid a fee. There are no benefits. I have a tough time making ends meet. But I really feel bad about the way it turned out. I'm really sorry."

Clare sympathized with her but she was not in a forgiving mood. Nor was Luna.

As Laurie stood to leave, Clare said, "Luna and I will talk about this …"

Luna interrupted to say, "There's no need to do any talking. We can't have someone who can't be trusted traveling with us. Laurie, I'm withdrawing the permission I gave you to ride along on the campaign bus. I'm sorry it has to be this way so close to the end of the campaign. But you screwed up, and you know it. Since we're going that way, we'll drop you off at state headquarters so you can get your car. Take a seat up front."

Laurie impulsively hugged Clare, said goodbye and sadly walked up the aisle. She sat by a window and peered at the people resuming their lives following the town's only excitement since a bottle containing a note from a boy in Singapore had washed up on shore about five months ago.

As she sat alone with her thoughts about her own life, Laurie felt a hand on her shoulder. It was Clare. "Come along and ride with us," she said.

76

HENRY TOOK THE passenger seat in front and Clare invited Laurie to sit in the back with her. The driver put Laurie's small traveling bag in the back of the SUV.

Clare had no special plan in mind when she offered Laurie the ride. She just remembered times in her young life when she had made wrong choices and paid the penalty. She knew how it was to have people angry with you and to feel terribly alone. Perhaps it was an inborn motherly instinct that made her want to give Laurie some comfort.

"Thank you, Clare. You probably don't even want to be speaking to me after what I did."

"It's all right. You've said you're sorry. No great harm has been done."

"I hope that's true. I don't think Luna feels the same way."

"Luna has had a rough life – being separated from her father in a divorce, being taken away from the only friends she had and taken halfway around the world by her mother and her new husband. They were both busy people so Luna was cheated out of the parental love and attention every child needs. She grew up very quickly – she had to. And that experience toughened her. In a way that was good, because she needed to be strong to meet the challenges she would face in the world. Perhaps someday she will have children of her own and that can make her more understanding and more patient with those around her," Clare said.

"I've had a life kind of like that," Laurie said. "Luna has a lot of good qualities. You can be very proud of her."

"I am. Now tell me about yourself."

They spent a good deal of the time returning to Santa Barbara in what turned out to be an unplanned counseling session, which made both Laurie and Clare feel better. When they had only a few miles to go, Clare asked about her plans – specifically if she would continue to cover the campaign.

"That's what I would like to do most," Laurie said. "I really do like politics. I find it both interesting and exciting. I was very happy going with you and your team, watching how you interacted with people. And I love writing. It was like everything was going right for me – and then I blew it by a stupid decision."

"I would like very much for you to continue on the tour. I don't mind saying that the articles you've written have been instrumental in getting Californians to know me very well."

"I really wish I could. But being able to ride on the bus made it possible. I don't think I can afford the expense of taking my own car everywhere you're going. I'll certainly attend any events close by in the L.A. area," Laurie said. "There's one thing I'm really grateful for. My mother keeps my three-year-old son for me."

"That's good. Actually, in the time that's left before the election, the surrounding area is where I'll be spending most of my time. We're conserving our travel expenses, too. So I look forward to seeing you as often as possible."

"Thank you so much," Laurie said, with tears welling up. "It means a lot to me that you care."

"Oh, I do, honey," Clare said, squeezing her hand.

On the following day, Henry and Clare flew to San Jose for a speech to an environmental group on protecting natural resources and a fundraising luncheon attended by junior executives of Silicon Valley firms – many of whom were breaking away from traditionally supporting only liberal candidates and, according to New Yorker magazine, turning to Libertarians and in some cases Republicans. In other words, they were becoming more open-minded about politics.

By Thursday, Laurie had decided to make it possible to rejoin the tour because Clare was campaigning in places like Inglewood, with large Hispanic and African-American populations; Whittier, a city of mixed politics; and predominantly Asian Alhambra. The week's schedule ended on the north side of Los Angeles with a rally in a suburb in Kern County.

The local "Clare for Governor" organization had arranged for an afternoon rally in a lovely city park. Volunteers had set up chairs to accommodate those who needed to sit. The rains had let up, allowing for a beautiful sunny day, which encouraged a large turnout. Being a Friday the entire "Clear Sailing" combo had arrived on the bus and had the crowd clapping and singing along on some of the tunes, including the campaign song.

Clare set her red shoulder bag down on a picnic table while she greeted her local hosts and with her standard introduction, "Here's Clare" she faced the crowd with a feeling of optimism and confidence. Spotting Laurie Miller in the front row, she gave her a friendly wave and began her remarks.

"Thank you all for coming. Are you feeling as good about this campaign as I am? (The crowd responded with shouts of "Yes" and cheers.) We're getting close to Election Day and I've got a feeling that victory is within our grasp. (More cheers) With 10 days to go I am confident that with your wonderful support, and that of 'Clare for Governor' volunteers throughout the state, we will make a strong showing in the June 3rd primary. (More cheers).

"If I am in the top two finishers on that Tuesday, as I expect to be, we will know that all of your hard work has paid off and that Californians have sent a signal that they want a change in the governor's office and the new governor elected in November will wear high heels and carry a red purse. And that's not Jerry Brown's normal attire." (Cheers and chants of Clare, Clare, Clare)

"When California voters mark their ballot for me on June 3 you will be saying you want better education for your children ... (Yes)

"... you want to make the best possible use of the taxes you send to Sacramento ... (Yes)

"... you want us to do a better job of conserving and protecting our natural resources ... (Yes)

"... you want to encourage economic growth without endangering our quality of life ... (Yes)

"... and you want our state leaders to make human resources a high priority and make sure the health and welfare needs of all Californians are met, without regard to race, color or gender ... (Yes)

"That's what all of us want. And if you elect Clare, that's what you'll get." (Cheers and chant Clare, Clare, Clare)

As the applause subsided a voice in the back of the crowd could be heard, muffled at first but soon becoming clear. A young man was shouting, "Lies! Lies! All lies!"

Clare wanted to make sure she heard right. "Sir, what are you saying?"

"You're lying. You're nothing but a lowdown liar."

"What am I lying about, sir? Come up here and tell me."

The man stepped out from the crowd and came into full view. He appeared to be in his 20s, with facial hair, wearing khakis and a camouflage jacket with a bill cap pulled low on his face. He walked forward, mumbling obscenities, and resumed his tirade: "Lies, lies, lies. That's all they are."

"Sir, I want you to tell me what I'm lying about. Come up here ... (she motioned him to circle the crowd to her right) ... and let's talk."

He kept advancing, but slowly. Clare noticed a slight limp. "Talking's no good," he snapped. "You won't listen to me. Nobody listens to me."

"I'll listen to you. Just tell me what's wrong."

The man was coming closer and yelling: "What's wrong is you and all the other politicians. You say you'll help me but all you do is lie."

"What do you need help with, sir? Come here and talk to me."

"I'll tell you. And you're going to listen." With that threat, he pulled out a handgun and waved it in the air. The crowd erupted with screams and began

266

scattering. He turned and pointed his weapon their way and people stopped in their tracks. "You are all going to listen," he said. "And don't touch your phones or I'll kill every one of you."

"Sir," Clare said. "Please calm down. And put your gun away. I'll listen to you and I'll try to help you."

"No. You're lying. I don't believe you," he said, pointing the gun at Clare.

She quickly surveyed the scene. Some of the people had managed to get away but a large number remained, frozen in fear. Not a single police officer was in sight. She saw Laurie hastily taking notes.

The crazed gunman was about 25 feet away and still steadily advancing. Clare slowly eased into position near her red shoulder bag on the table.

"Sir, please put away your gun. We don't want anybody to get hurt. We just want to help you," Clare pleaded.

"You're lying, like all the rest of them. You're not going to help me. AND I'M GOING TO KILL YOU!"

Pointing his weapon straight at Clare and with a wild, angry look on his face he moved toward her. A single shot rang out. The crowd gasped as a body fell to the grass.

Everything happened at once, but it appeared to be in slow motion. The assailant was down, grasping his right shoulder, which was oozing blood. Henry dived for the man's weapon and snatched it out of his reach. Luna came running from somewhere to Clare's side. Clare coolly returned her .38 special revolver to her shoulder bag where she had reached in and pulled it out when the man was about eight feet away.

The sirens that had been heard around the time the shooting occurred went silent and two policemen, with their service revolvers drawn, came running to the scene. Hearing Henry shout, "He tried to kill her," they handcuffed the wounded man. One officer ordered Henry to turn over the gun. Then he accompanied a stretcher crew which carried the man to an ambulance that had just arrived. A second squad car also came with sirens screaming followed by a fire engine. Two more policemen got out and came to the scene.

About half of the crowd, feeling lucky to escape, had run to their cars. The remainder, largely curious to see what happened next, stayed at a distance straining to hear what was being said. The newly arrived officers ordered the crowd to leave the park and they quickly put up yellow "crime scene" tape and began questioning as many as possible about what had happened.

Meanwhile, one of the first two policemen on the scene was taking a statement from Clare. Luna and Henry stood on either side of her and Laurie

Miller, showing her press credentials, got as close as she could and listened intently.

"I need to see some ID, ma'am," he said. She showed him her driver's license and state senator identification card. He entered information in a hand-held computer and gave the cards back.

"Thank you. May I see your gun, please, ma'am?"

She produced the revolver and, holding it by the barrel, handed it to the officer.

"You are the owner of this weapon?"

"Yes. And here is my permit." She handed him her concealed weapon permit.

"I got it in 2011 after I was elected to the state senate to succeed my husband, Gary," she said. "It was the same year Representative Giffords was shot in Arizona ..."

"It was in a setting similar to this one today, as I recall," the officer said.

"That's right. I bought the gun following a briefing by state capitol police about heightened concerns for state legislators at public appearances. A number of my colleagues did the same thing."

"Have you used it before today?"

"No. Fortunately I haven't had an occasion that called for it."

"I'll need to keep this for evidence," he said, unloading the cartridge of its remaining bullets.

"Evidence?" Luna exploded. "You make her sound like a criminal!"

Henry spoke up. "It was clearly self-defense. And there was at least a hundred witnesses," he said.

"It's simply a part of the investigation," the officer said. "We do have to conduct an investigation in any case involving the use of a firearm. Now, Senator de Lune, please tell me what happened here today."

Clare told him why she was at the park and how the man began speaking out during her remarks. "I tried to reason with him, get him to talk about his need for help from the government," she said. "But when he produced a gun I knew the situation was getting worse, not better. I was unable to persuade him to put down the gun and tell me about his problems. As he got closer I looked him in the eyes and I could see the anger boiling up inside him."

"What did you do then?"

"I had deliberately guided him into a position slightly away from the crowd. There was nobody behind him in the line of fire. When he came toward me threatening to kill me, I drew my gun and shot."

"Did you realize you could have killed this man?"

"Officer, I didn't shoot to kill. My only thought was to disarm him before he harmed anyone. I knew I had to protect myself and I also was concerned for the safety of all the others gathered here."

"You shot him in the shoulder, causing him to drop his weapon. That was a good shot. You must have had some training."

"I did. And it was very thorough. I did not want to own a gun without knowing how to use it in case I needed to."

"Thank you for your cooperation, ma'am. I think that will be all for now. But please don't leave the state. We may have additional questions."

"I don't plan to go far until after the June 3 election."

At the officer's request, she signed a form on the computer attesting to the truth of the statement she had given.

Turning to Henry, he said, "We'll also have to get a statement from you, sir. But that can wait. For now, if you'll please come with me to the squad car I need to take your fingerprints."

Henry then realized that his prints were on the wounded man's gun. "Were you able to identify the man who was going to kill Clare?" he asked.

"The man she shot was carrying some identification, yes. His name is Aaron Zane. He served in the Army in Afghanistan. He was awarded a Purple Heart for injuries sustained from the explosion of an IED which killed two of his fellow soldiers. There was also a copy of a letter he had written to the Veterans Administration about a disability claim."

"How long ago was that?" Clare asked.

"It was last summer."

"That's probably what set him off. He apparently hadn't received any response."

"One more thing," the policeman said. "Sergeant Zane was being treated at a VA hospital for Post-traumatic Stress Disorder."

77

CLARE HAD EXPECTED the confrontation in the park that ended in violence to be all over the news on Saturday. But the evening's rampage near the University of California at Santa Barbara campus that left seven dead, including the shooter, was the lead story. She was horrified but thankful that her encounter with a gunman ended differently.

As the only reporter present to witness Clare's showdown with the angry veteran, Laurie Miller had an exclusive story for the Los Angeles News. The AP picked it up and distributed it, with her byline, to its member newspapers and other media.

Clare had found her telephone answering machine full of messages when she returned home from the unnerving experience. She decided to remain unreachable by news media for the time being.

Henry had worked out an agreement to give his statement to the police in Kern County by phone and made it a part of the official record by an electronic signature which he emailed. He checked in with Clare and she asked him to come to the villa.

"How are you doing?" he said, noting the strain on her face.

"I didn't sleep very well, as you can imagine," she said. "I finally took a pill and that helped."

"It was quite a jarring experience. I couldn't stand seeing that man pointing his gun at your face. I felt so helpless."

"I would have, too, if I hadn't had my 'protective team' – Smith and Wesson – with me."

"Oh, so that's what you meant when you had that phone conversation with Luna right after we met in Seattle."

"Henry?"

"Yes?"

"I need a hug."

He took her in his arms and held her close for a long while. He could feel her heart beating fast and she was sobbing quietly.

"It'll be all right," he said, as she slowly pulled away.

"I really regret that it happened. But I had to do it."

"Of course. It was you or him. I'm so glad you had a gun and knew how to handle it."

She looked at him with an anguished expression, reliving the frightening moments of the previous day.

"I feel so sorry for that poor young man," she said. "He's been through the horrors of war and now he's suffering more because of a federal bureaucracy. I read that the VA has a huge backlog of disability claims that haven't been processed. He apparently hasn't even had an acknowledgement."

"But that's not your fault, Clare," Henry said. "He had no reason to take out his frustrations and hate on you."

"I know, but I wish there was some way I could help him." She paused and sat quietly, then added: "I'd like to check on his condition. I wonder how I can find out?"

"You might check with Laurie Miller," Henry said.

"That's a good idea. I'll call her." She punched up her number and put the phone on speaker. Laurie answered on the first ring.

"Laurie, this is Clare. How are you?"

"I'm fine. My heart skipped a couple of beats yesterday. But are you okay?"

"Yes. Your story really received a lot of attention."

"Well, I was the only reporter on the scene, thanks to you. So it was a scoop. And the editor of the News gave me a bonus," she said excitedly.

"I'm glad. You deserve it. Laurie, I called to get some information."

"Sure. How can I help?"

"I want to check on Sergeant Zane's condition. Do you know which hospital he's in?"

"He's not. It was just a flesh wound. He was only in the hospital a few hours. A doctor removed the bullet, bandaged him up and released him to the custody of his parents."

"Really? Do you have their number?"

"Yes. I wrote it in my notebook. Hold on a sec."

Henry broke in to say, "There's someone at the door. Shall I see who it is?"

Clare nodded, jotting down the number.

Henry returned with a uniformed LAPD officer who gave his name and said: "Sorry for the intrusion, ma'am."

"What can I do for you?" Clare said.

"We tried to call you. The Kern County authorities asked us to find out if you want to press charges against the man who threatened to kill you."

"Sergeant Zane? I hadn't given any thought to that. No. You can tell them I have no plans to do so. The man needs to be somewhere he can get some help for his condition, not in jail."

271

"All right. And they requested this to be returned to you," he said, handing her a plastic bag containing her revolver. "Thank you, ma'am. Have a nice day."

"And the same to you."

Henry escorted the young officer to the door. When he returned Clare was calling the sergeant's parents. His father answered and when she identified herself he seemed to be glad she called.

"I wanted to check on your son's condition," she said.

"He's sleeping right now. He's been sleeping a lot since the ambulance brought him here yesterday. I think they gave him a heavy dose of sedatives."

"But he's going to be all right?"

"From the wound, yes. It was only minor. But I'm afraid he has a long way to go to recover from the effects of the war. I hope you understand, that's what drove him to do what he did at the park yesterday."

"That's the other thing I want to ask you. He apparently has a VA disability claim pending for too long a time."

"Nine months. And he can't get anyone to tell him the status of his claim. He's been counting on that to help him get back on his feet. He wants to be on his own but he can't get a job. He had to give up his apartment and move in with us. His mother and I are happy to have him here, but we know he wants to be independent."

"What about his treatment for PTSD?"

"He was seeing someone at the VA hospital but he had to go and wait several hours so many times he finally just gave up."

"Well, I don't know how much I can do, but I do want to try to remove some of his frustrations. And one more thing: I'm very sorry I had to hurt your son."

"Sorry? Don't be. What you did saved his life."

"What do you mean?"

"Someone had alerted the police and they were on their way. If he had begun firing rounds at you and people in the audience, the police would have shot and killed him. I firmly believe that. So my wife and I want to thank you for your smart, decisive action – and your accurate aim – it allowed us to keep our son. And by the way, we intend to support you for governor."

Astounded, Clare said: "I don't know what to say. I'm so glad you see it that way."

"There's one more thing I want to tell you. A while ago, one of those lawyers who's always popping up in the news in sensational cases came knocking on our door and wanted Aaron to file charges of attempted murder against you and to sue you for damages. I didn't waste any time with her. I just sent her on her way."

"I'm certainly grateful to you for that. I fully expect one of my opponents to hit me pretty hard about this to try to knock me out of the race."

"We'll stick by you, Clare. Thank you for calling."

Clare put down the phone and sat letting the conversation sink in. All she could say was, "well, what do you know!"

She started to the kitchen to get some coffee and felt the phone in her pocket vibrating. Luna was calling:

"Do you have the TV on?"

"No. What's happening?"

"Jack Bull is holding a press conference. He's demanding that you withdraw from the governor's race?"

"That's ridiculous. For what reason?"

"He's accusing you of trying to kill – quote – 'one of our nation's brave wounded warriors'."

"Oh, for heaven's sake! That guy has absolutely no scruples. I guess I'd better see what he's saying."

She gave Henry a quick fill-in as she went to the nearest TV set and turned it on in time to see his closing statement."

"My fellow citizens," he said. "This candidate's actions yesterday were disgraceful. The very idea of shooting one of our country's fighting men – a courageous soldier who fought to protect our freedoms – a decorated combat veteran whose body is wracked with pain, who is struggling not only with his physical disability but also with PTSD.

"We should give victims of mental illness the kind of treatment they need and be nursed back to health. Instead, Senator de Lune wants to shoot them.

"That is abominable reckless behavior that is unfit for any citizen. It is intolerable for a public official to commit such inhuman acts.

"I repeat: I am publicly calling for Clare Sullivan de Lune to withdraw from the governor's race immediately to protect the good name of our state. Her failure to do so will prove that what I've been saying is true: she is totally unqualified to hold any elective office in our state. Thank you."

Bull walked away without taking any questions. He obviously didn't want to be put in the position of having to defend his foolish charges.

Clare resumed her interrupted trip to get a pot of coffee and two cups. She sat across from Henry and sipped slowly, mulling over the most recent developments in her roller coaster campaign.

"I can see it coming," she said. "Bull finally has an issue that he will use to the fullest extent to lift himself up by tearing me down."

"I hate to say it, but you're probably right. Maybe you ought to put out a brief statement to get into the Sunday stories with his blast."

"Good idea." She called Melody and dictated a short response to Bull's charges. "Jack Bull, as usual, is going off half-cocked. Sergeant Zane only suffered a flesh wound and his father tells me he'll be all right. I'm going to do everything I can to see that Aaron Zane gets the help he needs."

"That ought to do it," Henry said.

"Silly me," she laughed. "I had the crazy notion we could close out this campaign on a high note and coast to victory. But it appears we'll have to work harder than ever this coming week to counteract the preposterous crusade that Bull will be leading."

She called Luna. "Well, Jack Bull has finally latched onto something he can use to stir up the masses and perhaps turn the tide in his favor. I think we'd better scrap what plans were made for the final week of the campaign and mount a counteroffensive. We need to have a powwow in that online chatroom thing to discuss the best strategy. Do you think you can set it up for this afternoon?"

"I'll do my best," Luna said. "Hang in there, Clare."

The chatroom session was short but productive. There was general agreement that the Kern County incident was an emotional issue and had to be dealt with accordingly. It had to be put to rest quickly so Clare could regain control of the agenda. Hector predicted that editorial comment in the Sunday news would be split or slightly in Clare's favor – which proved to be right. Gene applauded Clare's fast response. "It was the best thing to do: knock it down and move on." He also proposed a strategy that was acceptable to everyone – in theory. Gene said, "We need to blanket bomb the opposition with 30-second spots on radio and TV, mixed in with some 60-second ads." His grand finale recommendation: a 30-minute documentary type program highlighting Clare's career, with testimonials from Tim Barnham and others, and a closing appeal for support by Clare. When he gave an estimated cost for all this, the reaction was quite different. Clare said she didn't think the campaign had enough resources to afford it. Henry agreed, but added that if the group agreed to follow Gene's advice he would find some way to raise the necessary money.

As anticipated, the dramatic encounter in the park ignited the gun control debate and the Sunday editorial and op-ed pages were filled with commentary on both sides of the issue. Liberals pointed to it as another example of gun violence. Conservatives used it to strengthen their argument for second amendment rights.

Some editorials praised Clare for her courage and coolness in the face of death; others took the Bull line and condemned her for being reckless and endangering the lives of innocent citizens.

First thing Monday morning Clare paid a visit to the Veterans Administration office in West Los Angeles and from there to the VA Hospital located nearby. At each place she used her state senate credentials to get in to see the person in charge. She doubted that any of the bureaucrats at either place recognized her as a candidate for governor. She requested and received, after some delay, a report on the status of Aaron Zane's disability claim and obtained assurance that someone would let him know it was being processed. At the hospital she observed the crowded waiting rooms and the only explanation she was able to get was the old "underfunded and understaffed" excuse. The doctor who had been seeing Aaron was not on duty, but she got a promise from the staff that an appointment would be scheduled at an early date.

While Gene's hard-hitting ads were running, Clare used a chartered plane to make "hop, skip and jump" appearances in vital areas of the state to boost the campaign's get-out-the-vote efforts. She was encouraged by the response she received and by midweek the shooting controversy had begun to die down. The polls showed her running about 10 points behind Brown, the TV star.

Meanwhile, Henry was racking his brain for ideas about money sources. He concluded he had reached the limit with California contributors and he couldn't think of any outsiders, like the Las Vegas casino, to put the arm on. He had almost given up hope when he got a call from Luna. She said they needed to talk.

They agreed to meet after work in a Santa Barbara wine bar. Henry was baffled about the reason for the meeting. Luna put his mind at ease right away.

"I'm going to tell you something that I've kept from Clare. I've been ashamed to do it, but up to now I thought it wouldn't make much difference."

"I'm intrigued," he said. "Tell me your secret."

"You remember how you and Clare met? She was on a mission to Seattle to see Mr. Zee, with hopes of getting a large contribution?"

"I do indeed. And she was very disappointed that she didn't get to meet with him. I do remember that she left her bag in his office as a reminder that she was there."

"That's right. Well, a few days later he returned it. Clare was still fuming about the experience and she tossed it in the trash can."

"Go on."

"I couldn't stand the thought of trashing a designer bag, even if it was a knockoff. So I rescued it for myself."

"Nobody could blame you for that."

"Clare doesn't know it, but that's the bag she's using now. I gave it to her for the 'campaign costume' Gene wanted her to wear."

"That was a good thing to do."

"Inside the bag was a sample packet of Forever Yung cosmetics, which I could use. But there also was a personal letter from Mr. Zee, apologizing for what happened in his office. He also indicated he would still like to discuss her campaign with her."

"I believe I see where you're going."

"I can't be sure, but I think there might be an opening there if you want to pursue it."

"I do. And thank you, Luna, very much. The drinks are on me."

By week's end there was enough money in the bank to pay for Gene's advertising blitz with a cushion for unexpected last minute expenses. Only after fourth quarter campaign finance reports were filed did anyone know that Mr. Zee and Henry Jackson were leading contributors.

At Clare's invitation, local members of the campaign team gathered at the villa to watch the 30-minute infomercial Gene had produced to air on TV stations statewide. They assembled in the great room and sat in a semi-circle around the giant screen. The program began following an ad featuring a Hollywood starlet pretending to be Lauren Bacall and breathing: "When I want a perfect MAN-icure, I don't whistle. I go to Helen Bach."

Using still shots from photo albums and videos of her later years, Gene had traced Clare's life as an honor student, continental adventurer, sculptor and public servant. With stirring background music, there were scenes of Clare in scenic settings, on Main Street, shaking hands at rallies, visiting small businesses, addressing women's groups, and finally on the villa overlook silhouetted against a clear blue sky. The segment ended with clips from her announcement for governor. Tim Barnham delivered a folksy but sincere endorsement of her as someone he knew closely and could testify to her knowledge of state government and her ability to get things done. "She's very conscientious, and an independent thinker," he said. He gave her a solid vote of confidence that she would make an outstanding governor.

"I also had the opportunity to watch her most vocal opponent, John Bull, when he served in the state senate," Tim added. "All I can say about him is that he hasn't changed very much. His time in Washington has only made him even more vicious in the way he plays politics. The latest example of his underhanded tactics was on display this past week when he unleashed an attack on Clare that was totally unfounded. Bull made the outlandish charge that Clare committed a horrible crime against a wounded veteran who felt he had been mistreated by the government. He painted this gentle woman as a hardened criminal.

"Let's set the record straight on this matter, for once and for all. Let's hear what the parents of this soldier have to say."

The next scene was this couple sitting in their living room. The father spoke:

"We are the parents of Aaron Zane. Our son served honorably as an Army enlisted man in Afghanistan. While on duty there he was severely injured in a roadside bomb blast which killed two of his buddies. Aaron survived but now he walks with an artificial leg. Like many other veterans he came home suffering from Post-traumatic Stress Disorder."

Alan's father described the frustrations his son had encountered in trying to get help from the federal government – the long hours in a waiting room at the VA hospital, the inability to get any information about his disability claim from the Veterans Administration after months of waiting.

Near tears, he continued: "Aaron is a good man. He has never done anything wrong. We raised him to be independent and he has tried hard to make it on his own. But because of the economy, and complicated by his health conditions, he has tried unsuccessfully to earn a living.

"All of these pressures built up to the point that he had thoughts of suicide. His mother accidentally made this discovery when she found a half-completed note in a pair of his trousers that she laundered.

"We believe, and doctors lend some credence to our belief, that his war experiences and his troubled life as a civilian drove him to do the unthinkable thing he did in the park a little over a week ago. He was not himself when he went into that crowd of people armed with a gun and threatened Clare Sullivan de Lune.

"Mrs. de Lune called me to check on Aaron's condition and I told her – and I'm telling all Californians within the sound of my voice now – she saved my son's life by firing that well-aimed shot, which caused him to drop his weapon. It was a minor wound and he is making a quick recovery.

"When this happened the police were responding to a frantic call. Had they arrived as he was firing his gun they would have done their duty and shot him dead on the spot.

"Alan is alive today because of the sound judgment and fast action of this good woman.

"My wife joins me in saying that we are proud supporters of her to be California's next governor and we urge everyone watching this telecast to pay no attention to the lies that are being told about her. Join us in voting for Clare for Governor."

An announcer says: "And now, Here's Clare."

Her remarks had been taped the previous day in a rented studio which had proper lighting and sound equipment. She was seated before a close replica of the desk in her state senate office, with the U.S. and state flags behind her, along with a bookcase and a world globe.

"Thank you for allowing me to talk to you for a few minutes about my hopes and plans for California's future. I want only the best for our state and I'd like to prove to you that I can deliver.

"In the past several months I have met many of you face to face as I have toured the state from north to south getting to know you. Through my travels to cities and towns, industrial and agricultural areas, college and university campuses, seaside and mountainside, I hope you've gotten to know me better.

"I didn't set out to make an impression. I tried to be straightforward and honest in telling you what I believe about some of the problems facing us – we always have something that needs to be fixed – and what I would do about them. I hope I convinced you that I see clearly what should be done. It's summed up in my five-point platform. (shown on the screen)

"We need to provide our young people with the best education possible.

"We need to make sure our financial resources are put to the best use.

"We need to do a better job of conserving and protecting our natural resources.

"We need to encourage economic growth while preserving our quality of life.

"We need to be mindful always of our state's most important asset, human resources.

"I am dedicated to achieving these goals.

"As I said in announcing my candidacy, I believe strongly in clean, ethical government. I have run a clean campaign and I will continue to uphold those standards.

"I am seeking to become the first woman to serve as governor of California. I know that is a monumental challenge. My detractors call it a foolish endeavor.

"But my friends, I ask you: why not give a woman a chance for a change?

"Now, I've got nothing against men. I like men. But just being male does not entitle anyone to lay claim to the governor's office. Other states have set an example. A woman presently chairs the National Governors Association.

278

"Certainly being governor of a state with as large a population as we have is an enormous job. California has been referred to as a nation-state. That ought to be enough to dissuade anyone of the so-called weaker sex, right? Not this woman … not Clare! (thumb to chest)

"If Margaret Thatcher could establish herself as the Iron Lady of Great Britain … if Indira Gandhi could take the reins of a country like India … and if Angela Merkel can head the economic powerhouse of Germany … that argument goes right out the window.

"I like what Amelia Earhart said: 'Women, like men, should try to do the impossible.'

"If you believe what the political pundits say, most Californians are happy with the man in office now and are inclined to let him have another term. He has done some good things, and some not so good. But are you aware that he's hinted at having higher aspirations? Is it okay with you to have a short-time governor, itching to toss his hat into the 2016 presidential ring? Not Clare! (thumb to chest). California needs a fulltime governor, focusing only on what's best for the state and not pursuing personal ambitions.

"This will be my last opportunity to speak to you before Tuesday's primary election. So let me just make this request:

"Please go to the polls and exercise your freedom to vote.

"It's your right to vote for the candidate of your choice … but please cast an informed vote. Know all you can about the candidates running. Don't just mark your ballot for a name your precinct leader or your union – or your best friend – told you to support. Your vote is private. Make sure it counts.

"And finally, don't automatically write me off without considering what I've said in this talk and what you've learned – independently – about me. Only you can make up your mind. Give this election some thought. And if you can see your way clear to do it, vote for Clare!"

(fade to long shot of the state capitol)

As the last strains of music were heard, Clare's team embraced her in a joint hug. Henry raised his wine glass in a toast: "Here's to Clare for governor!"

78

CLARE SPENT MOST of the day on Monday in the state campaign headquarters, making phone calls, exchanging emails and responding to news media requests for an election-eve statement. She sent a personal note to her Twitter followers and posted a longer message to Facebook friends to impress the importance of getting supporters to the polls. Melody had used these media to alert "Clare for Governor" fans to watch Sunday's 30-minute TV program.

Luna checked to make sure all county organizations had arranged to have poll watchers to guard against any nefarious activity at the voting places.

Luna had made arrangements to have a Tuesday evening election watch in a ballroom of a downtown Santa Barbara hotel, which the local volunteers decorated. She also rented a one bedroom suite for Clare and the campaign team to keep tracks on returns as they were reported on television.

For the candidate, the day of an election can be nerve-wracking, or the opposite. Clare chose the latter option. She felt that her fate was in the hands of the voters and the gods (which some politicians believe are one and the same).

Clare decided she wanted this day to herself. So she turned off the phone, put aside her other communication devices, got her car keys and went for a drive.

She drove up to Rattlesnake Canyon Park and took a hike on Tunnel Trail, which offers gorgeous views of the city. Since it wasn't the weekend, the number of mountain bikers wasn't enough to make her regret the excursion.

Reversing course, Clare decided to take a stroll on the long strip of sand at Leadbetter Beach. She paused frequently to look out to sea and breathe the ocean air. She got a sudden urge to go sailing, as she and Gary used to do when he had a moment of free time. She parked at the nearby Santa Barbara Sailing Center and priced a small vessel for the one-hour minimum. A white J-24' was suitable for her needs. It had an auxiliary motor for easy launching and docking as well as insurance against any sailing difficulty.

Remembering what Gary had taught her, she handled the craft masterfully and relived an experience that she had loved long ago. She could have remained on the water for hours but was getting hungry so she headed to shore for a quick bite at one of the many waterfront eating places.

Back at the villa she changed into a swimsuit, mixed herself a mojito, grabbed a stack of magazines and settled into a poolside lounge chair. It wasn't long before she was totally relaxed – to the point of drifting off into dreamland.

Her nap was not lengthy. She awoke with a start when she heard Henry calling her name. "I couldn't reach you and I thought there might be something wrong," he said.

"No, I just wanted to get away from politics and spend some time in a world I haven't visited in quite a while. I feel like a dip in the pool. If you'd like to join me, there are some trunks in the pool house. Unless you'd rather go skinny-dipping," she said teasingly.

"Some other time," he said, and headed to get a suit.

They splashed in the cool water for half an hour or so, and then decided it was time to get out and shower. It was too early to get dressed for the evening, and there was one other thing she wanted to do.

She disappeared upstairs and reappeared shortly wearing shorts, a T-shirt and topsiders. Henry had changed back to casual shirt and slacks. Noting his shoes were loafers, she invited him to join her on a walk around the villa grounds, which he had not done before.

Clare was not in a mood to hurry so they took time to admire the gardens with their variety of blooming plants, the fountains, lily ponds and birdbaths. Holding hands, they paused on the steps leading down to the overlook and looked back at the villa – a view that was new to Henry.

The sun was bright, the air warm and the scenery breathtaking.

A little farther down the slope Clare felt a chill from the sea breezes and snuggled close to Henry as they gazed at the almost clear sky over the vast blue ocean. The waves crashing on the rocks below created a rhythmic sound that reminded them of that evening long ago on the villa balcony looking at the full moon and listening to the sound of the loon.

Finally, the businesslike Henry reawakened and he broke the silence by asking, "Would you like for me to wait and take you into the city?" Clare replied, "If it's all the same to you, I think I'd rather drive myself." With a flirtatious smile, she added, "I do recall there's parking at your apartment building."

"And also at the hotel," Henry said. "See you later."

As he was halfway out the door, he turned back and said, "You did remember to vote, didn't you?"

Her hand flew up to her mouth and she gasped, "I almost forgot! I'll do that on the way to the watch party."

She didn't forget she had a late afternoon hair and nail appointment. That done she hurried back home to get dressed.

It was difficult to decide what to wear for this special occasion. Gene probably would want her to stick to her campaign costume, but she had worn it so many times she just couldn't bring herself to do it this evening. After all, the campaign was over. She finally opted for black slacks and a red silk blouse with a patterned neck scarf.

The lines were long at her precinct and she took that to be a good sign. Election workers confirmed it. A TV crew was on hand getting comments from voters and naturally wanted a statement from the candidate.

"I am delighted to see a large turnout," she said. "That's an indication of high interest in this important election. I would just like to say to your viewers, if you haven't voted, it's not too late. So get out and vote!"

When she arrived at the suite in the hotel, she found Luna, Houston and Melody already there. They were glued to the television set, although there was little to report at the time. They had seen Clare's comments live and now the stations were replaying an earlier interview with Jack Bull. He was still pounding away at his prime target.

"Senator de Lune should have withdrawn from the race, as I suggested. She could have avoided the embarrassment of coming in last," he puffed.

Luna said, "Well, after today we won't have to put up with any more of that b.s. Anyone hungry?"

A table was laden with sandwiches, vegetables and dip and other comestibles. There was also a well-stocked bar. Houston offered to serve Clare a drink.

"I'll just have some club soda for now, thanks," she said, helping herself to a carrot stick.

"Where's Henry?" Luna asked. "I tried to call you to check on your plans."

"He'll be along," Clare said. "Sorry I was out of touch. I figured you and the team had things well in hand and I couldn't do any more than I have for the election. And I just wanted to get away for a few hours."

She took a seat on the couch, kicked off her shoes and put up her feet on the coffee table. One of Pat Brown's voluminous TV ads came on the screen.

"All he's done since he entered the race is to flash his bright smile and recite a few lines from a script his handler gave him," Luna said, sarcastically.

"And he's got enough money to do it over and over," Houston added.

Melody looked up from her tablet and said, "We're getting reports from our volunteers about heavy turnouts everywhere."

"I'm going down to the ballroom and check on things there," Luna said. As she went out the door, Henry entered. He was carrying a paper bag with three bottles of his selected wine. He set it down and opened another large softsided bag.

"No wisecracks about plastic cups," he said, pointing at Clare, as he produced half a dozen carefully wrapped wine glasses.

The watch party was scheduled to begin at 8 p.m. but Luna came back and reported there were already some early arrivals. It had been decided that Clare would follow the general pattern and make an appearance only after the election had been decided. So the group settled in for what was to be a long evening.

"Who else are we expecting?" Clare asked.

"Hector said he would be here. And Tim said he would try to make it," Luna said. "Gene and Shirley are watching the returns in Seattle."

Henry opened some wine and poured a glass for Clare and left the bottle while he put a couple of sandwiches and some veggies on a plate and sat down beside her.

"How do you feel – excited?" he asked.

"Numb," she responded. "It has been an exhilarating experience but I'm ready for it to be over."

"Only if it turns out well," said Hector, who had just arrived and was pondering the choices of food, as only a professor would do.

"I suppose," Clare said solemnly.

There was little to do but wait until the polls closed at 8 p.m. and the time was spent in munching and idle chatter. The suite phone rang and Luna answered it. "It's Tim," she said, and pressed the speaker button. "Yer lookin' real good," came the familiar voice.

"I'm sorry I'm not with you," he said. "I just can't get there. But I'm present in spirit."

"We miss you, Tim," Clare said. "What are you hearing?"

"Not much. It's too early. I'm sure you're aware of the reports of a large turnout across the state. I heard that in one or two places Bull's paid sign carriers were threatened with arrest because they were too close to the polls."

"We might have known," someone muttered.

When the time was getting close to 8 p.m. Luna and Houston went down to check with the county volunteer chairman to see if she needed anything. The room was filling up quickly. Ronnie and Rosa had arrived and on the hour broke into the "Here's Clare" campaign song. The TV set was blaring with profound announcements that "The polls have now closed and we're looking at some early returns." (All of which were with fewer than 100 precincts reporting.)

Back in the suite the group was seeing the same thing. Clare got up from the couch and began pacing. She walked to the window and stared out at the lights of the city. Houston came over and said, "I know it doesn't mean much but in all the returns we've seen you are running very close to Pat Brown."

"Thanks, Houston. These are largely from rural precincts. I thought I might do well there," she said.

"I think you'll do well everywhere," he said, cheerfully. Clare gave him a smile and returned to her seat.

As the time dragged on, Clare became more restless. She stood and said, "I know it's not the plan, but I think I'd like to go down and welcome our supporters and thank them for their efforts. If they're feeling like I am, they could use some cheering up."

"It's not looking that bad," Luna said.

"But it's not looking that good either. I'll be back shortly," she said to the group.

Henry and Luna fell in behind and flanked her as she entered the ballroom, touching off a chorus of cheers and chants of "Clare! Clare! Clare!"

The county chairman shook her hand and turned to the crowd, saying, "Here's Clare!"

Clare looked up at the giant screen, still showing a relatively small number of returns.

"It looks like it's going to be a long evening. I just want to thank you all for coming to the watch party and also to tell you how much I appreciate all the work you've done for my campaign. You and others like you across the state are responsible for the votes in my favor today. I hope we can see the numbers rise as the night wears on. I'll be back later on. Thanks again." Waving at her followers all the way to the exit, she and Henry departed. Luna decided to wait a little while longer.

By 9:30 p.m. the urban returns were beginning to show up and the group in the suite began to have smiles on their faces. Clare was showing well in San Diego and Orange County, where she was running about even with a Republican candidate. Both were leading Pat Brown.

By 10 p.m. the figures had returned to what they were earlier, in spite of some surges for Clare from Silicon Valley and the Inland Empire counties. At 10:30 p.m. she and Pat Brown were still close but that left her in third place. Prospects for Clare being one of the top two finishers were looking grim.

"There are still a lot of votes to be counted," Hector counseled, "and a good many are in counties where you should be running strong."

The group gathered around Hector at a table where he had some maps and charts laid out. He pointed out counties he thought would bear watching.

The suite phone rang and Henry, being closest, answered it. "Hi, Pop," he said, and put the phone on speaker.

His gruff voice could be heard clearly. "Jean and I just wanted Clare and the rest of you to know that we've been following the returns all evening – as much as we can get on Washington stations. There is some national interest in this race, as you know. But how does it look from where you sit?"

"I haven't given up hope, Pop. But Brown No. 1 is very popular and Brown No. 2 had his TV fame and his fortune going for him. I had a lot of dedicated hard workers, but I don't know if it's going to be enough. We'll just have to wait and see," Clare said.

"Well, just know that we're pulling for you. I still don't know why you'd want that tough job, but if you win you'll be the best governor that state has ever had."

"Thank you, Pop. Give my best to Jean."

At 11 p.m. the stations had gone to full election coverage. Panels of pundits were going full blast, pontificating on all the various factors that were at play, including this being the first open primary for a governor's race. One by one the news anchors boldly projected victory for the incumbent for one of the two top spots. Pat Brown's lead over Clare was gradually widening.

With one eye on the TV reports, Clare huddled with Hector. They pored over his charts, tables and maps and the others in the group observed a frown on his face. Clare called Luna on her cell phone and asked her to return to the suite. When she arrived, she met her at the door and they exchanged some quiet conversation.

They both came to the center of the room and Clare looked from one anxious face to the other.

"My dear friends, I'm afraid it's over. The returns that are still out are all in areas where Jerry Brown has always won by a large margin. Most of those votes naturally will go to him and just increase his lead. The gap between me and Pat Brown is too large for me to overcome.

"There's one bright side. The way it looks now John Bull will do well to finish in fifth place."

Members of the team managed a weak cheer at that news. They all headed downstairs to break the sad news to the throng of loyal supporters. Clare did not give a concession speech. That remained to be done by the loser in the general election in November.

Carrying herself erect with pride and smiling broadly as she went to center stage, Clare motioned several times for the crowd to end their cheering and chants and gamely began her remarks. She had made no notes and spoke from the heart.

"My friends, my loyal supporters throughout the state of California, this is the night we've all been waiting for. It's difficult to put into words the way I feel. I know I can't express my thoughts in a clever sound bite.

"This has been a long, hard struggle. You and I both know that the odds were against me from the beginning. But in county after county, people had enough faith in me to join in an uphill climb to bring a new era of government to California. Dedicated citizens in the 'Clare for Governor' movement put in long hours and made great sacrifices to their personal lives to make a dream become a reality. Like the gold prospectors of a time long past, we had high hopes. And we came close. But we didn't make a strike. Not this year.

"But my friends, it's not because we didn't try. We put forth our best effort. We offered Californians a 'Clear Vision' for our state, now and for future years. We ran a clean campaign.

"I had the best campaign team (pointing) that a candidate could ever have. Give them a hand. I had the best statewide campaign organization that a candidate could hope for. I don't know of anything we could have done better to make the outcome any different.

"I'm disappointed, as you are. But I have no regrets. I am not looking back. I hope you will join me in looking forward to the time that Californians will choose a new kind of leadership.

"Thank you. God bless you. Goodnight."

The ballroom floor shook with the sounds of feet stomping, hands clapping, voices cheering, as the musicians played and sang the "Here's Clare" campaign song for the last time. Clare brought the team members to the front of the stage to take bows. She gestured toward the musicians, who also received hearty applause. She shook hands with the county volunteer chairman and thanked her again, then walked into the wings, smiling and waving.

The group returned to the suite to collect their things. The phone was ringing. It was Laurie.

"I'm sure the last thing you need is to be pestered by a reporter. But I'm calling as a friend to tell you how sorry I am that you lost."

"Thank you, Laurie. That's sweet of you."

"And I want to tell you how much it means to me that you helped me turn my life around. I've been offered a job as a reporter for the metro section of the Los Angeles Times. It's fulltime, with salary and full benefits."

"I'm so happy for you, dear."

"I wish I could say I'm happy for you. But that day will come, I'm sure."

"I lost my husband. I lost a race for governor. What else could happen?"

Clare thanked her for calling and turned to the small close-knit team that had shared this experience with her.

One by one they hugged Clare and each other and sadly left the room. Houston told Luna he would wait for her in the lobby, knowing she needed a few private moments with her best girl friend.

Henry busied himself repacking the wine glasses and generally clearing the snack table while they talked quietly.

"Well, mom, what next?" Luna said. It was the first time in many months she had called her "mom."

Clare's Georgia memories framed her answer. "In the words of Scarlett O'Hara, 'Tomorrow's another day.'"

"You probably need to get away," Luna said. "I'll take care of shutting down the campaign operation. I'd like to give bonuses to Melody and a few of the others."

"Sure," Clare and Henry said together.

"Just let me know where I can reach you if absolutely necessary."

"I will," Clare said, meeting her in a hug. "I thank you from the bottom of my heart, my precious daughter." With tears streaming down their faces, they parted and Luna went out the door without looking back.

79

WHEN CLARE DROVE out of the hotel parking garage to return to the villa the next morning, rain was pouring down. Rushing water in the street gutters was testing the capacity of the drains. Traffic was slow getting out of the city. The overcast sky gave no promise of clearing. The dismal day only heightened her somber mood.

She and Henry had wound down from the evening's suspense and stress sitting close together sipping wine and watching half-heartedly the victory speeches, the analyses and commentaries. Clare had thought she would be wired but Henry's calming presence – and the wine – helped her relax. They exchanged little conversation. With his arm around her shoulder and her head on his chest, she had fallen asleep. She didn't know when he had slipped away to turn down the bed covers and then gently awaken her and carry her into the adjoining room for a few hours of comfortable rest.

He was gone when she aroused herself. He had thoughtfully unplugged the phone and left her a note saying he would check in on her by late morning.

Thoughts of the evening and of the past year raced through her mind as she drove to the villa. She parked the car in the garage and went straight to the kitchen to brew coffee. She also was slightly hungry and satisfied that craving with a peach from the fruit bowl on the counter.

She felt intensely alone and gave fleeting thought to the idea of having a pet – how nice it would be to come home and be greeted by a bouncing puppy or a cuddly kitten. After all, she would have time for that sort of thing now. But she quickly dismissed the notion, saying to herself, "Clare, you're not ready for the rocking chair yet."

Sitting on the terrace, enjoying her coffee, she heard her cell phone ring. It was as if Henry had been reading her mind. She was so happy to hear his soothing voice and overjoyed at what he had to say.

Henry reminded her that Luna had advised her to put the campaign behind her and get away. He offered a suggestion.

"You've been to Greece, I'm sure. The Greek Islands are among the most favorite places I have visited. I especially am fond of Santorini. How would you like to go and spend a week there?"

She perked up immediately to his proposal. She had been to this beautiful island but only briefly when the cruise ship she worked on had anchored there for less than a full day.

"I am thrilled and delighted with your idea," she said. "How long do I have to pack?"

"You won't need to take anything but a couple of swimsuits – preferably bikinis."

"Ha, ha, ha," she said sarcastically.

"On the outside chance you would agree, I made reservations for a flight to Athens leaving LAX tomorrow afternoon."

"That's wonderful. That will give me plenty of time to get ready. With the weather the way it is I have no plans to leave the house."

"I was going to offer to take you to lunch," Henry said.

"Why don't you come here and I'll fix something for us. And we can talk about catching up on our lives."

"I'll be happy to," he said.

Checking her watch to make sure it wasn't too early, she called Luna and caught her at state headquarters.

"Hi, honey. So you're up and around?"

"Been up for hours. Lots to get done."

"I know. And I really hate that you got all the grunt work of the campaign."

"That's my job. There's no reason you or anyone else should do it. Melody has drafted a personal thank you note to email to all of our volunteers. She rewrote it for use on Twitter and Facebook. I sent these to you by email. If you could take a look and sign off on them right away, then we can move ahead on that."

"Melody is a jewel. I hope she has gained something from this experience that she can use in her career."

"She has. She has told me how much it has meant to her. Houston and I are taking inventory of what's left in the headquarters so we can move it out and stop paying rent. We'll sell as much of it as possible and put the rest in storage temporarily."

"Again, I can't thank you enough for doing all this. I hope you can take some time off before getting back to your ad agency business."

"Houston and I are going to talk about that as soon as we can get our heads above water."

"Well, I don't want to keep you. I do want to let you know we're taking the advice you gave me last night to get away. Henry has lined up a weeklong trip to a Greek Island – Santorini."

"Yeah, I've read about it. One of the most beautiful places in the world. I'm glad to hear that. When are you leaving?"

"Tomorrow afternoon. I don't know whether I'll get to see you before then."

"Probably not. But we can talk again. Gotta go now. Bye."

Henry had stopped by a travel agency and picked up some maps and other information on Santorini to look at after lunch.

Clare had decided to do Western omelets with turkey bacon, wheat toast and fresh fruit and that suited Henry just fine. They dined indoors because of the persistent showers and after finishing the meal with some homemade cookies out of the freezer they dived into the materials.

Henry read from one of the brochures: "Santorini is essentially what remains of an enormous volcanic explosion, destroying the earliest settlements on what was formerly a single island, and leading to the creation of the current geological caldera."

"Caldera means a large crater, as I recall," Clare said.

"Right. And there was a huge amount of lava that buried some towns. A rush of water into the void created a hell of a big tidal wave which turned the island into a semicircle and left what is today a deep blue lagoon."

"Sounds marvelous. I'm beginning to remember. Tell me more."

"This is from a travel guide: It says 'today's Santorini is a stunning island, with its white villages clinging to volcanic cliffs above black sand beaches.'"

"The way it's described it must be paradise," Clare said.

"Well, Santorini is widely believed to have been the lost Kingdom of Atlantis," Henry said.

"Wow! I can hardly wait."

A 16-hour overnight trip put them into Athens in late afternoon where they caught a 45-minute flight to Fira, the capital of Santorini. Henry had made a reservation at a five-star hotel in Oia. He chose it rather than Fira because it was quieter and has the best sunsets. After a late dinner they were ready to settle in to their room, which had a magnificent view from their cliff-top location. It reminded Clare of her view of the Pacific.

Oia (pronounced ee-a) is a pleasant village for walking and they spent the next morning wandering through the narrow, cobblestone streets among the whitewashed houses with blue-domed roofs. The town is built on a steep slope and the dwellings and shops are in niches hewn in the volcanic rock. Clare was delighted to see that Oia, being a haven for artists, had a number of art galleries. She purchased a small ceramic work that wouldn't be much trouble to pack.

They had lunch at a café with a view of the neighboring islands, enjoying meal-sized Greek salads accompanied by a carafe of Nykteri, a dry white wine.

They looked forward to dinner and tasting Vinsanto, the sweet and strong dessert wine which is the pride of the island.

One reason Henry chose Santorini for their post-election getaway was because of his interest in the island's small but flourishing wine industry, based on the indigenous grape variety, Assyrtiko. "The vines are extremely old and resistant to phylloxera," he explained. Clare rolled her eyes and took another sip.

The afternoon included a visit to an old mansion that has been converted to the Maritime Museum. It has displays, ship models and other objects that trace the island's history. Mostly they enjoyed the Cycladian fresh air and the spectacular panoramic views from the heights of this romantic destination spot in the Aegean Sea.

On the second morning they took a local bus to Fira for more sightseeing, which included the Mt. Profitis Ilias monastery and a wine museum located underground in a natural cave. They also visited the Boutari winery for a tour and a sampling of their award-winning wines, followed by a sumptuous buffet luncheon featuring Santorinian cheeses, tomato balls, roasted oven pork with potatoes, bread and barley rusks and more wine.

They weren't hungry enough for dinner that evening so they sat on the balcony of their room admiring the sunset while shelling and munching on renowned Aegina pistachios they had bought in town.

Clare finally broke out her swim suits and put one on the next morning for an outing on the island's beaches, known for their black, volcanic sand. She packed a small bag with towels and other necessities, put on an orange striped coverup over her two-piece yellow suit, added a wide-brimmed hat and started for the door when she became aware of Henry's fixed gaze.

"Sorry to disappoint you, bud, but I don't own a bikini."

"That's the farthest thing from my mind," Henry lied.

They took a bus back to Fira and got off at Kamari, the first of the large beaches on the southern side of the island. They were early enough to beat the main crowd, although there were a number of families with children at play and a few surfers enjoying the waves. Clare spread a beach towel and Henry put up a large umbrella he had rented and both took relaxing positions feeling the warmth but not the direct rays of the sun.

A while later Henry said he'd like to test the temperature of the water and challenged Clare to join him. The only valuables they brought were their watches and they sneakily buried them in the sand in a plastic bag and pulled the towel over to cover the spot.

Clare raced Henry to the water's edge where he, naturally, splashed her. To her surprise the water wasn't too cold, so she waded out a few yards and dived into an incoming wave. Henry came right behind her and they ventured into deeper water while reminding themselves of the danger of undertow. Impressed by Henry's muscular breast stroke, Clare wondered if he had engaged in competitive swimming at some time in his past. They had fun frolicking in the surf but finally had enough and returned to their spot on the sand, relieved to learn no one had disturbed their belongings.

Clare had thoughtfully brought bottled water and after relieving their thirst they reclined on the beach towel until their suits had dried enough to pull on shorts. By late morning they were ready to abandon their spot and join other vacationers on the bus back to downtown Fira.

As Henry and Clare continued their exploration of the shopping area they happened upon the Hotel Katris, a two-story white building with blue shutters and rails. A sign told them that inside was a cocktail bar, Terpsi, which offered an opportunity for further relaxation, but away from the sun and sand.

Terpsi was a most charming place – small but bright and cheery with deep red walls and tan-streaked tabletops. One wall had a gigantic brass-rimmed clock with Roman numerals, surrounded by silhouettes of musicians with various instruments. They ordered Greek coffees and pastries, which were just right for that time of day.

Presently they headed back to the bus stop, pausing to sniff the red and yellow wildflowers in bloom, but Clare spied the cable car, which was there to convey cruise ship passengers and other visitors from the pier up the steep slope – those who disdained the pleasure of riding a donkey.

"I want to take a ride!" Clare said, and Henry shrugged (probably wondering how she could ride a cable car but not the monorail in Seattle). So they took the short trip down, getting a different perspective on the ocean view. Once on the ground, there wasn't much to see but the tenders waiting to take passengers back to the cruise ships in the harbor. Clare had a brief thought that she'd like to take a cruise again, maybe this time with Henry.

A short time later they were back on a bus heading for the hotel in Oia. Once there Henry felt like a nap and settled in on a recliner on the balcony. Clare brought a novel and joined him. It wasn't long before she dozed off, too.

As dinnertime approached, Henry roused and called the desk to get a recommendation for a restaurant with a good view of the sunset. Rejecting the standard answer – "any spot in Oia has a beautiful view of the sunset" – Henry pressed to find out the clerk's preference and obtained directions to "the best view." He tipped him on the way out.

The Ambrosia restaurant had more than a wonderful view, which could be enjoyed best from the terrace or the outdoor dining area on the balcony. The candlelit interior, which was filled with antiques, made it easy to see why Conde Nast Traveler named it one of the world's most romantic restaurants.

They delighted in reading the menu, which was "neoclassic Greek cuisine enriched with international flavors." They had had their fill of souvlaki, spanakopita and baklava and were ready to phase back in to a more varied Mediterranean style of dining.

Clare selected sauted shrimp in a mastic sauce on avocado; a green salad with local tomatoes, capers, Kalamata olives, green pepper and chloro goat's cheese; and fillet of sea bass grilled in a light lemon sauce, served with seasonal vegetables.

Henry's choices were sauted baby calamari scented with ouzo; rocket salad with spinach and French lettuce and a pomegranate dressing; and tender beef fillet with Vinsanto wine and fresh truffles, accompanied by mushroom trifolate risotto and caramelized grapes.

For dessert, Clare had dark chocolate leaves on a white chocolate mousse with fresh strawberry and Anglaise sauce. Henry was intrigued enough to order "Moroccan sweet with a tower of Greek honey flakes, nuts, yogurt mousse with dates and apricot, accompanied by mastic ice cream and rose preserves."

From the Ambrosia wine list Henry chose a Vivlia Chora Assyrtiko and an Agiorgitiko from Nemea. They finished off the meal with snifters of Metaxa brandy.

With such a satisfying repast both Clare and Henry enjoyed a restful sleep.

While having their breakfast coffee on the balcony and looking ahead to another day of fun in the sun, Henry asked if there was anything special that Clare would like to do.

"I can't think of anything offhand. I've sort of been leaving those plans up to you. Do you have anything in mind?"

"Well, since Santorini has such an interesting history of winemaking, going back to the Bronze Age, I think I'd like to take the opportunity to visit another one of the island's wineries," he said. "There's one here in Oia, Domaine Sigalas, that I'd really like to see. But if you'd rather do something else ..."

"I enjoy winery visits, but if you don't mind going by yourself I believe I'd just as soon kick back – maybe go down by the pool and read my book. It's so good to be able to get away from the real world for a change," Clare said.

"Of course, if that's what you'd prefer. I'll get a cab and be back before lunch." With a quick kiss he left. Idly she reached and got the information about Domaine Sigalas he had been reading. She learned that Sigalas has been a pioneer in organic viticulture and has combined that with the best in winemaking technology, quality products and experience, to become a leader in the field. Clare didn't regret her decision to stay behind, but she looked forward to hearing Henry's impression.

When he returned shortly before noon, he found Clare reclining in a poolside lounge clad in an aqua swimsuit, her exposed skin glistening with sunblock. She had a UV protective sun shield covering her face, but he was fairly certain it was Clare.

"Well, if it isn't Darth Vader," he said heartily.

"Very funny," she said, removing the shield.

"Shall we take a walk and find someplace to have lunch?" he said.

"I need to go up to the room first and make myself presentable."

"If you insist."

As they opened the door, Clare thought she heard her cell phone ringing. Truly on vacation, she had to think quickly to remember where she had left it. When she answered she heard Luna's voice. Clare instinctively felt something was wrong. She quickly put the phone on speaker so Henry could hear.

"Why are you calling, Luna?"

"You need to come home," she said. "Something terrible has happened."

"What's wrong? Did somebody die?"

"No, it's not that."

"What, then?"

"It's about the villa."

"The villa? What about it?"

"It's gone."

80

WITH HENRY'S ARMS holding her, Clare fell silent, trying to find the meaning of what Luna had just said.

"I don't understand, Luna. What do you mean, the villa's gone."

"Gone. Destroyed."

The color drained from Clare's face and she was near fainting. She struggled to gain control.

"What happened, Luna? Was there a fire?"

"No. Mudslide. It was raining when you left, you know."

"Yes."

"It didn't let up, it just got worse. A couple of days ago they started putting out warnings, especially for owners of mountainside and ocean front property. This morning …"

"Wait, wait. I can't get my days straight. What time is it there now?"

"It's a little after 3 a.m. I had a sleepless night and decided just to stay up."

"Oh, you poor dear. It's noontime here. Now, you said this morning …"

"A police car went through the streets with a loudspeaker saying an emergency had been declared for certain areas. Yours was one of them. Houston and I got there as soon as we could. We told Joe and Maria …"

"Are they all right?"

"Yes. They escaped with their car and some clothing. That's about all."

"What a relief."

"We loaded as much as we could in our car and your Lexus. So glad you left me a key. We looked for irreplaceable things like scrapbooks and photo albums. We managed to save most of the art and some of your sculpture. But we didn't see de Lunus and there wasn't time to hunt for it. I grabbed your laptop and its case – I believe you keep your flash drives in it. Around midafternoon water was running down in rivers and police ordered everybody to clear the area. We were carrying arms full of things to our car, but they made us get out."

"I'm still trying to cope with this. I can't quite grasp what you're telling me."

"I'm so sorry I had to give you the bad news. But I thought you should know."

"Of course, honey. You did the right thing. We'll leave right away and get there as soon as we can."

"Okay."

"And thank you for all you did."

Clare collapsed on the couch. "My God, Henry!" she said.

Henry was already on the phone checking flights from Santorini to Athens and then to L.A. He waited to call a cab until they could get their bags packed.

He sat down beside her and put his arm around her. It was a time when words were meaningless, but he managed to say what he thought might comfort her temporarily.

"This is a terrible tragedy, hard to believe. But you'll get through it. Just know that you're not alone."

"I'm so glad I have you, Henry," she said, weeping.

"I'll start packing," he said.

"I need a few moments to compose myself," she said.

"Take all the time you need. The earliest flight we can get is at 4:45."

"Did you get reservations?"

"Yes, and also for a hotel at the Athens airport. We're on the first flight to L.A. tomorrow."

Clare pulled herself together and began rolling her clothing for the suitcase. When she was to the point of looking to make sure she hadn't missed something, she told Henry he could go ahead and call a cab.

They got to the airport in plenty of time. The plane was on schedule, both taking off and arriving in Athens. Clare didn't get much sleep either overnight or on the 16-hour flight home. She had a lot of thinking to do.

They were a few minutes late arriving at the gate at LAX and by the time they claimed their luggage and picked up Henry's car it was around 1:30 p.m. She called Luna to let her know they were back and on their way to the villa — or rather, to the place where she used to live.

"Are you sure you want to go there?" Luna asked.

"I have to do it. I have to see it so I can quit pretending it never happened."

"All right, I'll meet you there. We'll probably have to talk our way past the guards that are trying to keep the gawkers away from the damaged areas."

On the drive from the airport Clare scanned a Los Angeles Times Henry had bought. A familiar byline caught her eye. It was a story by Laurie Miller:

> One of the victims of the hellacious mudslides that destroyed a number of oceanside homes in Santa Barbara County is no stranger to loss. Less than three years ago, Clare Sullivan de Lune lost her husband. Just last week she lost a primary race in a bid to become California's first woman governor. Now her beautiful villa overlooking the Pacific, where

she hosted gatherings ranging from political strategy sessions to a Christmas party for children, is lost forever.

Luna de Lune, Clare's stepdaughter, was an eyewitness to the destructive force of the mudslides which left nothing standing in their path. I interviewed her at the "Clare for Governor" headquarters. She was in the process of closing it down.

"As soon as I heard that police had declared an emergency for that area I rushed to the villa. I knew Clare was away but I wanted to make sure nobody else was inside," she said. "A friend helped me remove some of her sculpture and paintings, as well as a few personal possessions. But we didn't have much time."

Her description of what followed was reminiscent of what happened in the small coastal community of La Conchita, which was described in an Associated Press report as "From Peace in Paradise to Hell in One Day."

"The police were shouting, 'get out, now' so we ran with armloads of things to our cars. I heard a loud crack, similar to a gun shot but much louder. I looked up and saw the hillside above the villa turn into a thunderous stream of trees, shrubs, dirt and mud plummeting down to the dwellings and people below. I hoped that everyone had evacuated by the time it hit."

Authorities said the cliff had been weakened by a series of earth tremors and that, combined with the force of the mudslide pushed the villa off into the rocky shore.

As they approached the disaster scene, what Luna said was true but the police recognized Clare and allowed Henry's car and Luna behind him past the barriers, with a stern warning to be careful because of highly unstable conditions.

As the cars turned onto the boulevard that was so familiar Clare saw a scene she had not seen before – a sight of incredible devastation A row of homes that once stood a few yards off this street no longer were in sight. The cars crawled slowly along the way until they came to another roadblock. The guards there refused to let them through in their vehicles. Only reluctantly did they permit them to get out and walk closer. "Keep a good distance back from the line," shouted an officer, pointing to a long red tape marking the remaining edge of the cliff.

Hand in hand, Clare and Luna inched closer to the spot where Villa de Lune had welcomed so many visitors over the years. Clare peered beyond the space where the ground had given way to the mudslides and peeled off into the ocean, bringing the villa tumbling down to the rocks below. All she could make out were huge piles of rubble with pieces of the house and the roof showing here and there along with chunks of the white concrete of the pool and tiles from the terrace. Here and there were glints from bottles of expensive wine.

She watched in horror as she saw the trunk side of the town car emerging from the rocks and among the waves splashing against the wreckage she thought she saw a tiny piece of red, which could have been her signature shoulder bag.

Clare wept softly as Luna squeezed her hand. Then she turned away and buried herself in Henry's arms. Luna rubbed her shoulders, saying, "I'm so sorry." After a moment she added, "I'm sorry we couldn't save all of the paintings."

Clare reached for Luna and hugged her tightly. "That's all right, honey. They were mostly of sentimental value." Both Luna and Henry looked at her quizzically.

"When I was handling Gary's estate as the executor of his will I had to have an appraisal done of everything including the complete contents of the house. My lawyer arranged to have an expert art appraiser come in. He reported to us that while the paintings gave every appearance of being originals, in fact they were excellent copies."

"I'll be damned!" Luna said.

"That explains the Renoir in the bedroom that I thought I had seen. Pop and I talked about it and we remembered seeing a painting like that in the Phillips Gallery in Washington."

"Yes," said Clare. "The original of the 'Luncheon of the Boating Party' hangs there."

"I can't believe my dad would do such a thing," said Luna.

"Please don't think badly of him," Clare said. "Gary was not reluctant to spend whatever it took to get something he wanted. And he did want to surprise me with masterpieces on the walls of the villa he had purchased for us to live in after we married. But he also was a very impatient man. And when he realized how difficult, if not impossible, it would be to acquire the art he wanted, he found a highly skilled artist to make copies, with the intent of replacing them one by one as he could."

"They are worth something, aren't they?" Luna asked.

"Oh, yes. And I don't want to keep them. They're yours if you like. Or you can find an art broker who probably could get top dollar for them," Clare said. Then she added, "And Luna, don't fret about de Lunus. I had moved the bust upstairs and it's just as well it was lost. It was a reminder of my past – a life I'll always treasure." And looking at Henry, "But I have a new life ahead of me."

Taking a deep breath of the ocean air, Clare faced toward the clear sky over the blue waters and said, "I'll always have this view to remember. A natural disaster can't destroy that."

As they started to leave the scene, Clare felt something rubbing against her leg. She looked down and saw a yellow cat. "Goldie!" she exclaimed "You've come back!" She picked up the affectionate animal and cradled it in her arms. The cat instantly began purring. "This was Gary's cat. She disappeared on the day after he died." Luna and Henry gathered around for this emotional reunion.

"Goldie, I'm so sorry but I can't keep you," Clare said. "Maybe Luna would like to have you."

"I'm not a cat person," Luna said quickly. "But Houston is. By the way, Houston and I are living together." Clare's face lit up with surprise and delight.

Walking slowly back to their cars, Luna said, "You probably haven't given much thought about what you're going to do."

Henry answered, "We can stay at my place for the time being. Where are Joe and Maria staying?" Henry asked.

"They're in a hotel. I don't know what their plans are. I think they'd like to remain in this area if possible."

"I took a year's lease on my apartment and paid in advance," Henry said. "But I'll be giving it up. They can stay there rent-free for the months remaining while they decide what to do. They might want to build their own home, and I'll be glad to help with the financing on that," he said.

"You're too good, Henry," Luna said, squeezing his arm.

"Damn! That may be the first time you've called me Henry."

81

CLARE AND HENRY had little conversation on the way to his apartment. They were alone in their thoughts about what had been and what the future might hold for them. They had dinner in a small neighborhood café – a simple meal with a good bottle of wine. After finishing off a piece of lemon meringue pie for dessert, Henry spoke up.

"Where do we go from here?"

"That's what I've been wondering," Clare said. "I don't think I want to stay here. I don't have any real ties to Santa Barbara or California … except for Luna, of course. And there are too many bad memories."

"I can understand how you're feeling," Henry said. "And the only reason I would have to go back to Mt. Jackson is family. I've never had any genuine interest in the business."

"But you're still the president of the company. Didn't Pop expect you to resume that role after the campaign was over?"

"Perhaps. And I probably led him to believe I would. But he's a changed man after meeting and marrying Jean. You've seen that."

"Yes. He's much happier, I'm sure."

"After my mother died I think he felt he had nothing much to live for. His enthusiasm for work faded. He had always thrived on the challenges of running a large enterprise. But the spark vanished and he was ready – eager – to turn it over to me. So I reluctantly did his will. But I was just going through the motions."

"So you think he might have changed his mind?"

"I won't know for sure until I can talk to him. And if it's agreeable with you, I'd like for us to go spend a few days at Mt. Jackson and then travel for a while until we decide where we want to be." He took a sip of wine and, seeing Clare's contemplative look said, "Listen to me going on about 'us' and what 'we' will do. Perhaps I'm assuming too much. Maybe you'd rather go your own way and I go mine."

"No, no, Henry," she said, placing her hand on his. "I love you and I don't know what I would do without you. I do want to be with you, wherever that might be."

"I am so glad to hear you say that. Because I feel the same way. My love for you grows stronger every day we are together."

"That's settled, then," Clare said. "As to the future, there's not much I need to do to pull up stakes and leave. I know a good lawyer who can handle the insurance settlement on the villa. I do need to make a trip to the bank to get some things out of my safety deposit box. That's where all my good jewelry is, including the beautiful necklace you gave me – at least I didn't lose that."

"We can do that first thing tomorrow."

"I'll go ahead and resign from the state Senate. I can do that by letter. I have to do some shopping, too – for things like clothing, makeup and other grooming supplies. As you know I packed light for our trip to Santorini. That was such a wonderful trip," she sighed.

"We'll do any shopping you need to," Henry said. "Unless you'd rather wait and do it in Seattle."

"I'll think about it, but some of it can't wait," she said.

"You are so lucky to have Luna to look after things here," he said.

"I know. I want to make sure she gets a fair share of the insurance proceeds. I think Gary provided for it in his will. I also want to give her my Lexus. I'll tell her it's an advance wedding present," she said with a smile.

"Are you sure you want to open that subject?" Henry asked.

"You're probably right. I'll just say it's a bonus for the great job she did as my campaign manager. It's tough getting your life back on track after the string of unexpected events that have occurred. But I feel better after making a few plans."

"So do I. Let's go home – well, home for now."

"I hope we don't run into those flirty women in the elevator. This day already has been trying enough without that."

"They're probably out partying," Henry said.

The following day Henry and Clare made a run to a suburban shopping center to go to Clare's branch bank and shop at some of the major department stores located there. Henry patiently waited while Clare tried on various garments and he turned down sample sprayings of cologne while she stocked up on cosmetics. Finally they returned to the apartment with a backseat full of packages, including a new piece of luggage for her to use to pack her purchases.

Henry could put everything he needed to take to vacate the apartment in his large suitcase and they set off for the airport. On the way he turned in his leased automobile and they took a courtesy car to the terminal.

"There's one more thing I have to do," Clare said, reaching for her cell phone. "I need to let Tim know I'm leaving."

The conversation was brief. He had heard the terrible news about the villa and expressed his sympathies, as well as the sadness he and other close friends in the Senate felt about her misfortunes.

"We'll all be sorry to see you go, Clare," he said.

"It just seems to be the right thing to do. I'll miss you, Tim. Your friendship means a lot to me. I can never thank you enough for all you've done to help me through some troubled times and to support me in my campaign. You'll always be 'lookin' good' in my book."

"Same here."

When they took off on the flight to Seattle, their ties with L.A. had been severed.

Andrew met their flight again and he was glad to see both of them. He expressed his sorrow for Clare's election defeat and the loss of her home and said he was speaking for the entire Mt. Jackson family – Henry's relatives and the winery staff.

Clare had decided she didn't need to do any additional shopping in Seattle. She had put together a mix-and-match wardrobe that could at least get her through the immediate travel they had planned. So they headed straight for Mt. Jackson.

Henry took the opportunity to feel out his younger brother about his role in the family business. He really enjoyed the grape side of winemaking and much preferred to work in the vineyards than be cooped up in an office. He had come up with some new blends of different varieties of grapes that had produced profitable wines.

Although Andrew had turned down offers from Pop to move up from Vineyards Manager to a higher executive position, Henry detected a slight weakening of his firm resistance. As he had matured and begun to give more thought to a future that might include marriage and children, he acquired a different perspective. He would want to provide the best for his family, as his father and grandfather had aspired to do.

That was good enough for Henry to make the proposition to Pop that he put Andrew in the line of succession in place of Henry. To "grease the skids" Henry would offer to represent the winery at trade shows and other sales events. That conversation would come on the second day at Mt. Jackson, following a warm welcome and another outstanding dinner by Jean.

By the time they were ready to load Henry's car and leave, both he and Clare felt they had achieved an amicable separation from a life at Mt. Jackson, which neither of them wanted.

As usual, Henry had put in motion a plan for a second escape from reality: a stay – for a week or more – on Whidbey Island off the coast of Washington in Puget Sound. This long and mostly narrow island 30 miles north of Seattle and two hours driving time from Vancouver, British Columbia was once inhabited by the Skagit and other Indian tribes. It was explored by Spain in 1792 and two years later by an expedition of the British Royal Navy. Henry discovered Whidbey when he visited a friend who was stationed at the Naval Air Station at Oak Harbor. He was taken not only with the rugged beauty of the island but also with the serenity he found there.

The politically-mismatched man and woman who had met by chance, united in a bold adventure and formed a common bond while coping with their losses through love and devotion were about to begin a new life together.

III

Don't let yesterday use up too much of today.

Cherokee Indian proverb

82

HENRY AND CLARE said their farewells to family and friends at Mt. Jackson and climbed into his Cadillac with sadness at leaving but high expectations for what awaited them on their new journey.

They headed west toward Seattle, through Woodinville and north on I-405 to Mukilteo where they drove the car onto a ferry for the short trip to Whidbey Island. Once on land, state route 525 took them to Coupeville, which is near the center of the island and at one of its narrowest points. With a little help from GPS, Henry quickly made the way to the place where he had made reservations.

They found the historic Crockett Farm Bed and Breakfast to be a charming and peaceful spot with sweeping views of the countryside, fitting the description of a perfect romantic hideaway. The Victorian country house situated on a homestead dating to 1851 – one of the oldest in Ebey's Historical Reserve – had wide grassy lawns and marvelous flower gardens to be enjoyed by guests as well as deer, rabbits and other visiting wildlife. Occasionally eagles could be seen soaring and gliding in the skies above. A previous visitor had written in the guest book that no other lodging on the island could beat the quiet and beautiful setting, adding "instead of traffic noises all you hear is the rustle of the wind in the trees and meadow grasses."

The dwelling was known for many years as the Col. Walter Crockett House, named for a Virginian whose family went out west in the 1800's. It was turned into a B&B by a couple who owned the house from 1984 until 2005. During those years they hosted guests from all parts of the world, including some well-known movie stars. The present owner had the house remodeled and updated a few years ago. With a flair for promotion, she advertises: "Just bring love, we'll do the rest."

The old farmhouse had five private bedrooms, a large dining room where hearty breakfasts were served each morning, and a wood-paneled library with a fireplace for reading and relaxation.

Henry had chosen a downstairs bedroom because the ceilings upstairs were angled to conform with the slope of the roof and therefore would not be suitable for two rather tall adults. He told Clare that was the reason rather than the tales of the house being haunted because a son of the original occupant had killed himself in one of the rooms.

Their room had a large antique bed with a tall mahogany headboard and a flowered coverlet. A full-length mirror that could be tilted stood next to the dresser. The peach-colored walls rose above white paneled wainscoting. There was no phone or television set. The proprietor told them actress Kathleen Turner once had slept in this room.

After they got settled Henry pulled out some brochures and travel articles about Whidbey Island. They were both interested in seeing the nearby Fort Casey State Park with its lighthouse and adjoining Spanish style house, the cannon emplacements and other features of the historic port, plus the scenic views of Admiralty Inlet and the Strait of Juan de Fuca.

Henry's eye was drawn to a mention of the Whidbey Island winery, but it was located in the fishing village of Langley on the southern end of the island so it had low priority.

Knowing that Victoria, British Columbia was easily accessible from the island, they talked about going there to see the world-famous Butchart Gardens and on to Vancouver for a few days. It was wonderful not to have a rigid schedule.

For their first day on the island they decided to check out the old town of Coupeville and perhaps sample some Penn Cove mussels for which the area is known.

They lucked out on a parking place and set out for a walking tour of the historic waterfront town. Coupeville is a mecca for artists so a number of studios and galleries beckoned and they stopped in a few. They also poked around some of the many antique shops until Henry mentioned he was getting hungry

Clare spotted a sign for Toby's Tavern and said, "Let's go there." It turned out to be a good choice. They were seated in a booth overlooking tranquil Penn Cove, known for its abundant crop of mussels. The décor reflected the history of the building, built around 1890, which had housed many businesses. After prohibition it became a beer parlor but had been a restaurant since the early 1960s.

Only house wine was on the menu so Henry suggested they try the tavern's own micro brew, Toby's Parrot Red Ale. He told the waitress they would start with the steamed Penn Cove Mussels with garlic bread. She returned shortly with the ale and two huge bowls of mussels.

For the next hour or so, Clare and Henry had the heavenly experience of alternating sips of ale with the seafood delicacy and bread dipped in the delicious butter sauce. The mussels seemed to multiply the more of them they ate so they ordered a second round of Parrot Red Ale. By the time they could see the bottoms of their bowls neither of them gave any thought to any of the other appetizing items on the dinner menu.

"I think I need a walk after this feast," Clare said. Henry agreed and they went back out on the street. Darkness was falling by then and the lights of the shops gave the town a romantic glow.

They strolled leisurely, holding hands, until they came to a spot where they could walk out on a wooden deck to the edge of the shore. They stood there, cloaked in moonlight, and enjoyed a quiet moment.

"Henry, I have to ask you something," Clare said.

"What's that?"

"It's about that woman in England."

"All right."

"You really fell for her, right?"

"Who told you that, Pop?"

"Well?"

"Yes, I suppose I did."

"Was she that attractive? Blonde, brunette?"

"Brunette."

"Your dad said her name was ... uh, Katie?"

"Kate."

"He said she dumped you."

Nodding, with a grimace, he said, "I guess you could say I got a royal screwing." To her disapproving look, he added, "I didn't mean that literally."

"Yeah, right."

"She found her Prince Charming, and," looking into her eyes, "I found my Queen."

He put his arms around her and held her close, her cheek against his. Suddenly she pulled back and looked straight at him.

"You said her name was Kate?"

"Yes."

"Kate ... royal ... prince ... Oh, my G..." His warm hand covered her mouth, then his lips met hers in a long, lingering kiss.

"I'm with *you* now, Clare, and I want to be with you forever."

The all-knowing "man in the moon" smiled down on them and the only sounds were the waves lapping onto the shore and a loon in the distance singing, "good night."

Epilogue

IN THE FOLLOWING days on Whidbey Island, Clare and Henry did some of the things they talked about doing, plus some they hadn't planned. But despite these distractions, Clare couldn't get "the woman from England" out of her mind. She needed more answers to the question of how he came to be so close to the future daughter-in-law of the Queen.

In Henry's mind it was a matter that had best be forgotten. But he didn't have the luxury of that choice. Clare persisted in knowing the full story of his association with Kate: how they met, what they saw in each other, why he would hit on a woman whom everyone but him knew was on a path to marry a prince.

He stoutly resisted talking about this episode in his bachelor life because it would expose him as a witless sap who would become helplessly entranced by an exciting beautiful woman.

She had to drag the story out of him but as he told it she gradually became more understanding and even sympathetic.

In the spring of 2007 Henry had just returned to London from an extended stay in France with visits to Italy and other adjoining countries.

With his rugged good looks and continental charm, he easily moved into the London party scene. One evening at a popular night club all eyes turned to an attractive brunette wearing a short skirt and a low top who obviously was out to have a good time. She came with her younger sister and some other women. No escort was in sight. During the evening she danced with a number of men, and one of them was Henry. They danced more than once and they exchanged names – first names only. She mentioned another night spot she liked to frequent and he made a point of going there the following evening. To his disappointment she didn't show up, but the second evening she did. Again she wore a sexy outfit, pink top and skin tight white jeans. The woman was there to party and to show a certain someone what he was missing by having broken off their relationship more than once.

She and Henry danced again and then spent some time over white wine coolers talking, mostly about him. He thought her eyes led him on. Why didn't he know the identity of this world famous figure? He didn't read the daily newspapers and on television he watched sports and travel channels, not news and entertainment.

It could be said that Henry never quite reached the age of maturity, but this stage in his life was the closest he had come. While he enjoyed his carefree lifestyle he had begun to think seriously about having a romance with more meaning – about (horrors) a more permanent relationship. He just had not met the right woman. Until he met the woman in England.

He saw in her a very attractive woman who loved having fun, who appreciated good wine and the other finer things of life, who appeared to enjoy his company and who at that point had given no indication she had another man in her life.

All those fantasies came tumbling down when one evening, after the dance band took a break, he told her of his feelings for her and proposed a steady relationship. He realized there was a 10-year age difference but in these days that doesn't seem to matter much. But he didn't strike out on that account. Surprised by the unexpected proposal, she let him down gently, he told Clare, telling him that he was a nice American guy but that her future belonged with a special English gentleman.

Totally heartbroken, Henry refused to accept the finality of that response until he returned to the same club later that week and saw her on the arm of another man. The answer became clear. Henry had been dumped.

Shortly thereafter, he began making plans to go back to the United States and to his family in Washington and try to forget what a spectacular fool he had made of himself.

Despite the incredible revelation of Henry's unbelievable crush, Clare had decided their bond was strong enough that she could live with the reality that she had fallen in love with a man on the rebound.

From Whidbey they took the car and boarded a ferry to Victoria, British Columbia, and after visiting the magnificent Butchart Gardens they enjoyed tea in the Empress Hotel where they had a room overlooking the harbor. Then they took another ferry to Vancouver, the vibrant and exciting city which is Canada's third most populous metropolitan area. Many opportunities for fine dining were available, from five-star restaurants featuring fresh salmon to a café in a culinary arts institute on Granville Island that Henry knew about. They had a luxuriating stay in the Pan Pacific Hotel at Canada Place, with its distinctive roof of five white sails, and watching the cruise ships come and go aroused some desire to see Alaska. But both of them decided that could wait for another time.

Instead, Henry donated the Cadillac, with over 100,000 miles on it, at a Vancouver Salvation Army center, and they took a trans-Canadian rail trip, with stops in Banff and Jasper, to Toronto, where they picked up another car and continued their travels to New York City for several days there, enjoying the museums, Broadway shows and excellent dining adventures.

Travel was to be their lifestyle for some time to come.

Meanwhile, back in Santa Barbara, Gene McQueen bought Luna de Lune's advertising and public relations agency to have a presence in California and hired both Luna and Melody Turner. Houston Conover finished his degree and joined the faculty of Millard Fillmore University's Western Campus, where Hector Perido had been appointed Dean of the School of Political Science. Tim Barnham retired from the state Senate and began raising emus on his "Lookin' Real Good" ranch. Ex-congressman John K. Bull was convicted of campaign law violations and is serving time in a federal prison. Peter Pepper is still selling red tape to the government; Risa Yamada is still fitting brides-to-be with "Gowns to Go"; Mary Anne Parker is still turning out "Chowchilla Chow-Chow"; and "Elves on Call" are as busy as ever.

Acknowledgments

As an Oklahoma-born male who has worked for Republican candidates, I was ill-equipped to write from the perspective of a California Democrat seeking to become the state's first woman governor. I needed some expert advice. I received much helpful guidance (and some candid critiques) from Barb Best, award-winning comedy writer from Los Angeles; Cynthia Borris, San Francisco novelist and blogger; and Suzette Martinez Standring, a former Californian, now in Boston blogging, speaking and authoring how-to books for writers. I'm grateful to my cousin, Dr. Donald Haught, longtime California school administrator and leader in accreditation, for educating me about education issues.

Closer to home (Virginia) I picked the brains of Linda Carpenter, former resident of Santa Barbara, Calif.; Jill Quinley, avid reader and traveler with a teaching background; John Quinley, retired Virginia State Police division commander; and Brad Hansen, Winemaker at Prince Michel Vineyards, Leon, Va., formerly at Chateau St. Michelle and Columbia Crest in Washington.

Much appreciation to columnist friend Dave Lieber, a master storyteller, for his influence on my writing. Thanks also to author Bruce Cameron for allowing me to associate his good name with a bad joke, and to professional photographer Lynn Dykstra for making a cameo appearance.

The personality of state Sen. Tim Barnham is modeled after an Oklahoma legislator and newspaperman – a close friend, long deceased.

I beg indulgence for the use of generous doses of satire from cover to content as well as shameful displays of word play.

My heartfelt gratitude to all of the above, and most of all I thank Mary, my patient and ever-supportive wife, whose eagle-eye proofreading, valuable suggestions and tolerance of the time I spent with Clare made this first venture into fiction possible.

About the Author

ROBERT L. HAUGHT has written news, sports and feature articles for a worldwide wire service; editorials and a political humor column for a state's major newspaper; daily commentaries and travel, food, gardening, writing and humor articles for an internet magazine; humor books; business stories; book reviews; newsletters; essays; children's stories; cartoon gags; comedy routines; photo captions; television scripts; news releases; advertising copy; speeches; talking points; proclamations; resolutions; grant applications; government, university and association reports; legal documents; song parodies; original lyrics; and now, a novel.